B.J. KREIGER

A SHINING BEACON IN A POOL OF DARKNESS

DARKNESS

Reflections of a Journey Unimagined

This is a work of fiction. Names, characters, places,and incidents either are the product ofthe author's imagination or are used fictitiously. Any resemblance to actual persons, living or dead, events, or locales is entirely coincidental.

First edition

Editing by Heather Rivera Coverdesign by RafaelAndres

ISBN: 979-8-9865883-4-6 (hardback)

ISBN979-8-9865883-3-9 (paperback)

ISBN979-8-9865883-0-8 (ePUB)

ISBN979-8-9865883-1-5 (iBook)

ISBN979-8-9865883-2-2 (Kindle)

First edition

This book is dedicated to my ex-wife Sherry, and my daughter, Kari. Throughout all the darkness that I faced through those very trying years, they were a beacon of light, that kept me going, and always guided me back home.

Contents

Chapter 1

The Beacon is Lit

It was a sunny day, late in the summer of 1991; I sat on the dock in Alitak, a processing facility based at the southern end of Kodiak Island, Alaska, watching shipping containers being filled with frozen sockeye salmon – both meat and eggs - and loaded onto a large, green Japanese tramper ship. This was the beginning of my journey into the darkness.

I had been a commercial fisherman for 14 years and had been attending college since 1988. But the journey started for me that day in '91. We had watched the ex-vessel price for sockeyes in Kodiak go from $2.75 a pound in '88 to just $0.90 by the summer of '91. $0.90 was more reminiscent a price of the late 1970's than the beginning of the 1990's, and most of us were wondering what was going on with the market. We wanted answers; I wanted answers. Watching that processed sockeye getting loaded that day was the last straw – I promised myself that I would find out about the market (which was dominated by the Japanese at that time) and try to do something about it. In retrospect, it was like the old adage about the village that chose one of its citizens to leave the village; and go out into the world in order to save the village.

So off I went; I had been enrolled at a community college in Washington for three years. When I had originally begun college, my intention was to focus on pre-medical studies in order to major in dive medicine. But after that day on the dock in Alitak, I began to shift my studies more towards pre-business. I was going to major in marketing, as well as minor in Japanese studies. I enrolled in Japanese language classes in the fall of 1992 and began to prepare to transfer to a four-year college.

I completed my Associate degree and transferred to Seattle University in 1992. Shortly after enrollment, I spoke with a counselor who suggested that I might be a good candidate for the General Studies program. This was a program that had been made available in order to 'fill the gaps' for students with needs that couldn't be satisfied by any one of their college programs. So, I wrote my own custom degree in international marketing with a minor in Japanese cultural studies. I was going to learn everything I could about Japan's history, culture, language, politics, and economics. Along the way I took studies about China and Europe, a knowledge that would help to round out my education that I would use to my advantage later.

During my first year at Seattle University, I met the woman who would end up being my wife; I knew the moment that I met her that she was the one. She brought so much joy to my life – and helped provide me the focus and direction that was much needed then – and would be needed even more in the future. I completed my Bachelor of Arts in late 1995. Shortly thereafter, I headed back out into the working world, sending out resumes left and right to seafood companies all over the Seattle area, hoping to get someone to hire me. I also contacted the Alaska Seafood Association (ASA) at that time, hoping to get a chance for employment at the place I had dreamed of working at since learning about the agency back in the 1980's. The director of the export program had told me, "someone will have to die around here before a position opens up." Little did I realize that within four years, I would be going to work with the program.

1996 was a tough year; I tried going to work for a medium-size trading house called Nemo Seafoods. They were the marketing arm for a harvesting group known as Alaskan Victor Fisheries. I did some research and attempted to start a fresh halibut market in Germany for Alaskan Victor. And when that project faltered; I tried my hand at expanding sales in the U.S. market for Nemo. I sold a little halibut, and a couple of containers of king crab (due to my father's connections with a major processor), but I soon found after a couple of months of trading that there wasn't much of a competitive advantage in trying to sell someone else's product. The market is all about connections, and the only reason why anyone would want to buy from you is if you had a lower price (which we didn't); that left us with buyers who had bad credit, or were looking to burn us on a deal.

Learning these hard lessons, I became frustrated, and I went back to commercial fishing for a couple months in order to make it through the winter. I participated in the opilio crab fishery in early 1997; I still remember the other crew members, joking with me on deck, asking me how valuable I thought my college education was now. I agreed with them to placate them, but I knew deep in my heart that I was going to do something with that hard-earned degree. That season was a long one, as we went on strike due to low prices. The strike lasted for almost a month, so we didn't go fishing until February. The season got tougher as we went along. We had a number of mechanical breakdowns, and we had a hard time finding crab. Then, to make matters worse, while throwing the picking hook to catch the crab pot buoys, I caught my hook on a rail and tore ligaments in my shoulder. While in terrible pain, I informed the captain of my injury, and told him that I needed medical attention the next time we were in port for delivery. Twice we went in to deliver and get parts for repair, and twice I was denied medical attention.

I worked for two weeks in debilitating pain, compensating for my bad shoulder with my back; but it proved too much for my back, and I suffered a major strain. My back has not been the same since, and I still have to be careful not to re-injure it while lifting. Due to the injury, I couldn't finish

3

the rest of the season. I flew home to Seattle to heal my wounded back. In hindsight, it was the event that set me back on the path in the right direction once again.

Chapter 2

Time for a Change

Shortly after my return, I moved into an apartment with my girlfriend and began to look for work. While I felt the pull to return to fishing (the salmon season was quickly approaching), she had wise words for me: "If you keep running back to fishing and don't stay here, you'll never find that marketing job that you have worked so hard for." I knew she was right. I got a job as a checker at a local grocery store and kept looking for that dream marketing job. Barely a month after starting work at the store, I was hired at Magic Mermaid Seafoods. At that time, Magic Mermaid was being heralded as the new 'king of value-added in the seafood industry. They were launching a whole new line of products: fish burgers, seafood fajitas, crab cakes, and more; they were going to change the industry with their new, innovative approach. It was an exciting new venture, and I wanted so much to be a part of this movement. I went to work for them as their new sales and distribution coordinator for their distribution division – the first new position that the organization had created since anyone could remember. While the pay wasn't that great (only $24,000 a year), it was a 'foot in the door', and an opportunity to finally really start to apply that marketing degree I had worked so hard to get. I would be reporting directly to Derek O'Malley, VP of Distribution. Later I was to find that he had a number of nicknames, including of all things, 'Dad.' The first day of work was July 7,

1997 – 7/7/97. I took note of the date and took it as a good omen. It was a Monday, and the sales staff always met at

8:00 am. They opened the meeting by introducing me to the staff as the new hire. Immediately after, the VP of sales took the floor and announced that the Bristol Bay salmon fishery had officially collapsed. No one could have been as dumbfounded as me, considering this is the fishery I had just foregone to get this new job. While I paused to think of all my friends and family being impacted by the collapse of this fishery, I couldn't help but think how fortunate I was to make the choice I had.

I went to work with a great procurement team, led by Larry Black, the procurement manager, and his procurement specialist, Ed Mackey. Ed and I sat right across from each other in a cubicle, facing each other. It was perfect for coordinating the purchase and distribution of product. We gelled immediately and went right to the task of moving tons of product through the 'pipeline.' Things were clipping right along, and then on the third day, I had my first 'bump in the road'.

The VP of Seattle production came to me and told me that they had some fresh Dungeness crab meat leftover from value-added production (in three-pound vacuum-packed bags) and that they wanted to know if I could sell it to another division. I found out that the head fresh buyer from the Seattle distribution house, Dick Thompson, could use the Dungeness crab, but he needed it in one-pound cup containers for sales. I put in the production order to change the three-pound bags to one-pound cups. Unfortunately, the order did not get processed properly, resulting in Dick getting 75 pounds of three-pound bags delivered to him, directly to his desk (literally).

He wasn't amused. He immediately came upstairs to the corporate sales floor where I was located and commenced to chewing my ass out in front of the entire staff. When he was done raging, I apologized for the mistake (even though it wasn't on my part) and told him that I would have the problem taken care of. Dick quietly marched back downstairs. Most of the staff looked at me with pity, then went back to their work. Ed looked over at me and said," He was a total jerk to you; I can't believe you took that. If I were you, I would have asked him, 'do you realize who I am?" I looked back at Ed and said," I see your point, but I am going to make that man my friend." And I did; it took a while to get Dick to warm up to me, but I soon gave him the confidence to trust me, and we worked very closely until my departure. Here was an opportunity to make my first enemy at the company, but I chose to turn the other cheek, and befriend him. This would not be the first time or the last time I would use this tactic.

The excitement of the new position was electric for me. Though many of my fellow employees were very concerned about the Bristol Bay situation; and the concern continued to mount – especially with the upper management, as we learned that there were record water temperatures being tracked in Alaskan waters, as well as up and down the entire West Coast of the Pacific region of the U.S. and Canada. It turned out that the ocean and atmosphere was experiencing an 'El Nino' effect – a weather pattern in which sea surface temperatures are warmer than normal. The concern began to reach a fever pitch when the president of Magic Mermaid convened a staff meeting where he stated his concern about what was taking place in the Pacific Ocean, motivating the staff to find out what was going on before matters became worse.

I took it upon myself to start researching what was taking place in the ocean. I gained internet access right away from the IT department (no small task at that time, considering that at that time, there were only three or four internet accounts in the entire building). I spent hours researching what I could online; I spent even more time at my old alma mater, the SU, researching every bit of information that I could about the history of El Nino events, sea surface temperatures, and their impacts on fish and marine life populations. What I found was that these 'El Nino' events run in oscillations, or cycles, every decade or two, and that this one taking place during the

1997-98 years was the hottest one ever recorded in the 120 years since scientists had started collecting data.

Research indicated that extremely elevated sea temperatures act as 'hot black top' on the top layer of the ocean waters, preventing currents of cold, nutrient-rich waters from cycling upwards from deeper levels. It was also noted that water temperatures allow for more predators to travel into northern ocean waters. Additionally, I found during this research that sockeye salmon have a certain temperature threshold; if the sea temperature becomes too high, it acts as a thermal 'wall' in which the fish will not pass.

So, it was easy to imagine what contributed to the great collapse in Bristol Bay. Picture sockeye swimming through the ocean, already stressed by high sea temperatures and lack of a proper food source, trapped in pockets of colder water, concentrated for predators to congregate upon them. This is a possible explanation for the very low sockeye returns in 1997 (as well as in 1998). I distilled all the data from my research and release the information to all of the staff at Magic Mermaid. This provided some insight into what was taking place and helped the employees and management to get a better grasp of the situation, as well as to help to plan for the future.

After the hype started to die down from the sockeye run crash, we all settled back into the business of selling fish, including all of the new value-added products that were beginning to be launched. Spirits were still high into the fall, and I relished the excitement of my new job, putting in very long hours in an effort to do a great job. And the harder I worked, the more responsibility I received. Soon I found myself helping with not only procurement and sales for the eight distribution locations, but I was also helping to fill in for distributing early morning fresh production from the Astoria and Newport, Oregon plants on select days of the week. Additionally, I was helping to manage the sale of flake ice produced at the Seattle facility (it was previously given away for free). As a part of this new responsibility, we had to figure out the actual cost of producing ice so that we could charge the proper amount to customers. As a part of this analysis, we realized that we were being charged by the city for tons of wastewater that was not actually going down the drains; it was going out the door on our delivery trucks, into boats, and to customers. This turned out to save the company hundreds, if not thousands in wastewater charges every month.

Just a month after I started this job, my first experience with a management crisis took place – I later nicknamed it the 'Great Coho Catastrophe of 1997'. There was a chain of retail stores in the Montana area named Callahan's (it was later bought up by Bernie's). Every year they conducted a big fresh salmon promotion at their stores – right in the middle of barbeque season. It was now my job to coordinate the entire effort, ensuring that we were to secure wild salmon of all the major species to be sold during the promotion. All product sources were set up for the promotion, except for the coho salmon.

Coho is a late season fish in Alaska (they are harvested beginning in late August and September). Since it was still early August, we couldn't find any yet. Luckily, we found some to purchase out of the Bella Coola region of British Columbia, Canada. Ed arranged for the purchase of coho from a Canadian vendor, and had the product flown by air to Seattle. I then made arrangements with the freight forwarder to have the product received and shipped by truck to Montana. It was a Friday, and it looked like all the details were taken care of for the promotion that was set to go off the next week.

But on Monday morning, the 'shit hit the fan.' 'Dad' called me in and told me that he had just received a call from Callahan's, and all of the coho were ruined. He was pissed off and wanted to know why this had happened. I went right to work on it, going over all the orders' details – everything looked in place, so I wondered what went wrong. But after a little more investigation, we found out what happened: We had designated on the transfer order with the freight forwarder to "ice for truck." This means that when the coho arrived via air from Canada, the product was to have the gel packs removed (for air shipments, they usually place two frozen gel packs in with the product to keep it cool), and then it was to be covered with flake ice for the truck trip to Montana.

This did not happen – the product had been loaded on the truck with no ice, just the old, thawed-out gel packs. It was 100 to 105 degrees Fahrenheit that weekend; fish can spoil pretty fast in such weather. While the truck was refrigerated, the ice was needed to help protect the product from the high temperatures. To make matters worse, when the product arrived, it was delivered directly to Callahan's warehouse. If it had been the Magic Mermaid distribution center in Helena, the staff would have inspected the product upon arrival and made sure it had been chilled properly. Callahan's staff did not have the seafood expertise, so they did not inspect the product on arrival, and the coho sat for a couple of days with no ice, and the damage was done.

While we had finally found out what had caused the 'coho catastrophe', more important was recognizing the need to better educate retail staff on handling and receiving fish. As a result, my boss and I sat down and wrote out a plan for how to deal with this, and out of this issue came another great project – a retail education manual, for teaching retailers the finer art of working with seafood. Dad and I collaborated closely on this project, and I worked closely with several staff members to garner and distill as much information as possible for this education piece.

While I was truly enjoying all the action in the distribution and sales end of the business, I really wanted to get more involved in the company's marketing processes. I began to take inventory of all the collateral materials that were available and found the collection to be a mess. For years staff members had just stacked the materials in the back, and the entire inventory sat in total disarray. I recruited a couple of other employees to help out and went to the task of re-organizing everything, including creating an electronic database of all the materials.

Next came the newsletter; I had noticed that a newsletter had been printed up as a summer edition, focusing on the Copper River salmon run, etc. I went to my boss and proposed that begin to create a newsletter for every month – and the Magic Mermaid 'Seafood of the Month' newsletter was born. Each month was to focus on a new topic, such as seafood from a geographic region, like Latin America, or certain species, like king crab. It was originally geared towards retail consumers, including recipe ideas for certain products. But the trade partners took a liking to it as well, and we soon added food service menu ideas for chefs and their staff. The readership continued to grow every month, and next thing you know, I was creating editions for all of the different distribution locations across the western U.S., as well as for the corporate office at 'mother' Magic Mermaid. It was just a black and white version, but it included graphics, and I tried to make it as fun as possible for having a 'shoestring' budget to operate under; it was truly a labor of love.

I also began to write a quarterly market report for internal distribution. There wasn't anything that I was not willing to do to raise the level of enthusiasm. The days were long – usually 12 to 14 hours, but I was really enjoying the opportunity to create all these new forms of communications.

It had been only a month or two into the job, and then the next crisis sprang up. The market for frozen imported shrimp was starting to take a dive, and Dave Simpson, VP of Sales and Marketing, came to me and shared his concern about the declining value of shrimp. He was especially concerned as there was a major shipment of imported shrimp that Magic Mermaid corporate had purchased that was inbound, and he was worked up about his division taking a big hit on the loss. He told me that he wanted all of the inventories that had been ordered for the distribution group to be transferred over to them immediately – so they were off the corporate books, and on the various distribution houses' books, so they could absorb some of the loss in value. I went to see what I could do – the value of shrimp was dropping off the map at a tremendously fast pace, and so I worked closely with procurement, logistics, and accounting to move the inventories over to the distribution houses.

There was just one problem - the generally acceptable rule of accounting basically requires that all documents and bill of lading (shipping) be provided when placing sales orders between entities. None of that was readily available considering that the product was still sitting on a container ship in Long Beach harbor. But I put the sales orders in the system based on the inventory numbers and pushed them through as I was instructed. It was Friday, and was relieved for the weekend, having completed the arduous task that had been placed before me. Then on Saturday, I received a call from Bonnie from inventory control. She asked me about the shrimp sales orders, inquiring how and why I had placed these orders. Then she calmly explained that by placing those orders with no paperwork to back them, I had made $4 to 5 million disappear off the credit line for the weekend.

On Monday morning, I received a visit from Priscilla, head of the credit department. She asked me what I thought I was doing and let me know that the sales orders had been suspended. Shortly thereafter, Simpson entered the office and asked me tersely why the shrimp inventories had not been removed from the corporate books as he had instructed me to do on Friday. I calmly let him know that Priscilla had suspended all of the sales orders. And off he marched to Priscilla's office for the sparks to fly. This was my first real experience with being caught up in the power plays of some powerful egos —but it would not be the last.

While there were so many great people working at Magic Mermaid, one of the first people that I introduced myself to was a beautiful blonde-haired lady with a brilliant smile named Susie Fogle. Susie happened to be the sales assistant to Mark Montrose, which basically made her the international sales assistant to the entire world outside of the Japanese market. I introduced myself to her during my first week or so; she was quite the pleasant, bright, and inviting person. We became very good friends, and we would talk frequently, and we even carpooled for a while together, until our fiancées started to worry about spending us so much time together (in fact, she helped me to organize the entire marketing materials inventory), so we stopped the carpooling, but still remained close friends and associates both during our time at Magic Mermaid – and even to this day.

There were two other young, attractive ladies that were on the sales floor that I became associated with, purely out of professional necessity. One was a lovely slim redhead named Margie, who was a marketing assistant for the marketing manager, and the other was a curvy and vivacious brunette named Jane. I found myself coordinating sales and marketing efforts with all three ladies, which required frequent visits to the 'box room' where the marketing collateral materials were located. Here I was, venturing behind to the backroom with these three beautiful young ladies to secure materials on a daily basis.

I thought it was totally harmless and professional until good old Larry Black pulled me into my office (on a separate matter) and pointed out to me what a 'dog' I was, having only been at the company for barely a couple of weeks, and there I was, taking three of the best-looking ladies on the corporate floor into the back room alone almost every day. I turned red in embarrassment and began to laugh out loud. I had been so busy working that I had no idea what it looked like to others watching me move about the sales floor. I could understand instantly how my very innocent and professional (but very energetic) journeys behind closed doors with these lovely ladies could be so easily misconstrued as 'carnal ventures' to the backroom. It was another lesson on how easily it is for someone's action to be so easily misconstrued – especially when being a young male working in conjunction with such beautiful ladies.

What was ironically funny, was that a few months later we found a makeshift 'bed' in between a bunch of boxes just behind the location of the marketing materials. Whether this had been someone's secret napping area, or a 'love nest' we could not tell; but I sure was glad that I had clarified my intentions with Black during the summer before someone thought the makeshift bed was my sales 'workstation.'

Personally, my relationship with my fiancé, Sherry, was still flourishing. Most memorable was a trip in late July to Mt. Rainer. It was beautiful weather, with great picture-perfect days on the mountain, hiking through alpine meadows, and nights sitting around the campfire, drinking beer and wine, and dancing to music. It was youth at its finest. Bingo, my dog, was still in her prime and would hike with us (even though it was against the rules to have dogs on the trails).

We did have one run-in with the authorities. We had just hiked on the trails behind Reflection Lake, and Sherry was letting Bingo take a swim at the edge to the lake to cool off. All of a sudden, a ranger showed up. He flew out of his vehicle and stomped down to the lake to catch Sherry and Bingo in the act of regulatory defiance. I called out to warn her, and Sherry very wisely and quickly darted with Bingo through the trees up to a stone wall. Two of the other visitors lovingly helped her, and Bingo to quickly scale the wall. We rushed Bingo into the Mustang. We had obviously outsmarted the ranger, which just made him madder. While I sat on the edge of the stone wall with a bottle of raspberry wine at my foot, I chuckled as the ranger checked out Sherry, while explaining how it was against the law to have dogs down on the trails and in these marked areas, as it draws out the bears.

He went on to claim how just the year before a 'mammoth' (black bear) had killed a German Shepard in front of its owners on Paradise. The whole time during his rant he continued to have a conversation with Sherry's scantily covered chest. In the end, he ended up writing her a ticket. She was a little peeved at first, probably mainly because he kept talking to her tits, but because the whole situation was so ridiculous, we just laughed about it throughout that night. The weekend on Rainier was one of the most memorable in my life and was the beginning of many trips we would take that summer, and during the following summer.

It was an 'El Nino' summer, and we were having quite the heat wave. Fridays were heralded as 'casual' dress days at the office, and it was so warm that I sometimes wore jean shorts on Fridays. The ladies seemed to really like it, but O'Malley told me that it could be considered sexual harassment to be dressed so revealingly as I might arouse other staff members. I remember him saying this in passing in front of a couple of the girls I was chatting with; they said they didn't feel harassed (I think they liked what they saw, and I was still in good shape being in my early 30's). I told Sherry about the incident, and she laughed, and said that it was probably Derek that was aroused!

Chapter 3

Crushed Between Two Rocks

S hortly after the trip to Rainier, the real intrigue began. Dirk Fidalgo, the manager for the Portland distribution house was caught buying shrimp from competitors for a better margin. Staff from the Newport facility had alerted me to this fact when they spotted shrimp with Dirk's name on it from a competitor in a truck that they were loading. Considering that mother Magic Mermaid had an over-supply of company-produced fresh shrimp, the distribution houses were supposed to be supporting purchases of corporate products before going out to buy from competitors. Unfortunately, some of the distribution managers had a history of putting their individual facility profits ahead of what was best for the company.

At first, I was torn over what to do, as I was an employee and agent for the distribution group; but still felt the need to support the overall corporate mission for the organization. I made the revelation about Dirk and the shrimp purchase to Steve Poundworth, who was not only one of the category sales managers, but was also in charge of all production from the Oregon facilities.

Steve had me given me access to the 'Reach Out' system on the company's

Get Right inventory system. He then instructed me to go look into the inventories and purchases of each distribution house – quietly, very quietly. So, without 'Dad's knowledge, and with Simpson's blessing, I was now officially assigned as a double agent – caught between the two grinding boulders of corporate sales and distribution. From there out, I regularly 'reached out' to the individual distribution houses and started spying on their purchasing and inventory activities and compiling the data for Poundworth and Simpson. I was truly becoming totally immersed in the heart of Magic Mermaid, now virtually having access to almost every account and sales profile in the entire organization.

And the two rocks continued to grind. How was I to know that I was working to facilitate a huge confrontation and blow-out between O'Malley and Simpson. It was the Fall of '97, and the time for the annual distribution manager's meeting in Seattle was commencing. We had a full agenda, which included the introduction of the full line of new value-added products being produced and launched by Magic Mermaid. The distribution managers were all served a smorgasbord of these new products, immediately followed by a full-on session by the president himself, Bob Blackhead. I will never forget the words that Bill uttered to the distribution team: "I challenge you to sell these new products and make them a success." If only it would be so easy! The distribution team did take the challenge with full attention, and they made a valiant attempt to position these new products solely through personal efforts alone.

Bill left shortly after his speech, and then the shit really hit the fan. Simpson and Poundworth came storming into the meeting, armed to the gills with the purchasing and inventory history for the distribution houses that I had gathered for him. Only I could have any inclination as to what was unfold, but I had no idea the magnitude of fury that was to be unleashed. The meeting started with the usual pleasantry, the 'hi how are, and how have things been going' conversations, but then quickly into an ugly display of revelations and accusations. The room swelled with anger and frustration as the facts were laid upon the table about a number of the distribution houses, and their less than corporate-supporting approach to product purchasing. Tempers raged, faces got red, and I wondered for a minute if a fist fight was about to erupt. And there I sat, watching it all unfold, knowing that I had acted as the agent and catalyst to this confrontation. In a way, I felt like I just betrayed the distribution group, but in reality, I had only done what I had been told by a direct superior. This was my first real experience of being caught in between the conflicting agendas of two bosses – it was a great experience to learn about negotiating conflict, and it galvanized my emotions for the future.

After the big showdown, a calm descended upon the group, and we began to move forward to plan the future for the organization. This was my first, and really only opportunity to speak in front of the distribution group as a whole. I did my best to ensure them that I was there for them, and that I would do everything in my power to support and empower them to be more successful than ever. The managers took my offerings at face value, and I really think that their confidence and trust in my abilities increased, which would be directly reflected in a variety of scenarios as we moved forward.

Consequently, we came away from the big meeting with a new sense of purpose, not just from the 'subtle' reminder that the needs of 'mother MM' was a priority, but also with the priority of leading the charge to launch MM's new value-added product throughout the western sector of the U.S. I took to this new task with great vigor and set about to coordinate and manage the production, as well as the product launches throughout the region. I found there was only two real problems: there was no marketing budget, and the director of marketing took a rather disinterested approach to the entire effort. Still, I did not let this daunt me; I instead re-entrenched my efforts to make these new product lines a success.

Shortly thereafter came my first effort as a community organizer within the organization. I led the charge to organize the MM team for the annual Seattle

Aids Walk. I put out emails to the entire staff, and I placed registration and donation forms on everyone's desks. And I was able to secure approval by corporate to allow us to display a Magic Mermaid banner at the event.

While I was not able to secure a large base of support, we were able to raise some funds, and establish some form of a presence at the event. While the outcome might not have been as successful as envisioned, at least the attempt was made to further the cause. And isn't that what is really the most important result? That you believed in something, and you gave it your all, believing in a cause?

The next thing we knew, it was Halloween, and I found that MM had a yearly costume contest. In my memories, this was one of the lighter and funnier elements that I remember at the company. For Halloween, I dressed in a retro seventies outfit. I was looking tight – from the paisley shirt with pizza-slice-sized collar lapels, to the Robert Redford hair (wig), sideburns, on down to the cheesy Village People mustache and fake chest hair, as well as some God-awful green plaid polyester pants, the kind that makes your skin crawl after a couple of hours of trying to maneuver in them. I knew it was going to be a winner even before I left the house, as Sherry screamed her head off when I woke her up to say goodbye that morning, thinking I was some stranger that has snuck into her bedroom.

When I hit the office, no one could keep a straight face. Everywhere I looked people began to crack up and roll on the floor with laughter. Even my boss took a liking, as he quickly made me a gold necklace and medallion to complete my utterly tasteless '70's costume. By the end of the day I was voted the best costume, joining a very select club of individuals to win the contest during their first year at the organization. I can still see the laughter in people's eyes when they saw me that day, and it still brings joy to my heart to remember their looks. In reflection, that is the greatest gift that God ever bestowed upon me – to make people forget their worries and have a good laugh. We should all try to do a little more of that every day.

So, there we were, leading the industry in a new wave – the value-added movement had begun, and we were at the forefront, what seemed like light years ahead of the rest of the industry. And the best part was, we were building it all right in the Good ole U.S. of A, right on the production lines right below our desks. It was with immense pride that I worked diligently to get these new products out in front of the public. In retrospect, they were some great products (salmon burgers, crabcakes, home meal replacements, etc.) that should have done great in the market, if only we had committed to a little more marketing.

Chapter 4

A Change in the Tide

Then the boom came down. We should have seen it coming. First there were the big financial meetings taking place with the banks (the creditors); everyone could tell because all the vice presidents and the CEO all came to work in white button-down dress shirts. It was like an evil white omen. Then the word came off the street from all our contacts on the outside. The comments were, "time to stick a fork in you guys, cause you're done." The word was out that Magic Mermaid was in financial trouble, and that we were going bankrupt.

And sure enough, they layoffs began. First the corporate retail division was called into Simpson's office. The look on their face made it clear as they left the office; they made a trip to their desk to clean it out, and then they were gone. This set all the rest of us off, as everyone wondered who was next. The upper management soon called a meeting to tell us that the layoffs were over. Then a day or two later, Simpson called more people into his office, and laid off even more sales divisions. The assistant for the procurement division, Ann, was laid off as well. I know it was really hard for Black to do it, but it was not his choice, just his responsibility. I felt so bad for her that I personally walked her out to her car and gave her a hug goodbye.

In the midst of all this, Montrose came to me and asked, "aren't you afraid for your job, you were the last one onboard?" I said, "no, I have confidence in my abilities, and besides, I work for the only division that is keeping the lights on."

Funny thing was, I don't remember them laying off anyone in accounting. So typical, let's keep all the bean counters, but get rid of the sales staff. In retrospect, not a very good plan. I can understand having to reduce overall head count, but why get all rid of all the people that were bringing in money, but none of the people counting the money. Funny how in many cases, finance protects its own department. It reminded of me what my stepfather once told me – when the bean counters are in charge, it is time to get out. I guess I should have heeded this warning, but I was still too busy enjoying the challenge of the new position and opportunity.

Shortly thereafter a message was released by Blackhead (or as I soon lovingly referred to him as – 'Black Tar') that we were cutting costs, which included releasing the janitor. I was just happy that we still had free coffee, which I drank readily from my arrival at 6 am all throughout the day. Since the janitor was gone, that meant we had to empty trash ourselves. So about twice a week I took it upon myself to get a big trash bag and go from desk to desk on the corporate floor, having everyone empty their trash bins into the bag. It was really no big deal, and upon reflection, a great team building experience.

About this time, we were prompted to distribute some samples of some fresh shelled Jonah crab from the East Coast. Jonah crab is a 'stone crab', which is very closely related to the Dungeness crab that is readily available in the Pacific Northwest region. They came in one-pound tubs, and so I sent a couple of tubs to each facility for sampling. Feedback was lackluster at best. It was just a little cheaper than Dungeness, didn't have the same 'nutty' after taste, and had some product defects. I think that Portland summed it up best with their comment when I followed up with them: "Yeah, it's great, if you like the taste of shells and pubic hair." Turns out the supplier was a good friend of Blackhead's, which is why they pushed it on us to begin with, but it was not well adopted into our product line.

Since I had been an actual fisherman in Alaska, some of the distribution managers and salespeople started asking me questions about product from Alaska. BJ started inquiring about what the difference between hook and line-caught cod and trawl-caught cod was, as there was sometimes a considerable price difference, and the customers wanted to know why there was such a difference. Was it a different quality? What makes the price so different? So I explained, "It's like this; you can buy a fish that was brought on board, one at a time, and individually handled and bled, or you can buy a fish that was caught from towing around a giant sock through the water, and brought on board in one giant mass. Which one would you rather eat?" While this might have been a pretty graphic description that many trawlers would not appreciate, it basically is the truth. While some trawl producers do their best to attain the highest quality of product as possible, the quality potential from a hook and line fishery is at an entirely different level than that from a trawl fishery.

In September Sherry asked me if I wanted to start playing soccer with a co-rec team. A friend at work was starting to attend a soccer clinic where teams are formed. So off we went to the intro clinic, and shortly thereafter the group we were training with formed a team we named Red Army. We played a couple of seasons, and then the team disbanded; but by then I had met enough people in the soccer community that I had gravitated to another team, and had firmly entrenched soccer as a weekly to bi-weekly activity for years to come (and still to this day).

As another element of my team building experience, I started going on the road to all the various distribution locations. First was Portland, which I visited with O'Malley; we drove together in his BMW. I think it was always important for Derek to visit the Portland facility, as it is where he had started his career at the 'Portland Fish' facility, so it was symbolically his home. He had only moved to Seattle to take the promotion to VP of the distribution group. I could tell when we were there that he there was a tinge of melancholy for the town he once called home. During this visit I realized the strategic importance of the Portland facility, as it operated in the face of Magic Mermaid's biggest competitor, Western Fish (also known in close circles as 'West Fish'), whose headquarters were just down the road in Warrenton.

I spent time getting to know the staff. The one person I clashed a little with was the assistant manager; he had a real attitude about Seattle eclipsing Portland as the base of operations for the group, and Seattle having a larger sales base than Portland. I enjoyed 'stirring the pot' with him on this subject constantly. One day on the phone he said to me, "When are you going to get it through your head? Portland is the center of the seafood universe!" Of which I quickly and slyly replied, "Actually, the official Center of the Universe is just down the street from the plant here in Seattle. It's called Fremont, and there is a sign hanging up in front of the town to prove it!" He had no reply.

Then came the spot prawn experiment. Spot prawns are actually shrimp, and they are hands down the best shrimp I have ever tasted. During November of 1997, Magic Mermaid decided to buy spot prawns from harvesters that were fishing in Southeast Alaska. The idea was to get a higher price for them by selling them in a fresh format. Since it was a limited quantity and the intention was to go fresh with them, the plan was to move them through the distribution houses. All the managers were ready to move on it, when the first shipment came down from Ketchikan.

The problem was that it had taken so much time to move from the boats, through various locations in Southeast, before getting shipped. The fresh prawns were in sealed bags (tied shut), and by the time they had been received at the Seattle plant, they were already starting to decay and build up gas. So not only had it taken a lot of time in transit for the shrimp to move to Seattle, to make matters worse, many of the larger size spots had egg clutches, which were making them build up gases faster, which intensified the rate of decay in a fresh state (spot shrimp, like sea urchins, are hermaphroditic, so when they start life as males, but when they get older and larger, they switch sex into females).

Black and I were there the afternoon the spots arrived. We were both very excited about starting this new fresh program, so we were really disappointed when we opened the bags and smelled the gasses starting to build. We knew the shrimp weren't going to last long at this rate, so we opened all the bags, let the gas diffuse, iced them down, and then made the decision to sell them all to Seattle Distribution to move them quickly on the market because of their short shelf life. I secured a purchase order from Dick Thompson, and then they moved over to distribution's side for sales. The next morning, I dropped down to Seattle's chilled floor to see what was going on with the spots. Seattle had sat on them all night, they weren't on their sales sell sheet, and they were just sitting there on a cart, ready to go rotten. When I pushed on the sales managers, they said they did not have interest in moving them. If something wasn't done, they were going to be a total loss.

I ran upstairs and told Black about the situation and dropped the idea on him to either throw them in the freezer or sell them all to the staff at a little over cost. At least this way, they wouldn't be a total loss, and the staff could enjoy some tasty Alaska spots. I quickly cobbled together an employee price list and send a message out over the internal email system. Orders from all over the building came in almost instantly. Now it was time to get the spots rinsed, re-bagged and ready for pickup by staff. I had the production staff on the corporate set up to rinse and re-bag. It should have been a simple transfer from Seattle distribution to corporate side. It was only 25 feet or so, from two sets of doors, from one room, the cold room, and onto the other floor. I went to the corporate floor and asked where they were. They said, 'tell distribution to send them over. I walked over to the distribution floor to see where the spots were. They said, "tell them to come and get them."

Ridiculous. We were at a total standstill (and it wouldn't be the last time).

We were at a WTF moment again. Consequently, I grabbed the cart, and I literally pushed it through to the other side. This was one of those moments when I was really felt like I was earning that coordinator title. But at least we got them all sold off and out the door. In hindsight, I suggested that if we were going to try moving spots again that we try to move them live – but we never did.

About that time, I noticed the sign hanging up in the shipping office downstairs – some of the wisest words I ever learned and have constantly applied throughout my career and life: "Your lack of planning does not necessitate my emergency."

Chapter 5

Hitting the Road

As winter set in I traveled by myself, first to Spokane. It was not the largest of the distribution houses, but the staff was very colorful. The manager at that time was Kevin, who his staff lovingly referred to him as 'the Belly Man'. We visited various customers, including a visit to Bernie's, where I first recognized Bernie's method of 'premier' retail merchandising, which included separating the various different species in the display cases with ugly bright bands of light blue plastic strips, and stacking the product to the top of the display case like a pile of firewood.

Spokane had a good staff, and Kevin was very cordial. In fact, I stayed an extra day for the weekend and spent time sightseeing in the back country with his son. The time spent built great rapport and gave him the confidence to know that I would take care of him.

Shortly following I traveled to Boise. This visit opened my eyes about the 'hidden history' of Magic Mermaid, mainly due to the manager at the time, BJ Michaels (who I soon nicknamed 'BJ Neanderthal'). BJ didn't pull any punches. He had been with Magic Mermaid for some time, back when the Boise facility was still owned by Idaho Seafood, which was later purchased by Magic Mermaid. BJ had been childhood friends with the Simpson brothers and knew them all too well. He told me how Dave had started out with him as a delivery driver and had soon worked his way up to the Boise manager position before moving on to Seattle with his brother. He told me about how they had gone to school with one of the sons of an executive of Bernie's (whose corporate office is based in Boise), which revealed to me why Magic Mermaid was so supportive of Bernie's as a customer.

BJ also told me a deep, dark, unspoken secret about the Simpson family – which was actually rather amusing when you think about it. It seems that Dave and Alex's brother-in-law (married to their sister) had at one time been hired as the manager for the Boise facility. Accordingly, he had a little problem with 'nose candy' and ended up skimming the books to cover his habit. When it came time for the team from corporate to perform the yearly audit, he knew he was going to be in trouble. So, in an act of desperation (no doubt fueled by drug-induced paranoia), he tried to burn some of the frozen seafood inventory by pouring gasoline on it and setting in on fire.

Well, frozen fish doesn't burn too well, even when helped with a little gasoline, so all it did was make a big, stinky mess. From what I was told, he was quietly 'let go', and the whole thing was swept under the rug to avoid loss of face by the Simpson family. To this day I still get a chuckle visualizing this cokehead, sweating in a panic, dragging frozen blocks of fish out of the freezer, dumping gas all over them, and setting them on fire, only to watch the flames go out after the gasoline had burned off. I wonder how long it took him, and how many times he poured gas on the frozen product, before he realized he was totally fucked. God, what a mess that must have been.

I audited a Bernie's store again while in Boise. And again, the seafood in the display case was wrapped in ghastly shade of blue, and stacked to the top of the case like wood. The blue really gave the white fish a strange-looking hue, reminding me how important colors play a role in branding and marketing.. I also got to play 'collection agent' for BJ. We visited a food service customer in downtown Boise, a small restaurant that was way behind on her bill to Boise. They had made a number of attempts to collect, but the owner had continued to shine them on. So BJ and I paid her a little visit. I was introduced as 'being from corporate in Seattle'; we created the image that I had come to Boise just to collect from delinquent accounts like hers. I reminded her that she was way behind on paying her bill to us, and that we valued her as a customer, and would hate to have to take further action. It worked, because she pulled out her check book and wrote a check right for the overdue amount right away. Sometimes being 6'4" and having an intimidating stance can come in quite handy!

Derek had told me when I first started that we didn't treat our own distribution group outlets very well, when they were some of corporate's best customers. So, I decided to take the Boise staff to a great dinner while I was there– on Magic Mermaid corporate's dime. I was to be chastised for it later, but it was worth it to see the staff feel the respect that had been due for a long time.

BJ and I really hit it off. He had revealed so much to me, including that the distribution group's secret nickname for O'Malley was 'Dad', due to his overly paternal management style – kind of like a 'father knows best' attitude. Yup, BJ was definitely an in-your-face, no-bullshit kind of guy; the type of person I could really respect. And he was very cordial like Bellyman in Spokane. In fact, BJ had me stay at his house during my visit. I repaid his kindness by giving him something to really laugh about, as I slipped on my ass on his ice-covered driveway while walking in my cowboy boots. He didn't let me live that one down for a while. But I didn't mind, because I realized that if he could make fun of me openly, that he really liked me. My heart went out for him, as he had grown up with Mark, and knew him so well, but I sense that there was a feeling of betrayal between old boyhood friends. Dave had moved up the ladder in corporate but had left his old buddy BJ behind in Boise to be forgotten.

My next visit was to Salt Lake City Distribution. I guess the purchase of facility was a tremendous deal – which I was told should be credited to O'Malley, who negotiated the deal; essentially the old owners were way behind on the bills, etc., and Derek essentially negotiated it so that the owners actually paid Magic Mermaid to take it off their hands! This facility was a real cash cow. It had one of the highest margins on average, and very little competition. It had a great customer base – lots of high-end ski resorts in the surrounding mountains. A lot of well to do Mormons in the area didn't hurt business either.

Mark Devonshire was the manager and was a really nice guy – and a sharp one to boot. The assistant manager was a guy named James Jeffries, who was a really sharp cookie himself. It was a large facility that was very clean and very impressive. The one thing that really stood out about Mark when I first walked in his office was that his desk was spotless. Not a single paper on it. Maybe he was just a clean freak. But someone had always taught me that a clean desk meant you had nothing to do, and not in a good way (or that you have too much time on your hands). In retrospect I think that Mark was just a very organized individual and ran a really 'tight ship'.

While I was there, I visited one of their top food service customers – one of the resorts at Park City. After visiting with the staff, I consulted with one of the resort's top chefs. He was suspicious of wild salmon because it came in a product form with no head. Since he was so used to working with farmed salmon, which always came fresh, and with its head on, I could understand his concern. I let him know that the head-off format for wild salmon was just an industry standard that had been in place since the inception of the fresh/frozen production (I assume as a cost-saving measure, since so much production takes place in very remote locales throughout Alaska, and storage and shipping costs can add up quickly). As a result of this exercise, Magic Mermaid actually attempted to produce some fresh, head-on production specifically for the Salt Lake market.

It was a great example of having a customer-driven marketing approach that had been so rarely instituted in the industry. Kind of like Burger King's ad campaign of the 1970's: "Hold the pickles, hold the lettuce, special orders don't upset us." The industry could and (probably still could learn) from such approaches. For as I was to confirm later while at ASA, the production-based mindset was not isolated just to Magic Mermaid but was permeated across most of the rest of the Alaska seafood industry.

They probably couldn't help it, as historically the industry had started by a bunch of greedy carpetbaggers that saw dollar signs (salmon) milling around to get up creeks and rivers in the summertime, and just set up traps and canneries around these major tributaries in order to catch and shove as much salmon in the can (and salted barrels) as they could during a three to four-month period. The ruthless bastards had no idea of the biology of the salmon, so in many cases they managed to destroy some of the largest salmon runs in the world in a seven-year period (like Karluk and Akalura Lakes on Kodiak Island, that were respectively the 1st and 2nd largest sockeye salmon runs in the world at the turn of the 20th century. To this day, they are still attempting to rebuild Karluk to a substantial level again, and Akalura is basically a 'ghost lake' with a tiny little salmon return every year). Yes, they probably thought the salmon would just keep coming back forever but were rudely awakened when the runs dropped off to almost nothing after they killed off the brood stock and totally destroyed the life cycle process.

Anyway, after finishing talking with the chef, the sales rep and I went and got a bottle of Jack Daniel's (great for 'loosening the legs up') and proceeding to go night skiing at Park City. The next day I visited some more retail customers and food service clients and took their top sale rep to lunch as a bonus at their best customer restaurant. I was trying to do like O'Malley had told me, and that was to treat the distribution houses like they were our best customers, not like the red-headed stepchildren that they had previously been treated like.

I think it was the last night I was there that I decided to walk the streets and check out the Mormon Temple; I have to admit, it was an awesome sight – those giant dark pillars jutting up into the sky, all strategically illuminated by lighting, almost like it was some alien altar from 150 years ago. But that was about it; it was like 8-9 at night on a Thursday night, and the streets were strangely devoid of people. Talk about 'rolling up the streets at night.'! It was dead, except for one of the diners on one of the corners, and one bar/club that appeared to have some signs of life, with people milling around out in front of it. I drove up and down the street a couple of times in my rental car to check it out, but I had a strange feeling that something wasn't right about it.

So, I drove back to my hotel and went to bed instead. Which was not like me at all, as I had always been a night owl, and was always looking to find a good watering hole for drinking, dancing and carousing. The next morning, I was back at the Salt Lake office, and while sharing a cup of coffee, I pointed out my observations of the lack of nightlife – even on 'ladies' night' (Thursday). I told them about the one bar I had found. They all began to chuckle and reassured me that I didn't miss anything by not stopping in, as it was notoriously known as being the local gay bar. Gay Mormons anyone?

No doubt there were other clubs and places to party in Salt Lake City (or maybe are now), but to this day, when I think of downtown Salt Lake City, the images I conjure are of strangely empty streets, with the exception of one little happening building with a bunch of dudes standing around outside, grabbing each other's asses. Surely not the 'curb appeal that the Salt Lake City Visitor's Association was envisioning...

Shortly after returning to Seattle, I submitted my receipts for reimbursement. And right after that I was called into O'Malley's office; I could tell by the look on Derek's face that he was less than pleased. Out came the stack of receipts. And I began to catch hell for my actions in Salt Lake. And in a way, rightly so. I had submitted receipts for the bottle of whiskey, and the ski lift tickets. I had assumed that these would be acceptable 'entertainment' expenses, since I was basically entertaining one of the distribution food service salesmen. But he drew the line and said, "This is not acceptable." And then he continued to lay into for the expensive lunch I charged to Magic Mermaid when I took their top salesperson to lunch at one of their top customer restaurants. I reminded him what he had told me when I first started about treating the distribution locations more like a customer; he conceded a little, and agreed to reimburse for the lunch expense, but told me that there would be no more of that in the future – any future entertainment meals would be pre-approved only.

After being dismissed, I shared what had transpired with Ed. Ed shook his head and said that was not right. He had a good point – if parameters and expectations had not been very clearly identified, then why should I be crucified for it? Better that they set expectations and limitations first, instead of sending me out into the field to establish it by trial and error. It was a valuable exercise for me in communicating expectations, instead of just assuming.

One of the things that I had noticed when I was at Salt Lake City was the infrastructure being built to accommodate the upcoming 2002 Winter Olympics. I told Derek that we should start working to secure the sales and distribution contracts to supply the athletes at the Olympic village. Visions of Magic Mermaid products being used to fuel the world's premiere athletes began to swim in my head. But as usual, the idea was totally ignored, and went nowhere.

Helena was next. It was a fairly long flight, and I sat next to a pretty native girl that I chatted with until stopping over in Butte, where she got off. And then on to 'sheep country'. Lots of sheep – and snow everywhere along with wide open spaces. It was fucking cold, and full of cowboys. But they were really nice, down-home types, that were very warm and inviting. Helena was like so many other state capitols, another small town that was far from being the largest city in the state or any type of perceived center of commerce or industry, but had happened to retain the state government, probably form early days as a territory. Funny how that is so true of so many state capitols I have known and visited:Olympia, Salem, Sacramento, Montgomery, Juneau, Tallahassee; the list goes on and on....

We visited the Magic Mermaid facility and met the staff and then went and visited the headquarters for Callahan's. I apologized profusely for the 'Coho catastrophe' that had taken place in August (even though it was partially their fault for not checking the boxes of fresh fish the entire weekend, as it had been a direct shipment to them, and they had officially taken title of the product), and took the opportunity to review our new retail education manual and how such a tool would avoid similar incidents in the future.

Then it was onto Great Falls. Through the snowstorm, we drove. Past long, endless fields of snow we drove, with white sheep barely discernible amongst the snow. I joked that they needed to paint the sheep during the winter, or else the cowboys were going to go lonely all winter. And then we passed occasional buffalo too. It was picturesque, just as I had remembered Montana as an early child, when I had spent a winter in Great Falls with my mother and brother when my mom decided to live with some guy out there for the better of a year.

We hit Great Falls and did some retail audits. Inside a Callahan's I saw Magic Mermaid's home meal replacements in a retail setting for the first time. A customer had actually bought them and put them on display in the fresh section (customers in Boise and other locales had placed them in the frozen aisle, and then complained that the product didn't look appealing because it was 'iced over' – something they had not been designed for).

Great Falls was just what I had remembered in my mind. Lots of single-level buildings, and spread out all over God's creation. I saw lots of trucker and cowboy bars and massage parlors. Todd politely invited me to visit one of the massage parlors; we walked in the door, but then I got a strange, sleazy feeling, and politely declined. We ended up having lunch at bar with a really cute Mexican girl tending the bar; we flirted with her for a while, had a couple of shots of tequila, and then drove back to Helena. On the way back Todd told me how it was always another bad year at MM – according to corporate.

He explained how his brother had been working for him for the past two years or so for dirt cheap and how he really wanted to give him some type of raise. Even though the facility was continually more profitable, he was still being informed that he couldn't give his brother (or any other staff) any raises, because it was 'another bad year at Magic Mermaid'. This seemed to be a resounding trend at most of the facilities I had visited (at least with those that felt open enough and trusted me enough to talk about it). I enjoyed my time with Todd; he was a kind and humble person and had really put his trust in me. He had invited me to stay another night and told me I could stay at his house. I thanked him for the offer, but I wanted to keep on schedule, and I wanted to get back to home to Sherry.

Chapter 6

Trying Something New

Next thing I knew it was January 1998. This is traditionally the slowest time for the industry – at least in the sales sector. It was so slow that I started to think that the company would have saved money just by sending everyone home for the month on paid leave – at least they would save money on the utilities for having the power on all day for nothing. But then the creative side of my mind kicked in. I had a good look at the frozen inventories (which I had been became very intimate with as I had participated in the quarterly inventory audits every quarter – which were marathon, round-the-clock, all weekend long affairs – but lots of overtime).

Sure enough, there were thousands of pounds of frozen sockeye salmon in inventory in the Seattle freezer. Then I started to ask the question – why not sell some frozen sockeye at the retail level? I started asking around; checking with the distribution managers. Such a thing had never been done before, so they wondered if it would work. But if the price was right, why not give it a try? Boise, Spokane, and Seattle said they were in. Astoria, Helena, Portland, and Salt Lake chose to pass. And Pocatello decided it would feed off of Boise's supply. I didn't get the perception that those outlets didn't want to participate, it's just that the dynamics weren't right and they had limited customer interest (except Astoria, and Portland, who always seemed to be more interested in keeping their profit margins high as their sole measurement, versus Boise and Spokane who were both real 'team' players that were always willing to take the chance).

I went to O'Malley and got approvals to set a frozen sockeye promotion into play. And away we went. If I remember correctly, we set the prices at around $2.00 a pound wholesale. It was enough to make a small profit for corporate, a little for the distribution facilities, and still make a reasonable price at retail. And besides, this was product that would have just been sitting in the freezer, getting freezer burnt (and high oil fish like sockeye remarkably suffer from 'oil migration' when held at less than -60 Fahrenheit; the oil in the flesh literally migrates to the outer edge near the skin). A great sign that this promotion was going to be a success was the fact that Western Fish literally lashed right back with their own offer, and a price war ensued.

While Boise and Spokane were doing good with their sales, the demand in Seattle exploded overnight; Kevin told me he needed every last fish we had in inventory. As I went downstairs to the flood to talk with Bob Wyman (the production manager) about 'feeding the monster' known as Seattle, here came another great lesson for me about one of the greatest challenges still faced by a number of major salmon processors in Alaska – inconsistency in grading standards and processes.

Bob had all the remaining inventories of Alaska sockeye. I can only describe this as a very well-used acronym: FUBAR – Fucked Up Beyond All Recognition. We had lots of headed and gutted fish from three Alaska facilities: Cordova, Kodiak, and Petersburg (in those days every single fish from the Naknek facility in Bristol Bay went directly to Japan on tramper vessels). Almost all the fish from Kodiak were listed on the inventory as #2's, and almost the fish from Cordova (the home of the world-famous Copper River salmon) were listed as #1's. And Petersburg fish were a mixed bag, listed as #1 and #2.

The Petersburg fish were off on their grading; there were #2's that were in the #1 inventory and vice versa. But the grading of the Cordova and Kodiak fish were appalling. The #2's from Kodiak looked way better than the #1s from Cordova. It was a mess. But the crew did the best they could to grade to product out in its proper format for distribution. With the exception of a couple lots that were so poor that they fell into a # 3 category, (and were re-directed for other use, like value-added, flaking etc.) we were able to move the remaining lots for sales through the Seattle facility. But it really opened my eyes into far off the industry could be when it came to their grading standards.

Sales started to pick up as the winter moved along. I continued to work on improving the monthly newsletters, the market reports, as well as working on finding ways to promote the new line of Magic Mermaid products. I formed a website committee and began to develop a draft website for the company (but wasn't embraced and implemented).

Next thing you know, it was early springtime. And it was time for me to go and visit the Astoria plant. Magic Mermaid still had a little production facility in Astoria, but it was in its final stages of being shut down perma-nently. The real money in Astoria was 'Diamond Dave's' distribution house. And you couldn't hide this facility when you came rolling into town. Dave's wife had picked the color for the building – bright purple; I shit you not. I could not believe it when I saw it; I sat in my Mustang and rolled onto the floorboard to laugh myself silly for a minute – the kind of laughing that makes your ribs ache from laughing so hard!

Astoria had a small market, but very high sales margins – the highest margins in the entire distribution group. Dave knew how to squeeze a dime out of a dollar really well. And the area had a lot of high-end beachfront resorts, as well as a lot of 'fish and chips' stands, so it was also a great home for all of Magic Mermaid's chalky halibut. Chalky halibut is a condition where the halibut meat takes on a less than opaque appearance, similar to the color and texture of chalk. It is perfectly edible, but it is totally unsuitable for use in the high-end food service or retail sectors, where the customer would not be pleased with lack of visual appeal. But chalky halibut is perfectly fine with lathered with batter and deep fried!

I toured the small 'purple plant' and spent some time getting to know the sales staff, including Kelly, whom I had met when she visited Seattle – and was a real 'looker', and had a lot of fun to joke with boot. One of the real eye-opening experiences for me during this trip was visiting the crabmeat production plant that was based just to the north, on the Washington side of the Columbia River. The majority of the plant was mothballed, a sad but telling sign of the mighty fisheries of the Northwest region that once existed but had been terribly overfished to the point of almost commercial extinction. But in one end of the plant a little life still existed four days of the week – at least part time. I walked into the plant, and on the floor, there was an army of minions garbed in white, cracking and shucking Dungeness crab like there was no tomorrow.

The workers were paid by weight extracted, not by a simple hourly wage, so the quicker they shucked, the better the pay. The workers filled trays of extruded meat, which would then be scanned thoroughly under a black light to spot any stray shell particles for removal. Then it would be packed into either one-pound bags, one-pound plastic cartons, or canned in five-pound steel cans. It was quite the impressive but seemingly thankless process, a lost art that is rarely seen these days here in the U.S. But one should not take for granted the precision work performed by those that extruded the meat so readily. Next time you enjoy Dungeness crab meat at a restaurant, remember that it did not come easily!

After the tour of the plant, I returned to the plant to visit the staff again. Kelly and the others asked what I was doing after work. Dave, who was a very profound Christian, made it look like he was taking me out (or to his house for dinner) – this is the impression he gave his staff. But all he did was take me to the vista point on top of the hill overlooking the town, and then dropped me off at my hotel room (unlike those 'heathen's' in Boise and Spokane that opened their homes to me). Kelly thought I was going out with Dave for the night, otherwise she and the staff would have taken me out and showed me the town. The next morning the staff and I said our goodbye's and I headed back north to Seattle.

The one distribution facility I never visited (and was sorry I never did) was the one in Pocatello, Idaho. Frank was a nice enough guy, but his shop was pretty small, so corporate felt that I could skip the visit.

Each locale had its own special flavor. Salt Lake always focused on needing a profit – which came mostly from high-end food service; this had been made explicitly clear by its managers. Boise were both not huge markets, but were little powerhouses in their own right, especially due to their management's attitudes. Helena was an 'outpost', again not a large market, but still a revenue maker, and a presence is the sparsely populated state that is Montana. Pocatello was probably the one house that was still a question mark. It had been inherited when MM purchased Idaho Seafood and had been maintained all this time; it made money but had a very small footprint. The conventional wisdom was that as soon as the manager retired, it would be shut down, as the territory could be easily covered by Boise and Salt Lake.

Astoria was also a margin-driven shop, and was on the cusp of the battle-ground, just up the road from Western Portland seemed like an outpost in enemy territory, and what a challenging position that had to be. I always needed to keep this mind when working with Dirk and the Portland crew. And then there was Seattle, the 800 - pound gorilla of the distribution group; it by far had the largest market, and the greatest resources at hand. It was another battleground with Pacific, but at least it had the strategic advantage of being situated at the same physical location of 'Mother MM'.

Boise and Spokane were the more fun houses to work with, for they exuded and lived the team spirit of Magic Mermaid regularly. Whenever we were long on fresh product, I knew I could depend on them to absorb a good chunk of the excess inventory. My favorite recollection was one morning when the Oregon production center called and told me were long on the inventory of fresh shrimp – over 800 pounds. I had called all the rest of the distribution locales, and none of the rest wanted to move on it. All I had to do was pick up the phone to Spokane and Boise, and the bidding war was on for who would buy the most.

I would call the Belly man in Spokane and tell him about the shrimp. The first question out of his mouth was, "How much did Boise take?" I told him that I hadn't gotten to him yet. So, the Belly man says, "You tell BJ in Boise that I am taking 300 pounds." Then I would call BJ. He would ask, "how much did my brother in Spokane take? Whatever it is, I'll take 50 pounds more." This would ensue, with me going back and forth on the phone, until all of the product was spoken for. If only everyone was so easy to work with. These two were truly gems in the Magic Mermaid crown, and I still smile when I think about working with them.

And let us not forget Seattle Distribution! Quite the cast of characters. Alex Simpson. Nice guy, but as described by more than one fellow MM employee, he provided the mental image to most that he was sitting in his office most of the day, blowing bubbles. It was probably unfair, but the general feeling in the office was that if it wasn't for the fact that he was Dave's brother, he wouldn't have a job there. I used to joke with him years later, when I would visit as an ASA employee, and ask him if he was still taking up oxygen.

And then there was Dick Thompson, the fresh purchasing manager for the distribution house. Great if you want him buying for you, but if you are a vendor, or anyone else that is around, he was considered a nightmare. Dick was probably abused as a child (locked in a closet or something), as he really didn't give a shit what anybody thought about how he treated others- and he we would be the first to agree with that statement. I also thought he would look really good with a Nazi brownshirt or SS outfit on – it would be perfect, he was short, had an evil scowl on his face, and he even had the little, groomed Hitler mustache to go along with it. But Dick was one hell of a buyer, and one of the most efficient managers I ever met. He and I used to do mass product transfers together and I needed purchase orders from him so I could create sales orders for the transfers. I would sit next to him and whip the product orders out to him so he could create the purchase orders in masse. I started to call him the 'one finger wonder'. Dick could only type with one finger, but to this day, I have never seen a person type so fast with one finger – really amazing. Dick and I actually became pretty close once he let his guard down a little, but he was always pretty gruff, and he never had a problem chewing my ass out (or anyone else's for that matter) in front of everyone.

But then there was the 'anti-Dick', David Richie. David was salt of the earth. Very witty, and funny, and a real leader. I can't say enough good things about David. He was basically the frozen purchasing manager and sales manager for Seattle Distribution, all rolled up into one. David used to give me shit, but it was always well-natured, and with a sense of humor. And he and I ended up working on a number of projects together, including the creation of the full-color, MM holiday newsletter. There was a general consensus on the floor that David should be the general manager of the Seattle facility (and he was basically the de-facto manager); he would have been if not for Alex Simpson being planted in the spot. In fact, it was David that gave me my final performance review, and also was the one that gave me the news that I was being laid off. Still, I have the utmost respect for him, as the rest of the salespeople at Seattle Distribution did.

I had received a wide variance of feedback from the various locations, but overall there was one resounding theme – we needed to do more marketing! Managers would share stories about people that would call Magic Mermaid, thinking it was a beauty salon. Yes, indeed, it was time to raise awareness about the MM brand, time to create the proper image. And the sales staff would get frustrated when new products would be presented to them to sell, with little or no product information, no point of sale (POS) materials, let alone any promotional support. I could feel their frustration and more than once I found myself putting in the overtime to generate POS materials for them to use with their customers. And I was always going the distance for the sales guys at Seattle Distribution, since they could bend my ear directly on a regular basis.

When a new value-added product was launched, I started having the test chef (who I lovingly referred to as the 'Mad Scientist') cook up samples for me to serve to the Seattle sales floor. At least they couldn't say they didn't know anything about the product anymore. Training the sales staff with new products is essential, and in this case, tasting it was the quickest way possible to get them educated and excited about the product.

One victory for me was the creation of the Magic Bonita logo. One of the great new value-added products that MM had created was salmon fajitas, which were made from keta (chum) salmon. These, as well as fajitas made from tuna, had been created on a custom-order basis (like a number of other products) for sales and distribution by a third party (in this case Trade Joe's). Magic Mermaid was conceptualizing creating its own line of branded salmon fajitas but was struggling with a new brand that would represent this line of 'Latin' products. Someone was throwing out the idea of using one of the canned brands, Icy Point, for the sales brand. I laughed to myself and thought, "that doesn't conjure up images of a spicy and tasty salmon fajita!" They have got be kidding!

I put my mind to it, and out popped 'Magic Bonita Salmon Fajitas'. It was perfect, not only was 'bonita' an almost perfect translation of 'beauty' in Spanish, but it even rhymed! Away I went on the old Mac clone sitting in the 'marketing' cubicle; I took the MM logo with the maiden and did sketching in Photoshop to switch the lettering around, put a sombrero on the maidens' head, and a maraca in her hand – and the Magic Bonita logo was born! I drew up a mockup of potential packaging bag for the product concept, and then we turned it over to the advertising agency to complete.

While the fajita line faltered later (probably due to lack of marketing and promotional support), years later after I left MM, they continued to use my logo to represent additional Latin product, including an awesome salmon chorizo. To this day, the Magic Bonita line is still listed in their product brand lineup on their website. And it still makes me feel good inside whenever I see it; I just love it when one of my ideas is put to good use.

I was really starting to get fired up with creative energy (spring always does that to me), and I really wanted to see the value-added products get the promotional support they deserved. One morning I was sitting in traffic on the way to the office, and I sat there behind a Seattle Metro bus; and there it was, staring right in front of me – a huge print ad on the back of the truck (and all over the sides). That was it! Seattle Distribution alone must have at least twelve to sixteen trucks on the road, almost every single day of the week. And every distribution had at least a couple trucks. Visions of mobile Magic Mermaid billboards splashed with the colorful images of our new value-added lines of products rushed through my head. What an affordable way to get our products out in front of consumers!

We could take those plain white trucks and make them our mobile messaging platforms. I went out and secured bids from Baker Industries, which was one of the leaders in mobile graphics at the time. We had a lot of options, as the film was available in various thicknesses, so we could affordably change our imagery every six months if we were to choose. I put together a proposal and put it in front of O'Malley, suggesting that we use Seattle as a test market with a few trucks. He gave me the same spiel about how we didn't have the budget for marketing. And again, another great idea that could have provided the new products some semblance of a chance was shot to hell. This was really starting to get frustrating for me.

Then there were the spring halibut promotions. The commercial halibut season would typically start on March 15 every year (since the institution of the individual fishing quota) (IFQ) and there was this huge buildup by retailers to drive customers to their stores, with big ads in the newspaper promoting fresh halibut at ridiculously low prices. And guess who was expected to absorb a huge chunk of the loss? MM Distribution was expected to drop its pants to meet the ad prices. Corporate would try and help absorb some of the loss by reducing the transfer price, but it was the distribution side who was expected to take the bulk of the hit to its margins.

The retailers would leverage them hard, knowing that they would concede in order to keep the year-round business. And all so that Bernie's, GVF, or some other retailer could drive customers to the store to buy their frozen peas. It seemed like madness the first time I watched it happen; but in retrospect, it is just part of the retail game that is played. This is a valuable lesson to anyone looking to get into selling to retailers – expect to get beat up bloody on the price and try to make it up on volume; it's either that, or bypass and sell it to customers directly. But realistically, how many people are going to buy fresh halibut online? "Yes, I'll take two half-pound fillets. Could I get that delivered to my house today via UPS for free?"

And let's not forget the (fairly) new kid on the block: farmed salmon. It was quite an education working directly with this product (as well as a plethora of others). I must admit, one could see how it was quite appealing to consumers to have salmon available in fresh, uniform formats on a year-round basis. And the farmed industry did build a whole new market for salmon by making it available for the masses around the world on a regular basis. But the more I learned about it, the more I questioned it.

Salmon are carnivores. Which means they need to eat protein to flourish and grow. Estimates from studies indicated that it takes three to four pounds of food fish to make one pound of farmed. This 'food fish' came typically from cheap, high-volume fisheries (like the anchoveta fisheries of the southern oceans), or from ground-up fish remains that had been turned into meal.

So basically, the farmed producers are robbing the ocean on one side of the planet so that they can grow it for a profit on the other side. It doesn't take a rocket scientist to figure out that this is not a sustainable practice for the long term.

Many may contend with the following statement... from what we have learned from the mad-cow crises over the past twenty years, when an animal is fed its own kind, bad things start to happen. To this day, I have warned consumers about the potential for 'mad salmon' disease. Farmed salmon might actually have been raised on the remains of wild (or even farmed) salmon. And similar to other mass-market protein industries, farmed salmon are typically raised at high densities levels in pens, which creates an environment for the growth of contagious diseases (like infectious salmon anemia). Therefore, the industry has adopted widespread use of anti-biotic agents, which is a major point of contention with consumers seeking pure and natural foods.

To make matters worse, there is also widespread use of synthetic coloring agents like astaxanthin, which helps to provide the flesh with vibrant hues of orange and red that you might have recognized at the grocery store. It reminds me of the time that Ed announced for us all to come and see the new farmed, 'fire-engine red' steelhead, fresh from Chile. And it was damn red at that – to the point of looking far from natural. But as I was later to learn, Japanese consumers adore red-flesh colored salmon, which can no doubt be attributed to their long-standing love affair with wild sockeye salmon (and they still haven't figured out how to farm a sockeye, thank God).

I remember seeing the first generation of 'organic' farmed salmon, which didn't' use any artificial coloring agents, and the flesh was 'white as a sheet'. Wild salmon derive their true color from naturally occurring astaxanthin, typically derived from the consumption of shrimp. But in most cases for farmed salmon (for cost savings) it is derived from synthetic sources; mmm, have some more chemicals cooked up in a lab and brought to you by companies like Roche.

And then there is Kudoa. It is an occurrence in farmed salmon (and other marine fisheries) that is tied to a parasite infection. And it is nasty. I first saw it shortly after I started at Magic Mermaid. Seattle Distribution were filleting some farmed fish, and Ed got the call upstairs that we had some Kudoa on the floor. He and I went downstairs to see what it looked like. It was reminiscent of something one would see in a sci-fi movie. Essentially the infected fillet laying on the table appeared to have started bubbling and liquefying and started draining off the table and onto the floor. Talk about disturbing. And there is no way of detecting it until you have the product in hand and are filleting it. Another fine reason why you will never catch me eating farmed salmon – besides, I don't like the taste of it either. Call me a salmon snob if you like, but for me, eating wild salmon is cheap health insurance.

During my orientation at Magic Mermaid, I had been educated about the organization, and specifically the needs and requirements of the distribution group. O'Malley had impressed upon me a sense of integrity, and the importance of bringing things to his attention that looked out of place. It was months later, and I accidentally stumbled upon something that really looked out of place. It started when one of the distribution houses needed some 6 oz. fillet portions (if I remember correctly, it was salmon). There was none available from corporate inventory, as the only inventory remaining in-house was already committed to another sales order – which happened to be for one of BM French's customers. Usually, I would have just gone to BM and asked him if he could just release a couple boxes (since his order was not slated to ship out for another week or two), but he was out of town, so I was going to have to go into the order myself on Get Right and de-commit the product I needed.

It's when I went into the order that I noticed that all of the prices for each of his products was considerably under the threshold price that was established on the current corporate sales list. It was a pretty set policy on what the corporate sales prices should be (distribution could get a slightly lower price, since they were affiliates, and would need to stay competitive in their respective markets), and it clearly outlined what volume discount rates would be, and at what volume level a discount could be provided. But all of the price on BM's sales order were well below the prices outlined on the corporate sales sheet; in fact, they were substantially lower than the lowest discount prices outlined by policy – and the volume for each item was well below the threshold for a discount.

I was in disbelief at first; but I knew that the prices were way too low. I'm no angel, and I've made plenty of mistakes in my life, but I have always tried to be as honest as possible when it came to business. I just couldn't look the other way. I printed out a copy of the sales order and took it to Derek. I started out by reminding him that he had trained me when I first started to come to him and report if I saw things out of line. I started questioning, "How was it that these prices were way below the corporate list?" "What was going on here?" And then I think I crossed the line; I cited that this looked like it was a violation of the Clayton Act (in this case the provision being price discrimination). O'Malley looked a little flustered when I mentioned the Clayton Act; he dismissed me quietly by saying he would research the matter and then get back to me. He never did; this was the beginning of 'Dad's attitude towards me starting to chill.

Next up was the bi-annual distribution meeting, which was being conducted in Spokane. The meetings started out with great energy, and the big announcement was that it was the first time in Magic Mermaid's history that every distribution location demonstrated a profit; this was truly a historical occurrence, and one that I felt we all took a lot of pride in. While I of course had to take notice that this historical event had taken place during after my first nine months with the organization – was this just a coincidence, or had I played a pivotal role in this taking place? Of course, my ego would like to take all the credit, but in reality, it was truly a team effort by all those involved in the distribution group to make this happen.

Still, it is a testament to be a catalyst that can generate a new sense of positive energy in an established environment. And it is always a reminder to me that one person can make a difference. Also, in retrospect, O'Malley should be given a lot of credit for having the vision, foresight, and capacity to hire the right person to come on board for the distribution group that would address the issues that it faced. This is especially important, considering it was the first truly 'new' position that had been created for the organization that anyone could ever remember.

After we finished patting each other on the back, we moved on to the necessary strategic planning, which included crafting a new mission statement for the distribution group, which proved be a very elaborate exercise. We did massive amounts of brainstorming, and placed it all on giant lunch board sheets, and pasted them to the walls all about the room. Hours into the exercise, good old President Blackhead stopped in two give us his elevator speech of what was going on from his vantage point from the top. The first thing he said when he walked in the room and noticed all the paper decorating the walls was, "I can see that Derek has been at work here again" (One of the comments I heard to describe O'Malley one time was that he would pontificate about an issue or opportunity so long that by the time he made up his mind, the moment had passed. Keeping this in mind, it is no wonder why O'Malley and Simpson clashed so much, as I found Dave to be very impulsive – in fact so impulsive that I nicknamed him 'Quick Draw McGraw').

Blackhead went on to give us an update about how overall it was going to be another tough year at Magic Mermaid, which kind of drew a big dark cloud over the news of the distribution groups' historic accomplishments. 'Black Tar' also went on to tell us about the political situation in Alaska with the impending rationalization (privatization) of the Bering Sea Pollock fishery resource, and how in hindsight Magic Mermaid had missed the opportunity to claim a stake in the resource; processors were going to be provided a quota of the processing rights of the resource, based solely on historical processing capacity.

This was a foreshadowing of things to come in other sectors of the industry, but the impact of such a dark process had not come to be fully understood by so many to this point (though I had studied a little about this suggested 'two−pie' quota systems when studying the effects of transfer pricing and monopolistic business practices while I was attending Seattle University). After Bob finished giving us the 'good' news, he quickly departed, and back we went to our strategic planning.

This was when I really got to the see what BJ referred to as the God Squad together, as Dave Murphy (I found this out with Dave directly when I was in Astoria) and Derek O'Malley were truly devout Christians. It became very apparent overhearing their conversation together, as well as Derek extorting that we give thanks to God for our success during the sessions. Personally, I don't have a problem with Christianity, or organized religion in general, but I am very careful about how it is displayed in the workplace.

One of our key value-added vendors was Aquawolf Smokers, which had launched a number of new value-added line of retail products, which Magic Mermaid was readily distributing throughout the network. Their West Coast sales manager, I think her name was Karen, was this darling little petite redhead that joined us for dinner the final night of our sessions. She gave us a nice presentation, extorting the value and benefits of working with Aquawolf products.

Shortly thereafter the God Squad broke off for their fellowship, while the rest of us ran off to get drunk at the bar. The conversation continued late through the evening until I found myself in BJ's room, out on his balcony, swilling cheap beer and ranting about Derek, the lack of marketing, and the future and direction of the division and MM in general. Here I was, drunk, young, and stupid, spewing venom about what I saw as major shortcomings. Even though I tried to keep a low tone, O'Malley was in the room next door in bed, and probably heard everything while I stood on the deck and attempted to quietly relieve my frustrations to BJ. What a stupid thing for me to do but I guess I needed to get it out.

Chapter 7

The Fall from Grace

Yes, I was frustrated, but my creativity was unabated after my return home. I was still thinking of ideas on how to promote the line of new value-added MM branded products. I had gone to the stores where they were, seeking them out, and after searching could find them. I knew they were there in the freezer case, but how would the average consumer know they were there? They need to first know they existed! I had talked with a number of staff members, inquiring about what type of promotional activities had taken place in the past (it was April, and by now our last dedicated 'marketing' person, Francis Forest, had resigned, and moved back to somewhere in the mid-West). I was told that we had set up a booth at the FishFest the year before, with very lackluster results; most of the people typically attending this festival were local fishing types anyway, so it was kind of like promoting to your own family.

I started thinking that we needed to do something a little more mainstream. Why not the Taste of Seattle? It takes place at the Seattle Center in the middle of July, and usually had at least 250,000 in attendance. This indeed would be the perfect venue for a cost-effective means for generating some awareness and interest for Magic Mermaid's new line of products. Fiestas, Inc., was the organizer for the 'Taste', so I contacted them to see what cost for a booth would be. It turned out that there was a very strategic spot that had just become available at the event, as the previous year's occupant, Razor Shellfish, was backing out of the space. This was a huge opportunity, as this was a double or triple-wide booth right in front of the entrance of Key Arena – with three days of a sold out Garth Brooks (one of the hottest country music stars on the planet at that time) concerts taking place at the same time. What an opportunity to get Magic Mermaid out into the mainstream!

I had it all planned out - we would promote the new salmon and tuna burger as our main items, and the sampler 'bite' item (which was required to be sold at the price of $2.00 maximum) would be the new crab cakes, and we would hand out discount coupons to purchase our new products at the retail outlets where they were currently stocked. I put together all the cost estimates for equipment, rental space, etc. I went to O'Malley and Simpson with the idea and gave them the cost structure, which if I remember correctly was going to be about $8,000. They said, "No, it will cost too much with the staffing costs". I retaliated by going around the office with a volunteer sign-up sheet; I quickly had almost 30 people signed and committed (including myself) to donate their time for free to man the booth during the event.

I showed them the figures that only would the sales of our products cover the cost of the fees, space and equipment, but that we would actually make a profit from this effort! The bosses came back with, "Some of our key restaurant customer that participate at the event might not like the competition from us." So, I went downstairs and checked with dear David Richie, who as the point person for all food service sales in Seattle. David checked with these customers and confirmed there would be no issue with us having a booth at the event, especially since we would be promoting only our retail line of products.

By this time, I had generated a lot of excitement with the staff; people were getting excited with the idea of promoting at the Taste, and the buzz was really building. Some were already asking if we were going to do the same thing in Portland, Salt Lake, etc. And the contact at Fiestas was getting back to me and asking if she could confirm booking the space. I had provided the proposal and all the necessary information to 'Dad' and 'Quick Draw', and I was waiting to hear back from them, as 'Black Tar' was going to have to approve the activity. I let them know that I had the spaces reserved with Fiestas, but that I needed to answer with them by a certain date. They said they would consult and get back to me. Days passed, and I patiently waited with anticipation.

The day of the deadline drew upon on. 'Dad' called me in that morning and said, "Sorry, but we have decided against conducting the event." I was mortified. I had done all the legwork, planning, estimating and persuading. Every one of their objections and concerns, I had countered, with good, logical reason or reassurance. It was like they were finding the reasons not to do it, instead of the reasons why. To this day I still wonder why. Was it how I went about doing it? Was it because it wasn't their idea? Or were they just afraid to take the chance? For whatever reason, the light for this opportunity was extinguished, and the darkness began to ensue.

Right after I heard the news, I received a call from the contact at Fiestas. She wanted to know if Magic Mermaid's participation had been approved. I let her know the bad news. She was floored; it was such a no-brainer to participate. She volunteered to come and provide a presentation about the benefits of participating at the show. I didn't want to sound too depressed about it with her, so I gave her the names of the bosses, and told her to go ahead and give it a try. I never heard from her again, and I am not surprised. They probably never even took her call (and these were the days before all the staff had external email accounts).

When I broke the news to the various staff members, they were all pretty bummed out, but some were not surprised. For the veterans, I am sure it was just another 'it will never work, I told you we shouldn't have tried it moment'. The defeat was so obvious in so many faces. I had had it! I

54

began to rant about what the hell was wrong with the management. I very caustically used this analogy to describe how the company had invested so much money and energy into creating these great products and then not promoting them. It was like a guy asking a girl out on a date, taking her out to a nice dinner and movie, then taking her back to his place, putting on the 'mood' music, pulling out the champagne, turning the lights down low, stripping down naked, and then still couldn't decide whether he wanted to fuck or not!

There was such a lack of vision, such a production-based mindset. It was almost as if they didn't want to make money with these products. I just didn't get. In reflection, I still wonder if the organization (or at least portions of it) wasn't just one big money laundering operation. It sure had a lot of the typical indicators! It's either that, or a bunch of people were too busy stealing from the cookie jar to worry about making such products actually possible. Or maybe they were just plain shortsighted – for which there is no cure.

But as frustrated as I was, I still had not given up totally. I really believed that there was such a fragmented approach to marketing (as Francis had only represented the corporate sales division when he was the marketing manager) that a position needed to exist that would act as the bridge between all sales divisions and departments at Magic Mermaid; this would be a position that would unify the entire organization, and truly move the brand forward in a singular fashion with a cohesive message. With all these thoughts in mind I crafted a new director of marketing job description. In hindsight, I should have released it before my performance review, but instead I saved it to provide during my review.

By now it was late April 1998. I carefully prepared for my review by listing all my accomplishments that had taken place during those first nine months. I shared them with Ed and Larry to assess and help me fine-tune for my review with 'Dad'. I went into the review, armed with the new job description, ready to make a good argument for the 'whys and hows' I knew I would face. The session started by Derek letting me know that I was, "... the student not the teacher." Then he went on to review my accomplishments, and my areas that needed work. He praised my enthusiasm, but also suggested that I learn how to contain it. I told him that I had proven myself and requested a pay upgrade.

He replied, saying there was no money for big raises, and then he started in with the same old song and dance about how it was another bad year at MM. Funny, considering it was the first time we (distribution) had ever been profitable across the board (and that the VPs all had new cars bought or leased). I was to receive a $2,000 bonus, and an $0.85 an hour raise (I knew the distribution managers had all received a $10,000 bonus each – BJ had told me). While it was better than nothing, it felt like a punch in the stomach, compared to all the work and overtime I had put in during those first nine months (so many 12-14 hours days I couldn't remember).

Then Derek shared a new project for me; Seattle distribution needed help downstairs, and I was just the person to help them out. He told me it would only be for the summer, and that I could keep both desks and handle both jobs, alternating back and forth. He would not give me the bonus check or sign my review until I agreed to do this. After I reluctantly accepted the assignment, he reminded me again, "Remember, you are the student, not the teacher." In hindsight, I probably should have quit right then, but I didn't. I didn't even bother pulling out the new job description, as obviously he had other plans for me.

Since my vision had been to push for a marketing position that would represent the entire company, I had laid the groundwork for a meeting with Simpson for that afternoon. As frustrated and dejected as I was from the session with Derek, I shifted gears to prepare for the meeting with Dave. When I came to him with the new director of marketing job description, his initial reply was "So you want to work for my team". I immediately replied,

"No, I want to work for ALL teams at Magic Mermaid." It was definitely my inherent desire to stop all the fragmented and separationist attitudes and efforts that existed between the divisions and create a truly unified approach.

Quick Draw revealed that there were not many real salesmen at MM, just mostly order takers. He told me that he thought I showed signs of being a great salesperson, and that I should think about taking that path. His view of the importance of marketing was different than mine, and he felt I would best serve the organization by leaping with both feet into sales (in hindsight maybe this would have been a better move). Still, Dave had position over Derek, being a senior vice president, and he had the opportunity to save me, but did nothing. I felt let down and disappointed. No director of marketing position for me – and so died my dreams and vision of formulating a real plan for success for the new line of value-added products, nor for attaining a pivotal role in marketing at MM.

For a rare moment, I did not have much to say. I felt broken. Ed was one of the first to ask me what had happened; I told him that it had not gone well. He shook his head in disappointment. Black and I spoke about the situation too. He was powerless to help me, and you could see it in his eyes when he told me he was sorry. Both of them knew how hard I had worked, how much passion and personal devotion I had put into the effort, and I feel that their hearts truly went out to me. Most of my associates were being respectfully quiet and supportive, with the exception of the MM controller, Harry Reems, who was a total jerk to me. I was in the lunchroom getting a cup of coffee and he walked right in and said to me with a big grin, "I heard you got your wings clipped. You're not going to be traveling anywhere anymore." All I could think was what an asshole he was to gloat over my situation. After that encounter, I was just waiting for the other shoe to drop.

For the April newsletter we had some real fun – I made it 'shellfish' month. And the image for the front of the newsletter featured the walrus and the carpenter (from Alice and Wonderland). The inside joke with the distribution group was that O'Malley had been associated to a walrus due to an incident that had taken place at the Portland facility years earlier when he was based there; BJ had told me the story about how Derek had been digging through some boxes of clams in the cold room (I think he was looking for the ID tags or something like that), and since he had a very full and bushy mustache, when he stuck his head up, he had portrayed the image of a walrus rooting around for some clams. I could visual the scene and could see the humor in it (as did the rest of the distribution group, which at that time included Dave Simpson). So, whenever someone saw or mentioned a walrus, they thought of O'Malley.

Due to this story (and my anger and frustration directed at him), I purposely went and found this classic Alice and Wonderland image of the walrus and the carpenter to represent the shellfish issue. It was perfect, as it was a very creative and fitting image, due to the fact that the picture has oysters visibly present. It was approved and went to print. While many at MM did not get the joke, those at distribution got the inside joke and were rolling with laughter. Right after the newsletter was distributed, Simpson came walking by me, carrying a copy of the newsletter and asked, "whose idea was this?" I told him it was mine. He smiled, shook his head, and told me I was a brave man. At this point, I had a feeling I was pretty much fucked, so why not have some fun? Besides, fun is way better than being angry. At least I was still making people laugh, and the April issue was quite popular.

Time rolled on, and all of sudden it was the middle of May, the day of the opening of the Copper River fishery in Alaska – probably the most important single day for fresh distribution of Alaska salmon; Black, Ed, the distribution managers and I had spent weeks working to prepare the pricing, distribution and logistics strategies. Everything was set, my allocation and distribution sheets were in place, which was especially important, considering that Black was going to be at the Cordova plant for the opening of the season. I came in that morning to find David and Billy from IT taking apart my computer to 'temporarily' relocate it on the Seattle distribution sales floor downstairs. I asked, "What the hell is going on here?". David told he had been instructed to move my equipment downstairs. I knew right then that I wasn't ever coming back upstairs. This wasn't going to be some temporary move for the summer; my gut told me it was permanent. Yes, I had the sickening feeling that I had fallen from grace – and downstairs I went.

A wave of feeling swept over me; sickness, dejection, shame, betrayal and anger. I had been totally lied to, and to make matters worse, I was being moved on one of the most important dates of the year. The message I had been sent was very clear: 'Dad' wash washing his hands of me. And it was all taking place during the opening of Copper River. How convenient it was to have Black absent from the office for it to take place. As I headed downstairs I began to mutter, "It is like Pontius Pilate, Derek had washed his hands of me." I found it a suitable comment, considering O'Malley's deep religious convictions. Yes, his hands were now clean of me, and I was now thrown to the sales floor of Seattle Distribution to wither away.

I received a cold welcome downstairs. Not that I had ever been cruel or indifferent to anyone on the floor. If anything, I had always been outgoing and responsive; I had just been operating at a different level, acting as the adjunct for the entire distribution group. It might have been that they all felt bad for me, didn't know what to say, and were respectfully letting me settle into the situation. All I could think was, thanks for the promotion – maybe I should have just quit. But I have never been known for being a quitter.

Trying to coordinate the entire Copper River fresh distribution program from downstairs was a mess; I was pulled between those duties and dealing with the Seattle group's sales needs. Anytime someone was sick or out on leave, I was supposed to fill in for them. This pulled me in many different directions and created even more stress. But from a positive view, I was able to gain exposure to the contacts and markets for most of sales outlets in the region.

The beginning of the summer of 1998 was tough. My grandmother died in June, and it was hard to accept. But I endured and moved on in her memory. I started thinking to myself, what next? And then about month later, my grandfather passed. It made for a rough time, but I did the best I could to stay positive.

During the Winter and Spring, I had planted the seed, working with procurement, sales and distribution, asking the question, "why are we selling and distributing just Copper River salmon for fresh sales and promotions?" Why not make fresh Alaska salmon available from all of our locations throughout Alaska. Funny how just by asking a question, a new process moves forward. Obviously, my persuasiveness worked this time; by April we had been gearing up for fresh Alaska salmon promotions (mostly sockeye) from all production locales.

After the initial surge of Copper River was diminished, it was time for Kodiak to come online (they have a sockeye run that arrives in early June). It would the perfect dovetail for what we hoped would be consistent promotions of fresh Alaska salmon throughout the entire summer. We were getting the first shipments out of Kodiak, and then it came to a crashing halt. It was probably due to the Japanese buyers, worrying about the sockeye supply, due to the massive Bristol Bay run failure the previous summer; the announcement came that the fresh production from Kodiak would be discontinued, and all further production was going into the freezer for the Japan market. This was a real disappointment, but we turned our hopes towards Bristol Bay, which was just a few weeks away.

But the Bristol Bay run was failing again, and the Japanese were raising the price enough so that all production was directed to the freezers. And Petersburg wasn't producing huge amounts, so corporate announced that the new Alaska fresh promotions were being terminated. Again, we were back to just Copper River being distributed on a fresh (and by now) a very limited basis. A number of distribution members voiced their frustration that again Mother MM was generating all this excitement and commitment, and then pulling the rug out from underneath everyone. And it was always the distribution houses that took the brunt of the abuse from the clients. The excitement and expectation had been established, and then there was no follow-through; not a good way to build trust with customers. I can understand that with the nature of wild fisheries, it is hard to guarantee supply, but there could have been at least some of the production channeled towards supporting the commitments that had been generated in the domestic markets. I had to just shake my head – there had to be a better way. Once more, where there had been the light of hope for something different, the darkness of disappointment was creeping in.

Having sat through an entire Copper River marketing season, I noticed that there was a lot of Copper River salmon being sold fresh on the market – like two to three times versus what was actually being caught (this was not MM, but mostly at lot of competitors in the market – not to 'name names'). There had been a lot of discussion about this on the floor, as similar circumstances were taking place with the even rarer, and more prized Yukon king salmon. Hmmm... I wondered, why not tag the fish? I had seen a number of farmed salmon coming through the distribution floor with tags. Why not make the wild product more traceable?

When I shared the idea, again received a less inviting response; it would be too costly, too labor intensive. Again, I faced attitudes of why not to do it, instead of why. I was told to quit dreaming and get back to work. To this day I would think by now that at least Copper River would have started a tagging program, but I still haven't seen. While the elements of traceability could be a major selling point, the majority of the industry has never really embraced the concept. With the radio frequency identification technology of today (that can even measure time and temperature), I still hope for massive adoption across the industry for at least the fresh sectors.

But I was constantly reminded this was not my job. "Get back to work to cover the retail sales for whoever is it out today" – in addition to all my other responsibilities. The days were a struggle for me, calling and taking orders from retail buyers: "Yes, did you need 5 pounds of clams, or ten today?" I was about to die of boredom, and I felt that I was going to scream (in fact sometimes I walked outside and walked around the corner and did). Slowly but surely, my role of coordinating the distribution group's needs was being eroded away.

But I was constantly visualizing a more cost-effective means of doing business. Why not an automated ordering system that the seafood buyer at each retail store outlet could utilize to place their order for the day? This would be so much more efficient in the long than having six guys sitting downstairs and taking orders over the phone.

And it didn't stop at the sales order side, I was conceptualizing a bar code electronic tracking system for implementing at all levels of MM. This would streamline efficiencies with inventory, logistics and tracking (it was working great with major freight carriers like UPS, FedEx, etc.). What probably sparked this idea was not only my time on the floor working with the staff, but also my participation in every single inventory audit session, which took place four times a year. This was always a marathon session, starting on a Friday afternoon, and going round the clock, over the entire weekend through Sunday, in order to count the over $5 million of inventory that was in the main freezer.

I always volunteered for the graveyard shift (midnight to 8am), as it was always hard to find people that would volunteer for that shift – what can I say, I've always been a team player. We would literally hand count every box/item in the freezer with two people, audit each other's number and then hand enter it on the sheets for inventory to enter into the system. This was extremely time-consuming and required a massive effort by a group of people over this three-day period. And like I said, it was being done four times every year. I imagined the efficiencies of using a bar code scanner system instead. But again, the idea was ignored when I suggested it to management.

Another idea that had emerged was extending the Magic Mermaid brand line to the retail outlets. Why not make the entire seafood counter at Bernie's or GVF (or whatever retailers that agreed) as Magic Mermaid Seafoods counter? After all, we were supposed to be the 'seafood specialists' (and in reality, we were). It was another novel idea, but one that was again ignored. But I kept trying, undaunted. Call me tenacious, or just call me stupid I guess, but I always have a hard time giving up; it's just my nature. No matter how times I was rejected or told 'no', no matter how much darkness surrounded me, the light of creativity continued to burn brightly in my mind.

Mornings downstairs could be very challenging. I would come into work and deal with the needs of the distribution managers, but at 7:00 am sharp, Dick Thompson would have the fresh sheet read. This was a sheet that was established every morning for Seattle Distribution so that all the salespeople know what the exact amount of fresh product was available. And for obvious reasons, this was very important to get this information out to all on the floor in front of everyone so they could get to selling it all off immediately. This made for an extremely fast-paced morning, which must be similar to the furious activity that takes place on a stock exchange floor.

One morning I was trying to take care of the needs of one of the distribution managers; Dick started his fresh sheet call, and we he saw me on the phone, not paying attention to him, he lashed out at me and attempted to humiliate me in front of everyone. He very loudly blurted out, "BJ, would you like to show some respect and join us for the fresh sheet this morning?" You could hear a pin drop. I promptly cut the call off and turned around for the count. And Dick, in his very efficient and demanding way said, "Thank you for joining us."

I never made that mistake again. I told the distribution managers about the situation and trained them that I had to go immediately with the phrase: "I must go now, the Fuhrer is about to speak." It actually worked really well, and everyone always got a chuckle out of it. I think if Dick knew I was saying that (and he probably did), he appreciated it as well, for he knew he was a ruthless little dictator when it came to his fresh program regime.

One of the things that migrated downstairs was a whiteboard for messages from others (kind of like a giant 'Post-It Note'), which I had prominently hanging over my desk. There had been a number of times that I found myself having a conversation with the surrounding staff, only to have them say, "You are going to have to speak English, I don't understand any of them words you were saying, we didn't go to college like you." I always referred to these less commonly used words as '$10 words' and '$20 words', implying that I had spent money at college to learn "...them words...". After this request took place a couple times, I decided that it was time to give the 'boys' an education.

I told them, "It's time to educate you heathens.", and I starting writing a new word on the whiteboard every day for everyone's benefit (including my own, as a number of times I picked words from the dictionary that I was not familiar with either). Many of the staff started looking forward to the 'Word of the Day' and would constantly come up and asked what the new word meant. And if I was too busy for the day and forgot to write a word, people would ask, "BJ, where is the word for the day, you're slacking." I was not only winning hearts downstairs, but I was also winning their minds. I was probably continuing to piss the management off by doing, too.

The stench in the building some mornings was unbearable when I walked in. While there was always a fairly putrid smell in the building (which was probably due to years and years of seafood juices leaking into the floors and walls downstairs), the worst mornings were when they were cracking Dungeness crab. Due to the overpowering smell permeating the air, I started smoking cigars every day on the way to work to kill my olfactory senses. It stunk so bad at MM (even upstairs in corporate) that when I would come home, Sherry would insist I change my clothes immediately. And when I interviewed for jobs elsewhere, or was going to attend events, I would change into different clothes in my car before going to meet with people.

To this day I wonder how many potential customers walked in the door, took one whiff, and turned around thinking, "I'm not buying anything from this place. I always found it kind of embarrassing, but the bosses obviously had gotten used to it, or they would have done something about it.

For the July 1998 issue, I decided to create the Bar-B-Q newsletter. Again, it was time to have some fun, while at the same time taking a dig at O'Malley (God, I can be such a vindictive asshole when I have been pushed the wrong way). I prominently placed cartoon characters from The Simpsons on the cover, featuring Bart, Homer and Ned Flanders. My inspiration had come from some of the Seattle Distribution sales staff telling me that another nickname (yet another) they had for O'Malley - 'Ned Flanders'.

Anyone who has watched the Simpson could recognize the startling resemblance in almost all aspects: The round glasses, the bushy mustache, the cardigan sweater with shirt and tie, and a very fundamentalist devotion to Christianity. The only thing that didn't match was the voice. Derek has a very deep baritone voice, with a slight Texas 'twang', whereas Flanders has a very nasally and higher pitched voice. Otherwise, the parallels were remarkable.

I had searched the internet and found some great images of Bart Simpson, Ned Flanders, and an image of Homer Simpson, cooking over a grill, totally flaming the burgers to a crisp. Again, I had another hit on my hands with the staff. People were literally rolling in the aisles again with uncontrollable laughter when they saw the newsletter. And again, it brought a smile to my face and eased my boredom and pain a little. Since the effort was pretty much an 'inside' joke with the Seattle crew, I figured I was safe from repercussions. It would be 'our' little joke. But then one of my favorite sales guys, Joey, enjoyed the joke so much that he had to cut the image of Flanders out of a copy of the newsletter and taped it to the side of his computer. He wrote 'Derek O'Malley' underneath the image and positioned it prominently for everyone to see. About a week or so later, O'Malley came walking by and asked, "what is this about? I don't get it." Joey bashfully said, "It's you, dude. You're Ned Flanders." I shrunk down in my seat in dread and continued to focus on my work. All I could think was, "Thanks Joey!" And after Derek cleared out, I went over and gave him crap for posting the image so prominently and therefore revealing the inside joke. O'Malley would know that I was the one behind this one again – or at least suspect it. 'Dad' either didn't know who Ned Flanders was, or was pretending not to. In hindsight, he probably didn't. For his faith probably forbid watching 'demented' shows like The Simpsons. I bet he went home and researched the show after that. After this episode, I chilled on the attacks for a while.

Chapter 8

Chihuahuas and Practical Jokes

And then came the 'Wet Cuts' episode. MM was launching a new line of portioned product (halibut, cod, swordfish, etc.) that was injected with a water-based brine referred to as 'Wet Cuts' (when I first heard of it, the dirty boy side of me instantly wanted to nickname the new product line 'Moist Sluts' – shame on me). The line was targeted at the food service sector. The big selling point was that it would prevent the product from drying out when cooking it, and it would presumably extend shelf life. When I thought about it later, it was another method for making more money by literally 'injecting' additional weight into the product, so the customer would be paying the same price for water, as it was for the fish.

They came to me and Laine (a kid that was working there as someone's minion, I believe it was Simpson's) with the idea of creating a POS sheet for this new line. Laine and I envisioned imagery that exuded something moist and wet. We found a cool, shimmering blue, pool background and Photoshopped some MM portion plate shots onto the image to provide the appearance that the plates were floating on water. It looked great and aligned with the 'moist and wet' theme; we thought it would be a hit. But Sheila, the U.S. food service sales manager, thought otherwise.

She recently commissioned a line of portion shots on plates with a burlap theme background. No, she insisted, she wanted a nice brown background to go along with the Wet Cuts promotion sheet, something that matched the rest of her product line theme. So out went the pool, and in came a desert/sand background. I thought, "Yeah, nothing says moist and wet like a fucking desert." But the boss is always right, and if I created any more fuss, I feared I might come in the next day to find my computer and desk relocated to the company blast freezer. So off we went to replace the pool shot with a desert background. They were letting Laine do the finishing touches on the piece, and then I got called upstairs by the bosses – "BJ, come and fix Sheila's POS, there is a problem with the color correction."

Anyone that has worked with color print work knows that screen color and print colors are entirely different; screen is three color (RGB), and print colors are four color (CMYK). The color on the screen wasn't matching what we were getting on our printed proof. While I had assigned the correct PMS colors (which were created years ago to deal with such color correction issues), Laine had been trying to correct it, to no avail. I went to see Sheila to clarify the situation.

Taco Bell happened to have a very popular promotion going at that time, one that was centered on a cute little Chihuahua that would say, "Yo Quiero Taco Bell" for the tagline. As a part of the promotion, Taco Bell made little stuffed Chihuahua toys available to customers; Sheila was obviously a huge fan, as she had half a dozen of them sitting on top of her shelf. When I walked in Sheila's office, I asked her what she needed; she whips out the proof for the POS sheet and says, "I don't like the color of the sand in the background!" (Whereas she had liked the color on the screen version). I asked her what she wanted the final color to look like. She looks around, and then grabs one of Taco Bell Chihuahuas off her shelf and says, "I want it the color of this Chihuahua!"

I said, "Give me the 'color correcting' Chihuahua, and I'll see what I can do." And off I went. We literally then used the 'color correcting' Chihuahua to compare the screen color to the print proof until we found the matching color that she found satisfactory. People in the upstairs office were walking by and watching this spectacle of us holding this stuffed Chihuahua toy up to the screen and print proofs and asked us what the hell we were doing. I just shook my head and chuckled; I had to explain repeatedly to people what we were doing. They too would shake their head in disbelief and walk off laughing to themselves. But in the end, it made Sheila happy, and I guess that is what mattered most. I finished the project, and got back downstairs to more pressing matters, like calling some Bernie's meat and seafood manager to see if he needed five pounds of clams tomorrow, or ten.

Even though it was almost a year since I had received an internet access account, I was still one of the only people in the building with access, and I was the only one on the sales floor with it. Whenever I went upstairs or went to lunch (when I did take lunch, as I usually worked straight on through the day, due to my workaholic tendencies - except when I would take an occasional walk with Ed to break to get some exercise and let off some steam) I would come back to my desk and find a swarm of sales guys hovering around my computer. They were surfing the Web, looking for some naked or revealing images of some celebrity (like Anna Kournikova).

I was not pleased. As I reminded them, wherever they surfed, the record was showing up on my account, and I didn't desire to get punished, or sued, for their curious natures. It got the point that I had to start logging out of my account before leaving for any period of time, for fear of them going places on the internet that would surely come back to haunt me later.

During that summer, Sherry and I had done a couple of trips to Rainier to escape, and I really enjoyed the sanctity of hiking up on the mountain and leaving the crap of MM behind for a couple of days at a time.

Next thing you know, summer was gone. But I remember it was a hot one – it was still an El Nino year, with more really hot weather in the Seattle area and throughout Alaska. I remember we started seeing a lot of incidents of chalky halibut, with a lot of it coming out the Kodiak area. The staff was perplexed, including my favorite buyer, Dick Thompson. In an effort to help him, I remember taking the time to source the sea surface temperatures chart for the Gulf of Alaska region and started to print them out in color for Dick on a regular basis. At least this way he could start potentially gauging where some of the chalky product might be coming from. It was small gestures of kindness like this that I think Dick really appreciated.

It was fall of '98, and one of my friends decided that we were going to start doing a 'boys' night out' on one or two Thursday nights a month. It was good to get out with some guys, and to mix it up, we would always try to go someplace new. One Thursday night I suggested we go to a notorious gay bar in Seattle – the Re-Bar. It was 'ladies' night' at the Re-Bar, which means the crowd would be all women, who would all happen to be lesbians (and some really good looking ones at that).

Of course, there is the male fantasy that exists of 'turning a lesbian' to sleep with a guy for the night. And this no doubt works with girls who are bi-sexual; but good luck with a full-on lesbian, you're just going to piss them off most of the time. I tried striking up a conversation with a couple of the ladies and was chatting away. Finally, one of them leaned over to me and said, "You're wasting your time, you know; isn't it obvious to you that we are not into guys?". I snapped right back matter-of-factly, "That's okay, I just want to be your friend." They fell silent. They probably never had a man throw the old line that ladies use right back at them.

And I was serious! I knew they were lesbians, so I knew better than wasting my energy trying to 'turn them'. After that, they relaxed a little, and enjoyed our company a little more; best to get the sexual dynamics/tensions dispelled so we could get onto enjoying each other's company. Besides, I love women so much that I have many times jokingly described myself as a 'lesbian trapped in a man's body', a statement that always gets a good laugh out of people.

It was at the Re-Bar that I noticed a straw tray full of what appeared to be a pile of oversized matchbooks. Curiously it was a promotional 'How to Use a Condom' kit that was created by the Seattle LBG Alliance, targeted at the gay community to reduce the spread of AIDS. I opened the kit and low and behold, not only did it contain a sealed condom, but the inside liner unfolded revealed actual black and white photos of an erect penis. The following images showed a condom being put on the erect penis, complete with instructions on how to slip it on. The next picture was the real fun one – it showed a photo of a 'wrapped' penis that had just 'seen action', right next to what looked like another guy's hairy ass, with instructions on how to carefully remove the 'soiled' condom. The imagery was right on the borderline of gay porn. After viewing this imagery, I quietly folded the kit back up and slipped it in my pocket to take with me.

This was my chance to get even with Joey at work. I'm not homophobic, but I figured a number of the Seattle sales guys were – including Joey, who was an avid outdoorsman and hunter. The next day at work I waited for Joey to step away from his desk. When no one was looking, I quickly placed the kit on his keyboard and waited for the 'shit to hit the fan'. And I wasn't disappointed. Sure enough he came back to his desk, and I heard him muttering aloud, "What the fuck is this?". He quickly opened it and saw the very graphic images and started to blurt out, "Oh my God, it's a picture of a guy's dick right next to another guy's ass! Who the fuck put this here?!??" Like a flock of seagulls, the sales guys around him dropped everything to see what Joey was making a fuss about. I quietly sat there, acting like I was on the phone, and enjoying listening to the rant. He went around the floor, asking the other guys, "Did you put this here?" Of course, the others were all responding, "It wasn't me!"

Joey's frustration and exasperation continued to grow as he couldn't figure the origin of 'The Kit'. I just sat there and enjoyed the show for a while. After I had enough fun with watching the whole episode of 'show and tell', I went over to his cubicle and let him know that I had put it there and explained to him how and where I had found it. He started laughing, relieved that it wasn't some coy innuendo by a secret admirer. He looked up at me and said, "I should have known it was you, you crazy fuck." Like I said, I am far from homophobic, and was probably one of the few guys on the floor that would have the balls and confidence to set foot in a gay bar. It was definitely worth the laugh; I just wish I had a copy of the kit still, as it was pretty funny (not to mention a great example of a very solid promotional effort by the Seattle LBG Alliance to reach its audience –something I could really appreciate from a marketer's perspective).

Chapter 9

Proposals and Philanthropy

Fall was upon us, and it was time for the distribution group to have its bi-annual meeting for the fall session, which took place in Seattle. I was allowed to attend the event but was playing way less of a role in the session, more one of being an observer. It was a very sobering experience for me, and I felt distance had grown between I and most of the managers – which I feel was by design. As I sat in the room with them during the sessions, I started to feel really out of place, like I didn't really have that much in common with the group, even though I had spent so much time aligning myself with all of them, and had worked so hard to build their respect and trust. It was at this moment that I really came to grip with the reality that this was no longer my path, regardless of the relationships I had built. This was the last time I ever saw the managers face to face (with the exception of Alex Simpson), and it was truly a bittersweet time spent with all of them – especially BJ, who I had grown very close to during the past year.

Suddenly October arrived. I secretly bought Sherry an engagement ring; we had been dating for four and a half years and living together for a year and a half. It was time to ask the question – either that or move on. A woman and her family deserves the respect from a man to have honorable intentions;

it is not what age you are, but more importantly how long you have been in the relationship. I have always believed that after that much time you are not ready to commit, then it is time to move on. I was getting ready to 'spring the question', and I started planning for her birthday, since it was only two weeks away.

The night I bought the ring was a Thursday, and we were both still playing co-ed soccer together. We were at Washington Park, sitting in the car before the game, having a fight. I don't remember exactly what sparked it, but the argument was getting pretty heated, and Sherry said, "Maybe this isn't working. Maybe we should think about calling it quits." I was starting to envision me returning the ring that I had bought that day. I said, "Let's talk more after the game.", as it was time for the match to start.

During the game I received a very rare yellow card (I've always tried to play very aggressively, but very clean) for heading the ball at an angle (not allowed by Co-Rec rules). I had forgotten my ID, which I needed to show the referee to re-enter the game. I came back to find the game stopped, and sure enough, there was Sherry laid out on the field. I ran up to check on her; there had been a collision with an opposing player, and she had gotten the wind knocked out of her. She was going to be okay, but just needed a couple of minutes to recover. I didn't recognize, but this was going to be the foreshadowing of an even darker event that was about to occur.

It was later in the game, during the second half. I was playing left wing up front (my favorite position to play when on offense). I had the ball and went to 'juke' the one defender that was left between myself and the goal; I would then have an unchallenged shot. Most of the fields in Seattle back then were still 'all weather' fields, which were basically sand lots. And Washington Park was one of the most notoriously soft ground fields. I went to turn, and my left ankle planted and turned the wrong way in the soft sand; I went down screaming in pain. I had rolled my left ankle before, but nothing like this. The adrenaline and pride kicked in as I hobbled off to the sideline. I thought first about trying to re-enter the game, but the pain continued to increase, and my ankle began to balloon in size. It was starting to swell so much that I was hesitant to even remove the shoe, which I reflected later, was a good idea. All the adrenaline and endorphins in the world were not going to fix this one.

After the game Sherry drove me home and helped me up the three flights of stairs to our apartment. We carefully removed my shoe to find a horribly purplish and swollen ankle – one of the worst I had ever seen. We iced it and propped it up for the night. A couple of ibuprofens barely got me through the night. It didn't look any better in the morning, and I called into work and let them know I wasn't going to make it. Sherry called her work too; as she was going to need to drive me to the clinic to get it looked at. We went and saw the doctor and he ran the usual x-rays, etc. He diagnosed it as a severe sprain, prescribed some pain medication, an air-cast, and a pair of crutches. It made it tricky getting up and down the stairwell at Magic Mermaid for when I did go upstairs for meetings, etc., as well as getting up and down the three flights of stairs at home, but I managed. I did not realize until years later that I had torn three or four ligaments, which was confirmed by an MRI. It was months before I was able to play again, but at least Sherry and I had forgotten all about our fight that night.

One of her favorite restaurants to dine at in Seattle is Palisades, so I booked a table for her birthday. She would think we were going for her birthday and would have no idea that I was going to propose to her. Even though I was on crutches, we dressed up for the occasion; she put on a nice dress, and I put on a suit and tie. We had a nice table up front on the floor, with an awesome view of the Seattle skyline. It was a rather busy night, and the restaurant was packed. I was trying to figure out when we best to propose – should I ask her at the start of dinner, and have her lose her appetite, or do I ask her near the end of the meal, and risk having her get nauseous and puke up her dinner?

We ordered some appetizers and were enjoying them, and then I pulled out the ring, in a box, cracked it open, and showed it to her, and asked, "Will you marry me?". She paused, started to blush, and then said, "Get down on your knee and ask me again." In her excitement, she had forgotten all about my injured ankle; but as painful as it was, I stooped down on my right knee and asked her again. By now, we were a spectacle to all the tables around us. Fortunately, she said, "Yes", and people around us started to applaud. It was not until after I had sat back down that she realized what she had asked me to do. But it made the story better as she told it; for as she would say, "He must really love me to go through that much pain to get down on his knee for me."

The next day at the office I started to let people know that I was engaged. This became the catalyst to a couple of engagements for a couple of the ladies at the office, as they promptly ran home and told their boyfriends, "BJ just got his girlfriend to marry him." Next thing you know, Susie and another young lady or two were sporting engagement rings. I guess I really started a trend in the office -there's nothing like being the icebreaker.

One of the greatest things that I contributed to while at MM probably would probably never have occurred if I had not been moved to the sales floor downstairs. This is an example of the serendipity factor; one must accept things for the way they turned out, and make the best of the situation presented before them. In this case, it was the creation of MM's donation program with Cascade Harvest. This is one of the projects that I fought for and won. While working on the floor in the fillet room (where staff was busy cutting fresh and frozen fish into fillet and portion forms for local distribution) I noticed a container with a giant pile of fillets that product was being dumped into.

I asked the staff in the room what was up with this pile of fish. To my dismay I found that there was a massive amount of fillets (especially from fresh product that was shipped in from all points across the globe) that was winding up in this pile – with the sole reason being that is was not high enough grade to be esthetically pleasing to the clientele. Defects such as separation of flesh, blood spotting, etc., were usually the reason for the product being rejected. This was understandable, especially for the food service sector, but also for the retail sector, as consumers tend to buy food with their eyes, and presentation is key (unless it is breaded and battered, like at a fish and chips shop).

Here was an excellent source of healthy protein, being thrown away into the dumpster, when there are families going to bed hungry at night or lacking the resources to purchase healthier food choices. I was appalled; it was really no one's fault, and it appeared to be one of those situations where it would require more resources to get the product into bellies than it was worth. Undaunted, I contacted Cascade Harvest, and started to discuss possibilities.

This time, before I approached management, I had 'all my ducks in a row' before I even started to approach them. I found out how much labor and materials it would cost to pack the 'defective' product in boxes for freezing and storage, which was minimal. Then I established the frequency window for Cascade Harvest pickups, as well as the means of tracking contributions, and then I worked with staff to establish what the best process and time frame would be for the pickups. And finally, I crafted a tracking system that the fillet staff could use to ascertain exactly the product being donated and its estimated value; I incorporated this into a digital tracking sheet that could then be stored for inventory and accounting to utilize. This was going to be a real team effort, as so many people in the chain were going to have to lend their energy to make this work.

After all this was in place, I drafted a short proposal that included the need, the opportunity, the expected outcomes, and the system for easily imple - menting the program. As with any successful corporate social responsibility (CSR) effort, for it to gain real traction with upper management, it really helps if the initiative adds to the bottom line (the making you feel 'warm and fuzzy' inside is compelling only to a certain point). The real selling point to corporate was going to be the tax deductions that were going to be realized by the tracked contributions. The first person in management that

I approached was Alex Simpson, and next was Derek and Dave. There were the usual questions and objections, mostly concerns about the amount of time involved to make this happen, and whether it would be a good return on investment. But this time, I was ready for these issues, and was able to persuade them all to give it a try.

Finally! Yes, finally I was able to convince management to take the leap of faith to try something different. It was easy to implement, as all the elements had been set up. We just had to give the green light to the floor to start tracking and storing the product and make the phone call to Cascade Harvest to do the pickups. Less than six months later, I was very happy to see that we had not only accumulated over $10,000 in tax-deductible contributions for the company but had more importantly supplied hundreds of pounds of healthy protein to disadvantaged Northwest families.

Time flew by, and next thing I knew, the holiday season was creeping up again. I had continued creating newsletters and market reports in black and white. I really wanted to do a newsletter in color, but management had forbidden it due to the extra cost of color printing. I was finally able to convince Derek and Dave to allow me to create a special Xmas holiday edition in color; but I could only do it if I was to convince a number of our branded suppliers/vendors to shoulder the cost, because corporate was still too cost-conscious to pay for it. I was able to convince a number of our suppliers to pay an 'ad fee' to have their logo included on the back page. It was actually a great exercise in generating a co-promotional effort – something that I would use again later. It was awesome to finally create a color newsletter, and I made it as fun as possible, and worked closely with David and Bobby so that it had a nice food service element added to it. Color was definitely a hit, and after that, it was hard to go back to a black & white format, but I had no choice.

Chapter 10

Closing the Door

In January I came up for another job review. Except this was one was not to be performed by O'Malley, it was to be done by Alex and David. This was the final nail in the coffin for my career at Magic Mermaid. For over eight months I had endured the 'temporary relocation' downstairs. This was the final confirmation that this relocation was permanent. And even though I had managed to face the additional challenges that had been set before me, somehow balancing the duties for the distribution group, helping with the feeble attempts at marketing at the corporate level, and helping to cover sales for the Seattle distribution house, it was not enough to salvage my career at the corporate level. I had done everything that had been asked of me, and more.

What's the saying? 'Let no good deed go unpunished'? And sure enough, my intuitions were again correct. For the review, any of my accomplishments were glossed over; more importantly, I was being offered a new position – sales assistant for Seattle Distribution. This was the final insult; this 'new' position was a dead end for me and was way outside the parameters of what I had originally been hired to do. I thanked them for the offer, and politely declined. I took the initiative to ask what the next step would be. They said they weren't sure, so I decided to make it easy, and let them know that I would start actively pursuing employment outside the company and would keep them appraised of the situation. They asked what I would do if I didn't find a job within a few months. I told them if I was still there, we would cross that bridge when we came to it.

I continued to do the same job that I had done all those months; while I felt even more dejected, I continued to stay positive, and tried to find something good in the situation I faced. Newsletters were still produced every month, and I developed some POS materials – including one for a new smoked salmon burger. But my drive and passion was slipping away. While there were sparks of creativity once here and there, the light was fading fast. I was resigning myself to leave Magic Mermaid, and as soon as possible.

Susie, Ed, and I had secretly made a pact to get out of Magic Mermaid the year before. While Ed had the advantage of having his own private business with his live crab company, which allowed him to have more freedom, he too desired to find a better environment. Susie was the first to fulfill the pact. She had been offered a domestic sales position by AquaWolf; she really enjoyed working in the realm of international sales, so she was struggling with the decision to leave. She came to me and told me of her predicament, and I advised her to get the hell out of Magic Mermaid.

I told her to take a good look at the people that occupied the window (VP and Director) offices and reminded her of what type of person you would need to become to gain a seat in one of those offices. I added, "Imagine Magic Mermaid as a tree. The tree is rotten to the core, and the only way to fix is it to rip the tree out of the ground and replace it with a new one." She looked at me and said, "You're right; thanks for providing me the clarity I needed, I'm going to leave." She resigned within a few days. And while I was going to miss her beautiful, smiling face, I was happy for her to escape. For Ed and me, it was a grim reminder that we need to intensify our efforts to find our way out.

For the many years as a harvester in Alaska, we questioned the fairness in pricing being paid by the processors to the harvesters. It had become such an issue in the salmon sector that by 1995 a pricing lawsuit was filed in Bristol Bay. The fisherman had always thought that they were ones getting the raw end of the deal. But after spending this time at Magic Mermaid, and hearing and seeing what I had, I now theorized the following - three elements were occurring: 1. Harvesters were being paid unreasonably low prices (at last at appeared that way at that period of time). 2. Most of the employees were being paid low wages (as we were constantly being paid low salaries and for most, no or very minimal bonuses, as it was always being portrayed by the top levels of management that, "....it was another bad year at Magic Mermaid."). 3. The IRS was getting hosed too, as it appeared MM was transfer pricing large volumes of product (sockeye, king crab, etc.) to their Japan office at drastically low values that were basically at a loss, or just slightly above the cost of production. It appears now that they were just ahead of their time, as the vast majority of U.S.-based, multinational companies (the list goes on and on) are producing their products overseas and retaining the products in offshore accounts to avoid taxation by U.S. authorities, which is also known as transfer pricing. Most people these days just call it 'creative accounting'.

By now, the job was really starting to get boring. I was searching for jobs outside and was starting to interview at a couple different places, but there was nothing concrete coming through. I was starting to volunteer to run small deliveries to retail stores with my car (usually for small orders, or 'emergency' runs). I was driving to places like Poulsbo, Marysville, Juanita, in my car – anywhere to get out of the office and its increasingly caustic environment.

One of the last deplorable acts that I witnessed while at Magic Mermaid was a disgustingly unethical and basically illegal event. Frozen cod fillet prices had been prices had been skyrocketing during the beginning of the year. In fact, the price was climbing so high, that the purchase price from our suppliers was now substantially higher than what the current list prices were for the last of our inventory we were selling off. Alex negotiated an ad sale with Bernie's to sell the last of the cod inventory; but he had forgotten to put a limit on the volume of the promotion. There were only a couple thousand pounds of product left, and we blew through it right away with the ad that had been placed. Many of us on the floor had no idea what was going on until calls started flooding in from a number of irate Bernies' fish managers. It turns out that we had run out of the old stock of cod fillet, and instead of filling the commitment with the new, way more expensive, product, the management had decided to send out pollock fillet in its place.

It probably would have worked, but there was one slight problem. The order had been put in for the night crew to take the pollock out of its original boxes marked 'Alaska pollock' and put it into Magic Mermaid boxes. But somehow the order didn't make it through to the crew, and they shipped out all the pollock fillet in its original boxes. The next day, the calls start rolling in: "Hey, you sent us pollock fillet when and we ordered cod; that is what's on ad right now." Some of the managers were getting irate, but most were giving us the benefit of the doubt. We (the sale guys) were very apologetic and tried to assure the customers that the problem would be resolved. Unfortunately, it was not. Management gave the order to re-box the pollock fillets back into generic boxes and send it back out again.

Maybe a couple of the Bernie's managers didn't catch it, but most of them were on full alert by now and were watching to see what they were going to get – and believe me, they were pissed when pollock got sent back out to them again. Some were cussing, and most were saying, "What kind of idiot do you think I am? You get this pollock out of here and get us the cod we are supposed to be selling." I for one was totally embarrassed, not to mention totally disgusted with this totally unethical act. It was just wrong, any way you looked at it. It was management's own stupid fault for not putting a volume ceiling on the sale, which they ended up having to eat anyway. But this move to 'quietly' substitute pollock was not only illegal and unethical, but also tarnished the company's brand and reputation. I couldn't wait to get out of there.

My final battle with management was over being appointed to the domestic research committee for the Alaska Seafood Association (ASA). I had been in contact sporadically with Betty Dorman, who was the executive director for ASA. I had intensified my contact with her during that spring, especially since I was looking to get out of MM. Due to my experience with, and enthusiasm for Alaska, she appointed me to ASA's new ad hoc committee that would define the scope of work for a major U.S. market research project, and then select a contractor. When I let the MM management know that I had been appointed, they threw a big stink about my participation. They made the comment that they were worried that my participation and input might impact MM's relationship with their harvesting fleet.

I found this ironic, considering my years of experience in the harvesting sector in Alaska, which including harvesting and selling product to Magic Mermaid in Bristol Bay. While they firmly attempted to dissuade me from participating on this committee, I was bound and determined to finally have some form of interaction with ASA – especially after utilizing their promotional and education materials for years (as well as being a major advocate for the Alaska brand). To ease the tension with management, I made the concession that I would not participate as a representative of Magic Mermaid, only as a highly interested, but independent seafood professional.

One day soon after that (it was April by now), David came to me and asked me to step outside. He told me that I was, "...free to go." I asked him to define what that meant. He was perplexed, because I believe that management had hoped that I would just resign, which would release them from having to pay unemployment benefits. David replied by asking, "what do you want?" I made it easy for him to take it back to management. I said, "I want to be laid off." This seemed fair to me, considering that the position they had hired me for was no longer considered a requirement, and I had always met or exceeded my metrics. David said, "Fair enough." And he went back for approval. He came back to me within a few hours and confirmed the lay-off was approved. The only thing to define was when my last day would be.

One of the last meetings I participated in was a session called for the Seattle distribution sales staff. Management was in discussion with Bernie's on how to raise their value and their sales. Most of the comments were pretty benign, so I thought I would take a 'hard stab' at it since I really didn't have anything else to lose anymore. Since I had spent a lot of time in the past analyzing various Bernie's outlets, I thought it was only fair to give an honest summation. So, I told them, "First, get rid of the blue plastic ruffles that are laid out to separate the different species of fish, because it gives off a nasty, unappealing glow to the whitefish. Second, quit stacking the fish and crab like cord wood to the top of the case; it's unappealing and more is not always better. And third, quit trying to sell swordfish at almost $18 a pound; half the customers I see in line at Bernie's are using food stamps. People shop there to save money, not look for really expensive fish. The room fell silent; you could have heard a fly fart. Sometimes the truth hurts, but it is still the truth. Don't ask a person who is being laid off (and one who has been ignored and disregarded for an extended period) what their opinion is if you don't want to hear the God's honest truth.

It was getting close to the time to go. I could feel it. Being the organized and thoughtful individual that I am, I started cataloging all of MM's marketing and graphics materials, so there would be no loose ends and a smooth transition for whoever the inheritor of the marketing efforts would be. I wrote company standards for how to place sales orders, how to enter sales credits, etc. No one could say that I was not leaving peacefully and cooperatively – and more importantly, on my own terms.

That last maddening part was the short notice of dismissal. It was a week before Copper River was going to start, and they gave me just five days to 'clean up shop' and train my 'replacement'. The poor bastard they had brought in was straight off one of the delivery trucks and was being 'thrown' right onto the computer. I was frustrated not for myself, but more for those that were being left in the lurch - I guess you could say that I am too caring of an individual. I put together the distribution tracking sheets and did my best to adequately train the guy in just five days.

I actually had a sendoff party by a number of the staff at the Nickerson Saloon a couple days before my last day at the office. None of the top managers attended. There were no Simpsons, no Black, no O'Malley. But many of the 'underlings' were there to send me off properly, including Dick Thompson and David Richie – they were paying me some form of respect for my contributions. I remember Dick coming to me and saying, "I hope that you can look back on this someday as a positive experience, that you got something good out of this." I shook his hand and replied, "Dick, for all of my negativity, it is the positives that I am taking with me; thanks for all you taught me."

Again, it was serendipity interceding again, as my last day was a Friday, and the day that the Copper River was starting – the same day that I had been ushered downstairs a year before. The skies were parting; the darkness was being dispersed. And to add to the lightness I was feeling that day, one of the people in accounting had free tickets to the Boz Scaggs/ Stevie Nicks concert that was taking place that evening at the Gorge in Eastern Washington, so I snapped them right up, and called Sherry to let her know that we were going to the Gorge that night.

As I made my round of goodbyes', I went up to O'Malley and said goodbye, and shook his hand. He looked at me and said, "I hope you find what you are looking for." Those words were to resonate for years to come and are words I still carry with me today for my darkest hours of doubt. I said my last goodbye to those downstairs, and I walked out the door with a very light step. A great weight was lifted from my shoulders.

I was free again! And the whole world was in front of me again. I didn't know where I was going, but I had a renewed sense of vigor again. The sun was shining, and Magic Mermaid was now to my back, and moving far away fast.

Chapter 11

A New Door Opens

That night Sherry and I drove to the Gorge and had a wonderful evening, enjoying the concert as the sun crept down over the mountains, providing a spectacular backdrop to the stage. There was no mobile phone ringing, no worries about some shipment that was lost. Just myself, and the woman I loved, sitting on a blanket, savoring the music that was drifting up the grass-covered knoll – with not a care in the world. That night could have been the end for us both. On the way home, just before hitting Snoqualmie Summit, we were passing a semi-truck in the left lane, and just as I was passing it, the truck suddenly drifted over into our lane. I immediately swerved out of the way onto the shoulder of the highway (and thank God there was room) to avoid the impact. I just narrowly avoided the collision, which could have potentially been a fatal encounter. Sherry had been asleep, and I swerved so violently to avoid the truck that she woke up immediately asking what was happening. I told her what happened, and she recognized that we were lucky we were not killed. Thank God we were able to escape what could have been a horrible tragedy.

Shortly thereafter, I began to search for a new job. Though I had much on my mind; Sherry and I were planning a quick trip to Hawaii, and we were also spending a lot of time on the necessary preparations for our wedding in August. Job searching was still pretty simple in 1999. The economy was still steaming along, skills were highly transferable between industries, and most importantly – internet resumes were still being read by human resource departments. The giant 'black hole' of resume databases and automated tracking systems were not in full swing yet, and one could actually apply to a job via the internet, with the expectation that their resume would be read by a real human being on the other end, and that if one had some form of qualifications for the job, one might actually get a call for a screening interview. I was being very selective in my job search process, and even then, I was getting responses, so I was confident that a good fit would appear in the near future.

In the meantime, I worked on a small project for the Puget Salmon Association. They were laying the groundwork for a marketing plan, and I was contracted to draft an initial plan for them, with the potential for a tagging identification program. Their budget was small, and the project was fairly short. The summer was quickly flying by, and Sherry was growing concerned about my lack of employment and considering that the wedding would soon be upon us, I could understand her concern of being in the predicament of having to explain to her family members how she was getting married to a man without a job. Empathizing her position, I began to intensify my job search efforts. About that time, a contact from Helly Hansen interviewed me for a marketing coordinator position. But the job paid only in the mid-$30,000s, so I politely declined. Just days later, along came some new opportunities at ASA. First an ad appeared for a domestic specialist position. Within days, two more positions appeared for their export program – both the program director, and the Asia marketing specialist. While my original intention was to apply for the Asia specialist job, many encouraged me to apply for the director position, so I did. I was brought in to interview for the director job, and spoke at length with the executive director, some board members, as well as the two domestic program directors. The executive director, Betty Dorman, called me and told me that another candidate had been chosen for the director position, but that I had been recommended for the Asia specialist position, and was on the list to be interviewed by the new program director. The new director was a man named Ryan Patrick. He had a long history in the Alaska industry, having spent over twenty-five years working in the processing sector as plant manager at various facilities throughout the state. I interviewed with 'Ryan' shortly after he was hired and was soon after was offered the position.

Finally! After all the education, and all the time waiting, my dream position had finally become available. And just in the nick of time, as our wedding was just weeks away. I was ecstatic, and so was Sherry. Now we could direct all our energies towards the big day. The wedding was a splendid affair. By Chinese community standards, we were having a 'small' wedding, with just over 200 guests invited. Most of them were from Sherry's family, and I had no problem with the imbalance, as I recognized how culturally important it was for her family to invited extended family to the event (in fact, we had pared back the list twice already). It was late August, and it was a beautiful, hot, and sunny day. Sherry was a beautiful bride, and everything went perfect – with the exception of the weather in the Gulf of Mexico.

Chapter 12

Barracudas and Stinky Fish

It just so happened that I had selected Cozumel, Mexico for our honeymoon. And when I arose the day of the wedding, the first thing I saw on the TV that morning was news that there was a fierce hurricane blowing through the Gulf of Mexico. I made no mention of the potential for a 'hurricane honeymoon' to Sherry, not wanting to take away from our special day. I figured I would let her know that night after the excitement had died down. But we didn't make it that far. We were about halfway through the reception, when one of her aunts leaked the news. We were just getting ready to cut the cake, and she heard the news. Her mouth dropped open, and she looked over and me, and said, "What are we going to do for our honeymoon?" I told her not to worry, that we would figure it out. We departed the day after, wondering if we would have a resort left to stay at when the hurricane subsided. We flew through Texas, and our flight was delayed in Houston for a couple of hours while the remainder of the storm played out. We got lucky, as the hurricane never reached full potential, and Cozumel was spared any damage – just made for a memorable experience for the future.

And memorable it was. The weather was gorgeous in Cozumel, but the conditions at the Diamond Resort I had selected were horrid. It was one of the last resorts on the island that had not been updated, and the smell of raw sewage often permeated through the air of the resort. And the 'private' cabanas we were staying in were had 'shared' ceilings. While we had walls to separate your rooms, the ceiling was wide open. We realized this when we could easily hear the passionate sounds of the couple next door as they 'wrestled' in bed together. We tried not to laugh too loud when we heard the noise but couldn't help but sit in bed and giggle as we listened to the noises emanating from the busy couple next door.

The waters in Cozumel were crystal clear, and during my first swim I immediately noticed a barracuda patrolling in the shallow waters off the beach. Barracudas have a very keen sense of sight and are attracted immediately to the glimmer and sparkle of jewelry. Knowing this I warned Sherry about wearing jewelry while in the water. We had a lockbox in our room, but it was kind of flimsy, and she didn't trust it, so she kept her diamond wedding ring on while at the beach. A day or two later, we were both snorkeling just a hundred yards or so off the beach. I had brought some food and was feeding the local reef fish. I looked up to see how Sherry was doing, and I saw her swimming full speed to shore. I shot after her and caught up with her and made her surface to ask her what was wrong. She looked past me with terror and pointed that it was coming after us. By the look in her eyes, I was expected to turn and find an advancing bull shark but was relieved to find that it was only the resident barracuda, which was only about three feet long. The fish was no doubt drawn in by the sparkle from Sherry's diamond ring. To be cautious, I followed her to shore to make sure she would be okay, making sure that the barracuda was no longer following. As we reached the shallows next to the beach, I looked behind and could no longer see the barracuda. Sherry was standing knee-deep in the water, telling the story about the barracuda chasing her to a woman that was floating in the shallow water a few feet from her. Just as I was starting to say that it was gone, the barracuda popped up out of the shallow water, right in between Sherry and the woman. They both started to scream and scrambled out of the water as fast as they could. I couldn't help but chuckle a little, considering no harm had been done. To her dismay, Sherry's nickname quickly became 'Barracuda Bait'; while she was a little shaken up over the affair at first, it's a story we still laughingly share with others to this day.

The rest of the honeymoon went pretty smoothly - we visited Chichen Itza in the middle of the jungles of the Yucatan Peninsula, toured the shops and bars of Cozumel, and relaxed and swam on the beach. Unfortunately, Sherry caught dengue fever during our stay, and she suffered horribly while enduring the malady upon our return home.

Shortly upon return from our honeymoon, I received confirmation from ASA that I had been approved for the Asia position. My start date was September 29, 1999, and I hit the ground running. With Ryan Patrick being hired as the new director of the export program, that left only one staff export staff member from the old regime. His name was James Krylos, and he was the senior European marketing specialist; James had been at ASA for almost eight years, and signs of wear were evident. To add to James's challenges, he had been in line for the director seat after so many years in the trenches, and here was after all these years, reporting to a man that had spent his entire career managing processing plants.

James and I got along fine from the start, so he spoke very candidly when sharing his concerns. He was astounded that Ryan had been hired for the position, considering he had no prior experience in marketing whatsoever. Within the first couple of days of being at the job, Krylos came to my office with a worried look on his face and said to me, "Ryan doesn't know shit about marketing. He just asked me what the difference was between advertising and public relations!" We both began to watch him closely. We noticed he was handwriting all of his memos and letters and handing them over to the receptionist to process into Microsoft Word format. And his emails were one giant paragraph that appeared as one giant rambling monologue. This was not good. Still, there was nothing to do to change the situation, so we continued forward.

And we had plenty to work on from the start. The export program had just been evaluated by a contractor, and the industry response was not good. Industry was not happy with the mission or the performance of the program and complained that the staff was not very responsive. It appeared that many had lost faith in the program, and with its downward budget spiral, it appeared poised to implode. The budget was especially disconcerting. Historically, about a decade prior, the program had received about $ 8 million from the U.S. Department of Agriculture's Export Agricultural Service (EAS) in the form of Market Export Program (MEP) grant funds but was now down to a little over $2 million. Another $2 million or so used to come from the State of Alaska – directly from the Governor's budget, but that was now $0. The remainder of funds for staff salaries, etc., - about $800,000 - technically came from the industry's raw fish tax receipts. So what was once a premier, $10 million plus program was now a $2-3 million effort. There was work to do, indeed.

And the salmon sector appeared to be in terrible shape. I had salesman calling me and complaining about the plummeting prices for pink salmon in Europe. One of them called me and said, "I have 50 container vans of pinks I need to move, what do I do?" While I was still so new, I made the following suggestion, "Instead of calling your customers and telling them you have 50 containers of pinks so sell them, might I suggest that you instead tell them that you only have three containers, and that they are a special customer, so I can only hold them in reserve for a day or two." Creating the perception of scarcity can be a powerful purchasing motivator, if applied properly. 'Act fast now, this offer is only good for the next four hours' – it seems to work well most of the time.

During my second week, Betty came down to Seattle and brought her executive assistant, Liz Claremont with her. She was coming to attend an Export Marketing Committee meeting. I sat and had lunch with them, and they started to ask me ask me what it was like to work at Magic Mermaid. It appeared that in many circles, MM was considered this mysterious, closed organization that did not play well with others. I provided them as much detail as I could during lunch. I then asked Betty why there was no one on the ASA board from Magic Mermaid. She told us the story about the last Magic Mermaid board member – Bob Blackhead, and how he never attended a single session the entire time he was appointed. For some strange reason, I was not surprised.

Ironically enough, Dave Simpson called me about a week later. He wanted to know what it took to get on the ASA board. I told him that it might be best to start cultivating a relationship with the executive director, and suggested he call her in Juneau. It was to be years and years until I was to hear from Dave again.

Next was my first Export Marketing Committee (EMC) meeting; this was the sole committee that the Export Program officially reported to, and meetings were on a quarterly basis. James walked me through the entire prep progress. It was a laborious process - first we printed out all the quarterly reports from each country/region program, and then we started putting together a stack of various trade and consumer publications, etc., that demonstrated our advertising and PR efforts. When we had the meeting, one of EMC members, Hans Heinz, spoke up and said, "As usual, we have a stack of materials to look at, reports to read – it seems like the same old thing every time." I took note of this and began to conceptualize how the flow of information could be improved.

For it was time for my first taste of crisis management. The place was Japan. And the situation was not good. Word was spreading rapidly that the Japanese trade was 'less than happy' about the quality of the sockeye pack that had been produced in Bristol Bay that summer. Keeping in mind that during the two previous years of 1997 and 1998 the Bristol Bay run had suffered catastrophically low returns, it had caused massive shortages of sockeye supply to Japan. Two years of drought created a gap in the market that began to be replaced by farmed salmon (mostly Chilean coho and steelhead). This new, consistently high-quality product began to generate a new standard in the market. Meanwhile, after two years of critically poor salmon returns in a row, the Alaska Department of Fish and Game was perplexed to the point that they predicted the 1999 Bristol Bay sockeye return to be in the range of 8 to 40 million fish. It was all over the board. The harvesters and the processors had no idea what to really plan for. Unfortunately, the attitude was pessimistic, and most were prepared again for another poor salmon run for the year. But instead, the fish came back with a fury that year, exceeding a return of over 40 million fish. No one was prepared for what was about to happen. The capacity was just not there to handle such a massive number of fish, and quality suffered horribly. The reports coming back from Japan were that it was some of the worst fish they had ever seen, and much of it was practically rotten.

My brother had just given me some Bristol Bay sockeye that he had bought back from Magic Mermaid that summer. I quickly pulled one out of the freezer and thawed it for inspection. It looked fine on the outside, but as soon as I began to cut it open, the damage was very apparent. The flesh was all broken and the smell was putrid. Indeed, the bulk of the pack must have no doubt been rotten. And all I could think was, "How are we going to talk our way out of this one?"

I confirmed with Betty what I had found, and we quickly formed a group to deal with the 'Japan Crisis', which included Bill Coleman (Chairman of the board), Sam Marker (the Vice-chair), Lanie Freeman (ASA PR Director), Bobby Olson (ASA Technical Program Director) and Ryan Patrick. Together, we formulated a plan to conduct a trade mission to Japan which would take place immediately following our return from the China Fish Expo in November. The mission would include a press conference, as well as visits to a multitude of major trade members to do as much damage control as possible. And the message would be clear: This will not happen again. The industry would take the steps to ensure that quality would never become so low again. And a new advisory panel was being formed by the

Alaska Department of Fish and Game that would act as a conduit between harvesters, processors, and fishery managers to ensure that quality would remain at peak potential throughout seasons. It sure sounded good. But how would the Japanese respond? I quickly went to task, crafting potentially one of the most important speeches I would ever write while at ASA – an apology to the Japanese customers and a promise that it would not happen again. I wrote that speech as I then wrote every speech while at ASA, as if I was to deliver it myself. Though I knew full well on this first one that it would be for Ryan to deliver. It would not be the last time that I wrote I speech for someone else to deliver.

Chapter 13

Chicken Feet and Heart Attacks

A few days later I flew to Alaska for a special Japan trade session that was being conducted by the Alaska Trade Program. Currently, the program was a direct extension of the Governor's Office- just as ASA once was. The director's name was Craig Salis, who I found to be an energetic fellow. He was working hard to promote all the products from Alaska, which included potatoes, honey, coal, and seafood – basically anything that was produced in Alaska to be traded. I also met two other members of Craig's staff – Pam Fields, and Betty Clampett: I would get to know both of these ladies very well throughout the years and would work with them to coordinate a number of Governor's missions. It was at these meetings that I was finally to meet Jim Tanaka. He was the Asia Trade Specialist for the U.S. Department of Commerce, but he had previously worked for the State of Alaska and had spent years and years in the field. I had known of Jim for a few years, as I had requested trade data from him during last few years of college, as well as while I worked on a few projects during the first year or so out of school. When we met, it was as if we had known each other for years – we were truly kindred spirits, and we would have a strong working relationship and friendship throughout the years.

After a day in Alaska, I returned home, and the excitement began to build.

We were preparing for my first mission overseas. Finally, after all the years of studying Asian culture, I was going to experience it first-hand. It was hard to contain the enthusiasm. Sherry could tell, and I knew that deep in her heart she was overjoyed for me. For that first trip, I remember how she lovingly helped me pack. One can take for granted the preparation that goes into getting ready for a two-week long business trip. What can I say, it takes a while to get used to living out of a suitcase? But I was about to find out.

The China Fish Expo was in Shanghai that year, and we were flying there via Tokyo (Narita Airport). The flight to Asia was monumental, as the flight from Seattle to Tokyo just so happened to be the inaugural flight for the new Boeing 777 for United Airlines. We received a commemorative baggage tag and got to enjoy the comfort of a literally brand new airplane. For some strange reason the flight was less than full, and I had room to stretch out and relax across multiple seats on the way over. That was the last time I would see a less than full flight on that run for years to come. I was too excited to sleep the entire flight. When we arrived in Tokyo, James got Ryan and I into the United Star Alliance business lounge. James and I went to get a drink, and we discovered an awesome Japanese creation – an automated beer dispenser. You set your pilsner glass on the serving tray of the machine, push the button, and automatically the machine tilts the glass at the perfect angle to fill the glass without making a head of foam, and then at just the precise moment the glass it tilted upright again, and a second spout shoots beer foam to give the drink the perfect head. Leave it to the Japanese to perfect what German's have been doing by hand for half a millennium or more; what innovators they are! As James and I stood and admired the machine, Ryan snuck off to the first-class lounge. The United attendant caught him, and sent him packing, but not before he helped himself to some free sushi from their food bar.

Then we boarded another packed flight to Shanghai. I remember the movie on that flight was the very popular 'Crouching Tiger, Hidden Dragon'. The strange thing was that it was the version that had been dubbed in English, so it had Chinese subtitles for the Chinese passengers. How strange it must have been for them to watch a movie that had originally made in Chinese language but was now dubbed in English that they had to read subtitles to understand.

We arrived at the Pudong airport in the early evening. It being the late fall, darkness had already fallen; as we taxied off the runway, we could see the brand new airport facility, bathed in a swath of lights. It was just our luck that Pudong had just opened for service that day, and we were the second airplane to officially arrive. The scene reminded me of an episode out of the Twilight Zone TV series. Here was this brand new airport, with no, planes, no ground crew, and basically no activity, except for us. It seemed surreal and eerie to see the huge complex that was totally devoid of humans and movement. As we pulled up to the terminal, all the passengers began to get up and prepare to disembark the plane. What should have been a few minutes wait turned into almost an hour, as the new airport staff was having difficulty maneuvering the jetway to the side of the plane for the first time. Several of the passengers began to get agitated and impatient over the extended wait, but they had no choice but to stand and wait as the poor airport employees scrambled to dock the walkway to the plane. Finally, we began to exit the plane; as we poured out into the new terminal, one could see and smell that it was indeed brand new; it was perfectly clean and empty, with only an employee or two standing to direct us towards customs and baggage. There was a huge wait at the customs and immigration checkpoint as well, as the staff and equipment were struggling with processing travelers for the first time. After another hour of waiting in line, we were off to the baggage area. Fortunately, the baggage handlers were quicker than the customs agents, so we found our bags waiting for us. Bobby and Billy were waiting outside the door in a huge crowd; they had been waiting for us for probably two hours, but they were smiling and jovial, nonetheless. We quickly loaded into a van and headed for the city. Pudong was very similar to the Narita airport in Tokyo in that it was planned and built well outside the range of the city center. As we left the airport, it appeared at first that we were in the middle of nowhere, as we drove down an empty highway towards Shanghai. I thought at first that there were very few cars and trucks on the road because of the time of the day; I did not realize until later that very few people owned a vehicle to drive. Nothing could prepare us for what we were about to see. As we began to approach the city, building and people began to appear more readily, and the lights became stronger. Soon we were coming upon the new city of the Pudong district. Skyscrapers began to shoot into the sky. And all around, there was massive construction taking place. The streets began to shimmer with all the lighting and new metal that had been erected. While I had read and heard about this new city of prosperity that was emerging in China, nothing could prepare me for amazing spectacle of this new and gleaming metropolis that lit up the night. And right in the middle of it all, upon the banks of the river, was the new landmark for the city – the Shanghai TV Tower. Here sat this futuristic tower, looking almost like a giant rocket that was poised to shoot into space, all bathed in awesome light. One could tell right away that it was a symbol to the world that Shanghai and China were poised to be a powerhouse for the future.

As we passed the tower, we began entering a tunnel that would take us under the river and to the 'old' side of Shanghai. Coming out of the tunnel it appeared as if we were entering an entirely different city; many of the building were old and worn, and the lighting on the street was much sparser. But one could see that there was quite a bit of new construction starting in this part of town, and that change was coming to this area as well, if not as dramatic as on the Pudong side of town.

Soon the van arrived at the Ritz-Carlton Hotel. It was one of dozens of four-star hotels that had sprang up in Shanghai during the 1990's. We walked to the front desk and being that I was the junior staff member, I went to the desk first to confirm our room reservations and begin the check-in process. The person behind the desk obviously mistook me for the boss of the group (being the tallest) and upgraded me to a luxury business room – something I did not realize until the next day when I saw Krylos' room and realized that mine was much larger and had a desk. Sometimes it is good to be mistaken as the leader – just don't let the boss find out. Later that night I was introduced to Johnny Chin, a sales executive for Harpoon Seafoods; Johnny was acting as an Alaska industry representative and would join our entourage for all of our functions.

The next day we conducted a series of meeting with the Food Export Office (FEO) in Shanghai; the head of the FEO was Leroy Berbosa, who had been in China for a number of years. Later during the evening, we hosted a joint promotion with the Washington State Department of Agriculture at Maxim's Restaurant, which was located at the base of the new Shanghai Opera House. This is where I was first introduced to Clint Houston – what a character. I thought I talked a lot. I don't know too many people that can out talk Clint. That night I learned that Clint goes 'all out' for many of his promotional efforts. For the kickoff for the Maxim's promotion, he had sequestered a jazz quartet for entertainment.

And at the promotion was Han Kimchi, ASA's representative for Japan. I had met Han earlier that summer when I was attending ASA annual international luncheon in Seattle. I remember her well during our introduction, as she inquired if I was going to apply for the vacant Asia specialist position, of which I replied, "No, I am applying for the program director position." She looked shockingly at me and said, "But aren't you a little young for that position?" Of which I replied, "we'll see." That evening, Han greeted us with a warm welcome, and after the ceremony had concluded we decided to take a walk to the Bund to see the city lights over Pudong. We walked for what seemed to be miles (and probably was) to reach the edge of the riverbank to take in the panorama. I would return to that same spot for years, and I was always taken back to that feeling of seeing the awesome skyline of the 'new' city of Pudong, all lit up, literally representing the showcase of what China was rapidly aspiring to be as a growing world power. After six decades of being trapped in suspended animation by the Communist Party, the city and country was flourishing and playing 'catch up' – and fast at that! One could feel the electricity of excitement literally flowing through the air. It was a magical and historical time to be there – sore feet and all.

After everyone else turned in that night, Johnny, and I went out on the town to check out the local bar scene. We went to some 'local' watering holes, and I was basically the only white person in the bar. Johnny was busy socializing away with the locals; meanwhile I sat there and took it all in, as I really didn't know any Mandarin at that point, and I could not really strike a conversation with anyone. What was memorable to me was stopping in at a quick service restaurant and dining for the first time on a local delicacy – chicken feet. They were coated in a sweet red sauce, and I enjoyed them thoroughly (to Sherry's later disgust when I told her I had eaten them – as she would say, "those things stand in chicken shit all day!").

First day of show, I was wearing a dark suit, white shirt, and dark sunglasses (the sun can be amazingly bright in Shanghai in October); as I walked behind Ryan towards the show entrance steps, several people began to step out of our way, and gaze at me fearfully. Then a man carefully walked to me and asked me if I was a bodyguard. I replied, "No, I'm Secret Service." Then I laughed and let him know I was just kidding. Sometimes it's great to be tall, because one appears ominous and imposing, and people tend to get out of your way. Barely 12 hours in Shanghai, and here another case of mistaken identity! I looked over, and there was Jim Tanaka, long time Commercial Trade Specialist for the U.S. Department of Commerce. Jim was native Japanese, but had worked in Alaska for years, first as a processor, and then as a trade specialist for the State of Alaska. Jim was and continues to be one of the foremost authorities on seafood in the Asia region. He is one of the people that cannot and will not be replaced when he is gone – they come once-in-a-lifetime. The show went well, there was a beehive of activity the first day, especially with two new staff members attending the event. Immediately following the first day, ASA sponsored a reception at a ballroom at the Jin Mao Tower. It was very well attended by both trade and industry, as well as government officials. Ryan was (uncomfortably) making the opening remarks for the dinner, and as everyone was starting to enjoy the food and drink, Bobby suddenly ran up to me with a very panicked look on his face. He said, "Come quick, come quick, something wrong with Mr. Jim." I jumped up and raced over to find Jim Tanaka, passed out on the floor, turning an awful shade of gray and white. Everyone was totally alarmed, and I asked for someone to get medical help. Just then, Hans – a longtime member of the EMC- walked over, looked down at Jim on the floor, pulled a drag off his cigarette and said, "Jim, you look like shit." Jim looked up and smiled. Immediately the tension in the room subsided, and everyone began to laugh. It turns out that Jim had gone the day without eating, and between all the action, the multiple cigarettes, and a drink or two, it was too much for his system, which led to him passing out.

After the reception, several of us went to a club called Roe Jam. The place was packed with locals, and the dance floor was filled with a flood of people, with all kinds of flashing lights beating down onto the crowded floor. And there in the middle of the floor was Clint Houston, all 6'4" of him, dancing away on the floor with a couple of Asian girls. We laughed so hard that we fell to the floor until our ribs hurt; the site of Bill, towering over all the Asians, arms and body flailing away, was a sight to behold. And then we all jumped out on the dance floor, and starting dancing and high-fiving Bill, and danced the night away.

The next two days were more of the same. Business at the show was quite busy. We were constantly deluged by representatives from local processors that were trying to buy a 100 Mt or more of headed and gutted Alaska pollock to fill their processing lines. I could see that we had a lot of work to do in China to make headway to build demand for actual consumption; but we had to start somewhere. Things seemed to be going well, and then after the first night or so I ran into my first 'ugly' situation. One of Bobby and Billy's staff, James, was spotted in the lobby with Johnny Chin, setting up meetings on the side with buyers. Bobby and Billy were furious, and fired him on the spot, as it was a violation of policy. James probably knew better, and Johnny should have known better as well, but he couldn't help himself – such is the nature of many salesman – anything for a buck. This became my first lessons about the thin line of what was proper behavior and what was not, by organizational standards.

Things settled down the next day, and then it was time for a little sightseeing. This was my first visit to the 'knock off' market. It was an open-air market located at a square, looking like a flea market back home. There were rows and rows of stands that had pirated 'knock off' versions of everything one could imagine – clothing, purses, belts, shoes, watches, sunglasses, CD's, DVD's, etc. There was every popular name brand under the sun, there were deals galore, and the funniest part was bartering to lower the prices. Billy was the best at this, and he would drive the vendors crazy when he would drive the prices through the floor. One vendor was so furious that he remarked about Billy, "your friend is drunk, your friend is on drugs." Billy would just laugh, and then ask for an even lower price. He was definitely the guy you wanted to take shopping with you.

After the knock off market, we went to the Yu Garden market – there was plenty of 'knock off' stuff there too, and in addition all kinds of Chinese artwork, tea, gold jewelry, and even authentic clocks, watches, and clothing from the 'Chairman Mao' era. There was also a beautiful, classic building in the middle of a pond that is a restaurant, one that was surrounded by ornate boardwalks on either side. It is a beautiful setting and is probably one of the more historic districts still left in Shanghai.

Returning from one of the days of the show I remember Han striking up a conversation with me – in a longing sense, probably out of the need for stable management from ASA, she asked me very politely, BJ, please stay awhile. At first, I thought it was an odd request, but then after quickly reflecting on the instability in the program that had been endured by the staff, I could comprehend the reason for the request. So, stay I would, and for quite some time, in fact.

Near the final days of the show, we toured the local fish market – known as Tonglachu. The standards were not overly hygienic, but considering that it was China in 1999, it was probably fairly clean by the standards at the time. There were all kinds of fish, both fresh, frozen and live. There were frogs, snakes, and several various proteins. Of all the things I saw in the market, the image that resounded in my mind the most was a pet chimpanzee on a chain. It obediently sat on a chair in front of a rusty old ice machine, that was taking block ice and shaving it into pieces that dropped in a bucket. After everything I had seen, the monkey didn't real seem that out of place to me; it was just another part of the spectacle of the busy market.

We also had the opportunity to see several more 'touristy' sites during our first stay in Shanghai. There was the Jade Buddha Temple, which housed the largest Jade Buddha in all of China – no small feat. This was the first Buddhist Temple that I ever visited, and of all the Buddhist shrines I was to visit during those days to come, this was always my favorite one, and would hold a special meaning in my heart in the future.

During the last day of the show, we were tearing down the booth, packing away the left-over collateral, and preparing to dump the fish from the refrigerated display case. There were several locals hanging out around the booth, peering at the four-day-old fish and crab in the display like vultures, waiting to pounce on the leftover product. This time, show staff came by and picked up the fish for proper disposal (hopefully), dumping it quickly in a wheeled container, claiming it was a quarantine/sanitation issue; this was the last time I would ever see officials or staff come by to retrieve product in China. Upon returning from the show site back to the hotel, as Krylos and I exited the cab, we were quickly approached by a street pimp, which was accompanied by a fairly tall, pretty girl (or should I say woman) in a red dress. He came up to me directly and started inquiring if I was interested in buying the girl for a 'date'. James began to laugh immediately, pointed at me, and remarked, "You should be paying him to sleep with your lady." I began to laugh, and we both walked across the street to the hotel; I couldn't help but notice several white men walking in and out of the hotel entrance, each with a woman in a red dress on their arm. It was indeed the red dress on each one of them that caught my eye. These 'girls' had no doubt been hanging around the hotel during all the days I had been there – but I hadn't really taken notice until we were approached by the pimp.

For our last night in Shanghai, Bobby and Billy – being the gracious hosts they always were – took us out to a wonderful restaurant that overlooked a little 'lake' lined by beautiful evergreen trees. The next day, they accompanied us to the airport to say goodbye – seeing us all the way to the security, giving us hugs and very warm wishes, and an energetic wave goodbye as we disappeared beyond the traveler checkpoints.

Chapter 14

'Browjobs' and $75 Melons

So, it was off to Tokyo; it was early evening when we arrived at Narita. There was no one greeting us - and understandably so – Narita airport is a bit of a distance outside the main city of Tokyo, and quite the journey just to greet someone as they arrive. We took a 'limo' bus to our designated hotel, which was the ANA Hotel, located in the Akasaka district - which is basically the 'government' district. But it bordered the Roppongi district – the 'foreigner district', which was just a brisk walk up the hill. I remember the hotel well, as it was only time I stayed there, and I thought it was funny that the hotel was named 'ANA'; it was named after 'All Nippon Airways', which owned it, but 'ana' in Japan also means 'ass' or 'butt'! For this reason, the hotel was referred to as the 'A –N - A' hotel, not the 'ana' hotel.

Han greeted us at the hotel and made sure we were getting checked in okay, and that we had our updated itineraries in hand for our busy schedule. She had much to do, and being the polite, Japanese professional she was, she asked us if she could be excused for the evening to deal with affairs. We had no problem that, and Ryan said he was tired, so we watched him disappear into the elevator for the night. James had never been to Japan, and really was excited to go see the sites, so we planned to check into our rooms, and meet back at the lobby in a half an hour. Being used to Chinese standards, when the bellhop carried my bags into my room, I offered him an obligatory tip. But Japanese standards are different, as they expect no tip, and he politely refused. I would realize later that this was just polite tradition, and that you must ask three times. If they still refuse to take the tip after the third offer, they really mean it. But I found in most cases, that they would take a tip on the second or third offer....

The room was much starker than the plush surrounding I had enjoyed at the Ritz-Carlton in Shanghai. And instead of a queen-sized bed, I had two small twins, with very short mattresses. I found later that unless I curled my legs up, my 6 foot plus frame made my legs hang way over the end of these little 'kiddy' beds. And even funnier was the hotel pajamas that were neatly laid out on top of the bed for me. As I unpacked my gear, I tried them on for the fun of it, and found the pajama pants hanging down only to barely clear my knees. Indeed, everything here in Japan was not quite geared for tall guys like me!

James and I met up in the lobby, and he indicated that he wanted to see Shinjuku. He had read a lot about it, and it he really wanted to check it out. We went down to the street and quickly found our way to the world-famous Tokyo subway system, which I must say is one of the best – if not the best on the planet. After a couple of run changes – the Shinjuku line is the 'red' line, we found ourselves walking up onto streets that were totally bathed in light. Shinjuku is truly something to see at night – it is image of Tokyo that has been seen in so many movies – there are rows and rows of colorfully lighted signs in all directions, lighting up the buildings and streets in an almost surreal fashion. We were totally amazed, and I found some of the people were just as surreal. At that time in Japan, the hottest fashion trend for young ladies was to dye their hair platinum blond, get a fake tan, and wear ultra-high heel shoes. It was almost absurd looking at all these beautiful Japanese women, walking around in these huge platform heels, looking like they had been dropped in a vat of hydrogen peroxide, and then left to bake in the sun for a week. It is an image that still makes me chuckle today when I think about it.

Meanwhile Krylos was walking around with his mouth wide open in total awe at the sight the lights and all. He looks at me puzzlingly and said, "Han said it is kind of sleazy in Shinjuku, I don't know what she is talking about." I agreed, it looked like a vibrant place, to me, with several big department stores, and lots of people meandering along; Shinjuku is a major shopping – in the daytime. But the flavor can change a little at night, as we were soon to find out. We walked up the street, and then crossed over to an alley where I found a vending machine that served containers of hot sake, of all things. I gladly threw a couple of coins in the machine, grabbed my jar of hot Ozeki sake, cracked the top open, and began to enjoy it as we meandered down the street. I was starting to agree with James," What is Han talking about, this place is great!"

We walked for another block or two, turned a corner, and then the fun really began. We walked past a local, who began to flank us and started to ask James in horribly broken English, "Sir, you like browjobba? Having studied Japanese in college and hanging out with several Japanese exchange students, I could immediately comprehend what the man was asking James – he wanted to know if we would like to purchase a 'blowjob' from one of his girls. But James strained to understand the words that were thickly layered with a heavy Japanese accent. The man attempted a few more times to pronounce 'blowjob', but all that came out was 'browjobba'. James continued to stand there was a quizzical look on his face, while I did the best I could do to contain myself from laughing out loud. Finally, the man resorted to a gesture of his curled-up hand in front of his open mouth that unmistakably looked like he was putting a cock in his mouth. James's eyes bulged out, and his mouth dropped wide open as he finally realized what the man had been trying to offer. After he came over the shock of being propositioned, I began to laugh loudly and he told the guy, "Hell no." It seems we had wandered 'off the tracks' by crossing the street and had crossed over into the red-light district known infamously as Kabuki-cho. This was the sleazy part of Shinjuku that Han had been trying to warn James about. As we took the subway back to Akasaka, we continued to laugh and chuckle at what we had just experienced. It was time to get to bed, as we had some serious work to do the next day.

And tomorrow came early. Our first official visit was to the world-famous Tsukiji Fish Market. This required getting up at close to 4 am so we could be down at the market for a visit bright and early, as the tuna auctions commence at about 6 am. Han met with us at the hotel and made sure we didn't get lost finding the market. Good old Jim Tanaka was there to greet us and be our official tour guide. As soon as we arrived, we moved briskly to check in with one of the managers from Chuo Gyorui, which is probably the largest and most prominent wholesaler in the entire market. We were suited up in white boots (which in my case were a little tight) and moved quickly to the floor to view the tuna auction. For anyone that makes the journey to Tokyo, the tuna auction is a must-sees event. Two entire warehouse floors are covered with rows of bluefin, yelloweye, and bigeye tuna in all shapes and sizes, coming from all points of the globe. Buyers meander about the avenues of tuna, carefully inspecting the quality of each fish, reviewing the flesh taken as core samples, and preparing their offers for the morning bidding session. Some of the larger fish command prices in the range of tens of thousands of dollars, and the speed of the auction will make your head spin – a highly regimented and organized process that has been perfected over the years.

After reviewing the auction, we toured the remainder of the market, which included a vastly immense variety of products – frozen, fresh, live, value-added, etc. The variety of categories, species, and formats that are brought from all over the world (and from all corners of Japan) is incredible – and for all the seafood markets I would tour around the world, none would ever match the range and grandeur that is Tsukiji. And while the sheer magnificence will be tantamount in my reflections, one of the other elements of the market that is forever burned in my mind is the huge mountain of Styrofoam that I spied during the tour – it was an incomparable sight that made any other stack I have seen pale in comparison. I asked our guide, how many days it had taken to accumulate such a pile from all the fish shipping containers (they are used readily for shipping fresh product, due to their highly insulating properties). And to our shock he replied, "That is only today's". This immense stack of polluting plastic was a daily development! I could only imagine what a year's worth of production liked like. This was an environmental tragedy in all actuality, but a necessary evil of the need to move fresh seafood worldwide. Thankfully these days a good portion of 'Styrofoam' is made from biodegradable products.

Our tour concluded with a visit with the president and head staff of Chu Gyorui. It was an honor indeed to meet with him for a hosted breakfast, which consisted of a variety of select cuts of sashimi, some of the finest that the market had to offer – toro (fatty tuna), whitetail, surf clam, and more. While many Americans might turn their nose up at the idea of eating raw fish so early in the morning, I recognized the quality and cost of such a breakfast, and ravenously devoured each select cut for the delicacy that it was. And then came the finisher – a perfect slice of honeydew melon to cleanse the palate. Neither James or Ryan recognized the significance of the gesture, for they had not studied Japanese culture to my degree, and therefore did not realize the expense of such items in Japan. This is indeed a breakfast fit for kings. During the feast the subject of the problem with Alaska sockeye salmon was broached. This was our first official discussion about this issue – one that would be revisited constantly during our visit to Japan. Our position was one of deference, apologizing for the shabby quality of product that the industry had sent to the Japanese market.

Shortly thereafter we thanked our hosts profusely for the tour and breakfast, and off we were to the Food Export Office (FEO) for Tokyo. The staff was very welcoming, and after they provided us with an update of the current economic and market situation in Tokyo and Japan, we quickly shifted over to a discussion about the preparation of our official meeting with the Japanese press. We soon reached an agreement on the order of talking points, and how we would address potential questions from the press. Members of the Alaska Export Service were also in attendance – this was an extension of the Alaska Division of Trade – Craig Salis's crew, and they appeared to be searching for a reason for still existing as an entity – besides the fact that they were the first U.S. state trade office to open house in Japan, way back in the 1960's.

To conclude the day, we met with Juyojyo, who is a specialty wholesaler in Japan that had a long and historic involvement in Alaska processing, having been the last owners of one of one of the old-time major Alaska companies – Jitney Point. For Ryan, this was a personally important visit, as he had worked at Jitney Point as a processing boss for a good portion of his career and had a long personal relationship with Nomura –san, who now happened to be the president of the company. We were ushered into comfortable chairs in the executive visiting room to consult with the heads of the company, while beautiful and trim young ladies served us cups of hot steaming green tea. While we needed to cover the subject of the sockeye issue with the bosses, Ryan and Nomura made the effort to make the visit much more cordial than any other visit with Japanese trade that we had during our mission.

And our stop at Juyojyo turned out to be a visit with my past as well. One of the managers sat and stared out me strangely – and then I realized that he looked strangely familiar to me. Throughout the meeting we kept looking out each other. When the meeting concluded, I walked up to him and said, "You look so familiar – where have I seen you before?" He said to me, "You look very familiar to me too." He asked me where I had been in Alaska before – I told him I was from Kodiak. His eyes went wide with recognition – he declared, "Jitney Point in the 80's!" That is when it dawned on me – I had worked in that case-up section at the Jitney Point processing in Kodiak during early 1983 for the tanner crab fishery (as I had just graduated early from high school). He had been the manager for a special team of Japanese technicians that were working at the plant that were making a specialized test market of fancy packs of tanner legs and sections. Here we were, almost two decades later, having tea at the corporate headquarters in Tokyo! It's a small world indeed.

We concluded the day by performing some retail audits, which included visiting a very high-end grocery chain, Chinufugina. Sure enough, the honeydew melons were carefully stacked, with prices starting at $75 each. And you think the food prices are high here in the U.S. – nothing what prices can find in Tokyo!

The next morning was the dreaded press conference that we had prepared for such a long time. The questions from the press were very pointed about the extremely poor quality of Alaska sockeye, and how it was impacting the Japan trade. Ryan read my speech that I had wrote him, publicly recognized the issue, and apologized profusely in behalf of the industry. The press continued to ask questions of him, and each time he would lean over to me and quietly ask me what to say. And every I would whisper back to him the proper answer. After a number of questions, it began to look ridiculous – Ryan had no idea what was going on, or how to answer any of the questions effectively. You could see Krylos's disdain and disgust with Ryan continue to grow during the session. But I kept calmly feeding him answers until the session was over.

We spent the rest of the time calling on major trade partners, apologizing again for the crappy sockeye that had been produced, and asking questions about current trends in the Japan seafood market. I couldn't help but find it ironic that we were being so apologetic to these companies, considering that several of them owned production facilities in Bristol Bay, and had played a role in the quality issues.

The first to visit was Ichimo, the parent corporation for Captain Hook

Seafoods, which has operations all throughout Alaska; their main line of products is salmon, though they also processed crab at their facilities in Western Alaska. Ichimo had a long history of involvement in Alaska – which was emphasized during our meeting. And Captain Hook was renowned for processing some of the most consistent quality salmon of all the major Alaska producers. I could attest to this personally, as I had tendered salmon for them in the mid-90's, and their program ran on very strict timelines. Their tenders would pick up salmon and would deliver it to the processing facility on a day-to-day basis. So, whether a tender had 50,000 pounds or 5,000 pounds, it would be processed in less than 24 hours from being brought on board; this assured the highest of quality as possible for wild-caught product – which seemed almost revolutionary at the time. The relationship between Ichimo and Alaska ran deep – and they indicated their continued commitment to the industry.

Next, we stopped by Crystal Seafood's sales office; Crystal was a U.S. owned company, formed by a group of fishermen in Southeast Alaska in the 1960's – and like so many other of the major Alaska producers at that time – they had dedicated sales offices in Japan. The discussion at their office ran dark right away. The sales manager spoke of the decline and woe of the Alaska salmon market in Japan, sharing how there was no longer real profit in the sale of Alaska salmon anymore; his metaphor in broken English was that his company was making only "...bread and water, but had no meat." – in other words, no profits. His predictions for the Alaska sockeye market – and wild market in Japan – were bleak at best. Farmed salmon had arrived and disrupted the entire market. After he had shared his grim perspective, the manager turned to me and said, "You seem like a smart young man, you better get out before it is too late." In retrospect years later it was a haunting omen on a personal level. Our visit was not a very elevating experience and could possibly have been one that convinced me of the futility of expecting Alaska's position in the market to ever recover. But instead, it was one that would galvanize me in my efforts to restore our industry's position in this essential market.

Our last visit was to Daijo Dani Magic Mermaid – for me, it was a little close to home, considering I had just left Magic Mermaid a few months before. The news was not good there either – the message again was that the sockeye market was in turmoil, and farmed salmon was quickly setting the new standard, and taking a huge chunk of the wild sockeye market share. (Knowing Magic Mermaid's willingness to distribute farmed salmon in the

U.S. market, it would be no surprise to hear just a few months later that they began to distribute farmed salmon in partnership with a farmed producer).

We came away with the message that the market in Japan was changing quickly, and Alaska's position in the market – especially sockeye - had seriously come into question. Our apologies were well received, but action needed to take place in the industry if we were going to re-position in the market. I had essentially taken notes on every point of discussion during every session (as I would do for years) and wrote a full report -which was not only a requirement for EAS-funded activities, but also for informing committee members (and anyone else that wanted to read the reports). This is when I also began to perform retail audits – tracking prices for various products in the marketplace. This would help to begin to establish consumer pricing trends that had not previously been tracked.

It was the end of our trip, and James and I were both running low on money, as we had spent a good portion of our funds on knock off items, pearls, and silk while in China. Prices were high in Tokyo and seemed even higher after being in Shanghai. I couldn't help but compare the two of the highest populated cities in Asia – to me it felt that Shanghai was a blossoming young lady, while Tokyo was an old woman. While still a vibrant city, Tokyo had developed and boomed decades ago before. Indeed, the energy and impression of each of the two cities were entirely different.

While walking the streets of Tokyo, I couldn't help but notice there were little flyer leaflets posted everywhere, advertising call girls (I was told later, don't bother calling, because they are for Japanese men only – not for 'gaijin' like me). Another thing I noticed was the number of older men being accompanied by much younger women. At first, I thought this might be a father and daughter walking together, but then I soon realized that there was a prevalent tendency in Japan to see older, affluent men with beautiful, young women in tow.

Not to forget about Johnny Chin – he had flanked us during the entire mission as an all-expense-paid Alaska representative. He worked for the largest seafood processor –Harpoon - and on the last night in Tokyo, Ryan noted that Johnny had not bought a single drink, meal or anything for the group, even though it was considered protocol for industry members to spring for a drink at least, especially considered almost all his travel expenses were being covered by ASA. Johnny went the safe route and took us to the Hard Rock Café in the Roppongi district. For those of you that don't know Tokyo districts, Roppongi is basically the 'gaijin' district – where all the foreigners hang out, as well as the Japanese that want to hang out with foreigners. We sat down and ordered drinks. I ordered a Typhoon – a trademark drink for the Hard Rock in Asia. I was joking with James and Johnny, and suddenly out of the blue Ryan grabbed my untouched drink and drank the whole thing in one giant gulp. Before I had a chance to say anything, he blurted out, "You waited too long." Considering my drink had been sitting for just a minute, I was a little shocked. This was my first indication of Ryan's love affair with alcohol. What he did was rude to say the very least. But at least Johnny paid for it – so I ordered another – and cautiously kept it out of Ryan's reach.

The next day we packed and staged for the bus to take us to Narita for the flight home. James and I were hungry, and we both found ourselves almost totally broke. In fact, we both were literally scrounging our last dollars from change so that we could buy a cheap sandwich from a 7-Eleven store; nothing like going home broke.

Chapter 15

An Unwanted Promotion

Shortly after the return from the trip I got a call from Johnny. He and Harpoon were in trouble in Taiwan- a shipment of frozen salmon was being held up by Taiwanese customs officials. It had been shipped from Los Angeles, but it was chum fillet portions that had been re-processed in China, and so the boxes were marked, 'Product of China'. Authorities didn't believe Harpoon's assertion that it was truly Alaska product. This was one of my first experiences with dealing with traceability issues and a need to clarify regulatory product origin requirements. What is confusing is that the origin standards are to require a product to be identified as the country of origin where the final processing takes place. While the product should have said, 'Processed in China/Product of USA (Alaska)', it instead just said 'Product of China'. So, I had to write a letter to the Taiwan customs office to explain the circumstances and verify that the product originated from Alaska. I would find product origin issues to be a reoccurring discussion during my time at ASA.

We hadn't been home for more than a week or so, and Ryan called me into his office. He asked me to come look at his computer. On the screen was a porn video of a woman with a giant magnum champagne bottle planted deep in her vagina; the bottle was pulled out, and champagne started spraying out of her, and all over the room. Ryan chuckled and said, "One of my friends just sent this to me." I was mortified. I remembered well the internet usage policy agreement we had signed with the State of Alaska as a condition of employment, and securing, viewing, or sharing pornographic materials with company equipment was a definite 'no no'. I said to Ryan, "That's amusing, but you might want to get that off your computer and tell your friends not to send such materials anymore, as it is a direct violation of the State's policy." While we could not control what our contacts sent us, after that I always made it explicitly clear to my friends not to email jokes or any type of inappropriate materials to me work address.

It was becoming obvious Ryan that was not qualified for the job, and that James and I were having to do all the work for him. We wrote the trip reports and did all the preparations for the quarterly Export Marketing Committee (EMC) meeting. He wrote long rambling emails to all in the program – with no paragraph breaks, just one giant, multipage paragraph, with subject matter all over the place. And he would hand write his letters and give them to the office manager to type up – totally old school. I was not comfortable with the lack of leadership either, but realized I had no choice in the matter except to continue to take on the work that was necessary to keep the program rolling forward. Ryan would show up in a suit and tie almost every day. My favorite was his mustard-colored blazer – which reminded me of a Century One real estate jacket from the 80s. And Krylos was becoming more frustrated by the moment by his ineptitude and incapacity for the position. I tried to keep him positive, and reminded him that I was there to help, and encouraged him to depend on me as a resource to help keep the program intact, in spite of Ryan.

It was November and it was time to go to the annual United States Food Export Association (UFEA) conference. This year it was being held in Baltimore; it was essentially a huge meeting, where all the U.S. agricultural cooperators groups met with the Export Agricultural Service (U.S. Department of Agriculture) – the agency charged with administrating the Market

Export Program (MEP) and Foreign Export Growth (FEG) programs. The two grant programs were funded at about $150 million annually at that time, and all funding was distributed amongst about 120 cooperator groups, represented by agricultural producers from across the United States. The event took place at the Hyatt Regency, which was situated right on the Inner Harbor; the entire hotel was awash with cooperator reps and government officials when we arrived in the evening. Ryan then decided that we needed to have a meeting at 7 am before the regular session started. Having just arrived from the West Coast, it meant that our brains would think it would be 4 am – not good. Krylos and I grumbled to each other about it, but Ryan wanted a meeting with the officials from the Wood and Seafood Product Division (WSPD), so we set the alarm clock for 6 am. I was a night owl by nature and considering that my internal clock was running 3 hours behind, I worked through the night, finally falling asleep about 2 am Eastern time. Rudely I awoke to the phone ringing – it was Krylos asking me where I was – it was 7 am! Shit! I jumped out of bed, ran my head under the sink, speed shaved, threw my suit and tie on, and ran out the door. By then it was almost a quarter after; I jumped into the elevator and there was Susie Denim – the WSPD Deputy Director. I was breaking into a sweat and started to apologize to her for being late. But she looked up and smiled, and said, "Don't worry about it, I don't know why Ryan felt like we needed to meet this early." I was relieved and made sure I walked into the meeting room with her. This was the first of many of Ryan's staff meetings that he would call when we would basically talk about nothing. Essentially, he would ramble on about "We are new here." and all kinds of other juvenile and unnecessary statements.

So glad I was in such a hurry to get there on time- not! And it appeared that the rest of the FFPD staff felt the same way.

The sessions commenced, and the first issue right out of the gate was about Genetically Modified Organisms (GMOs), in this case it was mainly about GMO-produced U.S. wheat. It was becoming a huge point of contention in Europe. It was reported that one of the latest container ships full of U.S.

wheat was waylaid upon entry into the harbor in Bremerhaven, Germany; local protesters had a boat run along the ship, using green lights to broadcast a skull and crossbones and the words 'biohazard' brightly on the side of the vessel. The point had been made. The Germans – and a lot of other Europeans - were not happy about GMO products. This was a huge concern for several producer groups, and during the break I was approached by reps that asked me what we were doing to address GMO issues. I couldn't help but chuckle and respond that this was not an issue for us, being 100% wild and natural products. We were one of the only cooperator groups that could boast such an advantage – we were indeed one of the 'last of the buffalo hunters'.

The UFEA sessions always covered several subjects. There were updates to the budget (of which the future was always in question) regulations, standards, processes, etc.; this included changes to the management and the features of the new online system for inserting Combined Marketing Strategy (CMS) applications. The CMS was essentially the master grant application document that is a marketing assessment, strategy, activity plan and grant request, all wrapped up in one neat format. While hard copies had been the traditional means for applying, the new online system application was becoming a mandatory requirement as well. Being my first time to UFEA, I was taking notes on everything – and Ryan, as usual, was barely paying attention.

And then there were the 'beltway bandits'. They were numerous groups of consulting/contracting agencies that were constantly vying for projects – both directly from EAS, as well as from cooperators groups. The main theme by a certain consulting group during these sessions – which we were all required to attend – was a pitch about 'Results Oriented Management' (ROM). I couldn't' help but think that it would be a 'no-brainer' to manage for results, but I guess that must have been a new concept for others – or maybe it was how it was being packaged – as something fresh and new. Regardless, it was the new mantra of the year, and one that we were to carry back home to infuse into our marketing plans and management efforts.

I also learned loads about the other EAS programs and started to conceptualize other programs that we could utilize besides MEP – as the EAS was strongly encouraging.

I had only been there for barely two months – it was early December, and things had been moving so fast – but I was still so excited to learn more. James was supposed to be preparing for the next trade mission to Australia – which was of huge importance, considering the ban on importation of fresh and frozen Pacific salmon into Australia had just been lifted after being in place forever. Then all of us a sudden, my world was to change.

James walked into my office and told me he had just 'resigned'. They had basically forced him to – nobody gets fired from ASA – one just resigns. Still, I was shocked; the one person left in the program that had intellectual history was being swept out the door. Ryan pulled me in quickly and explained to me that he and Betty thought that James was 'poisoning my mind' and that it was time for him to go, but the good news was that I was instantly promoted to the role of Senior Marketing Specialist. Still, I was very saddened by his departure. As Krylos stepped into my office to say goodbye, his last words to me were, "Don't stay too long; it will turn your brains to mush." Those words would prove to be prophetic.

I sat in my office in shock. I had come accustomed to change throughout my life – but this was crazy. There was no one left in the program to assist with the transition. It was just me and Ryan – which was almost as synonymous as being just me. I had my hands full just taking care of the Asia programs, and now I was managing all the day-to-day needs for Australia and Europe as well! How was I going to handle all of this?

Then I got my new laptop. Jay Wakeman, the domestic retail program director, had purchased several computers for the office and he bought the export program a pair of Dell Inspiron laptops. Nice huge bricks the domestic program had bought us — they must have weighed ten pounds each. Ryan never really used his. I used my laptop for a while, but it would constantly go to sleep and then not wake up. Essentially it would crash and require to be restarted all the time — what a piece of crap! It ended up turning into a very expensive doorstop.

There were two major projects to take care of before the holiday break — to organize the final EMC meeting of the year, and to get the latent Taiwan program back up and running.

Chapter 16

Leading from Behind

T hankfully, James had been there to help me to organize at least one committee meeting before I left. After what I had seen from my first session, I wanted to make this one special. This was the first committee that I oversaw - and I wanted to 'wow' the members. In addition to quarterly reports, I generated pricing reports and special reports about new possible funding avenues from EAS – both for ASA and private companies. I generated PowerPoint presentations for every activity and issue that had occurred or was relevant to the program. And during the sessions I presented all the slide decks to the committee – I had asked Ryan if he wanted to, but he declined. Included in each of their committee packets was a CD containing copies of all the presentations for them to review. When the session was over, you could have heard a pin drop. The members were in awe at what had just been presented to them. Bob Falrik said, "where did you find this guy?" And then Bob Johnson (a longtime associate from Kodiak) made the comment that it was the best EMC meeting they had ever had. The standard for committee sessions had just changed. The digital age had been ushered in, and there was no turning back. Industry members were going to start believing in the potential of the program again. Ryan sat and smiled and took the credit for hiring me.

Now that the EMC session was cleared off my desk, it was time to turn my attention to the Taiwan program. William Lee had been the previous contractor representing the program, and his contract had not been renewed in early summer. From what I was told, he had about 23 clients, and wasn't giving the program the attention it needed. I consulted with Betty on what direction to take. She told me about Elsie Chun, who was the contracted representative for the Alaska Export Service-also Craig Salis's crew. Getting the program back up and running was important, mainly due to a political push from the State of Alaska and EAS. I consulted with several industry members about Taiwan and found that there was little interest in the market. It was not a huge consumption market (only 23 million people on the island), and it had high tariff schedules. From what I was told, in order to do business, industry and trade would have two separate sets of pro forma invoices; one with low products values that would accompany the shipment and duties, and a second one that would be secretly faxed back and forth and would contain the real values to be paid upon. The picture being painted was one of an uphill battle.

Despite lack of industry interest, I was undaunted to restart the program, and to make it a success. This was going to be MY project, MY baby, and I was going to do everything I could to be triumphant. So, I hired Elsie, and started putting the program back into play. It had the smallest budget – barely $100,000 – which wasn't much; but enough to get started. According to the marketing plan, we were to conduct a consumer food show, consumer advertising, trade public relations, retail merchandising, and some food service promotions, and I put Elsie to task to get initiatives started.

As we slowed down for the holidays, I took the time to start the process of switching job jackets from hard copies to digital. Job jackets were the means for approving activities. The contractors (who were called Foreign Promotion Agents, but I later renamed International Promotion Representatives) would create a job jacket for a specific activity. The jacket would contain the name of the activity, the federal activity number (this is how EAS tracked activity budgets), a description of the activity, estimated timing, and then a breakdown of how the budget was to specifically be spent. Contractors signed the document and then faxed it to the Bellevue office for one of the export staff to approve and sign. After that, a copy would be faxed back to the respective overseas office and a copy to Juneau for the Export Finance Administrator, Jeff Prince. Hard copies would be filed, and the job jacket would be included on a master spreadsheet for tracking the budget. No one had heard of a PDF file yet, so they were a little perplexed about how we were going to switch to digital processes.

It was not too difficult. First, I created a job jacket template with Excel, and then I had each contractor scan a copy of their signature and save it as a bitmap file. Then I taught them how to insert their signature in the Excel file and email it to our office. I would then approve, add my digital signature, and then save it as a PDF and email a copy to Jeff Prince, and the respective contractor. It took a little while for them to get used to, but it did streamline the process, and meant less time in front of the fax machine.

Christmas and New Year's came and went. It was supposed to be the big Y2K event – computers were supposed to potentially crash everywhere, due to the changes in time code that existed for most computers. New Year's came, the new millennium was ushered in, and there were no catastrophic crashes that so many had predicted. But we had a great time that night – Sherry and our friends dined out on Indian food for the last meal of the old millennium, and then we danced the night away.

Chapter 17

Drag Queens and Seagulls

I t was January, and it was time for me to go to Japan for first ASA Consumer Seminar and Lunch Party. It was a new concept that Han had cooked up. Essentially, we conducted a retail merchandising promotion in the Miyagi Prefecture of Japan at a retail chain cooperative called Miyagi United. For a month at these locations, we held an 'Alaska Seafood Month' promotion, which included a contest to win one of a 100 seats at the first Alaska consumer seminar and lunch party in Sendai.

My job was to assemble a presentation and then come to the seminar and educate the contestants all about the benefits of consuming Alaska seafood. The technology was a little antiquated at the venue, so I had to put together a series of old photo slides of seafood – some from ASA's collection and some of my personal images. No PowerPoint this time – we were going 'old school' – really old school.

So off to Japan I went, wondering how the activity was to be received. After arriving in Tokyo, I stayed at the Capitol Tokyu hotel. Han had lined up some trade meetings, as well as the standard complimentary visit with the local EAS office. While in my hotel I was trying to retrieve my emails but was having a problem establishing an internet connection. I kept messing with the setting on my PC computer, carefully following the hotel instructions for dialing out. I would switch configurations, but it wouldn't work. After a few hours, I decided to take a walk. So, I did. Then I came back and tried again. A few hours later – still no connection. So, then I went for a walk again and thought about it again. Then back to the computer, I went again. Finally, I was able to establish a connection. It just took the better part of a day or so to figure it out. Establishing a connection to the internet (and retrieving and sending email) would be an ongoing issue that I would deal with for the next few years, as it was a new process for most international business travelers at that time.

Two days later, I took the Shinkansen (bullet train) to Sendai with Han and Jim Tanaka. After arriving at the hotel, we received a very warm greeting from the members of the local trade as we joined them for an official dinner. There were reps from Miyagi United, local wholesalers, and primary suppliers from Tokyo – all that were involved with the sales effort. This is when I was first introduced to our interpreter, who was to help me steer conversations throughout the night. We had a wonderful dinner of all types of local and Alaska seafood. The conversation was very cordial and lively, and the drink flowed freely as we continued to toast each other, as well as to the success of the new day's seminar. It was a traditional Japanese setting, with low tables, and everyone sitting on their knees. My long legs would grow uncomfortable while sitting in this position, but I would do my best to move back and forth in the two 'acceptable' positions, to be a gracious guest.

Most were starting to get a little drunk from all the toasting. As we got up to depart, I thought we would all be retiring back to our rooms for the night. But the locals had something else in mind. Our interpreter politely asked if she could be excused for the evening, as she did not want to have anything to do with what was about to occur – and she looked quite concerned. I graciously excused her, but her hasty exit had me worried – what was I in store for? I had heard stories of the infamous red-light districts, and being freshly married, there as a bit of concern about what I was about to step into. An entourage of about a dozen of us, including Han, her two staff members, and Jim, sauntered down the street, heading into the 'night district' of Sendai. Where were we headed? What was in store for us? All Han could say was that they were taking us to a 'special' place.

After walking for a couple of blocks through the traffic of street callers, bars, and beautiful young 'hostesses' we came upon a building and proceeded upstairs. Like so many other Japanese buildings, there were several floors, with a number of small establishments on each floor – none with any windows. In the U.S., such establishments would probably never pass a fire code standard, but in Japan, it was the status quo. Up a couple floors, and then deeper we walked into the building until we reached the very back. There was a sign above the door that said, 'Nonderarella'. All I could think was, "what the fuck does that mean?" I was about to find out. We walked in and there was a small reception area, with walls to the right with cutouts loaded full of bottles of scotch; to the right was a cozy little room, with a karaoke stand and a big circular booth. And on the walls were framed photos of ladies. Through my alcoholic-infused haze, I took a closer look, it appeared that the woman was kind of ugly, and wore too much makeup. Then it dawned on me – oh my God, these were men in drag! I started thinking, what kind of place was this? Was this some strange transvestite strip joint? Was I about to get a laptop dance from some Japanese tranny?

I wanted to bolt back to my room but didn't want to be impolite my hosts. So, I sat down and prepared for the worst. Then the music began, and as the first guest stood up in front of the microphone to sing karaoke, the proprietors of the establishment came out and started dressing up the guy in a wacky traffic cop outfit. Now it was starting to dawn on me, they dressed you up in funny outfits while you sang. I was a little relieved at first but wondered what they were got to dress me as. Soon I was up, and out came one of the staff members. First, she drew a mustache on my face, then out came a sombrero and a sarape. I was safe- they were dressing me only like a

Mexican! The hostesses continued to poor us scotch and water, and slowly but surely, each person in our party stood up and sang, and was randomly dressed in a unique and funny costume. Han got lucky – they dressed her in a bridal dress. Two of the men were not so lucky, and were dressed up in wigs, makeup, and dress – a couple of ugly women indeed. The night was winding down, and we were all having some great laughs. And then it was announced that I was to sing one more time – the grand finale of the evening. In fact, I had not escaped – they had saved me for last. The hostesses grabbed me and drug me in their back room, stripped my shirt and coat off, and then started the process of converting me into a 6'4" drag queen. A long green dress, long arm gloves, a blond wig, and a giant, flowery green hat, and a ton of makeup transformed me into one of the tallest drag queens they had ever seen. I was so drunk by then that I don't even remember what I sang. All I can remember was the laughs and howls, and the never-ending flash of cameras as they flicked away, taking dozens of pictures of me. I supposed I could have said no, but with all the hospitality and goodwill that had been built up, it most certainly would have put a damper on the night. Now the Nonderarella name was starting to make sense to me – it was a play on words for 'not Cinderella'. It was a test and a trial for me. It was a special treatment that they gave to visitors that they felt were worthy, and they told me that I had passed, and that I was now an 'official citizen' of Sendai.

The next morning, I awoke, and first thing I thought was, "Did that really happen?" But it had. It was time to get dressed, have some breakfast, and tend to the last-minute preparations for the seminar. The seminar began, and I watched the Japan trade members kickoff the event with several opening remarks. Here they all stood in their dark suits and ties, looking so formal, when just a few hours before they were dressed in zany outfits and looking so very different. We ran through the presentations – I shared all kinds of facts about why Alaska seafood is so healthy for people - especially for brain and eye development in kids. There were several questions, and then after all were answered, with no further ado, we moved the contestants to the room next door to enjoy the lunch party session. There was a giant square serving area in the middle of the room, with a dozen or so different types of Alaska-inspired dishes. The housewives wasted no time and descended like seagulls on the food. In no time at all the serving platters were empty. They had eaten every morsel! And they were loving every minute of it. Shortly thereafter we had them all complete surveys, to enter into a contest to win gift packs of Alaska seafood, with the grand prize being a trip for two to Alaska. This was the first time I had seen an event that incorporated every element of the distribution channel – from the primary supplier, all the way down to the end user. We had the entire chain in the room together. Han and I were so relieved as we watched the smiling faces; we had been worried about the outcome of the activity, but it was now clear that it was a huge hit. We headed back to Tokyo that night, feeling a great sense of accomplishment. We had taken the risk, and it had worked.

Chapter 18

Sunburns and New Friends

Meanwhile Ryan was heading to Australia with ASA's Technical Program Director, Bobby Olson, and a hand full of industry members. As I mentioned before, this was an extremely important mission to make inroads for fresh and frozen Alaska salmon. And it was not without controversy. At the beginning of the month, Ryan and I had traveled to Juneau to meet the rest of the administrative staff, including Bantu, who at the time was the finance representative for the domestic programs.

There was another reason for our visit. The Governor's office was questioning why there was a trade mission going to Australia in the middle of the winter; to them, it obviously appeared that staff was going 'down under' for a vacation in the sun. This was my first visit up the '3rd Floor' of the capitol, which is where the Governor and his immediate staff were based. Off Betty, Ryan and I went, to make our case. We met with the chief of staff, and explained the need to promote fresh and frozen, since the ban had just been lifted. Gladly, we were persuasive enough that we were able to secure approval - this would be just one of many incidents were I had to continually explain how and why we were doing our jobs for the international marketing effort.

Ryan was back in the office a few days after my return from Japan. I reported on the success of the Japan seminar and asked him how the Australia mission had went. He said it was good, but didn't give me much detail, besides that the trade was very open to working with fresh and frozen products; the only other thing he had for me was pictures of he and trade members playing golf on their day off. Since Ryan didn't want to know how to write a trip report – or even try – I followed up with Bobby to ask how things went. He gave me details about what has occurred at the trade seminars and receptions, as well as the impressions by the trade. Then he started to laugh. The big joke was that Ryan had missed the press seminar and trade presentation. This is the event that they had traveled all the way to Australia for, and he called in that morning saying he was sick. Anyone can understand the unfortunate circumstances of getting sick before a major activity. But the funny part was that Ryan showed up the following day for some trade meetings, and he was beet red – totally sunburned. It turns out that Ryan spent the entire day laying out on Bondi Beach instead of leading the activity. Unbelievable! It was disgusting to think about all the preparation and work that Bobby and I had put into this mission, to have him bale on the day of main activity. This would come back to 'burn' him later, as the word began to spread about what has transpired.

But there was no time to split hairs, as it was time to start writing the CMS plan, which was due in late March. Considering that Krylos was no longer around, it was going to be quite a task to craft a plan for the first time. Betty was concerned about our abilities, so she contracted a local Seattle area agency, The Research Agency (TRA) to assist in the plan generation. And along with TRA came a man named Richard Meister - for the first and last time. I had known Richard previously due to articles he had written about transfer pricing and collusion in the industry. We had met a few times and discussed the issues and shared perspectives. He had also secured a little moonlight contract work for me with TRA while I was at Magic Mermaid, editing CMS plans for cherry and apple groups. Richard had been an accountant for a number of the major processors and had sued one for wrongful termination. Where he and I differed is that he was negative and suspect of everything, and I was attempting to do something positive for the industry through my work at ASA. As he reviewed the programs on behalf of TRA, he began to make suggestions that the budget for Japan was way too high, and that we should shift a large portion of the budget to Taiwan. I was very frank in my reply, and told him that he was out of his mind, and that it was too drastic of a change, and that the industry, nor market, could support such a drastic shift of resources. It was soon to become a non-issue, as Betty caught wind he was working in our office. He was infamous within the circles of the Alaska industry, and she ordered Ryan to get him out of the office immediately. This would not be the last time I would see Richard.

But he was the least of my worries. I was busy trying to make sense of the export data – which was poor and very general at best. Ryan wasn't any help, and I was working with TRA to work on the CMS – which was huge. We needed global projections, industry production and forecast updates, market assessments, strategy, and activity plans; and I had been devising a new method for crunching the export numbers. And the draft country plans had come in from each rep. Daniel Green's was in perfect English – being that he was the UK/Northern Europe representative. And Roger McClary's plan for Southern Europe was also in great form, being an American by heritage. Han's was a little rough due her Japanese style of English, and Bobby and Billy's China plan was a little hard to follow, but Elise's was unintelligible. I lovingly referred to her style as 'Elisanese' from that point on. She couldn't help it; English was her third or fourth language that she had learned. And I couldn't write in French to save my life. It was going to be a challenge, but it was going to take a while before I could fully grasp the intent of the translated words from most of them.

Previously the export number had been provided by one of the EAS analysts that was securing very basic and limited figures from a main customs database, it was ambiguous categories that accounted for just salmon, canned salmon, and whitefish categories. These figures represented only a fraction of what the industry was exporting. So, I switched over to figures from the National Marine Fishery Service's databases. Their database was vast, covering every export and import number for every category of seafood that crosses the border. The first time around the task was gargantuan, as I began to research every single category that might be relevant to the Alaska fishery. It was a complex task – it required cross-referencing every species for each country destination against figures for the Seattle and Anchorage customs reporting districts. With some species, like king crab or snow crab, it was easy to capture all the export figures for the U.S. as Alaska origin – since 100% of U.S. production is from Alaska. With other species, it was a long and laborious process to ascertain what was Alaska production. But it was closest anyone had ever come, and it was consistent – and it painted a much more realistic picture of the importance of exports to the Alaska industry, as well to the U.S. export component at the macro level.

It was about this time that we were getting reports that the wild salmon sales sector was worse than ever. I walked into the office to find a crowd of gloomy faces. There was real concern about the future for the sector. One person made the comment that it was getting really dark. And then the words popped into my head, and I said, "Not to worry everyone, we will be a shining beacon in a pool of darkness." At least I got them all to chuckle a little bit. But it was at that point on that I committed to myself that we were going to turn the salmon sector on the path to the recovery. It was just going to take some time – and a lot of effort.

And then Molly Greyson was thrown into the mix. She was this petite lady that had been married to a prominent Alaska fisherman for years, and she had been out of the workforce for about a decade, dedicating her efforts to raising her two sons. She had no background in marketing or sales, but she did have a degree in accounting, and a short stint working for the State of Alaska back in the '80s when she lived in Juneau. The first thought that crossed my mind when Ryan brought her in for an interview is that she might be Ryan's girlfriend. I remained skeptical during the interview due to her lack of background in marketing, but it was Ryan's call to hire her, and he did.

She was so funny - one of the first things she inquired in her first week is why I oversaw Asia, and she oversaw Europe. Her reasoning was that she was half- Japanese, and that I was half –German – a more ethnic perspective, to say the least. I reminded her that my formal education was a minor in Japanese cultural studies, and that I had been hired to run Asia, and had been working on the programs for half a year. It quickly became a moot point.

Next, she started asking why her Europe reps weren't showing any respect to her. She had just arrived, and it was natural for the reps to be standoffish. I explained to her that they had been through a lot of upheaval the past year, were still in fear of losing their contracts with the organization. I cut right to point, the reps were not going to respect her just because they suddenly reported to her – she was going to have to prove that she would take care of their needs and provide them with the proper level of support. She was going to have to earn it. She headed my words and went to task to gain their respect.

But the thing that amused me about her the most was that she banged on the computer keyboard a lot when the screen or cursor would freeze. She was quite loud for being such a tiny little woman, and I could hear her from the other room, "What's wrong with this damn computer?", as she slammed away at the keys. After hearing this happen a couple of times, I walked into her office and said, "Let's go get a cup of coffee." She looked at me and said, "Why?". And I said, "Because you just gave your computer about 50 commands after punching on the keys so many times, and it going to take about 20 minutes for it to catch up with you." She said, "Really?" And I said, "Yup, really." She kind of figured it out after that, but sometimes she would get frustrated and start punching all the keys again. I must it admit, the computer she was working with was total junk – so I totally empathized with her.

As our working relationship began to blossom, we began to yell back and forth to each other from inside our offices. Marylou, the front desk clerk, started saying to us, "you guys are pretty loud." And the name stuck – Molly and I were soon the 'Loud Team', or as we liked to refer to ourselves, the 'Loud and Proud Team'.

It was last March, and the CMS was almost due. We were in our final stretch, but it was still needing final touches to complete it– even with the help of a contractor. Ryan was ready to 'escape' to Spain for a trade show, and leave the mess of the CMS application to Molly and I, but then Betty got firm with him and told him that he was managing the program, and it was his responsibility to stay in the office and make sure it was submitted on time. They probably should have sent Molly, but she was too fresh to the program, and I was the senior specialist, so I went to Barcelona to participate in the Alimentaria show.

Chapter 19

Pickpockets and Warm Cokes

I t was a long flight to Barcelona. I had to switch flights in Germany, and by the time I arrived, I was pretty wiped out. When I arrived at the hotel it was about 8 am on a Sunday morning. My room would not be ready until the afternoon, and the staff would not store my bags. Frustrated and tired, and slumped down into a table at the hotel I ordered a Jack Daniels and Coke to take the edge off. The waiter looked at me strangely and said, "You are ordering alcohol this early in the morning?" Like it was any of his business. I told him, "Please, I have been traveling for almost two days – just bring me the drink." And he did. Just a few moments later, who walks by me but Jack Juniper of Nemo Seafoods– I had chosen him as one of the industry representatives to accompany us on the mission. He was already checked in from the day before, and he gladly put my bags in his room, so we could for a walk.

We had walked a couple blocks and turned off the main arterial, heading to a park that Jack had seen on the way to the hotel. It wasn't an alley but was a side artery with little traffic. As we strolled along, I spied three young punks glaring at us and talking amongst themselves. Jack was gabbing away and was totally oblivious of them, but I watched them out of the corner of my eye with suspicion. Sure enough, they were following us, hanging back at first to keep from garnering our attention, but still moving towards us at a rapid pace. I continued to glance towards Jack, so I could spy behind me and carefully monitor their distance, while as not to reveal my knowledge of their presence. They continue to get closer, but kept just the right distance, as they waited for the most opportune point when Jack and I were to be trapped, stuck in between a wall to our left, and row of parked cars to our right.

One of the punks quickly split off into the street and circled around the cars to in front of us while his two compatriots ran up on us from behind. The first one came straight at us and blocking our path, so that we would have to stop. Jack was still totally oblivious. Then the two from shuffled right up behind us. I calculated it perfectly; at the exact moment they were upon us, I quickly stepped to the right so that my back was pointed to the parked cars on the street. Their plan was blown, and they had no choice but to rush up only on Jack, and attempt to grab his wallet from his back pocket.

As I stood and stared at them menacingly, the punk in the front and the one closest to my back realized the game was up and ran off as quickly as possible. This left just one of them, all of us sudden standing there alone between Jack and I, holding a map that he had taken from Jack's pocket. As I stared at him with a scrunched-up brow, he started shaking and said to me sheepishly, "You dropped your map," He quickly handed it to me and ran off to join his friends. Jack was standing there, still in disbelief and asked, "What just happened?" And I said, "Don't you get it, they were trying to rip us off!" He replied, "No, I must have just dropped my map." I explained to him what had happened. He got an 'oh shit' look on his face when the reality of the situation hit him, and he quickly took his wallet out of his back pocket and zipped it in his front coat pocket. From that day on, I have always carried my wallet in my front pocket. That practice has served me well throughout the years.

Later that day we met went to the Ramblas to get some dinner. It was about

4:30 in the afternoon, and Jack had been craving a dish of bacalao – which is the Southern European version of cod; we were trying to find a restaurant and found that the restaurants were all just getting done with serving lunch. They wouldn't start serving dinner for a couple more hours. So we went back to the hotel, where we ran into our other industry representative, Larry Magnum, who was a sales manager for Wintersea Seafoods. We decided to have dinner with him and was joined by our rep, Roger. Jack and I shared the story of our close call that morning with the pickpockets. He shared several stories of such incidents in on the Ramblas – including one where the thieves actually used a naked woman to distract everyone's attention in order the lift their wallets. After hearing about all these incidents, we felt lucky.

The show started the next day at 10 am. At the booth was Roger's assistant David. I remember him well became when we met, he asked if I was German. I said, "Yes, I'm half-German." He replied, "I hate Germans." After that, I knew we were going to get along just fabulously. The Alimentaria food show was immense- it is basically the largest food show in Southern Europe. Pavilion after pavilion stretched across the giant fairground – there were so many major brands, with huge booths. Champagne, beer, wine, seafood, meat, etc. It went on and on and on. And then there was our little Alaska booth – a little 10 x 20-foot rectangle sandwiched between a row of similar booths. Everything about it spoke 'generic' and 'insignificant. We had some framed pictures hanging up, and we had a display case with some salmon, and a couple of whitefish in it. And there were a couple of small tables in the back. And we had a little mini-refrigerator in the back corner for cold drinks – but we found the first day it didn't work. And across from us was some local beer manufacturer with some brand I had never heard of. He had colorful displays, a large lounge full of tables, and a bar with beer on tap – and about a half dozen gorgeous women serving beer to patrons.

All I could think was that Alaska is the third largest seafood supplier on earth. Here we sit at a trade show with a boring little broken-down booth, with some obscure, local beer company totally outshining us. There was something wrong with the picture, and I couldn't help but thing that we needed to do something different for the future.

The next morning, we came to find the refrigerated display wasn't working, and all the ice had melted – the display fish were swimming in a pan of water. And the mini-frig wasn't working – the canned Cokes we had to share with visitors were as warm as ever. We called the representative in charge of the displays – he said he would have a technician there in an hour; we did not see the man again until two days later. David would do something in a similar fashion. He would say to me, "I'll be back in 30 minutes," – and then come back three hours later. I was finding this was the trend for 'Spanish' time. Being a punctual person, I was not amused, and I must admit that it took me a while to get used to it. It was a five-day show, and it seemed to go on forever. For two days we had to bail the water out of the display in the morning, and then place fresh ice in the case for the display product. By the last day of the show, I had had enough. I went to a local smoker that morning that worked with Alaska king salmon, and I talked him out of two large fillets of smoked salmon. I set up a makeshift cutting board in the booth and started to serve smoked salmon to visitors from the top of display case. This was the beginning of the sampling program, which would grow to become a standard at all our international shows. Yes, I thought to myself, "We can do a much better job at these events." It was just going to take some time to make it a reality.

The funniest thing that happened while we were in Barcelona was on the second night. Jack and I went looking for a place to eat, and just a block or so down the street was a little shop with cheese on display in the window – and the place was totally empty. Curious, we walked into the entrance, which was wide and expansive, like a typical European café; we sauntered up to the serving counter where the proprietor stood. There were windowed cases of rows and rows of different types of cheeses on platters. The man asked in a heavy Spanish accent, "What can I do for you?" I tried to politely respond to him in Spanish, and he snapped at me, "You should speak Catalan!" of which I knew absolutely none. Then Jack made the mistake of asking, "What's good hear?" The man snapped back immediately, "It is all good!" He was not pleased. He blurted out, "Sit down, and I will serve you." Many might have turned and walked out after such rudeness, but we were intrigued – and I felt that Jack had kind of insulted him by asking what was good, so we sat down immediately.

As soon as we had sat down, he came to the table and asked, "What kind of wine would you like to drink with your cheese?" Jack responded, "I don't drink." The man rolled his eyes and stared at me, "What kind of wine are you drinking with my cheese?" Usually I am a beer drinker, but at this point I wasn't going to push it. I quickly replied, "How about a wonderful local red wine – I'll leave it to you to choose." In no time he was back with a tray full of a half dozen different types of cheeses, and a bottle of rioja.

The cheese was fantastic, and I was doing my best to consume the entire bottle of wine by myself. Two British ladies came in and we watched them go through a similar process with the man. They asked for a menu, and started asking what he would recommend, and the commanded them curtly to sit down, telling them he would bring them something. And just like us, they scurried right over to sit down at a table. Them it dawned on me – this guy was 'The Cheese Nazi' – just like the infamous 'Soup Nazi' character from a popular Seinfeld episode. He was totally rude and insulting, but people would submit to him in fear of not being able to enjoy his offerings.

Not wanting to piss off the Cheese Nazi more, I drank the entire bottle of wine myself. He came back and asked how it was. We declared it was the best cheeses we had ever enjoyed – which was basically the truth. He warmed up to us slightly and told us that he was glad we enjoyed it. Then he went back to berating the British ladies, who were continuing to make him angry with inane questions.

We went back the next night for more cheese and abuse, but his shop was strangely closed for the rest of our stay. Maybe he was getting drunk the rest of the week, or maybe he just opened one day a week – who knows what the Cheese Nazi's schedule was – he obviously did as he pleased.

Chapter 20

The 'Year of Creativity'

I returned to find the CMS application finally done. Molly and Ryan were preparing to go to Brussels. Ryan was also getting ready to attend the semi-annual Board of Directors meeting. He was out of the office at one of his 'meetings' in Seattle, and all of a sudden Liz called to ask where the international components for the board packets were, as they were already two days past due. Molly and I couldn't believe it! Ryan had said nothing about this task. What were we going to do? We moved quickly. Molly started printing out all the trip reports and status reports, while I went to task, writing a director's report for the board – which I then signed in Ryan's absence. All the contents were assembled and were out the door in a FedEx overnight packet before the end of the day. All we could think was what a lazy and incompetent jerk he was. After that episode, we made it clear with Liz that she contact us directly for future board reports – or anything else. We had just saved Ryan's ass, and he didn't even know it.

I found that Ryan was spending time constantly having 'meetings' with the industry, which were more than likely consulting gigs for other companies, or attending someone's wake. He would constantly come into the office in the afternoon, reeking of booze, and he was always saying he was at someone's funeral, so I figure he was there to get free drinks. He would also tell me, "If Betty calls, tell her I have an important meeting with industry members." This would become the standard lie.

A few days later, Ryan and Molly departed for the show in Brussels – the European Seafood Exhibition. I came into my office the next morning to find a giant stack of paperwork –including printed copies of emails with various requests from industry and trade members, invoices, and other items that had not been addressed. Ryan left a note on top of the pile, asking me to take care of all these items. This would become standard practice with him. He would let lingering issues, potential projects, and necessary tasks stack up for months, and then drop them on my desk. By the time they reached me, simple tasks or needs were now in an emergency state to be addressed – just like the board packet.

And in the middle of this first stack was a request from the Western Consolidated Food Export Association (WCFEA) for us to participate in a food service promotion activity in China. They wanted us to provide product for a chef education event, as well as supporting collateral. The deadline for commitments had come and passed, and they wanted a commitment immediately. In a spirit of cooperation, I agreed to help, and asked them to forward me the details. I would later learn volumes about negotiating co-promotional efforts from this little agreement – but did not realize what a mess I had gotten myself into until later in the summer.

Meanwhile at home, I was finally closing the sale on my house. I had owned it for about eight years, and I had been working on it for the past two years, making the repairs and upgrades necessary for it to pass a bank loan inspection. It was another load off my mind to finally sell it. Now Sherry and I would have the nest egg we needed to buy a house, if the right one became available.

Molly and Ryan returned from the Brussels show, and shared feedback about the show, the Alaska pavilion, and what needed to be done to improve the results of the event. Ryan though everything was fine – as we had agreed accustomed to his minimum efforts. As long as he received a free dinner, and was not expected to do much, he would be happy. Molly talked about the challenges to the pavilion, as well as the traffic patterns, etc. She spoke about the issue of non-Alaskan product being promoted at of some Alaska booths. She told me about the 'lounge lizards'- industry sales reps that wanted to use the ASA booth for conducting sales instead of purchasing a full booth in the pavilion. She felt that we could do more to make things better. She was exhausted; the show was a huge task, and she had worked so hard to pull things off, with basically no help from Ryan.

In late April the team had a giant board session in Anchorage. The first morning of the board session, Liz really screwed up. She was supposed to have all the board packets ready, but instead of getting it done at the printer the night before, she decided to go drinking with her mother all night. Molly and I and a few others were there early for the start of the board session, when we saw Liz come rushing in with all the different components of the board packets in various boxes. All the board members were sitting in their seats, waiting for the packets before the session started; and there sat Betty – with a really shitty look on her face – and I really didn't blame her. It was a real fuckup on Liz's part. Still, we felt bad for Liz, as she frantically tried to lay out and organize the different sections of the packets. Molly and I couldn't help ourselves; we jumped right in and started to help her assemble the packets. With us lending a hand it didn't take more than a couple of minutes once we got a rhythm going – but with the ominous silence of the board members sitting there waiting – it felt like hours.

During the session I helped Han with a special presentation that she gave to the board about some of the challenges that Alaska seafood was facing in the Japan market. The situation in Japan was pretty grave – especially for the salmon sector – which had been wholly displaced by farmed salmon, mainly from Chile. Lee's messages touched on several subjects. I remember the most profound was about the inconsistency in grading and quality. One message from the Japanese trade that she shared that burned in my memory was, "No more surprise boxes please." The Japanese recognized that wild salmon makes for different grades in quality. But they were tired of the lousy grading that most of the processors had been providing. My experience at Magic Mermaid could attest to these grading issues, and I could totally empathize with the position of the Japanese. I could only hope that the industry was finally going to get the message.

Immediately following the board was the ASA Summit 2000 – it was Betty's idea to bring all of the ASA team together in order to brainstorm on ways to improve the organization and its functionality. Throughout these sessions, Ryan would continue to call specials meetings for the export team. We would gather all the contractors and employees, and then Ryan would act like there was something important to talk about – but there really wasn't. In hindsight, I think that he just wanted to feel important, or that he was trying to act as a leader, somehow. But it was just a means of demonstrating that he really didn't know what he was doing. The beginning of the summit launched with a series of presentations by all the agencies and contractors. When Elise's turn came up, Ryan got up and walked out of the room, and did not return until she was finished. It was such a shallow and selfish act on his part. And Elise couldn't help but notice. As soon as she was done with her presentation, she bolted out of the room in tears and into the restroom. Molly followed her in and tried to calm her, but she didn't want her help. Ryan was shattering her confidence and she became convinced that she would soon be fired. Molly and I worked hard to constantly remind Elise that we would do everything to keep that from happening, and that industry members would not let it take place.

Betty shared her vision of what she wanted to see as an outcome from the summit and declared the year 2000 as the 'year of creativity' for ASA. We kicked off with a lot of discussion about the history of ASA, and what we thought was important for each of our specific programs. We had a big dinner at the Alaska Brewhouse, and then we all went up to the Crow's Nest at the top of the Captain Cook Hotel for an afternoon drink. The smart ones went to bed after that. The rest of us were stupid enough to mosey on over to the Woodshed – a sleazy old whisky bar across the street from the Hilton. There was A LOT of drinking that night. If I remember correctly, there were five of us – Liz, Lisa, Mark, Dave and I. It was one shot after another – tequila, duck farts, etc. We kept drinking and drinking, and then we took over the karaoke machine. The songs came flowing until we all finally launched into singing together in a drunken warble the song 'I Got Friends in Low Places'. Near the end, the manager pulled the plug on us – literally. Talk about party over! We all started laughing hysterically – we had just officially shut down The Woodshed. It was time for bed, but we stumbled back up to Lisa's room for one more drink. I had enough and headed back to my room to get some sleep.

The next morning was rough. As we all assembled for the meeting, the five us that had stayed up all l night looked at each other with long, silent stares – it was going to be a long day. The hangovers we were all suffering from were horrendous. This last day of the summit was started with the introduction of a rubber fish. Whoever screwed up, or spoke out of line, would wind up with the fish on the table in front of them. Whoever was last at the end of the day would be stuck with the fish – and nobody wanted that. Some great ideas came from this last day. One of the things we clarified was who we worked for – the industry; while we answered to certain government entities, it would be good to clarify who are real clients were – to help all of us to hone our focus for the future. I felt that by far one of the best things to come from the session was the discussion and establishment of trade show and event standards. This would be essential in assisting me in establishing standardized approaches to create continuity at our events across the globe. I would continue to refine the effort internationally over the next few years. We also started talking a lot about the possibility of increasing our PR efforts – which was part of the outcome of the major domestic research project that had been performed the previous year. The domestic program would develop a dedicated effort because of these findings – and because of it, they wound up spending hundreds of thousands of dollars on a specialty contractor - that would provide limited and questionable results.

Probably the funniest thing that came out of the session was Betty's idea to offer an incentive to promote the 'year of creativity'. I can understand why she was doing it – she wanted to encourage all the teams to come up with creative ideas to bolster our marketing efforts. And it was actually a good idea. But everyone one the staff was scoffing at the challenge - mainly because the incentive was to secure $30,000 in funding for the program winner. The winning program would use the funding to carry out their creative idea. This was perceived by most as not a reward, but instead just a means of being tasked with more work.

Roger McClary had the best idea – to create an interactive video kiosk that be used at trade/food shows and special events. Unfortunately, nothing ever became of his idea, or the creativity contest itself– except a few jokes. While joking at the office a week or so later, I came up with the slogan, "Come gum our chum" – for the senior market. Molly had an even better idea – "Bone in, bone out" – in reference to the two common fillet product formats for salmon: pin bones in, pin bones out. It least we kept a sense of humor about it.

Chapter 21

How to Buy a House

Next up was my first trip to Taiwan, which took place in early June. We had a booth at the Taiwan Food Show. It was a four-day show in Taipei; the first three days were for trade only, and the last day they would let consumers in to enjoy the event. I had several industry members approved to join us for the event. I had Molly Clatsop from Magic Mermaid, Susie Fogle, who was now working for Aquawolf, and Rick Smoker, a board member and owner of Skookum Pass Shellfish – a company in Southeast Alaska that produced oysters and clams. As a special treat we arranged for some of Rick's oysters and clams to be shipped over live for serving at the show.

Molly had arrived ahead of us, as she was taking some personal time with her family. Susie had arrived early too and was conducing some business visits in other parts of the island to attempt to initiate sales. The morning after I arrived, I met with Elsie Chun to fly to Kaoshiung, which is the second largest city in Taiwan, located on the south end of the island. On the way to the airport Elsie and I reviewed the new food service brochure was she had generated for the market. I had approved it month's before, but it was not until that morning that she revealed that the photograph of salmon on the front cover was a farmed salmon. I was not happy to say the least. I could not believe she had used farmed salmon to falsely represent Alaska product. She explained that she couldn't find any Alaska product for the photo shoot. I told her that she should have told me, and I would have secured her some product. I reminded her that this was a serious issue, and that she could never do such a thing again. Unfortunately, this was just the first example of her tendency to make poor decisions and act without prior approval.

After our discussion, we flew to the south end of the island. Molly greeted us at the airport, and we spent the day in Kaoshiung, conducting several trade meetings.

We took the early evening jet back to Taipei; I got back to the hotel and opened the door to find a 14-page purchase and sales agreement slipped under the door. It was from Sherry; she had found a house for us to buy, just down the street from her parents. Anyone that remember the housing market in Seattle at that time would recall that it was on fire. I gave her a call - Sherry had made an offer the same day it went on the market, and there were three other offers that came into the broker at the same time. Fortunately, the owners remembered Sherry from her childhood, as their daughter used to babysit her and her siblings, and so they chose to sell it to us – but they wanted to make sure that I really wanted the house too, so they wanted me to write a letter expressing my desire. I asked her, "Can I at least see a picture of what we are buying?" There was no picture, and no listing for me to see online (listing services were not that robust in the year 2000). So, I made a leap of faith – I chose to buy a house I had never seen, and I wrote the letter, and filled out the purchase and sales agreement and faxed it off to her. It worked- they accepted our offer – and if the financing went through, we would get the house.

The next day Rick joined Elsie and I for meetings with the AIT – the Agricultural Institute in Taiwan. They did not have an official Food Export Office in Taiwan; it was one of those strange political situations that existed, since the U.S. government wasn't supposed to be recognizing Taiwan as an official government. This was the result of President Nixon opening political relations with Mainland China in 1972, requiring that Communist China was hereon to be recognized as the 'official' China to the world, leaving Nationalist China (and Taiwan) as an 'unofficial' country. One day a valued ally – the next day, to not exist; what a fucked up world we live in. The rift would become more apparent when I shared my business card with a Taiwan trade member – he read the simplified Chinese on the back and quickly snorted, "This is simplified; we use traditional Chinese here in Taiwan- we are more refined!" After our visit with the U.S. officials, we paid a visit to the local fish market. We couldn't believe our eyes – most of the fish were lying out right on the cement floor with no protective wrap or chilling – totally unsanitary conditions in the sweltering heat. But I guess that was just Taiwan standards at the time.

The next morning, I got up to go to attend the trade show. I was scheduled to provide a presentation, so I was brought my laptop and computer case with me. Stepping outside, I found that the taxi line was backed up around the corner. I needed to get to the show to setup early with Elsie, so I started walking at a rapid pace to the show. Even though the sky was overcast, the temperature must have been up in the mid-90s, and the humidity was spiking. As I sped quickly along in my suit, I couldn't help but begin to perspire. By the time I got there I was totally drenched in sweat. Elsie looked up at me as I walked up to the booth and exclaimed, "Is it raining outside? You are totally soaked!" I couldn't help but to begin to laugh out loud – "No, I had to run to the show from the hotel!" She asked me if I would be okay, but all I really needed was to go to the restroom, rinse my head, and cool off a little in the air conditioning.

Susie, Rick and Molly arrived shortly thereafter. We started to set up the booth and making sure that Rick's live shellfish were okay. They were doing great, so after unpacking them we put them inside the back of the refrigerated display case for safekeeping. Not too long after that Mark Montrose showed up at the booth. He was his usual brash self, and he was eager to get to business. The AIT had a lounge right next to our booth, and I reminded Mark that he needed to conduct his sales meeting in the lounge, not the ASA booth. Shortly thereafter, I headed up to a hall upstairs to give the trade presentation on Alaska seafood. Upon my return, there was Mark, right in our booth, with Molly, conducting a sales meeting with a customer. I reminded him again that he was not allowed to conduct sales in our booth and asked him to move next door. He said that it was stupid that he had to do it, but I reminded that I have no choice, and that I had to enforce the rules. Susie was having no problem working with parameters of the rules. When she needed a break for a sales meeting, she would let me know in advance, and off she would go to other area in the pavilion. Rick was busy serving his live oysters to people and talking about his farm. The first day blazed on by.

I took a break or two throughout the day, and I saw some familiar global brands – like Nestle and Pepsi. And there was all kind of crazy products, like a honeycomb-based tea for sale. The girl at their booth told me to try some and handed me a sample. She declared that it was "Chinese Viagra" and that it was "Very good for the man." She talked me into buying a box. I took it home and drank it a couple of times, but never really noticed anything special below the belt. During the show I was to find out that Taiwan had some of the most aggressive young ladies I had ever seen. A number of beautiful young ladies walked up to me and staring flirting and asking me if I would like to take them out. I would quickly produce my left hand and show my wedding ring to them; they would reply that they did not care. One young lady came up to me at the end of the day – she had a milkmaid outfit on – and she handed me her business card and told me to call her. I started to laugh, and I told her to come back when she was legal age (she looked very young and pretty, appearing to be about 16 years old); she got very angry with me and retorted back, "I am 23! I am old enough for you." Still, all I could do was laugh as she stomped off all angry and insulted. In all my travels I would never see women so aggressive again – with maybe the exception of Thailand – but most of those girls were prostitutes, while these Taiwanese girls were just young ladies, looking for some fun with an exotic foreigner.

After the show's second day, Rick and I decided to go out to dinner. He had found a live seafood restaurant he wanted to try. It turned out to be a cool concept. At the entrance was a row of shopping carts. And there was rows of live tanks of fish and shellfish. You would just push your cart along the line of tanks, and there would be an attendant that would help you grab the live product you wanted, and then wrap it in a plastic bag and place it in the cart. Once you had selected everything you want, then you would to get in line at a checkout – like one in a cafeteria – to pay for the product. After paying for your selection, you sit at a table and wait for them to butcher the product and cook it for you. It was a little expensive, but we had a great variety of products to try – and it was guaranteed fresh!

Unfortunately, Rick called me the next morning and told me he was sick as a dog – he must have eaten something bad. So, I headed to the show without him, arriving to find that one of the service technicians had lowered the temperature in the display case, which essentially froze and killed the last of Rick's live oysters. At the end of the day, I went to check on Billy and brought him some Imodium and Pepto-Bismal. The poor guy looked like death warmed over, and white as a ghost. It looked like a case of serious food poisoning.

The next day was the last day of show – the day where the average consumers are allowed in. When I walked into the entrance to the hall that morning, I could smell the distinct odor of bad fish. All I could think was, "Fuck, I hope that's not our booth!" I scurried through the hall and arrived to find that sure enough, it was our booth. One of the techs had managed to blow the circuit to our booth, so the power had been off the whole night. Those poor fish in the display case had been already sitting there on ice for over three days, and now all the ice had melted, and it had leaked out of the display and onto the carpet. The carpet was soaked across half of the entire booth. What a disaster! Minutes later, Susie, Molly, Rick, and Elsie arrived. They all looked at me in disbelief and started asking what we were going to do to fix it. It was less than an hour before the show was to open, and thousands of consumers were about to descend on the show – and they were about to 'smell' what Alaska had to offer – not really the image we were wanting to brand!

What were we going to do? Elsie was trying to put some paper towels on the floor, but that wasn't going to do shit to resolve the issue. I thought quickly – we need a steam cleaner! Luckily, one of the ladies from the AIT next door had one up in an office close by, and she ran to fetch it. Meanwhile, I instructed Molly and Susie to help me cut up a bag of lemons. There were like two dozen of them, as I had asked Elsie to buy a bunch for serving with Rick's oysters and adding some color to the display fish. We quickly cut all the lemons in halves and started squeezing them all over the carpet. It's amazing what lemons can do to neutralize odors. The girl from the AIT returned, and we began to steam clean the fish juice from the carpet. After that we squeezed a little more lemon juice on the carpet, and it was almost like nothing had ever happened. Meanwhile, Rick and Elsie had been putting new ice in the display; we had everything back in order right before the doors opened. A disaster had been averted!

We learned a lot at the show. There seemed to be a lot of interest in Alaska products, and we were hoping to get a lot of sales from our hard work. One buyer even talked about using canned salmon as a pizza ingredient. Tastes were different in Taiwan – they like to put corn on the pizza at the local Pizza Hut. After the ice adventure, Elsie had the idea to next year put the fish on green AstroTurf – she got the idea from the meat booth display across from us. But I tried to explain to her that it was not a good idea. It wouldn't look right have fish on green turf - and imagine what it would look like a day or two later with the fish slime dripping onto it; I could only imagine the mess that it would make.

The last night Rick and I took Elsie out for dinner. While every day during the trade show the rest of us were in formal business suits, Rick had been dressed in a short-sleeved shirt with Hawaiian prints, and a pair of khakis.

For dinner, for the last night, I was dressing down into some khakis and a polo. And here came Rick – totally dressed 'to the 9s' - sporting a white Panama jacket and suit! He continued to baffle me. Dressing like a street vendor during the show, but dressing like a boss during our casual dinner? Rick was definitely a person of his own devices. We hopped into a cab with Elsie and found a nice place for dinner. Over dinner, we discussed the issues about the existing political strife between the Mainland and Taiwan. Elsie held the opinion that there would never be a war, because almost everyone in Taiwan had relatives in both Mainland China, Taiwan, and the USA. She was probably right.

The next day, I headed home. When I got to the airport, United asked if I would be willing to take a different flight through Tokyo later, as they had overbooked the flight. I told them no problem and waited in the United lounge. Later they called me up to the desk and said they could keep me on the original flight and rewarded me by upgrading me to business class. It was a nice treat instead of flying in 'cattle car' class for 14 hours back to San Francisco. By the time I exchanged flights and got home to Seattle, I was totally jet lagged and exhausted. Usually, I couldn't sleep on the flight, so I had been up for a day and a half or so. It was the late morning, and I took a shower and crawled into bed to pass out. Just then the phone rang – it was Sherry. She was all excited – she and her real estate agent were at the house we were set up to buy. She wanted me to come over and see it.

So, I dragged me ass out of bed and headed on over. I was basically rummy and almost comatose. She asked me what I thought – I laid down on the plush white carpet and said, "Nice." Then I got up – before I fell asleep – and walked onto the back porch. As I stood there and looked past the rock embankment lining the back of the patio. All one could see was bamboo, trees, and overgrowth – standing over ten feet tall – at least. I thought, "How far back does this yard go?" One could not see past the growth more than a couple of feet – it was just too thick. So, I looked to the neighbor's yard and started walking up a narrow trail along the fence line on the right side. Up and up, it went, for at least 50 -60 feet —and all along the way, was total overgrowth. Obviously, no one had tended to the backyard for decades as in twenty to thirty years. We were definitely going to have some work to do after we bought the place.

Chapter 22

How to Wear a Yokata

Back at the office, we were finally approved to get cell phones for Ryan, Molly, and me. The program had gone all these years without cell phones, laptops, etc., and it was time to catch up with the rest of the world. I had been working hard to establish electronic workflows for the programs.

Near the end of the month, the annual federal budget allocation figures began to roll in – we were taking another hit – the federal budget was being reduced to just over $2 million (it has been almost $10 million a decade before). We were suffering the outfall of a marketing plan that had been constructed by an outside agency and the aftermath of losing the prior director, who had a good working relationship with the Seafood and Wood Products Division staff at EAS. Susie Denim, the Deputy Director, did not like Ryan at all, and she was picking our plan to pieces. When I tried to approach her on what was wrong, she started to pick every little detail apart – grammar, punctuation, premise, etc. It really was not so much about the validity of the plan as it was about the personality conflicts that had grown between the state and federal agencies. I could only promise myself, that if I were put into the position, that I would do everything I could to remedy the situation.

At the same time, Sherry and I were closing on the house. So we went to together to sign all the paperwork. And I thankfully had the $50,000 nest egg to drop on the down payment. I signed all the papers I could, and signed power of attorney over to Sherry in case she needed to cover anything while I was out of town. And then off I went to Tokyo for another long trade trip.

I arrived in Tokyo to sweltering heat. It averaged about 100 degrees Fahrenheit every day, with humidity hanging around 90%. It felt you could cut the air with a knife, it was so thick with moisture. And the special treat was to stay at the Nikko Nikko hotel, which was a resort hotel on the bank of Tokyo Bay in the Odaiba region. This was a special area of reclaimed land, and the area was quite upscale – appearing totally different from the rest of the city – almost as if someone had created a tropical vacation spot, nestled on the edge of Tokyo Bay. While the locale was a little ways from the heart of Tokyo, it was a perfect location for attending the Japan Seafood and Technology Expo, which was located at the Tokyo Big Site, just a couple of stops up the railway. And the best part was that you could see the famous Rainbow Bridge from the hotel. For those that have never seen it, it is decorated with vibrant lights that constantly change colors, lighting up the waterway so elegantly.

The day before the show started, I met with Kelsey McIntosh, the Executive Director of the US Fish Board (UFB), and Ariana Werner, who was the Executive Director of the (Maine Shellfish Council) (MSC). We had an early morning press conference at the EAS Tokyo headquarters, so we had to take the train across the Rainbow Bridge and make our way to the Akasaka district. It was then that we were to experience the infamous Tokyo early morning rush hour. We assembled in line to get onto the subway, and slowly moved liked packed cattle, down the stairs, and towards the cars. When we made our way to the loading platform, one could see men in white gloves. Their job was to push people into the subway cars, literally packing each car, as full as possible. It was quite the experience being packed in so tightly. The air was stifling, and I felt fortunate to be so tall as I was, to get some fresher air near the ceiling of the cars.

At the Expo we had a fairly prominent booth, one that we would share with the UFB and the MSB. Han had planned it out well; ASA was represented on one side of the large booth space, and UFB and MSB were represented on the other. During the second day of the Expo I remember conducting a trade and media education seminar. Kelsey sat in and watched, and at the end she came up to me and said, "You were born to do this job." Those few, but very powerful words, would bolster me throughout the years at ASA, as well as serve to haunt me later after my departure.

There was also a technical component of the Expo, so we had Bobby Olson fly over to participate at the technical forum. While Bobby and I were on the subway, traveling from the forum, we spotted some girls texting on a phone for the first time – two Japanese girls on a train, sitting across from each other, giggling. They could easily speak out loud to each other, but they didn't. Instead, they typed away to each other like mad, back and forth. All I could think while I watched them was, "How long before we see this at home?" It was a sign of things to come.

On the show's last day, we held a joint promotion with UFB and MSB – the 'American Seafood Reception'. And what a party that was - king crab and lobster in all kinds of flavors and formats. The guests just loved it. Alaska king crab and Maine lobster combined? Who wouldn't' feel like they had died and gone to heaven...?

It was Friday, and Bobby had a couple of beers in him. He was feeling good and wanted to go out on the town. So, we did. We took the train over to the other side of the bridge, and I took him all the way to Shinjuku, heading for my favorite watering hole that I had found during my first visit. It was taking a while, transferring between all the different subway lines, and the beer was starting to wear off for Bobby. Considering that he had just come from a cool climate in Alaska, he began to be overcome by the heat and humidity.

Heat stroke started to set in on him, and we had to stop in a restaurant and cool off in the air conditioning and have him drink a huge volume of cool water. After he started feeling better, we continued to Shinjuku, situated on the border of Kabuki-cho. We were almost to my favorite bar, when we were approached by a local man that started to proposition Bobby He said, "You want big American blonde? She has big tits." Bobby replied back, "Hell no, I just traveled thousands of miles to get away from such women. Are you kidding me?" I couldn't help but laugh out loud at the exchange. We had a drink or two, and then on our way back the subway system before it closed. This is when I learned about the subway shutting down. It was midnight; and that is when was all the regular subways stop for the night – they shut them down for maintenance for five hours. We had made it most of the way back to our hotel but were stuck on the other side of the river in the Asakusa district, which means we had to grab a taxi to jump the short distance across the bridge. While it was a very short ride to the hotel, we ended up paying like $70 just to get across the bridge. It was an expensive lesson to learn about the subways. After that, I always made sure to shut down my night activities in Tokyo before midnight – it was either that, or prepare for a very expensive taxi ride, or a long walk back to the hotel where I was staying.

Bobby was on a tight schedule and flew back to Alaska the next day. The rest of those of in the group – Kelsey, Ariana, Stanley, and myself – were slated for a cultural retreat at Mt Fuji. We took the train up into the mountains (all of us except Stanley – he was going to meet us later). As we transcended through beautiful green forests on the way up, Han explained to me that these forests were infamous; many people (mostly men) would go to these forests to commit suicide.

When we arrived at the station near the mountain, I spied a little girl lost at the station. She was terrified and was crying for her mom. I felt so bad for her that I went and found Han to comfort her until we could find her mother. Her mother was much relieved to find us carefully guarding her – and I was relieved as well; I remember being lost as a small child and could empathize with the fear she felt.

We then went to stay at a very traditional ryokan, which had a beautiful Japanese garden, accompanied with volcanically heated steam baths. This is when Han pulled a good trick on us. She explained that this was to be a cultural experience, and to really get the full experience, we should dress in the traditional yokata robes - with nothing on underneath. So here was Kelsey, Ariana, Han and I, meeting together in the guardian in our yokatas. The hotel had given us sandals, but mine were way too small for my feet. So here I was, shuffling along through the garden path, in these tiny sandals that did not fit, and taking very small steps so as not to have my yokata fly open and expose my genitals. One local man saw me shuffling along and came up to me with a big smile and said, "You are very beautiful in that yokata." All of us – including myself – broke out in laughter. Later we found that Han had worn her underwear underneath her yokata. When we gave her shit about it the next day, she smiled devilishly and said, "I only suggested that the tradition was to wear nothing underneath – I did not force you." This is when I realized how sly she could be sometimes.

After our time enjoying the hot spring baths, we met for a traditional dinner. Wilkes was supposed to be there, but he was running late, so we started the formal dinner without him. The men sat across the room from the women, facing each other. In typical Japanese tradition, the men were served first. The most enticing dish had to be the abalone. The servers brought us a live, shucked abalone in a steel cup. We had a little burner on each plate, which we then used to torture the poor little abalone as we seared it too death. I had just finished torturing mine to death, when suddenly Wilkes showed up, apologizing for being so late. He started mumbling to me about all this cultural crap, like he wasn't very interested in the experience – I guess he had done it plenty of times before, and it had lost its appeal to him.

After dinner we proceeded to the main lobby to watch a traditional drum performance. Stanley said he was not interested in watching, excused himself and proceeded to the room. The rest of us sat and enjoyed the show, which was quite impressive, considering that there were about a half dozen drummers, with an immense range of different sized drums. After the show Kelsey and Ariana excused themselves to their rooms. Han and I decided to take a walk in the garden and enjoy the night air. It was a lovely evening, with a full moon beaming down onto the mountain. She and I sat in the garden and talked until midnight – about the various people, the program, and some of the challenges that we faced in the market. Upon my return to my room I found Wilkes, passed out on the tatami mat with a couple of empty miniature scotch bottles from the mini-bar, and the TV blaring away. I went outside onto the balcony and took one last look at the night. Mt. Fuji looked quite majestic, being so close, and there were lantern lights strung all up along the pathway up the mountain – it was a site I would never forget. I was tired and I went to sleep, as best I could; for those that have never slept on a tatami mat, there is little between you and the hardwood floor. It was not exactly the most restful experience of my life. I woke the next morning to find that Wilkes was gone. He had cleaned out all the scotch in the mini-bar, and then got up in the crack of dawn to leave – and leave me with the mini-bar bill. What a guy.

We returned to Tokyo the next day, taking a very long bus ride all the way back into the city. Kelsey and Ariana left the next day, leaving me alone to my own devices. Han wanted me to stay in Tokyo and make a few more trade visits and help her in negotiating some promotions – which I gladly did.

During the last few nights, I realized I had been gone almost two weeks. At night I walked the boardwalk of Odaiba alone. I would sit on the rocks in front of the bay and take in the beauty of the Rainbow Bridge, and feeling so alone, wishing I could share the view with Sherry.

Chapter 23

Lessons Learned

When I returned, I came home to a new home, as Sherry had performed all the moving while I was gone. I was trying to figure out where all my belongings were. It was the end of July, and we began to prepare for our first strategic planning session with the export team. All of the main contractors – at that time we called them 'export promotion representatives' would come to town for an industry presentation, visits with industry members, as well as participate in a strategic planning session. I was determined to make the industry presentation a better experience that what I had seen the previous summer. So, I pushed for PowerPoint presentations for all! I took total control of the project, and I ran them all on a schedule, laying down a strict timeline, allowing each presenter a strict 15-minute limit. I even sat in the front row, with 3 x 5 index cards, with one marked 5 – for five minutes, then 2 for two minutes, 1 for one minute, and then 0 for 'time is up'. We prepared hard for the event– we polished up the presentations and practiced for timing. And when they performed before the industry they did well. I found I only had to display an index care on a minimal basis to keep the schedule on track. The only one that really started to run over was Elsie – she rambled off on side subject during her time, and when I held up the zero card she exclaimed, "My boss says I have to stop now." And even though she was a couple slides from being done, she stopped and promptly walked off the stage. I was proud of all of them. They had come a longways from the disoriented mishmash of presentations I had witnessed the summer before and we were really starting to look more like a cohesive set of professionals.

We were slated to conduct an export program educational seminar in Anchorage immediately after the planning session. I went home to grab my bags to find Sherry crying on the bed. I asked her what was wrong, and she admitted that she was so lonely without me. While I was enjoying my new job immensely, I had to stop right then and begin to realize what type of toll it was starting to have on our relationship. I told her I would cancel the trip and stay home with her, but she insisted that I go. These are the types of decisions that I regret to this day. If I had to do all over again, I probably would have stayed. But she was kind of right – I had a job to do. So off to the airport I went.

Betty and Ryan had decided that we should use the export team locally to do some outreach and create some good PR with the banking and business sector in Anchorage. So, we altered the presentations a little for the audience, and then presented to a packed room at the Hilton in Anchorage. Ryan never liked the limelight, and at the last minute he asked me to be the master of ceremonies, and provide all the introductions, which I did gladly with full vigor. I opened the floor, gave the welcoming statement, and introduced all the presenters making sure that Ryan was introduced to give a quick intro as well. Things were running smoothly; it was near the end of the event, and then Ryan whispered in my ear that he wanted me to answer all the questions from the audience. While I had no problem fielding the questions, I had to draw the line and say "no." No doubt that I understood the program better by then, but it would not look right to have the marketing specialist answering all the questions with the director just standing there. Ryan stumbled through the questions, doing the best he could, but it was embarrassing to see his lack of knowledge so openly revealed during a public forum. Elise was really getting disgusted with him – and the rest of the reps were not too impressed either.

The WCFEA event in China was becoming a problem. The executive director of the organization, who was bit of a shady character, emailed me the entire list of seafood products they needed for the events. It was unbelievable what they wanted – it was literally about $8,000 in product that they wanted donated. This list would eat up our entire budget for product purchases that was earmarked for all our chef seminars activities in that market. We could only use our state contributing funds to buy food products, as MEP funds could not be used for such purposes. I had to take the blame for accepting such an open-ended agreement – I had tried to get WCFEA to define their exact needs, but they didn't until the last minute – which made poor Bobby run around Shanghai, trying to round up all the product at a premium. But at least I learned my lesson, and made sure that, in the future, all needs were stipulated clearly by a potential promotional partner before we entered into an agreement.

August finally arrived, and it was thankfully one of the 'lull' periods in the schedule. All of Europe was on vacation, and things were quiet in Asia. Sherry had been busy with her job and had still had a lot of travel back and forth to Salt Lake City and other West Coast destinations. We were finding that, even as newlyweds, we were not spending much time together, instead passing each other in the night, with our two busy travel schedules. We would spend time when we could, but it could be tough. And in early August, I found myself at home alone in the middle of the week.

Chapter 24

Walking Through Fire

It was August, and I decided that I was going to pay a visit to my stepfather in Shelton. He had been my mother's second husband, and he played a big fatherhood role during the years that I was 5 to 9 years old – very formidable years indeed. I left work early, hopped in my 1970 Ford Mustang, and headed to his cozy little house that sat on an old farmer's plot right on the edge of Goose Lake. We had dinner and caught up on what was going on. He had been busy working on a new graphical interface system for the State of Washington, one that was going to set a new standard for data overlay on geographical maps – in fact, what he envisioned and promoted is now one of the industry standards today that we take for granted.

That night we had a few laughs, and then we sat back and enjoyed a little TV. We watched 'Survivor', which was in its inaugural season, as reality TV was becoming the new hot trend. The next thing we knew, it was 10 pm, and it was time for me to head home. We walked out onto his porch, and his dog and mine were running around, chasing each other in the dark. Then Bingo ran off around the corner of the barn for a moment. Suddenly, she came bolting back around the corner, making a straight line for us; behind her was a deer running at full gait – and gaining fast. Bingo stopped right at our feet and was cowering down, expecting the worst as the deer raised up on its rear feet with its front hooves poised to stomp my poor dog into the ground. Thankfully, Warrens's dog, a short orange ChowChow. Named Fuzzer, jumped out in front of deer, and growled loudly. It was just enough to startle the deer that it stopped its attack and ran off. Warren and I looked at each other in disbelief – neither of us had seen a deer chase a dog like that. Warren figured that the doe must have had a fawn with her and felt threatened by Bingo's presence. Thank God Fuzzer had been there, or the deer more than likely would have killed Bingo. It was a strange occurrence, and it turned out to be a strange omen for the night.

After we got over the shock of what had just happened, we said goodnight, and Bingo and I got into the car and headed home. I stopped at a gas station and topped off my gas tank right before I got on the freeway. The old Mustang –which I had for 15 years- had a small block 302 in it, but it could get thirsty on the way home if my right foot felt too heavy. It was a hot and dry summer night, and there wasn't much traffic on the road. As we traveled up the highway, we jumped off I-5 to take the side route on highway 512 to get home. After we turned on to the highway, a mile or so up the road there were big, huge lights cascading over the freeway as we entered a construction zone. I slowed down while passing the workers and then the road curved to the left as we exited the zone. I came around to a long straight stretch and slowed down as I could see that both lanes had come to a standstill.

This was odd, as we had already passed the construction zone. I was in the left lane, staring at the rows of taillights and waiting for the traffic to start moving. Suddenly, I heard tires screeching behind me and glanced up to see headlights coming up fast behind me. And then I felt a sudden and massive impact, accompanied by an immediate explosion – all in an instant. Suddenly all I could see was the glow of flames all around me while I felt my car hurtling down the road while I was hanging onto the steering wheel and desperately pressing on the brake to slow the car as I was pushed towards what was in front of me – fortunately, I had left a considerable distance between myself and the next car in front of me. The feeling was almost indescribable – I felt as if all of sudden I was riding a flaming chariot on the road to hell.

Then in an instance, the car stopped, resting at an angle against the cement median to the left of the lanes, with the driver's door, thankfully, sprung open. There were flames, spouting out from under the door well to the left, and behind me, the flames were so close that they were licking at my head. My first instinct was to jump forward to get out of the car. The seat belts – that era of Mustang's had a separate lap belt and shoulder belt, which I thankfully had put both on – were firmly in place, and I bounced back in my seat against them. Instantly I released them and peered to my right to see poor Bingo sitting on the front passenger seat, looking at me with a questionable look – as if she was saying, "What do we do now, Dad?" I grabbed her and jumped through the flames that were waiting at the edge of the door opening.

After escaping my burning vehicle my next thought turned instantly to the condition of the driver of the car that had hit me. I ran back the 250 to 300 feet to find the other car sitting in the middle of the left lane. It was a Honda Accord, and the front end was smashed in, with black blast marks from the explosion wrapping around the front fenders. I looked inside the car for the driver, but the vehicle was empty. Then I looked around and spotted someone laying on the ground in the emergency pull out lane to the right side of the road. I ran over and found a young man laying on the ground, with a blank stare on his face as he peered up at the stars. I asked him if he was okay. He said, "I think so." I asked him what happened. He said, "I'm not sure, I wasn't paying attention." He was obviously in shock and looked totally out of it. I turned and looked at my car from the distance, the flames were continuing to engulf it, but you could hear the motor still running. It was a horrific sight as the flames lit up the night sky in an eerie glow.

The initial shock was wearing off and was quickly turning into anger. I felt like kicking him in the ribs as he lay there, but I tried to control myself. I looked down on the driver and said to him, "Take a good look at that burning wreck – you just stole 15 years of my life and memories. It was the best car I ever had – you remember that." Just then one of the workers from the road construction crew came running up. He was in a panic, and he started screaming, "Is there anyone in the car – we have to save them!" I told him right away that I was the only occupant, and it was okay. I turned and again and saw that the entire passenger compartment was totally consumed in flames. Thank God I had gotten out myself. If I had been disabled, trapped, or unconscious, there would have been no saving me – help would have come too late.

Then time began to speed up. A state trooper arrived, then another, and right behind them an ambulance. As one paramedic jumped out and attended to the other driver on the ground, one escorted me to the ambulance for observation. I had been clutching Bingo tight the entire time, and once inside the ambulance, I finally relaxed my grip and carefully set her on the floor. Being summer, I had been in a short sleeve shirt, shorts, and sandals. In the light I could clearly see that all the hair on the left side of my body had been singed off and big chunks of my hair on my head were singed as well. Black residue coated most of my face and limbs. The medic swabbed me down with saline and started telling me how lucky I was. I asked if I could borrow his cell phone to call someone to get me – my phone and everything else was in the car and had been totally destroyed; he handed it to me and started to look over Bingo to see if she had any serious injuries. I immediately called Warren and told him I had been in an accident, my car was totaled, and that I needed a ride. I told him where I was, and he said he was on his way.

To help me with Bingo, the medic was kind enough to give me one of his securing straps to make a temporary leash. Then he released me to talk to the police. I stepped out of the ambulance and noticed that the fire department had arrived, and they were starting to spray water on what was left of my car. The flames were still burning in the darkness of the night, and traffic was almost on as standstill in the opposing lanes, as the cars were slowing to look at what was happening. It was truly a horrific sight, with balls of flames consuming my old Mustang, appearing like a terrifying beacon, lighting up the black of the night. I will never forget the looks of horror and dismay on people's faces in their vehicles as they passed by.

One of the troopers pulled me back to reality, asking me to come with him and sit in his vehicle to take a statement. He asked my version of what happened, and I told my story, describing how the other car had hit me full on, going a speed of about 60-70 miles an hour, and I was lucky that I had been wearing my seatbelts. He told me how lucky I was and told me the gory story about a victim that had burned in their car just a few months earlier. The trooper then I asked me if the driver had been drinking. They asked me if I smelled any alcohol on him. I snapped back, "Isn't that your job?" They said they were transporting the other driver to the hospital for observation – I guess he was traumatized. I asked them if they were going to test him for alcohol. He replied that they had no probable cause. I was astounded by his reply. I shot back, "What do you call this wreck outside, that's not probable cause?" He had no reply.

The interview was over, and it was time to retrieve whatever was left in the car that might have value. I had just purchased a brand new Apple laptop for work; it was in my briefcase in the car, and I knew that I better grab whatever was left if it so that I could put in a claim to my work. A wrecker had come and had pulled what was left of my car over to the emergency lane on the right side of the road, and traffic was starting to move again. The trooper escorted me to the wrecker and my car. I reached inside and found my burned and soaked briefcase, as well as my collection of music CDs – all 200 or so of them. It was too much me to carry all of this with my traumatized dog in tow, so I asked the wrecker driver if he had a bag to put it in. He said he did not, but he suggested I ask the trooper if he had one. As

I walked around the back of my car to ask the trooper for one, I found that there was no one there. Just then the wrecker pulled away with my car, and to my surprise and my dismay I looked around to realize that there was no one left – and I mean NO ONE – except Bingo and me.

This was too surreal. I had just gone through this horrific accident, narrowly escaped with my life, and here I was, standing there on the side of the road in the darkness, with traffic rushing by. It was as if nothing had ever happened, and I was dreaming all of this had just happened. But I knew it was real – I just couldn't believe that I had been left standing there alone in the pitch black. The next thought that sprung into my mind was, "How is Warren going to find me?", as he has nothing to look for as he sped up and down the freeway in the black of night.

So, I started walking up the highway, as the next exit was at the end of the straight stretch, just a quarter mile or so away. As I walked along, the road construction crew that had been around the corner slowly came upon me. One of the supervisors approached in his truck and he asked me what happened. I explained my circumstances, and shook his head in disgust, and said, "Get in, I'll give you a ride." As we approached the exit, there was a trooper that had another car pulled over for a traffic stop. I hopped out of the truck and saw that the trooper was indeed the same one that had interviewed me and left me behind. My nerves were shot by then. I started yelling at him, "You left me back there – why did you leave me on the side of the road?" He replied that they had cleared the wreck, and they thought they were done. Just then Warren pulled up in his car. I was disgusted. I thanked the road crew supervisor and said to Warren, "Let's get out of here." We got in the car and sped off. I started explaining to him what happened. He had been driving up and down the freeway looking for the scene of an accident – but it was already gone. Thankfully, he had pulled up to the police lights to ask what had happened to me. I shared all that happened while he drove me back home. We went in my house, and he asked me if I was going to be okay. I told him I would be, thanked him, and then he headed home. I showered

Bingo and I, and then crawled into bed to get some sleep.

The next morning, I woke to the phone ringing. It was Sherry, and she was asking me where I had been, as she had been calling the house, and calling my cell phone – which of course wasn't answering anymore. I told her that I had been visiting Warren last night. She launched into me, complaining that I had time to spend with him, but none for her – as I was always working long hours, and spending little time with her. I quickly told her to stop, before she was going to say something she was going to regret. Silence on the other line – then I began to tell her that my car was totaled, that it exploded and burned into flames, but Bingo and I were still alive and okay. She immediately shifted her tone. She said, "Oh my God! Have you been to the hospital yet?" She was going to call up her mom to help. She hung up and called me right back to tell me that her mother was coming down to pick me and help me to go to the doctor and take Bingo to the vet to get checked out.

I went to a clinic that morning and the nurse practitioner that looked at me told me that I was fortunate that I had not seen the other driver coming, as I would have braced for the impact, which in turn would have broken my arms as I held on to the steering wheel. The element of surprise had saved me, as my muscles were relaxed when the impact took place. She too x-rays to make sure I didn't have any fractures. She noted that all my back muscles were torn – from my neck all the way down my back. They had acted as a shield to my soft tissues and had protected my spine and bones. It was a good thing that I was young, and in such good shape – most would have not fared so well. In fact it was truly a miracle that I had been able to walk away with such limited injuries. I asked her why I didn't feel any pain if my back muscles were all torn. She explained that due to the massive shock and trauma of the event that my body had released massive amounts of adrenaline and endorphins, and that I would not feel the pain from my injuries for another day or two. She was worried about possible Post Traumatic Stress Disorder from the event and referred to me a psychologist.

I saw him twice but stopped after that.

Poor Bingo was next; Sherry's mother and I took Bingo to the vet. They did full x-rays on her as well but could not find any major injuries. She had lucked out as well. Then we drove down the impound lot to see what was left of my car and take picture for the insurance claim. I jumped out to take pictures of what had once been my beloved Mustang. Sherry's mom was dumbfounded when she visualized the wreckage. After viewing the carnage, she fully comprehended what I had just endured – and could not believe that I survived. All she could say when we got back in the car to leave was, "I can't believe it; I don't know what to say." Words today cannot begin to explain what had taken place. The images of what transpired are burned into my memory forever, as they are with those closest to me.

Next was a call to the other driver's insurance company. Once I told them that my car was totaled and that it was a 1970 Ford Mustang, the line went silent. They put me on hold for what seemed like forever, and then asked if I had an appraisal for the car. I could write an entire chapter about what I endured with them. But it is not worth it. In short, I received 'crack street' prices for my cherished car, and everything that was in it. And I received another $7,000 for my pain and suffering after six months of extensive physical rehabilitation. I hired a great lawyer, and I heeded his words of wisdom: "You walked away, you have had a full physical recovery – you have suffered enough – take the money and walk away." And I did.

If there had ever been a single physical element that had existed in my life that people had identified with me, it had been that Mustang. It was the essence of me; I had never been closer to any 'inanimate' object in my life. For 15 years I had labored over that car, caring for it, maintaining it, improving it. There had been so many adventures, so many road trips, so many great memories. I had driven it all the way south to the border of Mexico; I had taken it up the Alaska Canada Highway, all the way to Kodiak and back. It had been a faithful servant, a true friend, and a virtual extension of me. People had said that I would be buried in it someday – and I almost was. Its final gift to me was to sacrifice itself to save Bingo and I. It was truly a miracle that I walked away. After my deeply religious brother-in-law heard the story, and saw the pictures of the wreckage, he brought me a toy Hot Wheels model of a 70 Mustang, and he imparted upon me some of the sagest words that resonate with me to this day, "God obviously has something else left for you to do." It was unexplainable how I could survive this terrible tragedy so unscathed. Indeed, God still had plans for me.

Chapter 25

A Misconstrued Affair

few days after the incident, I got back to work and the WCFEA activity was in full swing. I was getting reports back from China about the event. It was going well, and our boys in China were doing their best to support the activities, but they were somber in the realization that the entire product sample budget had been consumed. They were going to need to cancel our seminars that had been planned – we couldn't pull it off without product. I explained to EAS our reasoning, and we shifted the remaining MEP funds to other activities.

From this experience, I deemed the term: 'ASA the Miracle Caterer'. So many groups and interests would come to us and ask us for product for their event, their luncheon, etc. And from that point I would always jokingly respond, "We are not ASA the Miracle Caterer, we are not here just to cater your events – what are both our organizations going to plan on accomplishing with this potential activity?" I would always approach negotiations from this perspective. It was a great way to qualify potential partners, and to make sure our interests were properly served with our limited resources.

At the end of the month, I received more wonderful news – it was the infinite wisdom of all the other program directors that the export program would create the first program website. The board had requested that an updated website be created, so the other directors selected me to create the pages, and I found myself shouldered with the responsibility. The ASA website looked like shit; it had looked totally institutional since its inception. The administrative office had improved the homepage and put some images on it, but it was definitely in dire need for some content. Molly and I went to work on the new site with the webmaster that ASA had contracted in Juneau. It was pretty plain, but it was a start. Basically, we had a couple pages for each specific country/region program, with an explanation about what was special about the market, as well, as the type of marketing activities occurring in each market −with a representative image included. Another component that we added was an exporter resource page that started out with a dozen or so links to every site imaginable that could help seafood exporters, or those interested in starting to export; this would include anything from export databases to certification programs. This section would turn out to be the most useful addition to the website for some time; the other benefit of creating this directory is that when we had inquiries from people, we could just point them to the directory, instead of having to provide a link to each requested site over and over again. While our program finished our portion of the website on schedule for the Fall board meeting, the other domestic programs never followed up with content for their programs. In fact, it would be literally five years before the domestic programs would have their own pages on the website.

September fell upon us quickly. And it was time to head back to Japan again for the first Alaska Lunch Party in Sapporo. This would be our second experiment of this concept, and it would be a good test to see if the success of the event in Sendai was just a fluke. The setup for this promotion was very similar. Retail partners conducted an Alaska promotion in their stores, and winners were selected for a seat at the seminar and lunch party. I found the people of Sapporo a little more reserved than those in Sendai. Jimmy Buffett's words ring true: "Changes in latitudes, changes in attitudes." But they were extremely polite people to say the least. Most of the same team was present. Lee, her staff, our interpreter, Jim Tanaka, and even the MC was the same. Our MC was a beautiful young woman named Aiko Tanaka. She was a TV news reporter and had also performed in an Alaska seafood promo video that we had recently produced. When I had first met her in Sendai, I could help but notice her beauty. She had inquired about me when we first met, but Han had told her I was freshly married, so she kept her distance. I couldn't help but be entranced by her beauty, but reminded myself of my vows, and kept a safe distance as well. And here we were in Sapporo, together again. Han being the instigator she could be, she sat me next to her at the lunch table. While I remembered being a newlywed, I could not help but flirt with her during lunch; it's just in my nature.

Still, we kept it professional. The event went off without a hitch. The trade and consumers seemed to really like the promotion. And this time I had converted everything over to PowerPoint, so the presentation looked more professional and flowed a little better. It was a late morning affair, so we sat down in the lobby to have a cup of coffee before some of the team was to depart. The jet lag was kicking in a little bit, and I wound up grabbing the salt dispenser and dumping it in my coffee, thinking it was sugar. I took a big swig of the coffee and then a got a nice big taste of salt. Everyone noticed the contorted look on my face as I choked on the dark brine. When I told them what I had done, they all broke out in great laughter – and I couldn't help but laugh along with them.

From there we walked Aiko and one of the producers of the event back to the subway station for their return to Tokyo. As we said our goodbyes, Aiko reached out and gave me a big hug. My family had always done a lot of hugging, so I didn't think anything of it and gave her a big hug back. We waved goodbye and I thought no more of it. Han, Jim, and I finished our visit with some trade meetings and a trade dinner, then headed back to Tokyo the next day. I arrived back home and a week or two went by. Then Han sent an email to Ryan and I, stating that rumors had emerged about the event in Sapporo. According to Han, a few of the women that had been participants at the seminar and party had been in the subway station, and had saw seen Aiko hugging me goodbye. They had then contacted members of trade and made a big deal about it after – claiming we had hugged as lovers do. I was dumbfounded. And then Ryan called me in his office and made a stink about the whole affair and started to become a little threatening – like he had something on me. I was even more dumbfounded. Since when was hugging somebody in public such a big deal? I guess people see what they want to see. It also taught me that those in Sapporo possibly have a little more reserved standard than I was used to. Either that, or they were bored, and looking for something to gossip about. Regardless, Han discontinued using Aiko for ASA related business, and I never saw her again.

Chapter 26

A Stricken Leader

In early October, Molly and Ryan were headed to Vigo, Spain for the Conxemar show. This was a new seafood trade show that was going to hopefully open up a few doors for the industry in the Southern Europe market. Roger and Molly did a great job of organizing a mini-Alaska pavilion, selling spaces to industry companies that wanted to exhibit. During this show we had our first real clash with Clint Houston. Clint was competing directly for booth space with us and was offering Seattle area industry members space at cheaper prices, and more flexibility. We were limited to promoting only Alaska products, while Clint had no such restrictions with his booths (even though he officially worked for the State of Washington). Montrose decided to purchase a booth from Bill, as did Bob Falrik of Wintersea and Hans Heinz of Pointer. Molly was understandably distressed that these companies had chosen to secure booth space from Clint, but I encouraged her to shine it on, and reminded her that the companies that chose Clint instead of us worked with a wide scope of product beyond Alaska. I had to recognize that it was a challenge to our position, but one must choose their battles wisely. Upon her return from the show, Molly told me about a little joke that almost went sideways. Clint and Mark decided to play a trick on her and put a fake card addressed to Ryan in her key box at the hotel. They had written out the card with a fake woman's name, and glowing comments to Ryan about the wonderful time he had shown her at dinner the night before. She of course, opened the card, read the contents, and then took the bait, hook, line, and sinker. She was totally disgusted, thinking Ryan was cheating on his wife. She was almost ready to email Betty and tell her what had happened, and thankfully she confided to Mark, who let her in on the joke. And just in time! Clint caught wind of it and explained the joke to Molly before it boiled over. Now that could have been a real political mess in the making. And all the time, Ryan was totally oblivious to what had happened.

During the summer we had started planning with the Governor's staff for a trade mission to Asia. I had been preparing to support the mission, and originally, I was slated to attend the mission with Ryan. But by early October I realized that there was way too much on the agenda, and that it would probably be best for me to stay behind and continue to keep things running smoothly from behind the scenes – not mention that I was still was still actively in physical therapy, recovering from the injuries suffered from my car accident. It was a good call; right after they left for the show, we got the news from Betty that she was sick. She had cancer and was going to need to take a leave of absence for medical treatment. Bantu would be the acting director during her absence. It threw us all for a loop, but we were committed to carrying on in her behalf while she was dealing with treatment. Governor Ryan's mission to Asia was a big one. He and his entourage were going to visit Japan, China and Hong Kong. For Tokyo, we organized a retail promotion. For China we had him attend the China Fish Expo in Dalian. And last, we set up a food service promotion and trade dinner in Hong Kong. It was a huge task to coordinate, so I was really glad that I stayed in the office to make it come off without a hitch. And from what I heard back from the field, the Governor and his staff were very pleased with our efforts.

During the mission, it appeared that Ryan was up to his old tricks. While in China, he requested permission to return to Japan on the way back from Asia. As the basis for the approval, he said that Han requested he return to Tokyo to help negotiate some important promotions. He was granted approval and stopped in Tokyo on the way back. Knowing Ryan and his lack of enthusiasm or understanding about marketing and promotions, I found his return to Japan very suspect. So, I went to Han to get the real story. Ryan said in his original travel approval request that the reason for going back to Japan was to finish critical negotiations for a promotion with a key retailer. Han informed me that there was no meeting with any retailer, only meetings with his old friend Nomura-san at Juyojyo. He had gone back to Japan just to have dinner with his buddy! I tucked this nugget of information away and saved it for a different day. Han and Bobby (along with the rest of us) were starting to get fed up with Ryan. He made the reps write his trip reports for him, and he was continually dumping more work on the rest of us that he should be doing himself. And to top it off, he was continually becoming more hostile to me.

The year was winding down, and we went back again to Baltimore for the yearly UFEA conference with EAS. Jeff Prince joined us for the sessions again. He, Molly, and I conferred about the growing issues with Ryan, and the three of us began to monitor him closely to see what he was actually doing during the event. We found him constantly sneaking out of important events, while the rest of us were dutifully taking notes and participating in important discussions about program changes, compliance issues, etc. Ryan was not engaged at all, and was just loitering outside of the sessions, and bullshitting away with anyone that would talk to him. We reported to Bantu, who was attending the sessions in Betty's absence, but he was gone for most of the sessions; we assumed he was at meetings with other Alaska related officials, but I'm still not sure quite where he went for the duration.

During our individual meetings with our federal administrators, they started advocating for our entry into South Korea. Export figures to South Korea were showing a high level of surimi and pollock roe. And while there was some surimi making its way into the market for consumption, the bulk of the pollock roe was not really entering the market for consumption. It was going into bonded cold storage warehouses for grading, with the lion's share winding up in Japan for consumption. But it was hard to sell these facts to some of the EAS officials. I would not be surprised if South Korea was on someone's agenda for increasing overall trade – while else would they be trying to push us to go into a market that had limited demand, and little industry interest? ASA had a program in Korea a decade earlier, but it was unsuccessful and short-lived.

Over the winter, Molly and I started working with industry to re-tool the Brussels show. The company exhibitors all wanted corner booths, and they didn't like how things were set up. So, we came up with novel idea that we move the ASA booth to the center of the Alaska pavilion, instead of on the end. This would technically provide industry partners with eight corners instead of just two. This would also increase the size of the business lounge and provide more room for tables within the ASA booth. I also started conceptualizing the idea of serving samples of Alaska seafood, as well as complimentary Alaska beer and coffee. But since I was only the Asia specialist, I had no say so over the concept. Molly was busy reconfiguring the booth space, so I kept my ideas for myself for the time being.

Besides, I had plenty to do in Asia. Elsie was starting to drive me crazy. It was revealed that she had used the entire Taiwanese trade public relations budget to print out and distribute consumer newsletters, which was totally outside of the scope for approved usage outlined in our marketing plan. And she had this crazy idea to promote frozen sockeye salmon at a medical trade show. While I could see the potential for what she was trying to accomplish, it was well outside the parameters of our approved activity schedule. I had these visions of Elsie trying to educate doctor's that they should prescribe fish to remedy their health issues, "Tell your patients to take two sockeye and call me in a week." It wasn't going to fly, and I kept having to tell her no. I made sure that I informed Ryan of the situation, but he was pretty much leaving me to my own devices to handle the situation. So I did everything I could to get Elsie back on track.

The holiday season arrived, and in early January, I found myself back in Sendai, Japan to conduct another Alaska Seminar and Lunch Party. The usual cast of characters were there with me, except for dear sweet Aiko. This year the event was bigger and more sophisticated than the first event – and there were also more wholesalers from Tokyo than the previous year. This was a good sign, as it appeared now that the word was getting out about the effectiveness of such an activity, and now the major players were wanting to be a part of the action. It was another great event, and we had more engagement than previous years.

After we conducted this event Han and I traveled next door to Shiogama, which is a seaside town on the coastline. We met with the mayor, as well as several industry members to discuss potential promotional activities for the future. Shiogama was an important city and region from Alaska's perspective, as the region imported about 50,000 metric tons of Alaska whitefish products annually. We toured the city's Marine Gate facility, which was being proposed for an Alaska seafood fair promotion.

I returned home and began started working with Molly to prepare the new CMS application. She was very frustrated with Elise's European draft plan. Elise's strength was not writing, and considering that English was not her native language, her reporting could be hard to follow. I affectionately named her writing language as 'Ellanese' and tried to patiently decipher the meaning of her words.

I was getting a lot of practice in deciphering secondhand English while working with the Japan and Chinese draft plans. I never complained, as I was far from fluent in any other language besides English. I just did my best to translate intended meanings into formats that would be more readable by our American stakeholders. As usual, Ryan was not much help; in fact, it was his standard pattern to not be in the office most of the time. He would always call Molly and I throughout the day, while we were working fervently to try and keep on schedule with the application, while continuing to take care of day-to-day needs for the program. We had a lot of work to do with the plan, especially since an external contractor had made several formatting changes in the previous year's version. This fact, combined with several criticisms and requests by the EAS was proving to require a lot of editing and reformulations of constraints, opportunities, and activities. But Molly and I kept driving forward, in an effort to keep on track.

Chapter 27

Earthquakes and Upheavals

By February, Ryan was out of the office more than he was in. He would often call to check see if anyone had called for him. He always meeting with somebody. I wouldn't be surprised if he was free-lancing as a consultant during this time. Either that, or he was out drinking, as it seemed like he was always going to someone's funeral. And when he was in the office, he was reading the newspaper half the time. He even had a temp come in – on ASA's dime – and have them sort through all his canned salmon label collection. It was fucking unbelievable. Betty was finally coming back to work, after recovering from her cancer surgery and treatment. She was lucky to be alive after finding a tumor the size of a grapefruit inside of her. I wanted to share with her what Ryan had been up to, but I resisted.

Later during the month, Sherry had some associates from her company that were visiting from Boston, as there was a big tech trade show at which they were exhibiting. It was their first time in Seattle, so we all went out to dinner at Elliott's, which is one of my favorite seafood restaurants, located on the waterfront in downtown Seattle. During dinner the visitors were asking all kinds of questions about the Northwest, and the culture. Then one of them asked, "Do you get a lot of earthquakes out here?" I remember answering that we get one every now and then, but that it had been a while since we had a big one. After dinner we hit the bars in the Pioneer Square district, as it was Fat Tuesday and Mardi Gras celebrations were in full swing. We were having a blast, drinking, and dancing away at the bar; the atmosphere strangely felt more festive than usual. I would look outside the bar every now and then, and I noticed that the street was steadily starting to fill up with more people, which was out of the ordinary for Seattle. After an hour or two, we stepped outside to see what was happening. The streets were packed with people. I could feel a strange energy in the air — it was an exhilarating feeling, but at the same time dangerous. Sherry's intuitions were kicking in as well. She felt the danger in the crowd and suggested that we leave immediately. I at first resisted, my natural curiosity to see what going to take place. I said, "Let's stay and see what happens." She told me I was crazy and again insisted to everyone that we clear out. So, we did. Our car was parked under the viaduct, so we started walking towards the water. As we came upon the viaduct, we spotted dozens of police, in full riot gear, hiding around the corner. Sherry was so right. It is a good thing we got the hell out of there when we did. We got home and turned on the TV, and sure enough, there it was all over the news - that a riot had broken out and all hell was breaking loose. And here we had been standing in the middle of it just a half hour before. We were fortunate to leave when we did, thanks mainly to Sherry's urging.

The next day I was at the office, and everyone came in talking about the riots; I shared with them my first-hand account of the events that had led up to it. Jeff Prince happened to be in the office, paying a visit to go over the budget and financial issues with us. I remember standing in the doorway, papers in my hand, and saying something to him. Suddenly, the building began to shake. But what scared me more than anything was the duration. Most earthquakes I have been in before were finished within a half-minute or so. This one kept on going. My first intuition was to duck and cover (like they train people to do), but then something told me to run. I bolted out the door of the office, and down the stairs, and out of the building. There were huge glass panes above the entrance, and I watched the panes carefully as I ran out the door. Two women were standing right outside the entrance, smoking cigarettes like nothing was happening. I ran past them and said, "You might want to get out from underneath all that glass before it cuts your head off." They quickly followed me as I ran to the middle of the courtyard, trying to make a safe distance from the buildings. I still wonder to this day how they could just stand there during the earthquake and not think to get away to a safe area. I stood there and watched, as the entire building was shaking back and forth – I really expected it to start collapsing from all the stress. The earthquake lasted for almost a minute – it seemed like forever. After it stopped, I went back up to the office to check on everyone. They were a little rattled, but everyone was okay. They asked me why I ran out, as it totally against what we have been taught. I quickly replied, "I wanted to live." And then I described what the building had looked like, shaking so violently. As I described what I saw, the office grew quiet, and most of them looked a little ashen. To this day, I don't regret my choice. It was the largest earthquake in Seattle in almost 40 years. It was a 6.8 – a big one. I truly believe that if the earthquake had gone on another 15-20 seconds, the building would have started to collapse.

The next thing that leapt into my mind was, "Where the hell is my wife, and is she okay?" I knew she was probably at the tech show at the event center downtown, and I could not help but wonder if she was still alive. I tried calling her cell phone but there was no answer. All the circuits were jammed with people trying to call each other. All I could do was wait to hear from her. A little while later she called and let me know she was okay. She said that most people had run out of the show and left their computer bags, purses, and everything behind. She said it had been totally crazy, but that she was okay. It was a Mardi Gras week we would never forget.

The next thing you know it was March, the export data I needed for the application was released, and I was busy crunching it for the application. With a huge workload in front of us, Molly and I were getting stressed to the max. Meanwhile things were finally beginning to unfold for Ryan. We had ensnared Ryan in his own trap. Bantu had informed Barb about Ryan's travel discrepancies that had taken place at the tail end of the Governor's mission in the Fall. Betty called me and asked me to explain the situation at greater length. I explained the circumstances, and I reaffirmed what Han had confirmed about his actions in Japan, how he had gone back just to have dinner with his old friend. And then I began to recount what he had been up to since his arrival. I explained how we had to write his reports for him, how we had needed to put together his board packets, and write his reports in his name, etc. There was a list that I had been compiling for the past year or so. Betty was totally disgusted. She reassured me to hang in there, and that she was coming down to address the situation. It was time for our next quarterly Export Marketing Committee Meeting, so she made the announcement that she was coming down to attend the session. That morning you could hear a pin drop in our offices, as Molly and I sat there, waiting for the boom to come down on him. Ryan suspected nothing. And then Betty arrived, confronted Ryan about his actions, and asked for his resignation. When she was done with him, Ryan asked Molly and I to come into his office. He then informed us that he was resigning, telling us that it was a not a good fit, and that he had decided to take a different job. All I could think of was, "Yeah, right." We left the office to have a long lunch after that, feeling uncomfortable being there. When we came back, he was gone. Betty spent time with each one of us separately, explaining the circumstances, and apologizing to us for what had taken place. She was embarrassed that he had fooled her, making her think that he had been leading the program, when in reality, he had been taking advantage of the situation. I reminded her that it was not her fault – she had been lied to and deceived. And besides, the poor woman had just spent over a half a year fighting for survival from cancer. It was not her fault. Besides, a dozen industry members had given glowing support of Ryan when she was originally vetting him for the job. Betty told me that she was appointing me as acting program director during the interim, but that there was no guarantee that I would get the position. I thanked her for her trust in me and told her I would do my best until she could resolve the situation.

Our tech specialist, Bonnie, had a look at his computer after Ryan left; she revealed to us that he had not even opened Microsoft Word once. The man had not typed a single document, outside of typing emails, the entire time he was there.

The next morning was the Export Marketing Committee meeting. It was the conference room at Crystal Seafoods, and as committee members trickled in the door, they started to look quizzically, and started to ask where Ryan was. We just said, he couldn't make it. As soon as the meeting started, Betty announced Ryan's resignation. Then we carried through with the rest of the meeting. At the end of the meeting, several industry members came to Betty and told her that they were planning on telling her about what Ryan had been up to. I could only think, "Yeah, right." Betty, Molly, and I would just look at each other in disgust. Rumors had run throughout the industry about his actions – especially the episode in Australia when he got sunburned on the beach – but not a single person from the industry had stepped up and said anything to her. It was pathetic.

Chapter 28

Taking the Reigns

A week later, I was flying to Juneau for the Spring board meeting. It was then that I confirmed as permanent director of the export program. The Deputy Director of the Seafood & Wood Product Division, Blane Farrell, was there for a rare appearance; on behalf of EAS he awarded me a pen to recognize my appointment. Even Molly had been brought up to be there in attendance. I was honored – what an exhilarating experience to be named the program director in the presence of the board. There were several board members that I had known from the industry during my youthful days in Kodiak.

During my first report to the board, I started referring to Betty as 'Madam Director' – I was told later she did not like the reference, but I did it purely out of respect to her. I owed her for everything. She was the one that had originally called me in 1997 to apologize to me for misplacing my resume. She had appointed me to the ASA committee when I was at Magic Mermaid. She was the one that advocated for my first interview at ASA for the director position, and she is the one that put me in front of Ryan to hire me for the Asia specialist position. Now she was taking another huge leap in faith by confirming me as director.

Board members and industry members were all congratulating me on the promotion. At the end of the sessions, board member Nick Kresner – who my father and I had worked with for years in Kodiak- came up to me and said, "Congratulations. I'll give anyone 18 months to get things right, but I don't want to hear about you laying on some beach in Australia (when you should be doing your job)." Bill Coleman, who had been the Board Chairman, came to me and said, "I don't know why we didn't hire you in the first place." Hindsight is always 20/20.

The whole world was opening for me. It was hard to believe that just two years earlier, I was getting ready to leave Magic Mermaid, and was totally disillusioned with my career path. I was so proud – here was my big opportunity to really make things happen. Strangely enough, I grew a beard for my official picture – probably to make me look older and more mature. I was trying to get used to the beard, but then Sherry and I went to dinner at a Japanese restaurant down the street from our house. The waitress asked me if Sherry was my daughter – that was it – I shaved the beard off that night. And I never grew it back again.

But there was not much time to bask in the glow of these transitional events. Molly and I worked around the clock through the entire week and weekend to finish the CMS application, as well as to get the online edition submitted. We were taking the bold step to expand the European region from one section into three. Some - including Molly – thought I was just creating a lot more work. This was true, but I felt it was worth, for it was really the only way to create the customized strategy and initiatives for each specialized region. It was crazy to think that previously the program had been claiming that the same market constraints and opportunities existed in UK as in Spain. Personally, I felt such a generic strategy had been sheer laziness on the part of previous program staff. So, while it seemed like so much more work, I really felt it was worth it, and was sticking to my guns. We were also taking the bold step of including Decree 409 and Quality Samples Program (QSP) funding requests for the plan.

Decree 409 was a specialty funding program with a limited timeline. Essentially the USDA had supported several developing economies by loaning money to fund agricultural development activities – to the tune of $25 million. The problem was that most of these countries that had economies so poor that their currency was not easily convertible on the open market. These were countries like Algeria, Costa Rica, Sri Lanka. We were free to apply for activities to conduct in our existing markets utilizing Decree 409 funding. The trick was this – we would receive the funding in the locale currency, and that it would be our job to convert the funds to US currency for use in the designated markets. The QSP program was a little simpler. We could use this funding to promote the use of American agricultural products to educate trade about the benefits of using such products. Most of the uses were for technical education, but we got creative and were going to use the funding to support trade education activities in Southern Europe and China. It was our Southern European rep, Roger McClary, that seriously advocated for use of this program. If not for him, we probably would not have made the attempt.

Molly and I worked fervently to get the plan out the door to EAS to meet the deadline. And then I had to take the time to submit the entire application into the online system – which was now a requirement. It took me two solid days – working virtually around the clock, but I got the entire plan in ahead of the deadline. Relieved at finishing this huge task, we could turn our sights towards all the other needs of the program.

It was about this time that Sherry got the news that she was being laid off. We were not surprised at all, as the company that she worked for had been struggling. And the dot-com boom was finally turning into the dot-com bust. When she told me the news, I just laughed and said, "Good, now you can come travel with me a little bit." Molly was busy trying to get the Brussels Show organized (and it was a lot of work), so we agreed that I would go to Portugal for the Alimentaria show. This year it would be in Lisbon, so off Sherry and I went. It was a massive show, and a long one – five days.

When we arrived at Lisbon, we were amazed at how old the city looked. And most amazing was that streets were paved with marble chunks just like they had been built 500 years before. There were several construction projects, but one could tell that the city had been in a state of disrepair for some time. Life ran at a difference pace here. Roger and I went to get lunch together during the middle of the week – it took two hours to be served a simple sandwich and beer for lunch.

Roger had hired some students from a local culinary school to cook samples during the show. We were cooking up whitefish – cod and halibut, and we even had some Magic Mermaid salmon burgers to cook. Buyers were not impressed with the burgers in their plain, singular format. So, I went and found a bun producer, and a cheese producer, and a made them a simple trade – you give me some buns, you give some cheese, and you can come to my booth and have all the salmon burgers you can eat. It worked – we served salmon burgers on a bun with cheese and all the fixings – and the buyers loved them.

Just down from our booth we found a company that was using the Alaska name. We were excited at first until we found out that the product was purchased from Norway. I called them out for falsely using the Alaska name, but they didn't care. It was another example of the lack of authenticity and traceability that existed in so many facets of the industry.

I walked the show – as I always did– to see what others were doing and get some ideas. I came upon the Red Bull booth – it was hard to miss with all the beautiful young women in Red Bull tank tops. It was a total party, complete with a DJ and a cocktail bar. It inspired me to create a similar party atmosphere at ASA booths.

I took a rare, half day off before the last day of the show; I took the time to see a few sites, including the Se cathedral, as well as some of the monuments along the waterfront that were dedicated to all the Portuguese explorers.

Along the way we ran into a sick dog, which looked emaciated, and was literally bleeding from its ass. A policeman walked by, and I asked if they could help the poor animal. He said there are hundreds of feral dogs in the city, and that it was a common sight. I told him he should just take his gun and shoot the dog and put it out of its misery if it wasn't going to help it. He did nothing. It was a disturbing sight, but what could one do? The sight haunted me for years.

The last day of the show Sherry was in attendance. Near the end of the day a man walked up to me and pointed at her and said, "Igloo, igloo person." I couldn't understand what he meant, so I asked our interpreter to translate. He explained that the man wanted to know if she was an igloo person – essentially, he wanted to know if she was an Eskimo. I laughed, and said yes, and pointed at a poster of an Eskimo on one of our promotional posters and said it was her. The man grinned from ear to ear, shook her hand and skipped away. Of course, it wasn't true, but it made him happy, that I couldn't' help but perpetuate the lie. We stayed an extra day, and Sherry and I took a tour to see the town of Sintra. as well visited Cabo de Roca, which is the most western point in Europe. While we were on the tour bus Sherry told me a story about the racial animosity she had experienced by some of the locals. It seemed that earlier the day before she had stopped in a café to get something to drink. Being less than proficient in Portuguese, she asked the server behind the counter for a Coke and pointed at the display can of Coke on the wall. To her dismay, the server pulled the warm display can and gave it to her. She asked for a cold one, but she just ignored her. Then she looked around and noticed other customers with cold versions of the product – it was sad to see such racism still existing today.

Chapter 29

Beer for the Masses

Near the end of the month, I was attended my first European Seafood Exhibition in Brussels, Belgium. This is hands down the largest seafood show on earth – and once I was there, I could see why it was so important for the industry to have an Alaska pavilion and such a presence. We took the bold step this first year to bring product over for sampling. We set up a modest serving area for visitors to enjoy. This was also the first international venue that we served beer from Alaskan Beer Company, as well as Alaskan coffee from Blackbird Coffee Company. I had truly wondered if the beer would make it past customs inspection and totally intact, but it did! I had attracted so much resistance in attempting this experiment. Carol had insisted the kegs would explode in the plane, and many had said that the product would never make it past customs inspection, so I was quite relieved to find the kegs all safe and tidy, tucked away in the cooler.

Betty was gaining her strength back and was joining us for the event. I was wondering what she would think of the sampling, as I know Elise was a little skeptical. She had made the statement when we were setting up the day before, "We are here to sell seafood, not feed people." Of which I calmly and quickly retorted, "Ah, but Elise, by feeding them seafood, we will sell more."

On the first day of the show at 10 am sharp a large contingency from a major German smoker, Heinzmanns, appeared. Elise came to me immediately and announced, "The Germans are here, time for the beer, BJ!" Betty was sitting right in front of me and looking at me to see what I would do next. I wasted no time, and tapped the first keg of beer, which was a specialty smoked porter, based on a traditional German recipe. Betty did give me bit of a look at first, like, "Is this really happening?" But I assured that it was perfectly normal for Germans to drink beer early in the day. So, I passed beers around to all our German visitors, and poured one for Betty as well. They all wasted no time in making a toast to Alaska, and quickly enjoyed the flavor of the Alaska offering. The coffee was well received, but I spent a lot of time grinding coffee, thanks to the poorly designed coffee grinder. It was an elegant-looking device, but the outlet port had a tiny little orifice, which became easily clogged. So, I constantly had to pull it apart and clean out the port. I couldn't help but give Elise a bad time, asking her if it was designed by the French.

This was the first year that we experimented putting the ASA booth in the middle of pavilion, essentially creating an 'Alaska lounge' for all to enjoy. I even brought a life-size display from an Alaskan Beer Company promo that had a man holding a king salmon. Montrose gave the bold suggestion of cutting off the head and using it for pictures, so out came the pocketknife, and instantly it was a perfect display for people to take their picture. We were indeed starting to create a friendlier atmosphere that was more conducive to business, including a fresh product display on one side of the lounge, and a frozen display on the other. Elise created a fabulous display of Alaska seafood for sampling. It looked so nice that even Brendan Robins, VP of Harpoon Seafoods, came by to pay us a compliment. The gamble had worked, and the industry seemed genuinely pleased at the changes taking place.

Chapter 30

Protests and Presidents

May came, and I was slightly perplexed, as I was trying to find the right candidate to replace the Asia marketing specialist role I had previously occupied. We were starting the interview process, and asked Molly if she wanted to switch to managing the Asia program, and if she wanted to apply for the Senior Marketing Specialist role. She declined both – she had thought about taking the Asia role, but she had built strong relationships with Daniel, Elise, and Roger, and wanted to continue to work with them. And after watching me and the added pressures of the senior marketing role, she chose not to pursue it. But now it was time to travel to Hong Kong for the HOFEX show – which is one of the most prominent food shows in South Asia. Molly was joining us for this trip - this was our first step in implementing cross-pollination efforts – an idea that I had formulated right after becoming director. Sherry was joining us, having never been to Asia before. We stopped in Shanghai on the way for meetings with trade members and the FEO. The first night we arrived, as we sat down for dinner, Molly asked why there were no serving spoons. I had to explain to her that in China, everything was served and shared 'family style' – with everyone just picking at the various dishes with their chopsticks. I think she was a little disgusted with the prospect at first, but she quickly became used to it.

Next stop was Hong Kong. We were staying at the Grand Hyatt, which was right on the waterfront, which was very convenient, as the hotel building was attached to the show's exhibition hall. We had the good luck that the Global Fortune 500 summit was taking place at that same time. And the Falun Gong (a Chinese spiritualist movement) was taking advantage of the event by staging a major protest. And it was happening right across the street from the site. After the first day of the show, we walked outside to see the crowd that had formed, as it was almost to a point of becoming a riot. The ASA China staff and the rest of us took a picture of the scene; so here we all were, standing together in our suits and briefcases, with the throng of protesters across the street behind us. When we went back to our rooms we started to laugh, as the protest was splashed all over the global news networks, and here we were, right in the thick of it.

President Bill Clinton had just finished his presidency, and he was in attendance at the Global Forum. We found that most Chinese really liked Clinton as a U.S. leader, and Bobby and Billy had their staff staged in the lobby, keeping an eye out for when Bill might come walking through. It was late that night, probably past 9 pm, and Sherry and I were already crawling in bed to get some rest. Suddenly, the phone rang – it was Bobby, and he was excitedly saying, "Come quick, come quick, Bill Clinton downstairs!" So Molly, Sherry and I all quickly ran downstairs to see him. The lobby was packed with a crowd of people surrounding 'Slick Willie'. He was surrounded by concerned-looking Secret Service agents, with people trying to push their way in to shake his outstretched hand. I reached out my hand as well but was quickly pushed away by the agents – I think I was a little too tall and ominous looking to be that close to the former President. So, I stood back and watched the action. Bill noticed Sherry and couldn't help himself but walk up and introduce himself to her – after all, she was a pretty talk drink of water for being Asian. Molly was standing right next to her, and after Sherry was done shaking his hand, she burst forward and shook his hand and said, "I'm Molly Greyson!" He chuckled at her enthusiasm and said, "But of course you are." Bill was quite the showman. He noticed a baby in a carriage and quickly picked up the child and asked, "Where's the Momma? Let's get a picture." Everyone was so excited that no one had a camera – except Sherry. She had a disposable Kodak camera, and she took some great shots of him with the baby and his family. The family was very excited about getting copies of pictures, which Sherry gladly did for them the next day.

Bill finally freed himself from the crowd and made his way to the elevators. The crowd gradually dispersed, but Molly, Sherry, Bobby, Billy, and I were still sitting in the lobby, laughing about what had just taken place. I couldn't help but notice that there were still two Secret Service agents, standing on security detail in front of one of the elevators. I was wondering why they were still there, considering that Bill had been gone for a good ten minutes. And then here they came – two gorgeous, beautiful young blonde ladies came strolling through the lobby, making a straight line to the elevators. I tapped the others to watch, and we all turned and silently watched as the two ladies entered the elevator that the Secret Service had been guarding. The agents stepped into the elevator with them, and the doors closed. Everyone sat there silent, taking in what they had just viewed. And then I snapped, "I guess Bill ordered blondes tonight."

We all began to laugh at the prospect, and then headed for bed. The rest of the show was fairly tame after that, though we met some interesting trade prospects, including a processor from South Africa that wanted to purchase really pale pink salmon. It turns out that he would use the fish to make a wonderful salmon spread for crackers. He had samples, and I must admit, it was quite tasty.

A few nights later, I was exchanging some money at the front desk of the hotel lobby. I couldn't help but notice a young Caucasian man as has he walked into the lobby with a beautiful Asian girl under each arm as he proceeded to the elevators to his room. My eyes tracked them as they walked across. Sherry and Molly had been sitting in the lobby, watching me the whole time. When I walked over, they let me know they had been watching me, saying, "Do you wish you were him?" I was busted! Of course, I was envious, but I snapped back, "But I have both of you for dinner tonight." They didn't buy my comeback, but I bought them dinner anyways.

Chapter 31

Cooking with Poop

June came roaring in like a lion. I was in the final selection process for hiring someone for the Asia marketing role; the candidate I chose was named Nora Wang. She had come recommended by Han as she was working for Northwest Farms, which was one of Han's clients in Japan. I submitted her for approval by the Governor's office, and we were waiting to get the sign off on the hire.

In the meantime, I was still covering double duty, so it was time to head to Taiwan for the Taipei International Food Show. To continue my cross-pollination efforts, I had selected Carly Redfern to attend the trip. Carly had been with the domestic program forever. She was originally from Wyoming, and had not traveled outside the country very much, so I thought this would be a good experience for her. I had also selected Fumi Davis to represent industry for this trip. Fumi knew Molly well, and I was familiar with her as I had seen her in Kodiak about ten years earlier. She was famous for being the only woman that had run a crab boat in the Bering Sea. She was half Japanese, and petite like Molly, and very enthusiastic about promoting Alaska. In fact, Molly had encouraged her to apply for the Asia job. I interviewed her, and we had a good discussion; but I had been very frank that if she took the job, she was going to need to fully commit to the position – and would have to put aside her fishing career. She chose otherwise; but my consolation was to have her join us for the trip to Taiwan. I remember that I needed to get her an advance check, and she called my house looking for me. Sherry had answered the phone, and she was not amused. She said when I came home, "Some woman is calling for you, and wants her check. I thought you said you were taking a fisherman with you on the road." And I started to laugh and replied, "But she is a fisherman."

So, off the three of us went to Taipei. After arriving, I met Redfern for breakfast and the hotel restaurant and explained to her that there usually weren't any forks, and that she would need to learn to use chopsticks. She said, "No problem, I brought my own." And proceeded to pull a fork from her purse. I just grinned and said, "Clever girl."

The food show in Taiwan was crazy as ever. We had a booth right across from us that was promoting a hip new beverage. They had a stage and a group of dancers, and music blaring constantly from the speakers. It was enough to drive anyone crazy. Redfern was simply amazed. I was being my usual self and handing out flyers to people as they walked by, encouraging to come see our display. Carly kept saying, "We can't do that at the show." Of which I replied, "But Carly, you are not in Boston anymore. Relax, and go walk the show and get some ideas."

The booth looked great for having such a small budget, but I had one real problem. Considering the problems that we had with the refrigerated display case the year before, Elsie had taken it upon herself to order a 'coffin' case; a case like you see at the supermarket for displaying frozen product. I was not happy with her at all; again, she had totally gone against my instructions. I did the best I could to fix the situation. I had her get us ice for the display and turned down the temperature control as low as I could. Unfortunately, the fish kept icing over – just when I thought she could not frustrate me anymore, here she was at it again. So, we made the best of it, scraping a layer of ice off the fish every day for each of the four days of the show.

Again, it was quite hot in June, and with the time difference I could not sleep. So I went out to find a good place for a drink. I grabbed a cab and found a bar and had a few beers and then did a little shopping. I got the bright idea to walk all the way back to the hotel. In the sweltering heat I did not realize how dehydrated I had become. I continued to walk back, but with each step my feet got heavier and heavier, and I began to lose my balance. I barely made it back to my air-conditioned room, and then I started to get sick and violently throw up. I quickly passed out and did not realize until the next morning that I had been suffering from heat stroke – now I realized what Bobby had endured with me the summer before. After that experience, I always paid close attention and was sure to monitor my water intake closely when I was in such hot and humid climates.

A few nights into the show we decided to take a tour of the infamous Snake Alley. It is a night market in the Wanhua district that is famous for serving delicacies and drinks made from snake products. We were walking along in line, taking in the scenery. I was leading the group, and then I stopped to turn and look around and make sure everyone was okay. Just then, I felt an acrid smell that began to burn my nostrils. Redfern shouted out at me, "Don't stop now, they are cooking with poop!" Sure enough she was right, the putrid smell of burning poo was unmistakable. It was definitely a highlight of the trip and gave Carly and I something to laugh about for some time.

It was during this trip that I met Elliott Branch of Shelby Welsh – one of the major consultant groups that worked steadily with EAS and the cooperator community. He was at the show representing Idaho Potatoes. We had a good visit and a lot of laughs; Elliott was someone that I would continue to stay in touch with throughout the years, though unfortunately, his agency never did win any of our contracts.

Redfern headed back home, and Fumi and I continued our way to South Korea. As we sat on the plane, we discussed all that she had learned so far.

Fumi had started to understand the challenges of the program and shared a perspective that I would hold dear in my mind for years. She confided to me, "I don't know how you are supposed to do your job – it is like you are running a boat with 50 owners." I totally understood what she was saying. And I shared with her my philosophy. I knew that there was no way I was going to make everyone happy. Instead, I employed the 80% rule – if I could keep 80% of the stakeholders happy, then I felt I was doing a good job.

Our visit to Korea was interesting to say the least. It was one of the few places I visited where I had a hard time eating everything served to me. Particularly I remember having lunch with an FEO rep at a restaurant. They served each of us a tray that had about 30 separate bowls containing all types of various products. The taste of some items I found rather hideous. Soon I started watching my host closely, and I noticed there were some bowls that he was not touching. I carefully compared with my own tray and made sure that whatever he was not eating, I was not going to attempt to try either. After lunch we visited some trade members to talk about Alaska seafood. They had complaints about working with halibut, specifically that it was too big for handling, as they were buying very large size fish (I assumed due to cheaper pricing). I suggested that they cut the large fish in half with a band saw for easier transport. It was that, or they would need to start purchasing smaller fish. They also complained that farmed salmon was cheaper than wild Alaska salmon. This is when I formed another of my famous adages. I replied, "You may eat baloney all week long, but when your beloved family member or best friend comes to visit on Friday night, do you run down to the store and buy another pack of baloney for them? No, you go and buy the best steak you can find. That is how you need to think of us – a special product, at an entirely different price point."

My main reason for the visit to Korea was to investigate the potential for Alaska seafood, and to confirm if the export figures that the federal authorities had reported were correct or not. So, at the end of the visit, I pointed out to a number of the trade members that export figures demonstrated high levels of Alaska seafood entering the Korea market. Then I asked the trade members and the FEO rep where all the Alaska product was in the market the room fell eerily silent. After a long pause, they changed the subject.

The next day I had Fumi join me and the FEO rep for a tour of the Norangjin market – the major wholesale market for fishery products. We walked all through the market, but again could not really find any products from Alaska. The only exception was one small pickup truck with some Alaska Pollock fillets - but it was not marked well, so we could not even tell if it was from Alaska or not. Not really the booming potential that EAS officials felt existed. We performed some retail audits and found some surimi -based products, and some examples of Pollock roe, but not in huge quantities.

During our last day in Seoul, Fumi and I conducted a few more retail audits at a variety of stores. One thing I could not help but notice was some smoked farmed Atlantic salmon at a retail outlet that was labeled as Alaskan Bear brand. We found some frozen cod and Pollock fillets, but they were not clearly labeled, so we had no idea what their point of origin was. Again, all indications pointed to the fact that there was limited potential in the Korea market.

The next day we flew back through Tokyo, and while we were boarding the bus to get on the plane at Narita – which was common, as there were typically more planes there than jetway terminals – there was Elliott Branch. What was the chances of running into him again on the way home? We had a good laugh and chatted with him while on the plane home – sharing stories about our adventures in Seoul. I think that Fumi came away with an entirely new perspective about marketing Alaska products – so much so that shortly thereafter, she helped form a group called the 'Fish Girls', that worked with our domestic division to educate women about the benefits of Alaska seafood.

Chapter 32

Miscarriages and Adjustments

I returned home just in time to make sure the budget was getting closed out. We were able to get the budget closing more in line this year. We spent almost every last dime of federal funding. We literally only had $11 left in the budget for the end of the year.

We received our new funding allocation, with MEP funding at a slightly higher amount than the year before. And Roger's Quality Samples Program fund request for Southern Europe was also awarded – which had been ingenious on his part.

And even more exciting, were also able to secure Decree 409 funding. The overall budget available for all the cooperators was about $200 million, and the money essentially came from money that had been loaned to developing economies (Costa Rica, Tunisia, etc.). This was money that had been paid back to the U.S., but it was still 'trapped' in those specific currencies, which were officially unconvertible. So, the trick was that we would need to convert the funding back to U.S. dollars by our own means. In our case, we went after funds from Costa Rica. Bantu had set it up so that our bank in Alaska would be able to convert the currency for a nominal fee. There was just one problem – EAS had awarded us S1 million U.S. dollars (about $21 million

Costa Rican dollars) – but they wanted us to spend it all in the China and Korea programs only. This is where I perfected the art of what I like to call 'persuasive justification.'

Once I received the award letter, I called up EAS immediately and explained that we could not just award funding to these two Asia programs – our industry would not like it at all, and we really needed help in our major markets in Japan and Europe to get us out of the hole. The EAS staff was as pragmatic as ever; he said, "...write us a letter with your reasons." So, I went to work to craft a statement that argued the following: While China and Korea were definitely new development markets (even though Korea had limited potential), our industry had lost considerable market share and position in Japan and the European markets. While EAS considered these countries as 'mature' markets for us, in actuality they were now 're-development' markets for us, and we needed to use some of the Decree 409 funds to rebuild these markets. My persuasive argument worked. We were able to direct almost 70% of the funding to the Japan and European programs.

And at this time Nora had secured approval to be hired for the Asia program as the Senior Marketing Specialist. So, we got her ready immediately to go to Japan for the Japan Seafood and Technology Expo in Tokyo. We sent her over alone – I had too much to deal with to go running off to Japan with her for a week of two.

Even though I had proof that there was very little product in Korea, they wanted me to start a program there immediately. So, I started the process of contracting Gang Sung to re-initiate a program. Gang had been the previous in-country representative for the program during ASA's first attempt. It was just natural that we approached him first since he was so familiar with all the idiosyncrasies of the programs. He was highly responsive of the idea, and we went right to work on implementing activities. I also had to go to D.C. to attend the summer UFEA sessions. I took advantage of being on the east coast to fly to Florida to spend a couple days with Sherry at Disneyworld and Universal Studios. It was one of the few breaks I got to enjoy that year.

Amongst other things, we started preparing for the annual industry strategic planning session that would take place at the end of the month. I had insisted that all reps would have PowerPoint presentations for reporting their program results. While there was some resistance from the old guard, they still had generated rough presentations. Nora came back from Japan, and she, I and Molly got to task on revising the presentations with the reps as they arrived. Everyone worked diligently to make their slide decks perfect, and then the day before the session, I managed to misplace all the presentations when I hit the wrong key (I found the files in my system a month later). I was about to have a coronary, because as a result, we had to re-tool them all in a matter of hours. I really felt like shit, and I stayed through most of the night to make sure they were all revised and perfect again for the next day. It was time for the presentation. I had created a presentation too – this was my first turn officially as the program director, and it was time to shine. The focus of my presentation was about creating a differentiation strategy for Alaska seafood – and especially salmon. The market for wild salmon had been disrupted and overshadowed by farmed salmon, but we were going to 'springboard' off of the momentum created by farmed by differentiating ourselves as superior product based on a list of attributes – natural, safe, wild, sustainable, and healthy. The mix would be customized for each market, but we were going take advantage of the new markets that had been created – and the old ones that we had lost. We were going to invigorate the brand, and we were going to re-position the Alaska brand as a top-shelf offering. And how were we going to do it? We were going to focus intensely on the wild element – our 'wild' card, and we were going to perform guerilla marketing; we were going to go where farmed couldn't go, and we were going to say what they couldn't say. The room fell silent after my words, but you could see the swell of hope that starting to rise in the room. We were going to work together as an industry to turn it all around – and we had just provided them the vision on how we were going to do it.

After the session, Bantu talked to the press and made it sound like he stumbled across the Decree 409 funds on the internet by accident – which wound up being displayed in an article. At first, I was dumbfounded at the story he had just fabricated – after all the work I had done to research and secure funds for the program. Later I called the press and set the record straight. That's when I started noticing a different side of Bantu – one that I would see again later.

Right after the session had concluded, I headed straight for home to grab my suitcase, as the entire group was heading to Juneau that evening for the remainder of the strategic planning sessions with the Alaska staff. Arriving home, I found out that Sherry had her first miscarriage. She was at home, in bed, crying and totally devastated by the loss. I realized how much she was hurting, and I told her that I was going to cancel my trip and stay with her. But she insisted that I keep going and lead the team. It was hard to leave her alone, but I knew that she was strong, and would endure. Losing the child, she had been carrying was hard on all of us – I felt powerless, as there was nothing I could do to change the circumstances.

I met the team members at the airport; a short flight to Juneau, and we had arrived. No sooner did I get in a van with the Asia reps – Elsie, Lee, and Bobby and Billy – and I was bombarded by their frustration. Each and every one of them started going off about Nora and her antics. Han was not happy with her performance in Japan. She said she kept messing with all the displays at the show and was acting domineering. Elsie was not happy with her at all either – while she had not worked with her in the field, she was not impressed with her attitude and mannerism. But Bobby was probably the harshest – he did not mince words: "She is Hong Kong princess – so stuck up." She had been talking down to all of them and treated them with no respect. They said that she would literally point her finger at them, and then raise it, beckoning them to come to her, as if they were her servants. I knew I had my hands full with the new hire and started pondering what I could do to repair the situation – if it all.

Everything was a buzz in Juneau. Lanie had lined the press up with me, so that they could talk with the new director about our new strategy. Most were quite congratulatory and supportive of my leadership – Bill Coleman walked up to me in the Juneau office and said, "I don't know why we didn't just hire you to begin with (to run the program)." Which I replied, how, "How would you have known from the start? It had taken me the past 18 months to really get a grasp of the situation and formulate a solid plan." Regardless, it felt good to feel so much support for my efforts. We continued with a great strategy session, and except for the friction between Nora and the Asia reps, things appeared to be moving in the right direction. During our visit to the Mendenhall Glacier, Roger McClary noticed an interactive kiosk at the visitor center, which inspired him with a great idea to build a similar device for educating trade and consumers at events. He submitted the idea for Barb's 'Year of Creativity' initiative – but the idea never gained any traction, unfortunately. In hindsight, such a kiosk could have been an excellent engagement tool – it's really too bad we didn't get to pursue it further.

I returned home a few days later and did my best to raise Sherry's spirits. While I had a lot of activities in front of me, I wanted to make sure she was not alone during this tender time. It was August, and things weren't slowing done. As soon as we were back in the office, I had a chat with Nora about her interaction with the Asia representatives. I reminded that our relationship with them was not so much hierarchical, but more of strategic partnerships. I tried explaining to her that she needed to not only earn their respect, but to demonstrate respect to them as well.

It had just been a few days, and we had a major Japan press mission to conduct in Seattle and Alaska, so I booked her a flight and made sure she would come to Alaska and get a little 'fresh air'. It was the first of many 'reverse' trade missions for me, and while they were a lot of work – we made these visits as impactful as ever for generating vital exposure about Alaska and our exceptional story that we had to share with the world. We arrived in Kodiak and quickly started doing plant tours and seeing the sights. Part of the mission included a flight to the south end of the island to Fraser Lake to see the returning sockeye salmon in the river, as well as the bears feasting on them. Fortunately, there were a few bears at the river, so Sherry and the others got to finally see a real 'Kodiak' brown bear for the first time. The bugs were there to greet us too – they were horrible, just as I had remembered them in my youth. Thankfully we had mosquito hats to wear, otherwise our faces and heads would be covered in bites as the mosquitos, gnats, and 'no-seeums' descended upon us.

The next day we were stopping by the hotel to pick up the mission members, and something hilarious happened. As I walked up to the entrance to the 'KI' (the Kodiak Inn), right in front of me was Bob Falrik, of Northwestern Fish. He looked up at me and said, "Uh-oh, we are busted." Right behind him was Mark Montrose, and then Clint, the International Trade Specialist for the Washington State Department of Agriculture. You could see by the look on their faces that they had not planned to run into the likes of me. Clint, with a shocked look on his face, exclaimed, "What are you doing here?" I couldn't help but chuckle, and say, "That's the exact same thing I was about ask YOU." He stammered, "Well, we are a federally funded mission to conduct trade." He had his own little secret trade mission going on, bringing buyers to Alaska with two prominent Alaska industry members – led by a Washington State government official. It was a duplicative effort from funding that I knew was coming from the same federal pot of cash as ours. Possibly it could have been construed as an alternative activity – but what I really cared about was to avoid any semblance of duplicity and disorder between our two organizations. Still, it was funny to catch them red-handed in my hometown. In actuality, it was the genesis of a higher level of communication between Clint and I. Never again would we have such a situation again. Whether we agreed with approaches or not, our agencies would work in conjunction throughout the rest of my career at ASA. There was to be no more 'sneaking around' in my 'backyard'.

After another day or so, Nora, Han, and the Japanese press members departed. Sherry and I stayed for another two days and visited with family and friends on the island. An old friend of the family, Benny Nekeferoff, had a charter boat at that time. It was beautiful weather, so we took Sherry out fishing for salmon. Benny set her up with a sinker and a baited circle hook to start. It wasn't five minutes and Sherry's line lit up with a halibut on the end. She was so excited – and it was fun to watch her catch her first flatfish. Benny quickly switched her to a troll line and we started to tow for salmon. The water shimmered brightly as her line lit up immediately again with a nice big fat king. She was a natural fish killer. She reeled it in quickly and reset again. It wasn't another five minutes and she hit another one! And then again, and again. Her tally after just a couple of hours was two kings, five cohos, and a halibut. My haul for the day was two measly cohos – she laughed and taunted me for only catching two. So I reminded her that she had a lot of fish to kill before she caught up to me – considering the thousands of fish I had harvested during my days a commercial fisherman.

Since I was going to be out of town, I had instructed Nora to attend the upcoming Salmon Committee meeting in behalf of the program. We had been trying to make sure that a representative of the Export program was participating at all the species committee meeting (Canned, Salmon, Shellfish, and Whitefish), which had always been considered components of the Domestic programs. I had made it very clear that it was important to update the committee members about program activities and initiatives. But when I came back to the office, Carly approached me to let me know that Nora's attendance at the committee was one of the strangest things she had ever seen. She said that when it was time for the export report, Nora stood up and said, "I am Nora Wang, and I have nothing to report.", and sat back down – as if it were some sort of joke. Enough was enough, she had been acting stranger all the time, and it just didn't feel like she was fitting in. And the Asia reps had said her attitude had not changed for the better. And I had warned her that she had a six-month probationary period, so I figured it was time to cut my losses with my first hire. I consulted with Betty, explained the circumstances, and told her I was letting her go. Betty agreed with my decision and advised me that I let Nora know that we had a certain culture at ASA, and that she was not meshing with it. I went into her office a few minutes later and let her know that she was not fitting in, and that I was letting her go. My first hire had quickly become my first fire. I did not relish that part of the job at all, but I couldn't go on with the dysfunction, so there was no use putting it off. She cleaned out her desk and left within an hour.

I made the decision to move into her office. When Ryan resigned, I had chosen to stay in the middle office, as I had been used to being there. But after being the director for a half year, I figured it was time to move into the corner office. Molly took the opportunity to move into the middle office before I made the next hire. I also took the opportunity right then to ask her again if she wanted the Senior Marketing Specialist role – this time she accepted it. I also gave her the opportunity to switch her areas of responsibilities to the Asia programs, if she so desired. But again, she chose to stay with the European programs, as she had developed a strong relationship with the European reps and did not want to abandon them.

The following week we had an Export Marketing Committee meeting. Molly had just completed her first ever reverse trade mission to Alaska in August. Elise brought over some key buyers from Germany and Switzerland, and from what she had told me, it sounded like it turned out being a great activity with a lot of future sales potential. She had built her slide deck and was started to report to the committee about the mission. She started out her presentation by making the statement, "We had a really good time." You could feel the air get sucked out of the room, and I could see the look of displeasure on the committee members' faces. While she continued to elaborate the details of the mission, it seems like some were not listening very intently. Of course, the industry members that secured sales thought it was a good mission. For those that did not, they questioned the validity of the activity. Such was usually the case – it was usually considered a good activity if a member directly benefited from it. The members unfortunately had a bad habit of forgetting to 'take their company hat off' when they came into the meetings. The next day we were back in the office, and I asked Molly to come talk with me. I calmly pointed out to her what the reaction was in the room when she had opened with the "We had a really good time." statement. And I then said, "Please, I don't ever want to hear you start a report to industry with those words again." I suggested that she might start instead with, "It was a very productive mission..." I think she understood why, and I hoped that she took my criticisms the right way. Molly could not help herself; it was in her nature to share her successes in such a manner. I knew how hard she had worked to make the activity a success, and that it had generated some great relationships – with some becoming some key purchasers and promoters of Alaska products. It was just how she had made it appear. It was not easy for me to point out such discrepancies, as our relationship was transitioning from peer-to-peer to manager-subordinate. Transitions like this could be challenging, and we had our 'bumps in the road' along the way.

Chapter 33

A World Changed Forever

Next up was another Alaska Lunch Party in Sapporo – this time the audience would be parents and kids, and we had created a presentation that would be educational, but way more fun – we used a lot of cartoon imagery to make the story more 'kid friendly'. Since the Asia position was now vacant again, I would lead the mission. As usual, Han had put together a very busy activity schedule, with another lightning run through multiple cities. In just four days we would hit six different cities spanning two different islands. I left on a Sunday afternoon – losing a day by traveling across the International Date Line, I would arrive on Monday afternoon, and then take the long bus ride from Narita to downtown – hitting early evening traffic always made it a really long ride – usually at least two hours if not more to get to my hotel. I set in quickly for the night, as we were scheduled for an early flight to Sapporo. That morning we awoke to horrible weather. By the time I met Han and her staff at Haneda airport, the wind was blowing so hard that you could totally lean forward as hard as you could, and you would just float in the air. There weren't any planes going anywhere – all flights were grounded. A typhoon was blowing through, and all we good do was take refuge in the airport until the storm blew by. We sat and drank coffee for hours, then late in the afternoon they started resuming flights. We arrived in Sapporo in the darkness, and though we were very late, trade members from Sapporo United were waiting at a restaurant for us for a trade dinner. We rushed straight from the airport to the restaurant, which was at the Sapporo Beer Garden. The trade members were excited to see us, as it had been all over the news about how a really bad typhoon had blown through Tokyo, killing three people. I nicknamed the day 'Typhoon Tuesday' in jest, and we all had a good laugh. Shortly thereafter we thanked our host for the dinner, and then headed back to our rooms to retire for the night.

I was getting ready to crawl into bed, and I turned on the TV. On the screen appeared an image of a skyscraper with a hole in the side of it, with flames and smoke pouring out. I thought at first that I was watching a movie, but I noticed an identical building just to the left of the one burning, and I could see that superimposed at the top of the screen were the letter 'NYC'. The news reporters were talking very quickly in Japanese, and I was having trouble following what exactly they were saying. I called up Han immediately (who was in the room next door) to turn on her TV, and she started translating. She said the sources were saying that they thought a plane had flown into the building accidentally. No sooner had she said that, and we watched a plane crash into the other tower, creating an explosion with a huge fireball. My immediate reaction was to say, "That's no accident." It was so surreal. We sat there in our hotel rooms, so far from home, watching this horrific event take place. It was late at night, and after we watched the towers burn for an hour or so, as horrifying as it was, we realized there was nothing we could do, so Han hung up the phone to get some sleep. I sat there for another hour or so, transfixed on what was to take place, tears welling from my eyes at the site of the destruction. Though I was semi-lucid from all the jet lag and sleep deprivation, I continued to watch as the first tower collapsed, and then the second. I thought I might be dreaming, as I lapsed in-between consciousness and a semi-sleeping state.

I must have fallen asleep, as I awoke to the phone ringing. It was Sherry; after frantically searching for an hour or two for the location and phone number for my hotel, she had found me. She was in a panic, asking me if I knew what had happened. She quickly related what she knew: the towers had been struck by hijacked planes and then collapsed, that another plane had struck the Pentagon building, that all the airports and air space over the U.S. were closed, and that there was one rogue plane left in the air, and that the military was searching to shoot it down. She frantically began to ask, "How are you going to get home?" I tried to calm her and assure her that I would find a way to return home. That if I had no other resort, I would board a boat and travel across the ocean to return. I wanted to reassure her that - even though I was stranded in another country - everything was going to be okay. She begged me to hurry home, and I promised I would do whatever I could.

After her call, there was no way I could go back to sleep. On the TV screen, the Japanese media was displaying the faces and names of Japanese nationals that had worked in the towers that were now unaccounted. I started to weep again, but then I realized I needed to pull myself together and start communicating with the rest of my international team, to in some way form some sense of solidarity amongst all this madness. First, I called the head office in Juneau. Bantu answered the phone, and I let him know where I was at, and the situation at hand – that we were going to continue the mission as planned - and that we would keep in touch as the situation progressed. Then I sat down to my computer and began to type an email to the international team, recognizing this horrible event for what it was, and that Han and I were in Sapporo, and to remain vigilant during this time of crisis. Almost immediately, Daniel and Elise responded back to the group. And both stated their remorse, but how they had not forgotten how our American fathers and grandfathers had answered the call to lay down their lives to save Europe during the two world wars, and that they would stand with us in this time of horror. Their remarks made my heart swell with emotion, and I wept again, sobbing in waves as I thought of all the victims that had perished in the towers – citizens from all over the world – that had been working there. It was almost too much to comprehend as I sat alone in that small hotel room, so far from home.

After a minute or two had passed, I collected myself, and started preparing to head downstairs to carry on the promotion we had traveled so far to carry out. I was met in the lobby first by Jim Tanaka. He had a long, drawn face. We looked at each other, silently acknowledging the horror of what had just taken place. And then it began – one after one, the Japanese trade members arrived and came to me, and told me how sorry they were for the tragedy that had just occurred for my country and my people. I thanked them for their kindness and acknowledged that Japanese citizens were among the victims. I replied, "This is not just an American tragedy, but a tragedy for global citizens from all parts of the world." One of the Japanese were so kind, they brought me a squishy toy in an attempt to cheer me up. Sorrow and solemness filled the hall as we prepared to carry out the seminar and lunch party that we had come to perform. Regardless of the events that had just unfolded, the show must go on, and so it did – though with a very somber air about it. That night we had a very quiet dinner and turned in early.

The next morning, we got up early and headed southeast to Chitose. At Chitose we met with a medium-sized trade house to discuss the market and ascertain local needs. They were very candid with us and revealed a fact that was sadly not surprising but was nonetheless disturbing. The joke on the street was that if you were purchasing Magic Mermaid or Harpoon brand salmon, that it meant that you need to get a $0.50 discount – because the quality was so shitty. What a terrible brand image that the major processors had created for themselves. It was definitely another sign that things needed to change in the industry. After our meeting we headed back to Sapporo and flew to Kushiro.

Kushiro is located the East coast of the island of Hokkaido. That night at the hotel I got the taste of a real Japanese 'business' size room. It was tiny compared to the rooms in the hotels in the major cities. The bathroom was this prefabricated all plastic chamber that I had to stoop over in order to enter. Inside of it, neatly compacted together was a toilet, sink, and what appeared to be a small, square- shaped tub to climb into. It reminded me of the same kind of feeling you get when you go into a restroom on an airplane compact, cramped, and slightly claustrophobic.

The next day we started our visit with trade members at the historical trade facility near the harbor. After we concluded our meeting, they gave us a tour of the facility. There was a vast bidding hall at the port, which was now silent and empty. At one time, massive shipments of Alaska sockeye salmon used to land at this port to be traded and distributed all through Japan. But the business had shifted to ports to the south, and the great shipments and vibrant business that used to exist were nothing but a faded memory. Now there were just the small coastal fisheries to support the community. That afternoon we departed and flew to Sendai to conduct a few trade visits and negotiate additional promotions. Wherever we went, people all over kept asking me if I was an American, and then they would apologize to me – I will never forget the sorrow in their eyes. Every TV screen was filled was images of the events of 911. It was impossible to escape. I think that the worst thing to watch was family members looking for loved ones, posting their pictures and descriptions on placards – it was heart-wrenching to watch. That evening we returned to Tokyo. Han and I parted company at the airport, so she could be with her family during this very morbid point in time. I quietly took a taxi and checked into my hotel. There the hotel staff asked me if I was an American, and then shared how sorry they were for what had happened. Just down the street was a Shinto shrine, so I slowly walked to it and kneeled before the altar. I prayed for the victims of the event, and I prayed for the families of those lost. I couldn't help but begin to weep as I thought of all the loss and the suffering. That night I continued to watch the reports on TV from my room, wondering if I was going to be able to go home or not the following day. Never had I felt so lost, so trapped, so alone – I just wanted to go home and be with Sherry and my family.

The next morning, I got up early and made my way to Narita, not knowing if my flight to the U.S. would leave as scheduled, considering that U.S. airspace had been closed since Tuesday, and there had been no report that the status had changed. I had expected huge lines at the airport, but strangely enough the lines were very short at the United check-in desk. Thinking that the flight would be packed, I put in a request for an upgrade to business class. I walked to the gate, and I found the waiting area almost empty. To put things in perspective, United's daily flight between Tokyo and Seattle had been jam-packed every time with Japanese nationals for the past two years – due in part to Nintendo's ownership of the Seattle Mariners baseball team, in addition to the fact that two of Japanese's favorite baseball players - Ichiro Suzuki, and Kazuhiro Sasaki - were on the team. After boarding the plane, I looked around and was astonished at how empty it was. There was almost no one in the economy seating section, and just a handful of scared-looking American businessmen (like me) in the business section. I struck up a conversation with one of the few people sitting nearby. We began to converse about the 911 event, and how strange it was to be heading home in the face of all that had taken place. The drink service started, and the flight attendants served us cocktails in the standard glassware that we were accustomed to receiving in business class. But when it came time for the meal service, while we were provided a metal fork and spoon, the standard metal knife (which was typically a blunt butter-style) had been replaced by a plastic knife. The man sitting close to me, and I, both looked at each other and started to chuckle. Considering that the terrorists had used boxcutters to assist in taking over the 911 flights, we could understand the new policy. But as we sat there with our cocktail glasses in our hands, we couldn't help but reflect what was more dangerous – a butter knife that I would have to try and file down to a sharp edge, or a glass that I could break off immediately for a razor-sharp edge.

The anticipation of coming back home continued to build as we raced across the sky. As I watched our flight trajectory tracking map, I couldn't help but notice that we were not flying the usual route, which meant hugging the

Aleutian Islands chain and the Alaska coastline. Instead, we were flying a straight line directly across the Pacific to Seattle, and at a speed close to 600+ mph. I began to wonder if we would be able to land in the USA, considering that the airspace had been closed since Tuesday, but then why would they have let the plane take off to begin with? As it turns out, we were one of the first planes allowed back into the U.S. Of all the times I have traveled outside the U.S., it never felt so good to get home. We didn't know what to expect when we arrived what type of greeting we would receive. Being a US citizen, immigration and customs waived us on through, saying nothing but a somber, but very sincere, "Welcome home." Unfortunately, it did not look like the same type of reception for the arriving foreigners, who appeared to have a very long line, and no doubt a very thorough review.

I had returned to a nation in mourning. On all the news channels, there was nothing but news and stories about the event, the victims, and the families left behind. Tears abounded at every turn. Vigils were being held across the nation. Even though I was very tired from the jetlag and time difference, that first evening back Sherry and I joined thousands of others for a candlelight vigil being held at the fountain pavilion at the Seattle Center. It was a very sad and solemn time. It was one of those events in time that one realized would bring about changes in the way of life. In this case, it would change the way air travel, international travel and border security would occur. Life as we knew it was never going to be the same – and here I was, an international program director, facing the stark reality about traveling and performing business internationally, under a new, heightened sense of security.

Chapter 34

A Long Road Through China

There was not much time to reflect on all that had unfolded. Molly and I needed to travel to Vigo for the Conxemar show in early October, and we had a major trade mission to China planned for the second half of October – one that we had been planning and preparing for months and months. This was going to a big mission, Betty was going to attend, as well as board members Dan Gumdrop and Tommy Caldwell, as well as two industry members, Bill Holden and Dolly Lindsey. We had two weeks of a jam-packed schedules of trade and press visits all over northeastern China. After what had taken place with the attacks on 911, Betty was apprehensive of us conducting the China trade mission. But I assured her that China would be one of the safest places on earth to visit at the time. I shared the following logic: Who in their right mind would attack China? They could call up a million-man army overnight, followed by millions more if desired. The logic worked –she agreed that the mission was a 'go' as originally planned.

2001 had been a watershed year for me, I had been promoted to the program director, we had received a significant boost in new program funding, I had made my first hire and fire with Nora, I had just endured the tragedy of the 911 event far from home, and I had been running hard and fast. When we went to the Conxemar show in Vigo, I was pretty rundown. When we finally arrived at the airport in Spain, after a long series of flights, we caught a ride with one of the FEO attaches, Magdalena. We had made our way in her rental car almost all the way to the hotel, when I realized that my computer bag was missing. I was frantic – I must have left it behind. Magdalena quickly turned around and drove back to the airport. My mind was racing – surely someone must have taken the bag by now. But it was dark and late, and sure enough, there was the bag, sitting in the luggage cart in the parking lot. I was truly fortunate. Shortly after checking in at the hotel I crashed from sheer exhaustion.

The show at Vigo was going well. But we were having a problem securing an internet connection for retrieving and sending emails. There was no internet connectivity at the show, and the hotel had nothing but phone lines. I had a remote server list for dialup access, and I was frantically trying to secure a dialup connection (yes, dialup was pretty much the international internet standard in 2001) in order to gain access. I was dialing server numbers all over Spain – but nothing was connecting properly. Then finally I secured a connection from a server in Valencia. Success! While the connection was so very, very slow, at least I could get messages in and out for those three days of the show.

Next it was time to go to China. Sherry had never visited China, and she was excited to see the land of her ancestors, so I booked her a flight to join all of us. We started the mission in Beijing. For a change, we arrived a day earlier, so we could get settled in before the long trip. In the morning we started by visiting Tiananmen Square. It was amazing to finally see this famous landmark. There were people visiting from all over the country, and when they saw me, they would walk up and ask me if I was an NBA basketball star and inquired if they could take pictures with me. As I joke, I would wait until after they were done with taking the picture, and then I would say, "That will be $10." Most would have an astonished look on their face, and then I would start laughing, and tell them I was joking. When we finally made our way through the crowd of people, we made our way into the Forbidden City. The palace was simply amazing to see – and I was especially entranced with the Dragon Throne. I had seen it before in Portland, Oregon, when it was on tour with other palace relics, but it was truly amazing to see it in its original setting at the palace. After the long walk through the Forbidden City, we headed back to the hotel. We got back and I started blowing my nose – I was astonished to see black snot coming out. My nose was totally coated from all the soot. What we thought had been morning fog was actually thick smog from all the coal dust in the air. The pollution was that bad. Later that day I bought a coat from one of the street vendors. After returning home, I couldn't get the smell of coal out of it – even after washing it several times. All I could think was – they are having the Olympics here in 2008? The athletes are going to need oxygen bottles and masks to deal with the air pollution, or they will have the slowest times every recorded.

The next day we want on a tour to see the Great Wall. On the way up to the wall, there were several vendors lined up to sell souvenirs and trinkets. And then we came upon a camel - of all things! The vendor tried to talk us into mounting it and taking a picture, but Dolly was the only one brave enough to try. And the guy that had the camel was so funny. When we were coming back down the mountain he yelled out to our group again and again, "Dolly I know you!" To get to the wall, there was a tram that went up the side of the mountain. And we rose up the steep hills, I couldn't help but wonder what a tremendous task it must have been to have to haul all of the stones up to build the structure. When we got to the top, it was truly an amazing sight. The wall went in both direction as a far as the eye could see! It was rather steep at a couple of points, but we carefully descended to one of the guard stations, where we were greeted by a local that was dressed in traditional costume, with a spear in hand. He screamed war cries and dragged the spear along the rocks for effect. He was quite amusing, and we were more than happy to give him a nice tip for his performance. The next day we conducted some trade visits, as well as a visit to the U.S. Embassy to meet with the agricultural attaches and officials. The following morning, we conducted our first trade seminar and luncheon. We were totally bombarded by the press with questions after the event – Betty and I must have spent an hour sitting with them to provide them with answers to all their questions.

Then it was off on a quick plane flight to Dalian.

The visit to Dalian was something else. It was a port city on the coast, but the city was filthy. The cars and buses were visibly spewing dirty exhaust everywhere along the streets, and the street beggars were all around us. I had one little girl that was so persistent, trying to sell me a flower. I would try to step around her, but she kept jumping back in front of me. I was feeling bad, and then Billy finally shooed her away. We conducted some more trade visits during the day, and then that night Bobby invited us to eat at a Korean restaurant. There were quite a few types of meat being served, but the one that stuck out was the beef tongue. If you have ever had beef tongue, you would know how chewy it is. I really don't like it that much, but Bobby asked if I wanted more – I said sure (I was joking but thought it would be funny). Sherry was pissed at me, as she hated it, but she felt that she needed to be polite and eat more. We were staying at the Shangri-La Hotel in Dalian, and Sherry decided to go to bed early. Bobby and I planned to meet in the hotel bar downstairs. There were lots of Russian and Chinese hookers in the bar, and a lot of them were looking at us. Bobby warned me not to make eye contact with them, or they would come over to the table to proposition us, so I tried to keep my eyes to the stage. Which was easy to do, as there was a trio of beautiful Filipino girls singing and dancing. I found their performance intoxicating, and we sat and watched their entire set. When they finished, one of them came over and introduced herself and shook my hand – she smelled wonderful. As gorgeous as she was, I said goodnight and went back to room. As soon as I got back, I took a shower to get the smell of the girl's perfume off of me. But as I crawled into bed, Sherry woke up started sniffing as she smelled the scent, as the perfume was still so heavy. We left Dalian the next day; as we walked to the airport to leave, I started to detect a metallic taste in mouth – one that I had for days afterward. The only I can figure is that it must have come from all the air pollution we were absorbing during our visit. With all of the pollution we had just endured, I was happy to get out of there.

Next stop in our mission was Qingdao. This was going to be the new home for the China Seafood Expo; the show had been held in different cities every year (it was in Dalian the previous year, and Shanghai the year before). As we traveled into the city from the airport, Bobby remarked that Qingdao was a small city – having a population of only 8 million - only. The show was held in a brand new trade event center, and we had a great showing that first day. That night we held a reception to a packed room. The visitors immediately wiped out the supply of crab. People were walking away with heaping plates of crab legs, leaving nothing for the rest of the guests – but how could you blame them? The next day, Sherry, wanting to see the sites, talked some poor taxi driver into taking her for a tour for the entire day – all up and down the countryside to temples and such. She told him that she was a celebrity back in the U.S., and he was taking all kinds of pictures with her, thinking he had an American star in his car. And then she paid him only $25 for the entire day! Man, that girl could drive a hard bargain on people. During that day at the show, I saw Clint Houston. He had secured two more Alaska companies to be a part of his booth, even though he worked for the Washington State Department of Agriculture. I didn't mind, but he was always trying so hard to compete with our group. When he came to talk to me I let him know that I was okay with him having the Alaska partners in his pavilion – he was a little sheepish with me after catching him in Kodiak. I took him aside to talk with him. I wanted to encourage him to stop trying to sneak around my back, so I told him, "Clint, why don't you stop acting like a remora, and start acting like another shark to swim alongside me." I think that he took the comment the right way, as he changed his course of actions after that, and started working more open and closer with me. In fact, for the remainder of my career in the position, we started working closer than ever – more as a partner than a competitor.

On the last day in Qingdao, Bobby was having lunch in the hotel with his aunt and uncle. Considering how many times he had paid for our meals, I decided to get even with him. I gave the waiter my credit card and told them to put Bobby's bill on it. After paying the bill, we got up and greeted his family and quickly left. When he went to pay his bill, he was shocked afterward to find that I had paid the bill – I had got him good. He found me later, smiled, waived his finger at me and said, "Very tricky." Of which I replied, "I have had a great teacher." After that, it became a game to outfox each other on who could find a way pay the bill. It was a game we continued to play for years.

After three days the show was finished, and we made our way finally to Shanghai. Bobby and Billy had constantly been bragging about Shanghai – to the point that the trade members on the team were starting to get tired of hearing them go on and on about it. When we finally arrived in the city, the trade members were blown away by the magnitude of what had been built. With one exception – Bill had taken a good look at the Huangpu River that cuts through the middle of the city. He leaned to me and said, "If I fall in, don't bother trying to save me – I'd probably die of massive bacterial infections anyway." He might have been a little bias, for on the flight in he had shared an article with me from the China Daily – it revealed that Shanghai produced 39 million tons of wastewater every day but treated only 25 million tons a day. I couldn't help but chuckle a little when he shared his joke with me – the river did look pretty filthy. Otherwise, Shanghai was quickly converting to a gleaming new city – on both sides of the river. There were cranes everywhere. There were skyscrapers, high-rise condos, gleaming new shopping centers – the city had been exploding with growth since the late 1990's, and it was in full swing of growth and expansion.

The next morning, we had a meeting with Bah Ha Chong, a distributor/wholesaler. During the meeting they talked about how they wanted to import Alaska seafood, but no one in the industry had responded to their request. Dan Gumdrop, spoke up and acted like we at ASA were not doing our job properly, and wanted to know why we had not informed his company of the need. He totally embarrassed us in front the representative. Right after we walked out of the meeting, I lost my temper with him and reminded him that Bah Ha Chong had been sending trade lead requests for months which we had circulated to his company, as well as others, but they had gone unanswered. This event, and the continued inaction by the industry, became the catalyst for the beginning of reverse trade missions of Chinese companies to Alaska. If the industry would not respond to the Chinese trade, we would bring the trade directly to the industry.

During the whole entire mission, every time we went to dinner, Bobby and Billy had paid the bills. On the last night, during our final dinner, I had Sherry sneak off with my credit card to pay the bill – but Billy was following close behind her to make sure she did not pay it. The group was wondering what was going on, and I let them know that they had been paying the bills for almost the entire mission. While the rest of us sat there, Bill snuck off and paid the bill. Again, Bobby and Billy had been foiled.

The next day we headed home. When we arrived in San Francisco we were clearing customs, Sherry had gone overboard shopping and we had four large suitcases, totally packed. The customs agent noticed all the suitcases, and said, "You guys sure have a lot of luggage." Quickly I replied, "We needed a lot of clothes, as we were on a mission for an entire two weeks." My quick thinking had worked, as he decided to wave us on through. It would have been an unpleasant experience if they had found all the undeclared Chinese items we had purchased while we were there.

Chapter 35

A New Hire

Right after our return, it was time for another semi-annual Board of Directors meeting in Juneau. One of the highlights was to explain to the Board why we were going back into Korea again. The main reason being that EAS saw high export numbers, and that they were pushing hard from a political perspective. After the meetings had ended, while we were at the airport waiting for our flight, I had an open discussion, with one of board members, Brad Short, about Korea. Brad totally understood the challenge of what I faced with us having to go back into Korea. He brashly said: "How do put in the CMS that the main market constraint is that they are lying, cheating bastards?" Considering some of the unsavory industry experiences with the Korea trade that had taken place in the short time I had been at ASA, I could understand the sentiment.

I had barely arrived home, and it was time to hit the major annual UFEA sessions. This time they were in Baltimore, and I had a major presentation to provide to the entire cooperator group. This was the largest audience I had ever presented in front of, and I was a little nervous to be talking in front of so many people. The subject was about enhancing the use of federal funds by partnering with other cooperator groups. I shared the examples of how ASA and the U.S. Seafood Export Council had partnered together, sharing booths at the Japan Seafood Show, and had conducted joint receptions together. I had the crowd laughing, as I shared stories about feeding king crab and lobster to Japanese media and trade members. It turned out to be a lot of fun giving the presentation, even though in reality, I was nervous as hell.

We had been advertising to fill the Asia specialist position during the Fall. I had approached my old friend Susie about the role. She thought about it, but considering her family situation, she just could not commit to so much travel. And then came Ocean Buchanan. She had interviewed very strongly. Like me, she came from an Alaskan fishing family – in this case Petersburg. And she had recently graduated with a business degree and was passionate about promoting the Alaska brand. After enduring the long process of approvals, she was hired. She took right to task and was very enthusiastic about work. Just a day or two into it, we were creating Country Progress Reports (CPR) for each program. These were new reports, and Molly was complaining about creating even more new reports, it just seemed like a lot of duplicate work in addition to all the reports were already crafting. After a day or two, Ocean walked into my office and asked, "Why are we doing these CPR reports, we already have the money?" Of which I replied smugly, "Because maybe we want some more money next year." She started blushing, and I started to laugh. She was bright, but she was new, and she still needed to get her attitude in check about some things. We were talking about salmon promotions, and she said, "We don't eat dogs and pinks in Petersburg." Of which I replied, "Well you do now." She needed to understand that we were promoting everything coming out of Alaska, not just the premier offerings. This was a reminder to myself as well, not to have a cavalier attitude to the 'less than premier' species of salmon. In the past I had called chums and pinks 'utility fish', so I made a note to myself to check my attitude as well.

It had also turned out that Ocean had never eaten sushi before. So Molly and I took her to lunch and showed her how to eat it. And we also took the opportunity to teach her as much etiquette about Japanese dining and tradition as possible. Being a tall, statuesque blonde, we figured she would be very popular in Japan. This was going to be fun. This time I made the decision to keep the new hire in the office for six months to learn the programs well before traveling.

Right before the holiday break I had a discussion with Betty. We were reviewing the quarterly performance reports. She had been reviewing the retail merchandising activities in Japan, and she asked, "Why do we have such small results?" I had to point out that we did not have enough funding, even for our largest market, to do continual retail promotions year-round. I asked the question, "Do you want to a whole bunch of nothing, or a little bit of something?" I think then that she realized our plight. We just did not have enough funding to gain the traction that the industry stakeholders expected. The international program used to have $10 million a year, and now it had barely $2-3 million.

In January one of my first acts was to shut down the Taiwan program. I had been its biggest proponent, since I had re-launched the program two years before, but there were a number of issues with the program. First of all, Elsie had been running amok for some time, spending money on advertising activities that were supposed to be directed at consumer public relations activities. In retrospect, I don't' think she knew the difference between the two. And her latest endeavor was to promote sockeye salmon at a medical conference as a health product. This was another example of her not being able to stick to the strategic plan and approved activities. While I appreciated her creativity, she just could not spend the funds on unapproved activities – activities that would never pass audit with EAS and would not serve our expected goals. I had relayed this point to her a number of times, but I just could not seem to get it across to her. While her rogue behavior had been enough of a challenge, the program suffered from another issue: the lack of industry support. For two years I had worked closely with the industry to grow the Taiwan market. I had recruited industry members to join us for trade shows, and I had implored industry contacts again and again to engage in the market – but they would not. In hindsight, I realized that I had been like a young infantry officer, rattling my saber, and attempting to rally the troops to charge over the ridge, and on into the face of the enemy except no one would follow. No, I finally realized that the program had been a strong, but futile effort. It was time to let it go and shut it down. It was not hard to make the argument results had not been very strong, and it was easy to convince EAS to shut the program down. There was no resistance from the industry.

Besides, I needed to re-direct my efforts. Due to continuing pressure by the EAS, I was having to seriously entertain the prospect of starting up a new program in South Korea. We had performed research, both primary and secondary. We had made trade visits. We had interviewed trade and industry. All indications had pointed us to not re-start a program. But the federal officials continued to push for a program, and directed funds for it, so away we went. I started the process of bidding to hire Gang Sung to launch a new program.

Chapter 36

Kyoto Kipper Snacks

By late January, Bobby Olson and I were headed to Japan. We were going to conduct another Alaska Lunch Party in Sendai – with even more focus on quality and technical aspects. But before Sendai, Bobby and I were to pay a visit to the Kansai region. We landed in Osaka and made the journey to Kyoto. There we visited with several trade members. One of the processors we visited made a very unique product in which they wrapped sockeye salmon in wakame (seaweed) and then cooked it in a sauce and then packaging it to make it shelf stable. It was a very impressive operation but was even more impressive is what I was shown next. We were taken to their office for tea, and we had no idea what kind of treat we were in store for. We were about to be shown what the Japanese trade referred to as their 'dirty books'. They were picture albums that had been compiled throughout the years – pictures of seriously defective Alaska salmon that had been purchased. The images spoke for themselves – bruising, gaping, separating flesh. It was all signs of lack of quality control – and more importantly, the names of the suppliers were identified with each batch. Almost every single major Alaska salmon processor and brand was listed in the book. It was astounding. While it was unsettling, we could not help but to feel privileged. We were the first Alaskans to ever view these images – they had been kept in-house all through the years. I apologized on behalf of my industry and made the promise (as I had already done so many times before) that we would do everything in our power to avoid product of this quality ever being sold again.

The next day we were in for another special visit. We visited a factory in the outskirts of the countryside that processed Alaska herring into an exceptional product. They would fillet the herring and then take the fillets and marinate and cook them in soy sauce. As a result of the process, the flesh would take on a black color. And while it did not appear to be appealing visually, it was actually quite tasty. And surprisingly enough, the process helped to make it shelf stable. I nicknamed the product the 'Kyoto Kipper Snack'. The remainder of the day we conducted some 'cultural tours' of the region, including visiting the famous Kinkau-ji temple. And we also visited some of the local relics, including a Buddhist temple and showcase that had amazing, 1,000 year old wood carvings and figurines all throughout its chambers.

The following day we took the Shinkansen from Kyoto to Sendai. During the train trip we reviewed our presentations that we were preparing for the event in Sendai. Unfortunately, during the process, Han and Bobby began to disagree about certain elements. They had a falling out over this, and their relationship was never the same for the rest of my time at ASA. It is sad because the relationship had been jovial and so productive prior to this event. But Bobby unfortunately tended to hold grudges, and Han was pretty stubborn herself. It was hard to watch.

We had a warm greeting in Sendai upon our arrival. And after the trade dinner the first night, we again found ourselves heading towards our favorite karaoke bar – Nondererella. Bobby had heard my tales of previous visits, so he knew what was in store. As usual, the locals continued to pour alcohol down us, as well as themselves. They started by dressing us up in some goofy outfits during our first of karaoke singing – nothing too outlandish, but wacky nonetheless. And then they started dressing one of the trade members in drag, and soon after, they dressed Bobby and I in drag too. With three of us standing there in dresses, mascara, lipstick and wigs, we were inspired to do something special – we had them put on an old Diana Ross and the Supremes hit, 'Babylove', and we began to belt out the words. As we sang away, we noticed a few drunk guys stumble in the door. They took one look at three of us and turned right around and walked out. They were having none of that. Inspired by our performance, they named us the 'Sendai Supremes' – a name that Bobby and laughed about for years and years. When I later showed the pictures of the three of us in drag to one of my best friends, Teddy, I made the comment, "If these pictures get out, I'll never been an elected official." Of which Teddy replied, "But you'll most certainly get the gay vote."

The lunch in Sendai went off well. Bobby did a great job leading the charge to share health and technical information about Alaska products. The Japanese trade was more involved than ever, and as always, the consumers that attended the event ate everything that we provided. After the show we visited Shiogama to negotiate another event. During the trade dinner we were served some of the local oysters. I did not think anything of it until the next day, during our return to Tokyo. By the time I reached our hotel, I was becoming very sick. We were able to trace it to the oysters later, when we found that others that had eaten fill ill as well. It was food poisoning, and it was the worst case I ever experienced – I spent the entire day, and all the next in bed, writhing in agony. That next night I was beginning to recover, and we had an important trade dinner scheduled with FEO officials, so I made myself go to dinner, even though I was far from well. The next day I was starting to feel better, and Bobby I got together to work on some reports. The next thing we knew, it was getting late in the evening, and we decided we would go for a walk to find a bar for a drink. It was a cold winter night, and the streets were totally empty. We walked for a couple of blocks, but nothing seemed open. Then this girl came walking from the doorway of a building. She walked right up, and in broken English she said to us, "Would you like the sex? I am number one blow job girl. I will start with hand and finish with mouth." We both looked at each other and had to keep from laughing. She was totally serious. I looked back at her and started to feel bad for her. We politely declined, and then turned back for the hotel. It just seemed like it was going to be one of those nights. The next day we flew back home. It was time for us to get to work on the new Combined Market Strategy plan.

Chapter 37

Unintentional Porn

O cean was starting to catch on more all the time. And it was really great to have some help with the Asia component of the plan, as in the past I had to edit it all myself and compile all the harvest and export information for the 'front-end' of the plan. Finally, the international team was running at full-steam, and it allowed me to dedicate more time to work on strategy and program management.

March was upon us. It was time for another board meeting in Juneau. For this one we took the entire export team with us. Molly needed to go over some fiscal business with Jeff, and we wanted to introduce Ocean to the board and the Juneau staff. I was in for a special session with the board meeting. The board awarded me a letter of thanks. It was quite the honor, as it was the first time ever that an active staff member received a letter of thanks. Shortly after Bantu got up and provided the fiscal report. He pointed out that the export program budget had been run tighter than ever. In the past the annual carryover budget was about $200,000. For 2001 we had reduced the carryover to only $18! I knew that we had run it close – like the board had requested, but I had no idea it would be that close. These two announcements were one of the proudest moments of my life. While I was enjoying the recognition, but I didn't' want to outshine Betty. She was still the ED and had been the driving force of getting ASA back on task as a whole – and she had given me my start with the organization – for which I will be eternally gratefully. She seemed to take it well, as she congratulated me on the recognition. Later, I was sitting in the audience, and Ronald Reynolds (our new PR consultant) asked me what I thought of his new mockup ad to promote salmon with AFC funds. I started to review it and couldn't help but notice an Atlantic salmon as one of the images. I quietly suggested that he might want to get rid of the picture of the farmed salmon on the cover. He turned a beautiful shade of red. Bill's time with ASA turned out to be short-lived. After that encounter, I was not surprised.

Upon my return to the Bellevue office, I received a hero's welcome. Redfern literally led a procession into my office with a king's crown on a pillow for me. They were laughing and joking that I was going to be the next Executive Director soon. As I placed the crown on top of one of my file cabinets, I pondered if I would be. The energy was so positive, and everything was coming together. The hard work and dedication were really starting to pay off – the whole world was in front of me, with all the opportunity one could imagine.

It was a about a week later and I was approached by Redfern. Carly Redfern – what a character she was. She had been at the organization longer than anyone, so I called her the 'archive' department. She and I would spend hours talking about the history of the organization. This time she wanted my opinion. There was a new promotional effort for the domestic program that was focused on women – the 'Get in the Pink' promotion. To support the activity, they had created pink baseball caps, pink aprons, etc. So, Carly wanted to get my male opinion about the ad that was being run in female-targeted magazines, like Ladies' Home Journal, etc. I took one look at the ad, and I couldn't believe what I was seeing – at the top of the ad in big print were the words, 'Get in the Pink', and below it was a prominent plate shot with a pink salmon taco. I just couldn't believe it. As I gazed upon the ad, Redfern asked, "What do you think of it?" My response came as a question.

I asked, "Are you running the ad in Hustler, Penthouse, or both?" She was shocked at my reply. But I was serious. For those that might not understand the joke, a euphemism for a vagina is referring to it as a 'taco'. Of all the meals to tie into 'Get in the Pink', they pick a freaking taco. She thought I was being perverted, but she and her ad agency had managed to create what we might refer to as 'unintentional porn'. To make sure I was not being overtly sexist, I decided to gain a female opinion to confirm my view. I called Liz in Juneau, and asked if she had seen the ad. She replied, "Oh my God, they put a taco underline the tagline." I knew I was not the only one that recognized the faux pas. Still, they ran the ad. One can only wonder how many people saw the ad and had a similar impression. While it was an innocent mistake, as a marketer, one must never forget how easy it is easy to make the wrong impression than what was intended.

The following week, I stopped over at Magic Mermaid to visit some of my old co-workers. As usual, I was greeted warmly by many – reminding me that I had left with more friends than enemies. And of course, I stopped in to visit with Montrose. He was his usual smug self, with his Cheshire cat grin. MM had been on a roll; they had acquired a couple more businesses and distribution houses and their annual sales had increased to about $500 million. So, Mark said to me, "You should have stayed with us. We are a half a billion-dollar company now." For which I quickly responded, "If all of you had listened to me, you would be a billion-dollar company now." We both looked at each other and started to laugh. Mark and I always liked to give each other shit – but we had mutual respect for each other, and we were always both smiling at the beginning, and the end of our conversations.

Chapter 38

A Strange Experiment

It was April, and the time for the Brussels show was coming up. It was a magical time, we were riding high, and the tide was starting to turn in our favor. We started this trade mission off in Hamburg, Germany, and conducted meeting in Bremerhaven and Hamburg, including a visit to Heinzmanns, which was very well- established smokehouse in Hamburg. We gave some presentations, and then toured the facility. We found that they were treating the frozen fish a little rough when filleting them. Pulling back on the fillets hard while cutting them was causing cracks and gaping the meat. We suggested that they would reduce damage if they trained staff to handle the product with greater care.

After we concluded meetings in Germany, we traveled to Paris to conduct more trade meetings – including a major presentation with Marrefour, who at the time was one of the largest retailers on the planet. During our session, we promoted how pristine and clean the environment of Alaska was. One of the executives from Marrefour responded – but isn't the whole planet polluted now? Of which I quickly replied, "If the entire planet is polluted, then Alaska is the least polluted." It seems to be accepted with validity, and we were able to continue with negotiating several more promotions with them.

While in Paris, we also held meetings with FEO officers and attaches. After a day of meetings, we walked along the Champ de Elyses, until we reached a Monoprix store, where we stocked up on some beer and wine and snacks. As we reviewed with cold cases, we noticed some lox made from wild Alaskan coho salmon, as well as some lox made from farmed Norwegian salmon. When we returned to the hotel we decided to conduct a blind taste test – farmed vs. wild. Each one of us took turns being blindfolded and then fed to two different samples. When it was my turn, I could tell right away which was the farmed salmon – it had a mushy texture and left an oily feeling on my tongue. Both Molly and Bobby could also tell right away which one was which as well. The rest of the coho lox was consumed quickly, but no one had any desire to partake of any more of the farmed salmon. We broke into conversation and were chatting away. I got up to get another drink, and I noticed something weird going on with the farmed fillet. As the fish had started reaching room temperature, pools of strange colored oil had begun to rise to the surface of the product. We had never seen anything like. The sight always made me wonder about the content of farmed salmon after that (not that I had not already had questions about the product). To this day, I still have never knowingly eaten any farmed salmon.

Sherry arrived the next day as we were out at trade meetings. When we arrived back to the hotel, she was getting up from a nap from the jet lag. She had always wanted to visit some famous bars, and the Buddha Bar was right across the street. We walked across and got a nice table upstairs. We ordered some champagne and appetizers. Now usually I am the clumsy one, knocking over everything. But on this night, Sherry finally got her turn – as she reached across the table to get some snacks, she managed to knock over both glasses of champagne. Considering they were about $10 each, it was an expensive mistake – but I just laughed at her and ordered another round.

The next was my birthday, and for a special treat, Elise took Sherry, Bobby, and I to a nice little restaurant, just down the street from the Moulin Rouge. The owners/chefs were a very nice French couple that Elise had met an event shortly before. They were wonderful people, and they did their best to make it a special night for us. The menu looked very appetizing, and I ordered a vanilla chicken dish that was served right in the pot that it was roasted in – it was one of the most amazing flavors I have experienced. And they made me a special tort birthday cake, with sparklers and all. Paris was a lot of fun – as always, and it was extra special this time, having Sherry to enjoy the sights.

The fun in Paris came to an end, and we took a train to Brussels. The ESE was as grand as ever, and for this year we had a full spread of seafood catered at the booth. Every year the Alaska pavilion was better than ever, with more traffic than the year before. As we visited other booths at the show, we noticed 'organic' farmed salmon – the fillets were white and pasty looking without the artificial additives. It did not look appealing at all. This is when I tagged the line, "Farmed salmon is an industrial process." Honestly, I was always disappointed with the Norwegians for turning so heavily to farming seafood. They had come to Alaska and taught us how to fish (my father and I learned how to catch and clean halibut by a great Norwegian fisherman), and like Alaska had done in the past, they over-harvested their fishery resources. But instead of taking the steps that Alaska had done to rebuild the stocks and manage the fisheries for long term sustainability, they chose to go the route of farming fish, replacing what had been a natural process with an artificial and industrial method. Hence my term, 'industrial fish'.

Immediately following the Brussels show, we had a one-day session scheduled with EAS representatives from Europe. Someone had gotten the bright idea that we should consider Europe all one market, and they were making the case that we should consolidate all our programs into one – and that all the cooperator groups should just be a part of one big European program. So, it was our job to make arguments against this idea with EAS. We watched several groups make their case, explaining that each market has its own specifics needs, challenges and cultural sensitivities. Daniel, Elise and Roger all stood up and explained how their programs worked, and the challenges that they faced trying to cover the multiple country programs in each of their markets. I followed up by pointing out that we had made the bold decision two years previously to move in the opposite direction than what was being proposed. The Europe program had been one giant program in the CMS, with all the same constraints and opportunities. I explained how this had made no sense it all, considering the very broad and diverse cultural tastes and eating habits from one point of the continent to the next. Brits eat canned salmon, while the French liked to eat chum salmon fillets, and then the Spaniards liked salted cod. Therefore, we had committed to doing the extra work of breaking the European program into three components. We had tripled our workload with all the metrics to track, but we felt it was a worthy effort to do a more impactful and measurable job in the marketplace. Our arguments were well heeded, for we never heard another mention of the idea after that.

Right after the meeting, we said our goodbyes, and Sherry and I boarded a train bound for Germany. We were heading to Hannover to spend a couple of days with the family. It was a joyous time. My aunt drove up with our cousins from southern Germany, so we had a large portion of the family together. My cousins were in their late teenage years, and they both had long dreadlocks, and had a real Bohemian look to them. They look so ragged and stoned that I nicknamed them 'The Glimmer Twins'. They were indeed a sight to see – but a lot of fun, nonetheless. I had never been to Germany in May, so we were in for a special treat, as the May Day celebration was about to commence. My grandmother's house was located in a little town on the outskirts of Hannover named Olper. And just up in the street in Olper they were having a very fine May Day celebration, with a Maypole, and lots of beer and great German food. It was quite a festive environment, and just down the street my uncle had a friend that had a tradition; every Spring for the May Day celebration he would haul his palm tree outside onto the front patio of his house. So, we were invited to help. The palm tree was amazingly large – it must have been at least 10 feet tall, so tall that it could only fit in the high stairwell in his house. So about six of us turned the tree sideways and hauled it outside. I still wonder to this day how large that palm tree must be, decades later. We spent the rest of the day, drinking and eating way too much.

Chapter 39

A Trip Down Under

T he following month, some good friends of ours were getting married. I had been invited to be one of the groomsmen, and they were having the wedding in the Los Angeles area. It was perfect for me, as I had to join a trade mission to Australia right after the wedding, and flights to Australia originated in Los Angeles anyway, so it would work out perfect. And Sherry planned to go on a cruise ship with another friend to Mexico, so it worked out great for everyone. Except that I managed to catch the crud on the way down to the wedding. By the time we arrived – which was the day before the wedding, I was sick as a dog, and had to go straight to bed in the hotel room. All the guests were staying at the same hotel, and it was filthy and rundown. As I lay in my room, I looked around at the headboard – it was crusty and stained terribly – I could only imagine what from. I did not want to even sleep under the covers, and when Sherry came to sleep, she slept in her clothes. And the bathroom was in terrible shape; there was literally a paper clip holding the chain on the toilet flush handle together, which was easy to spot, as there was no lid on the fill tank. It would come loose after every flush or two, and then I would have to reattach it. The next day was the day of the wedding, and I was feeling a little better, but not quite 100% yet. We were out in the hallway, comparing notes with others about their rooms. They all said that they were just as rundown –

one person even said that they had rats or mice running in and out of the walls.

But the wedding – it was a beautiful affair. They did a wonderful job arranging it, and all the guests had a fabulous time as we all danced into the night. The next morning Sherry got up early to leave on her cruise, and unfortunately, she caught the crud from me – which she had for most of her vacation. As for me, my flight did not leave until 8 pm that night, so I went out to the airport that morning to sit and wait for Molly to join me from Seattle. I was there so early that they would not check me or my bags in. I literally had to sit downstairs in the baggage area for hours until one of the airline employees took pity on me and got permission to check my bag in early. The flight to Australia was the longest flight I have ever been on – it literally took 20 hours to fly from Los Angeles to Sydney. And when we got there an hour ahead of schedule, we had to circle the airspace until they would open the airport. Australia has some of the most stringent quarantine requirements I have ever seen. No food or beverages to be brought in – period. And they made us pull our batteries on our laptop computers to scan them separately. They were definitely not letting anything in the country that might be invasive.

Sydney is a beautiful city. The opera house and the harbor make for a very picturesque setting. For this mission we were joined by Monty Wood, who was the VP of Canned Sales at Harpoon Seafoods. Monty was very accommodating, and he took us out for dinner that first night. He decided to turn in, and Molly and I went out to get some drinks and see the sights. We drank and talked, and then she joked about how I was trying to get her drunk to seduce her. We kept drinking and laughing, and then the next thing you know, she was running off to the bathroom to puke. After she was done getting sick, she joked again about me trying to get her drunk so I could get in her pants. Of which I replied, "If that were the case, then that is not the reaction I was looking for." The next day we went to visit one of the largest canned customers in the world – James East. Poor Monty got chewed on by them so bad. They were giving him crap about not being innovate enough with shelf stable products. And to prove it, James East showed us their new line of skinless, boneless canned product. It was made from Alaska salmon, and the can had a pull top lid, and was inverted to sit upside down on the lid – to go along with the whole 'Down Under' theme Australia is known for. Monty bantered that there was no way they could be competitive by building such a product in Australia, but the James East reps insisted that would be the case. I couldn't help but feel bad for Monty– he was a nice guy and had no control over the type of product format the industry put out.

The following day we flew to Melbourne and paid a visit to another major canned distributor. Again, they talked about the need for our industry to innovate the product format, as consumer tastes were changing. And then out came the quality reports – and they were not complimentary. I think that there are a lot of industry members that believed that you can take a poor-quality salmon and can it, and no one will know the difference. But these customers definitely noticed; they had definitive reports that tracked the quality of the product from all the major Alaska suppliers. This was another wake-up call to us that the industry needed to work on raising the quality standard.

As usual, I was spending a lot of time working on reading and answering emails, as was Molly. When Monty saw us working on our laptops at a coffee shop, he asked us why we were spending so much time on it. We asked him how he could go an entire week out of the office without answering emails. His reply was that when he gets back to the office, he deletes all the message in his inbox – with the exception of the messages from his boss. He said that if it was important, his staff would send the message again. We were dumbfounded when we heard this – that was definitely some 'old school' style management. While we were there were performed several retails audits. It was very clear that our skin and bone in the canned format was losing market share. On the top few shelves was the new formats – farmed salmon in sleek foil bags; it was all skinless/boneless, and flavored – all kinds of different flavors. And on the bottom shelves was good old Alaska salmon in half-pound and pound cans. The words came back to me from my days at Magic Mermaid, "Our best customers are in the graveyard." Yup, times were changing, and the old format did not have the appeal it used to. This when we found a James East pink salmon can that had a OSB label and a 'Product of Canada' seal on the top of the can. Since it was OSB certified, we knew the product originated in Alaska. But since it had been canned in Canada, it wore the maple leaf seal. This was again another demonstration of the failure of a proper traceability system. Why couldn't the industry standard be to have two statements on the product? ' Product of Alaska. Processed in Canada'. The concept is so simple, but it is still not being done to this day – which just continues to confuse consumers.

During our visit one of our reps, Phil, was kind enough to take us to an Australian Rules Football match. The Sydney Swans were playing Melbourne – one of the biggest rivalries in the country. I have never seen such a game. It was like a mix of American football, rugby, and soccer. They run, they pass, and they kick the ball, and the oval-shaped field is huge. It looks like one of the roughest games I have ever seen – but fun to watch, nonetheless.

Chapter 40

Bouncing Between Continents

My schedule was busier than ever. As soon as I got home, it was time to get right back on another plane. It was the beginning of June, and I flew to London for a few press luncheons. The Queen Mum had died just days earlier, and I found myself landing in a nation that was in full mourning. There were to be millions in the city to pay their respects the day I arrived, as the Queen Mum's remains were to be on full procession throughout the heart of the city. The activities were about to take place when I arrived, and I even got to watch the Queen's motorcade drive by me on the freeway during the drive into the city center. It took forever to get into the city center, as my hotel was just across the street from Hyde Park. I checked in, met with Daniel and we quickly proceeded to the park to watch the spectacle. And what an event it was. The streets were lined by the thousands. As we walked across the park, into the view came a formation of planes. It was a single Lancaster bomber, flanked directly behind by two Spitfires – all WWII era planes. It was moving to watch as they continued to circle the center of the city while the procession made its way. There were mounted guards, and members of the military forces, and the Queen's Guard, marching along in succession as the Queen Mum was paraded through town to pay last respects by all. It was a very emotional moment for the people to say goodbye to a queen that had lived through both world wars and reined throughout one.

I was not home for long again after returning from England, for it was time to us to launch our first major (and turns out last) promotion in Korea. JK had set up a chef contest and a booth at the Seoul International Food Expo – right in the middle of the first ever soccer World Cup in Asia. We had some fun negotiating this promotion, as our co-sponsors wanted to give away major cash prizes to the top three winners ($5000 for first place, $3,000 for second, and $1500 for third) – this was to lure in more top chefs. I had to explain over and over again to the sponsors that we could not use government funds for cash prices. And we went round and round to the point that I thought that we must cancel the event. Finally, I was able to convince them that we would bait- and-switch. We would cover their sponsorship costs for the event for the amount equal to the cash prizes, and they would furnish the cash. When running government marketing programs, one must find a way to get creative!

So off to Seoul, I went for the show. As I was flying through Narita airport in Tokyo, the USA was playing South Korea in a heated match. And to our surprise, there was not a single TV in the airport that was broadcasting the match - even though Japan was a host nation too! So, I made my way up to the United VIP lounge and plugged in my computer to dial into ESPN. These were the days before broadband, so all we could get were text updates of the match – but people swarmed around me anyway to stay updated. It might be pretty low tech now, but having such functionality at that time seemed state-of-the-art. I arrived in Seoul at night. It was hot and humid, and as I made my way through the city, one could see the revelry in full swing – it was packed with tourists from all over the world, sporting their country team colors. I had arrived two days before the kickoff of the event so that I could support a state mission that was being led by the Governor's wife, First Lady Peggy Ryan. I was beat with jetlag when I woke up the next morning but was called up anyway by her staff to meet with dignitaries. Besides being a little foggy that morning, it was an enjoyable experience. The First Lady was quite a gracious person, and I enjoyed helping her efforts (she even sent me a thank you letter afterwards for my participation – she was a real class act). In the fact the Alaska State Office had an Alaska promotion going on in the hotel that were was staying at, so it made for a wonderful boost to our efforts to promote seafood.

And what a hotel it was it was the connected with the COEX Exhibition Center. I had never seen anything like it. It was a complex that covered at least 4 or 5 city blocks. On the backside of the hotel, there was a huge open pavilion, with a temporary amphitheater with for viewing World Cup matches. It was composed of a giant half circle of stadium seating that faced three huge screens wired as one, with a stage as well. I found myself stopping and sitting to watch games on a regular basis – this was the life. And the rest of the complex was amazing, underneath the entire complex was a multi-level mall. The selection of stores and food courts was stupendous; I got lost more than once trying to navigate the giant labyrinth. And on the other side of the compound was the COEX Convention Center – where the Seoul International Food Expo was taking place. Conveniently our chef contest was taking place there as well, so it was one of easiest commutes to a show I had ever had.

I still had one day before the expo started, so I went to one of the soccer matches. I was able to watch China and Turkey play. I had worn my white Germany jersey for the fun of it, so I fit right in with the Chinese fans, as they were wearing red and white colors. It was a lot of fun to be at a World Cup match, as I have never been to another since.

The next day the show started, and we set our exhibition booth up. GS had ordered a small display case, and we were not sure how we were going to get all the fish laid out in the display. So again, my creativity kicked in. I laid the halibut down on the bottom as a platform, then I stacked the salmon all around him, and then I placed the king crab in the center on top of the halibut. It was a little crowded, but at least this way all the major species were on display for all the visitors to see. The show had several really cool items on display. Since it was a cooking show, there were a vast number of booths that were preparing food, as well as magnificent displays that were made of food.

The next day we held the cooking contest. There were several great recipes made from Alaska seafood, and as the contest came to a culmination, I made an obligatory speech, and then we handed out the prizes to the top three winners. The World Cup continued to be in full swing, and I toured the town at night, watching all the crazy fans from all over the world.

Friday arrived, and as I worked out at the hotel gym early that morning, I could not help but notice that crowds were beginning to assemble in the COEX Center square outside. As I made my way to the exhibition center, one could see Korea fans in red shirts starting to camp out in spots all across the square. People continued to pour into the area all throughout the day. By the time we finished that day of the show, the square was becoming totally packed with people. In fact, there were so many be the early evening that the back entrance to the hotel had been locked shut to keep the crowd from pushing into the building. I went upstairs and changed out of my suit and went outside to watch the fun. Korea was playing Portugal that night in the final group stage match, and the locals were get worked up into a frenzy over the game. It was a wild match to watch. Portugal was highly ranked and heavily favored, but then early in the match one of the Portugal players received a red card. Then another Portugal player received a red card; while they continued to play valiantly with a two-man disadvantage, Korea scored a goal, and then held on to win the match. And then I watched the whole town go nuts. People by the thousands were cheering, laughing, and celebrating all over the place. A sea of humanity dressed in red swarmed the streets in elation. It was one of the greatest celebrations I ever witnessed.

The last days of the show winded down, and it was getting close to depart back home. GS invited me for a drink and then gave a beautiful and thoughtful going away gift – a World Cup watch, shaped like the Seoul stadium. To this day, it is one of my most treasured possessions from my journeys while at ASA. I departed the next day for home. During the flight from Seoul to Tokyo I experienced the worst weather that I have ever flown through. The 747's air frame shook horribly as it drove through a terrible storm. I sat right behind the left wing and watched it shake in tremendous fashion. The turbulence and violent shaking were so severe, that as I watched, I expected one of the motors to break free from the wing itself. Even the flight attendant seated in front of me looked worried – I started to wonder how much more the plane could take from all the bad weather. It seemed like forever as we pounded through the cloud banks. And then we finally started to descend to land. The clouds were thick, and we could not see anything until the landing gear was down, and we were in final approach to land. I expected to see the rice paddies of Narita to appear below, but instead, suddenly water appeared. This was not Narita – instead we had been re-directed to land at Haneda.

It appeared that the storm was just too severe, so several plans had been sent to land at Haneda, as they were all lined up in rows on the tarmac. There we were, stuck on the tarmac at Haneda for about three hours. After the first hour, people could not stand the delay any longer, and they got up out of their seats and began to move around the cabin, and using the restrooms. After so many hours of just sitting and waiting for the storm to pass, we finally took off again and headed to Narita. By the time we arrived, I had missed my connection back to Seattle. I stood in line with so many others to change flight reservations, and by the time I got to the desk they told me I had two choices: I could stay overnight and wait for the next day's flight to Seattle, or I could take the midnight flight to Hawaii, and then fly to San Francisco for a connection home. I chose to take the redeye to Honolulu to get home. There were other U.S. passengers that chose to take the flight to Hawaii as well. They were complaining that they had an eight-hour layover in Honolulu, as I only had a three-hour layover. I laughed and asked them why they were so upset? With eight hours they actually had enough time to go to the beach or do some sightseeing! I would not have enough time to leave the airport. And good thing anyway – as soon as I arrived in Honolulu, I received a call from EAS. The new federal grant budget had arrived, and they wanted me to allocate the funds to the various activities immediately. So, I sat there in one of the airport gardens and crunched the numbers – along with a Mai Tai or two to sip. At least I got to enjoy a little Hawaiian sunshine and the scent of the ocean air before I headed to San Francisco for the trip home.

Chapter 41

A Changing of the Guard

I came back into the office the next day to be told that Betty was resigning. She had fought a valiant battle against cancer the year before – which she had won. But after ten years at ASA, she had had enough. She told us not to worry, that there was a good candidate for the position. I thought that a little strange, as she had just announced her resignation, but was indicating that there was a replacement already in the wings. I could not help myself; I assembled the other two program directors – Kylie and Larry – and we agreed that we should talk to the Chairman of the Board about encouraging the Board in taking it's time to recruit and select a suitable candidate. I called Sam and begged for he and the selection committee to take their time finding a suitable candidate. I, as the other directors did, assured him that we could run the programs proficiently during the absence of an executive director. Betty caught wind of what we did, and she called me to chastise me. She told me, "The body wasn't even cold yet, and you guys are calling the Chairman to position yourselves." But I responded right back, "Betty, I really loved having you as my boss, but you are leaving, and we still here really have to think about the future." I think she understood where we were coming from (she probably would have done the same thing). It was hard to watch her go. I had developed a strong relationship with her, going back to when she found my misplaced resume in May of 1997. In those five years -especially the last two — we had grown close. I had always respected her as the leader of the organization. She is the one that had been so supportive and had given me the opportunity to rise to where I had at ASA. She would be sorely missed (at least by me). We were now heading leaderless into unchartered territory. Initially, I thought about applying for the job, but I did not want to weaken my marriage by moving to Juneau. And while part of my ego yearned for the title and role, I really felt deep down inside that I was not quite ready for it.

There wasn't much time to ponder the circumstances. We were preparing the receive the first ever, Chinese reverse trade mission group. Ocean had worked hard with Bobby and Billy for months to set up this mission. Much time had been devoted to select and vet the members for this team — which came from companies across eastern China. We greeted them in Seattle and started by conducting trade meetings with industry members. Instead of parading them around to a few companies, we set up a conference room at the Westin Hotel downtown and set up 'mini-booths' so that each of the mission members could have private visits with salespeople from the various companies. They were all really fun people to work with — all of them were very polite and very excited to be visiting the USA. After we finished the sessions in Seattle, we took the group to Petersburg. It was time for Ocean to shine, as she was taking us to her hometown to visit. We toured most of the processors and held a nice reception with the community in their town hall. Petersburg is a beautiful little community, with one of the most diverse set of fisheries of any coastal community in Alaska — if not the most. It was a great opportunity for the mission members to see and learn about a very broad line of different seafood products, and the weather was very nice. I had never been to Petersburg before, but my parents had told me about it, as my mother had flown to Petersburg – pregnant with my brother — to marry my father.

Ocean of course was happy to be in her village, sharing her community with all of us. And she had reason to be proud – Petersburg is probably one of the most diverse coastal towns in Alaska. At least at that time, it probably had the broadest categories of different seafood species – followed by Kodiak. And I must admit, it was fun to enjoy the flavor of this wonderful little community – the 'little Norway' of Alaska.

Next stop was Kodiak. We took the trade members through a number of different processing facilities, just as we had in Petersburg. And we also held a reception, where we invited the mayor, council members, and key members of the seafood community. It wasn't quite the town hall reception we had in Petersburg, but we still established some good connections for the Chinese delegates. It was funny to watch the Chinese in action. They would ask the most inappropriate questions at the reception. They would ask people, "Are you married?" And they would ask women how old they were, and men how tall they were (even the short ones). Many of the locals were so taken back by the line of questions that I had to pull the trade members aside and explain to them that while their intentions were to make conversation, their questions were considered inappropriate by U.S. cultural standards.

After we had conducted all the activities in Kodiak, I let the mission continue back to Seattle without me. I stayed behind to spend some time with Sherry and her dad in Kodiak. We did some sport fishing and spent a little time with family and friends before returning to Seattle. As a result of the mission, not only were we able to establish immediate sales to China, but we also realized a secondary benefit. The Chinese mission members had built their own internal 'Alaska-China' network between themselves, and many of them partnered for joint purchasing and assist each other with their business. Overall, it was money and time well spent. While the reverse missions were always very time and labor intensive to organize and commence, we always considered them a 'labor of love', due to their substantial benefits and results.

July snuck up on us, and it was time for one of my favorite activities – the Seafood and Technology Expo in Tokyo. It was Ocean's first trip overseas, and she was very excited to finally visit Asia. After the previous experience with Nora, and due to Ocean's limited exposure to the global market, I had not allowed her to do any international travel until I felt she was fully prepared. But she was by this time! Away we went to Tokyo, to stay at the Nikko Nikko Hotel in Odaiba. This was the same spot that Bobby and I had visited the year before during the previous show, but the view never got old to me.

It was the middle of the summer, and as usual, it was very hot and humid. As always, the trade show was being held at Tokyo Big Site. Ocean was very excited to see all there was to see in Tokyo, and during our spare time I tried my best to show her as many sites as possible. The World Cup had just ended, and there was still a lot of merchandise in the stores, including a giant World Cup soccer ball in one store. I tried and tried to talk the store salesperson to sell me the ball, but I failed. The show went well; once again we partnered with the Maine Lobster Board and U.S. Seafood Export Council to have the 'Great American Seafood Alliance'. We had a lot of seafood samples at the booth, and we even did a co-promotion with 'Alaska' brand beer, which was a special edition beer brewed by a local brewery. It turned out to be another great promotion – but the last one we ever did with the Maine Lobster Board and U.S. Seafood Export Council, as both organizations dropped their programs during the following year. But it was a great first experience for Ocean, and it demonstrated her ability to integrate with the team.

We returned home to Carl. It had barely been a month, and already the role had been filled. Carl Peterson had just been confirmed as the new Executive Director for ASA. His entire career had been in the Navy, and he had just retired as a Vice Admiral. While had not worked directly in the fishing industry, he had heritage, as his grandfather had been a gillnetter on the Columbia River, and his mom had worked in a cannery in Oregon. I promised myself that I was going to do whatever I could to support my new boss. Almost immediately we were called up to Juneau for planning sessions.

We were all trying to get to know each other and feels things out, and then he pulled me aside the first day and told me, "I don't want you talking to board members without me." A chill went up my spine. Betty had always encouraged me to speak with the board meetings privately. And why not? Several of them I had known for years already, and it was just natural for me to speak with them openly about the program and the organization. And now I was being instructed to not talk with people that I had known and worked with for years. It made me fill sick inside. The message to me was that I was threat. Why? I had not applied for the Executive Director role, even though I had been encouraged by many. But after receiving the recognition from the Board during that Spring session, I can understand how it would cause some to speak of my meteoric rise in the organization. The words of my previous mentor, Larry Black, began to wring in my head. When he first met me at Magic Mermaid, he nicknamed my 'Mercury' (he called me 'Merc' for short all the time after that), because I was "...rising to the top." And here I was again, at that moment a shining star, burning brightly. In retrospect, I could understand Carl's apprehension of my growing influence and presence. Still, I was never the same from that day out during the rest of my career with the organization. That was the high-water mark of my feeling that everything was moving in the right direction. From that point on I started to proceed with growing caution of my future. I couldn't help but reflect that maybe I should have applied for the role. One will never know what might have been. Instead, Carl's entrance cast the first shadow on the road to a different era that was about to unfold for me.

Right after I came back from Juneau, Sherry had her second miscarriage. She had been so excited to be pregnant, and suddenly, again, almost an exact year later, she was once again losing the child she had been carrying. It was devastating – for both of us. We morosely shared the news with the family, and then our friends. And then I shared the bad news with those in the office. It was not the news we had hoped for. It had been almost two and half years of trying to have a child, and we all felt a sense of loss. We started wondering if we would ever be able to have children.

Chapter 42

Juan Diego's Wild Ride

In September, we traveled back to Japan to Shiogama; we were joined by Devin Carpenter, who at the time was a VP of Sales for United Fish; Together we traveled to Shiogama for another Seafood Rendezvous event. Between Ocean, Devin and I, we actually provided some very extensive presentations, covering the full gamut of all the species and fishery management systems of Alaska – it was probably the most comprehensive informational presentations we ever provided during all my years at the organization.

And then there was Jimmy – he was a local Japanese lad and trade member that just loved US culture so much. He was pretty intense, and he actually showed up at the consumer event with a wrestling belt band, and bandana on his head, and no shirt. He was quite the sight to see, running around, talking about how much he loved Alaska – what a sight to see! And then there was the food; the residents of Shiogama were quite the utilizers of Alaska seafood – especially whitefish products. There were a huge variety of kamaboko products made from Alaska surimi – including a wonderful fried cake that was infused with pieces of ginger. It was so tasty that I declared I would eat it for breakfast every day – and I probably would – if it were available back in the US.

The last night there we hit the bars after the trade dinner, and we sang karaoke and danced all through the night. I found myself dancing with a group of old ladies, laughing with them until the wee hours of the morning. The next day I of course woke up to a massive hangover, compounded by the lack of sleep; as usual, Han usually had every day packed with trade activities. So it was up to get some coffee and breakfast, and head out for the day. One of the visits was to the kamaboko plant that had made those awesome fried cakes. A few nights earlier when we were having a drink, he had showed us his remote camera feeds on his phone – he could watch everything that was taking place throughout the factory, day or night. And considering it was 2002 – that was quite an impressive piece of tech to have on a phone. The owner was a third-generation kamaboko producer, and the plant was very impressive. Many of the systems were automated, and he changed the cooking oil almost weekly, and donated it all for use at food banks. He was one of the most renowned kamaboko producers in Japan, and the products he produced were definitely a 'cut above' the standard offerings.

The last morning in Shiogama I got up early. The word had been shared about my miscarriages that the wife and I had suffered, and the local trade members had decided it would be good to take me to the Shinto shrine. Shiogama is renown throughout all of Japan as the center for fertility, and the Shinto shrine in the town is dedicated to the rites of fertility. So, it was only natural that I would be invited to the shrine, in order to help resolve my issues back home. It was a very solemn visit for me, and I took it very seriously. We paid homage and said prayers, and I made sure and purchased a fertility talisman before leaving. It obviously helped, as our first child was born the following summer, and three more followed after that! So if you are ever needing to boost your sense of fertility, be sure to visit the shrine in Shiogama.

We departed Shiogama that day and traveled to Sapporo for an Alaska Seafood Lunch Party. It was similar to the past events we had conducted there, but this type we focused on kids. Regardless, the activity was already starting to lose some steam. It was the third year in a row, and the novelty of the concept was wearing off. While it was fun to work with the kids, we ran through the motions and made our way home. That was the last time we did a Lunch Party in Sapporo. Every time I went back to Sapporo, I always remembered the events of 9/11 – those moments of disbelief and grief that I experienced there will haunt me the rest of the days of my life.

Shortly after I returned home, and I was playing soccer with Sherry and our friends Jesse and John Norman. I was driving us all back from the game, and I said that the game we played was a lot of fun. Jessie replied back jokingly, "Yeah BJ, we like it when you visit." That is when it hit me how much I had been gone. I was so caught up in all the travel and work, that I had forgotten to recognize what a toll it was taking on my personal life.

But I did not have much time to dwell on those thoughts. Just a few days later we were on a plane bound for Vigo, Spain for the CONXEMAR Trade Show. Sherry had come with us for this trip, and we were actually going to try and take some time off after the show to do a little sightseeing. The show was the typical affair, we had a standard corner booth, and Clint Houston had brought a couple more Alaska and U.S. companies to the show – this year they had a Wild West theme, with an old saloon-style bar, and a couple pretty booth muffins to hand out brochures and drinks. One thing about Clint – he was always trying to be creative and make the shows fun.

The day after the show we grabbed a rental car- a little Opel with a five-speed - and headed south into Portugal to Avierno, which is the major cod processing center of the country. The highways in Portugal were brand new and were very impressive. We traveled at a high speed on these new roads, slowing only to pay tolls about every 20 miles. We were heading south to visit Juan Diego, who was a major cod/bacalau processor who purchased a lot of cod from Alaska. His plant was incredible to see. Bacalua is a centuries-old method of salting and drying cod in order to make it shelf stable. It is truly an art to create this product, which was made very apparent by touring the plant. He had taken old school methods, and combined them with new tech. He was still drying product in the sun, just like his ancestors had done before, but he was able to use new methods to set the perfect salinity levels for each specific market (Italy likes higher salt levels than Brazil, etc.). Not only was Juan a great businessman, he was also quite gregarious and had quite the sense of humor – as we were about to find out.

After the tour, Juan invited us to come have dinner and stay at his condo on the beach in Porto. He asked for us to follow him into town, so we headed towards the freeway. It was Friday night, and traffic was starting to stack up heading into town. But that didn't slow Juan – in fact he started speeding up. Now we had watched some pretty crazy driving in Portugal and Spain before – but nothing like this. Juan was pushing it to the limit, accelerating like crazy, and swerving back and forth, weaving between all the lanes. And here I was, trying to follow him. I had done some pretty crazy high-speed driving in my youth, but this was right up there with it. I could not afford to lose him – we had no mobile phone to call him with if we lost him, so I had to do everything I could to stay on his tail. He flew off exit ramps, and through tool booths – right through the automated card lanes – I had no choice but to follow him through. And then he would head right back on another freeway, swerving all between the traffic, driving like a total maniac. Molly and Sherry were holding on for dear life the whole time, and Molly's husband muttered, "What the hell is he thinking – how are we supposed to keep up with him." But I did – no matter what maneuver he made, I stayed right behind him. Finally, after about twenty miles of sheer madness, he finally pulled over to see if we were still behind him. He actually looked surprised to see that we were still there – almost as if he was trying to lose us. But then he started up again, driving his Mercedes SUV as fast as he could. We continued to follow him for quite a few more miles, until we were finally driving along the shoreline on a two-lane road. Still, he kept speeding along, with no end in sight. Then all of a sudden a motorcycle shot out in front of me, taking a left out of an intersection. I slammed on the brakes, screeching to a halt – just narrowly missing the cyclist. I had had enough – I screamed out, "Fuck!" I could have killed the motorcyclist; it was that close. But still I had to collect myself and keep going. So I poured on the gas again to catch up to Juan. Fortunately, he did not have much farther to go, and just another mile or two down the road, we arrived at his condo. After that night, we always referred to that adventure as 'Juan Diego's Wild Ride'. To this day, when we talk of it, Molly always said, "I don't know how you kept up with him that night." Juan was a gracious host. We stayed at his condo for the night, and then toured Porto the next day, hen headed back to our hotel in Vigo for the night.

The following day we visited Santiago do Compostela, which one is one of the most elaborate and impressive cathedrals I have ever seen. Built about 800 years ago, it is supposed to be the burial place of the apostle James the Fisherman. If you are a devout Catholic, it is supposed to be one of the great pilgrimages to be performed – in fact it is supposed to be the third most holy cities for the Catholic faith, after Jerusalem and Rome. And it was apparent when we arrived, in the front of the mighty cathedral was a line of followers that were lined up to touch and say a prayer at a 'holy spot'. And one could not be prepared for what they were to envision when walking into the main cathedral. Above the pulpit was a humongous gold-encrusted angel. It made me reflect on the opulence and power that Catholicism wielded for so many centuries. We spent hours touring this grand complex and then headed north to La Coruna, which is located on the northwest corner of Spain. As we drove north, I could not help but note all the evergreen trees in the region; if one did not know any better, they would have thought they were in the Pacific Northwest in the U.S. – the climate was that similar. La Coruna was a quaint little coastal city, but most of the most impressive landmarks to see was the Tower of Hercules. The tower was actually an ancient lighthouse that had been built by the Romans back in the first or second century, A.D. It was claimed that it is probably still one of the oldest existing lighthouses in the world, having been a point of reference for mariners for almost two thousand years! We toured the tower, watched the sun start to set, and then headed back to Vigo to rest and get ready for the tour home.

Chapter 43

Avoiding Issues

After this trip to Spain, I finally had some downtime. It was time to get caught up on all that was happening at home. About a month later, and we were preparing for another trip to China. It was time to attend the China Seafood Expo in Qingdao again, which almost always meant a journey through Shanghai. Sherry came for this trip, which turned out to be her last trip to China, or anywhere overseas for that matter. She, Ocean and I arrived in Shanghai, were we met up with Kerry, who at the time was still the President of the Fisherman's Cooperative. Kerry had been in the industry forever and was a solid travel veteran. The trip did not start out well. Kerry had flown through Beijing for some reason, and the airlines managed to lose his suitcase. The poor guy didn't even have any underwear, so we took him shopping immediately. And I took the opportunity to have a couple of suits made at a tailor overnight– including a really sharp-looking green one. Unfortunately, none of the suits were made with the right fit, and I refused to pay for them. There was no time left to make new ones, and we headed off to Qingdao for the trade show. Han's staff, Haruko and Kim, flew in from Japan to learn more about the Chinese program, and traveled with us to the show.

The show was the standard situation. We had a brightly colored display that drew in a crowd – to the disdain of the Norwegian Fish Export Board, who had spent a lot of money again on sponsoring the show, but was not getting anywhere near the promotional traction that we were getting. For the second year in a row, we had a picture on the front page of the local newspaper – this time with Kim holding a king crab. The rest of the show went about without too many more surprises. We performed some trade visits on the way out, and then headed back home.

Right after we returned, it was time for another Board meeting. A few Board members told me that they had expected to see my name in the stack of applicants for the executive director position and inquired why I had not applied. I jokingly replied, "Because my wife would divorce me." Sam was still the Chairman, though his term was coming its end. We had a great session with the Board, and we appeared well positioned at that time. It had been a watershed year, with a change in leadership, but we were still well positioned. Sam made a very profound statement during this session. He said, "In all the years I have been with ASA, I have never seen a stronger team to execute the mission. It is as if we have a tuned-up Ferrari in the garage, but we have no gas in the tank." What he was alluding to was that we needed more funding from the State to accomplish the mission. ASA had been running on fumes for some time – which was sheer madness, considering the importance of the industry to the State's economy. These words would come back to haunt me again and again throughout my remaining years at ASA.

Right before the holidays started, Mitch Cantrell quietly contacted us and faxed a confidential memo that had been sent to a processor that he had intercepted. (Mitch had been a big ASA supporter in the past and was now working for a Canadian canned processor). It turned out that there was a new entity that was being formed from a new source of funding. There was a war chest of funds that the U.S. Department of Commerce had gathered from seafood import tariffs, and Senator Red Clemons was working to have the funds dedicated to the marketing and promotion of Alaska seafood products.

The memo identified that there would be a portion of funds that would be allocated to processors in direct proportion to the amount of salmon they had purchased during the summer season. The funds could be used to cover cost of business, including retail slotting fees, which looked to be a form of direct corporate subsidies.

A new Governor had been elected in the Fall - Terry Baxter. Terry was also known as 'Terry the Bank', due to his prior career in the banking industry. He had been the other U.S. Senator for Alaska for over twenty years, and his long-standing relationship with Alaska helped to sweep him into office. And with the new Governor came a new wave of appointees, including our new Commissioner of Commerce, Kevin Steele. He paid a visit to us at the Bellevue office with Alena Brown, who was now the new Director of the Governor's Office for International Trade. We flooded them with information about the organization and its accomplishments, and then they went on their merry way. Alena had been an owner of a hotel in Cordova and had been a big supporter of the Governor during his campaign – but we were still scratching our heads as to why she was going to run the international trade programs, as it appeared she had no background for it.

It was January of 2003, and Ocean and I were in Japan for another Seafood Lunch Party event. We were at our hotel, going over plans for a promotion, when we received a call from the Governor's Office. They were inquiring what we thought of conducting a promotion in Korea, which was being driven by Moon Park. She was a friend of First Lady Baxter, and somehow squeezed her way into being given $1 million to promote Alaska salmon, and she was targeting Asia. Moon had approached me about this subject a month or two earlier, and I had encouraged her that if she wanted to support new efforts, that she should focus on Taiwan and Korea, since we no longer had a program in the prior country and had a very limited presence in the latter. So, she had picked Korea, which was natural, considering she was originally from Korea. This potential activity they were inquiring about sounded kind of hokey, as it seemed like they wanted to pay industry members to get together to provide subsidies for sale of Alaska products with key distributors, including elements of the military - and they wanted us involved smack in the middle of it. I politely declined, reminding them that our organization's charter forbid involvement in such activities. And good, thing, as I heard later that the promotion was a total disaster.

In February, the Alaska Fish Council was officially formed on the Congressional Record. There was to be a fund as high as $75 million to use to promote Alaska seafood, and this new entity would have a board comprised of 10 members that represented the industry – harvesters, processors, distributors, etc.. Ronald Reynolds, an employee of the National Marine Fisheries Service, was hired to be the Executive Director. We could not help but stand back and scratch our heads? Why didn't they just give the money to ASA – or at least a portion? Weren't we just re-inventing the wheel again? And then I remembered the memo Mitch had shared. This new entity could run unrestricted, with no oversight by the State of Alaska, without the limits of a charter such as ours, which restricted use of resources for direct corporate subsidies, or individual brand promotions. But I did not have much time to think too deeply about it. We were building the new CMS plan – which was always so consuming.

And was busy enough, but then suddenly I was called to fly to Juneau for a visit to the Governor's office. Carl escorted me up to the 'Third Floor', and memories came back of time when I had been sitting next to Betty, in the same office, explaining to the Chief of Staff why we need to conduct a program in Australia in January. This time it was different faces (Alena and the new Chief of Staff), but the same office with the same table. We were being pressed again to support the Korea activity that we had been approached about back in January. I shared my concerns, especially the support of anything that appeared to be a branded promotion, or to support military operations; we could not use money to support any one brand. I never liked to say no to helping, but I did my best to explain how it could possibly jeopardize our relationship with EAS, and we could not afford to do that. When I got back to the office the next day, I wrote a very thorough, 'thanks, but no thanks letter to the Governor's Office, very carefully explaining the reasoning that the ASA should not participate. It worked, and we escaped having to tiptoe through that minefield.

At the Spring Board meeting in March, Harry Pitts was elected the new Chairman of the Board. I had known Harry for years and years, as he was from Kodiak, and my dad had fished and tendered alongside him for decades. I knew him all too well. Harry was fairly well educated, but had been a harvester most of his career, so he did not appear to have the 'polish' of the previous Chairman. Still, it was a harvester's turn to be Chairman again, and so there he was. We finished the new CMS plan right after that – we were asking for more money than before -with the exception of the Korea program. Not much trade was taking place in Korea, and our arguments were ringing true. While I felt bad for our rep, Gang Sung, we just could not get the industry to support the effort.

Chapter 44

A Lesson in Persistence

We had a big trade mission to Europe planned for the spring, so we invited the new Chairman to join us. I headed over a couple days early before the mission was to start. I flew into Frankfurt, and my brother picked me up and drove me south to the Bondesee, to our aunt's house. We were to meet our grandfather's second wife and her son, my father's half-brother, for the first time. It was Easter weekend, and we all gathered to celebrate, just the day after my birthday. My aunt, my cousins, and my uncle, were all there to enjoy time as a family. It would be the only time this side of the family was ever together again, but it was really great to get introduced to a part of the family we had never met before. The next day my brother and I left to head to the French border to visit with some of his friends. We enjoyed a very scenic drive through the Black Forest as we headed to Strasbourg, situated right on the French and German border. My brother's friends were quite amusing they lived on the French side of the border. I found it funny to watch them park their car on the French side of the street and watch them walk across to the German side to buy cigarettes, as they were cheaper. After a day or two of hanging out – including visiting the town of 'Bitche', we headed to our uncle's home in Hannover. I spent another day or so with the family, and conducted some retail store audits, before heading to Hamburg by train.

In Hamburg I met up with Elise, Bobby Olson, and our new Chairman, Harry. The first day we paid a visit to Simon Dunkel's smoke factory, in Bad Homburg, which was on the outskirts of the city. The factory was deceiving – from the outside it looked like a 150-year-old barn (which it originally was), but on the inside was a state-of-the-art processing and smoking facility. Dunkel was renown as one of the most high-end smokers in all Europe. In fact, his product was served at the European Union headquarters in Brussels. He was a big supporter of Alaska and was always in attendance at our trade show booths. I always joked that he was our PR department for Western Europe. He had heard that my wife was pregnant with our first child, which was supposed to be a girl. Having three daughters himself, he shared with me a very wise German saying, one that I was to never forget: "A boy has a boy, a man has a daughter." At the time, I did not fully recognize the power of these words. But as time went on, the words would truly resonate.

The next day we took the train to Bremerhaven, where we toured processing facilities throughout the harbor, including viewing fresh iced cod and redfish that just arrived from the North Sea, which was just sitting in bins, unprocessed. When I inquired why the fish had not yet been processed, the buyer said they like to let the fish sit around for a day or two, giving it 'more flavor'. I guess everyone has their own tastes. The following day we visited our old friends, Heinzmanns. We toured the plant, and Bobby provided a technical presentation again. That evening we went to the Hamburg media center and conducted a press dinner. It was a wonderful venue, and we were scheduled to give a presentation, but first, our new Chairman was to give a speech. He had written a long, drawn out five-page speech; I reviewed it just before the dinner started and tried to convince him to pare it back. But he was undaunted and decided to try and read the full speech. He made it about a page and a half, droning on, reading all the words verbatim, while the audience struggled to keep attention. It was getting painful to watch, as he started to break a heavy sweat, and after struggling through another page, he finally threw the speech down and said, "Well, please enjoy our seafood, thanks for coming." The poor guy – I tried to warn him.

The next day we headed to Lorient by train. Lorient is a fishing town on the coast of France. We had some interesting trade meetings there, negotiated a promotion or two, and then toured the local fish market. We headed back by train to Paris, crossing through the historic town of Le Mans, where they have the famous 24-hour race. We happening to be sharing the train car with a couple dozen schoolchildren. After we stopped at the station, we heard a commotion, and then we quickly heard that someone had committed suicide by jumping in front of our train. After sitting for what seemed like an hour or two we were told that we were going to have to disembark from the train, as it was now a death scene for investigation purposes. And it turned out that the remains of the victim were directly underneath our car. Of all the train cars, it had to be the one with the schoolchildren. So, we all left the train, and walked over to the next platform to wait for the next train to Paris. It arrived shortly after, and then we packed ourselves on board. There was no room at all, and people were crammed throughout the walkways, stacked in with our luggage. It took a few hours to get there, but it seemed liked even longer as we stood cramped together the entire time.

After arriving we checked into our hotel and went and grabbed a cab to go shopping for supplies and get something to eat. We hopped into a taxi, and I again tried to get into the front seat, which we were denied – as we had been so many times before. I had forced my way into the front seat more than once in Paris, so I always thought the driver was just being a self-absorbed prick for their pet dog (many Paris taxi drivers have dogs in their car), or to keep their jacket from being disturbed. Finally, after all these years, this taxi driver informed us that passengers could not sit in the front seat, as it was against the law. All this time, no one had bothered to explain it to us! Once this was revealed, we were more than happy to pile into the back seat.

After we stopped in a Monoprix to get some groceries, we sauntered our way to a bar off the Champs de Elysees. The strip was always such a tourist site – and it was always so crowded, with drinks that were way overpriced. So, we decided to step into an establishment down the street, a little off the 'beaten path' -which turned out to be a path to a goal that took three years for me to accomplish. The venue appeared to be a normal bistro, with a bar and a restaurant. We walked in and ordered a few beers. Then I went back up to the bar to get another beer, and I noticed the look of disdain from the bartender. Like some Parisians, he was rude to me because I looked like a tourist. I told myself right then, "I am going to make this guy my friend – whatever it takes." For the next three years, I would stop in the place every time I was in Paris. The next time I came in – about a year later- I brought Molly with me. As soon as he saw us walk in, he rolled his eyes in recognition. Molly got us off to a bad start right away on that visit, asking him, "What is good here to eat?" He spat back defensively, "It is all good!" Without realizing it, she had insulted him and his menu. Still, we tried to let things chill down, and ordered some items off the menu. Then Molly went and spilled her red wine all over the table. The bartender's eyes rolled in his head when he saw the mess. Well that did it – we were not getting through to him on that trip!! And we didn't. So I kept coming back for the next few years, every time showering him with smiles and politeness, no matter how badly he would treat me. And then it finally happened – during my last visit to Paris . Bobby Olson was with me and I explained the whole situation to him. So we walked into the establishment, once again. And again, we were greeted with disdain – but a little slighter after all the visits. Bobby and I sat down at a booth and ordered some drinks. Then when the bartender came back, Bobby introduced himself, and started to ask him about what type of food that was served at the restaurant. And it finally happened the man let his guard down, and he started to explain the culinary processes of the establishment. As his demeanor started to ease, we invited him to sit down and have a drink with us. And he did! Finally, he let down his guard, and he began to share the story of his family and how long they had owned the restaurant. And then started to share his life with us. He even went downstairs and personally cooked a special dinner for us. After all those years, I had finally reached him. I had resisted reacting to all his rudeness all those years, showing him nothing but respect and deference. It was another example of the power of persistence, and the strength of the human spirit.

The next day I paid a visit to Notre Dame. I had walked by the grand cathedral several times, but I had never gone inside. I was still pretty shaken up by the suicide that had taken place the day before. The victim had been someone's parent, someone's child, or someone's sibling. Somebody had loved them, and now they were gone – and it weighed heavy on my mind. So, I walked into Notre Dame, and I took in the grand paintings, ornate woodwork and relics. And then I went and purchased a candle, lit it, knelt, and prayed for that poor person's soul. It was a solemn moment, but it allowed me to move on, and release the heaviness I had been carrying.

A day or two later, and we were off to Brussels. It was another great show, and the Alaska pavilion was as thriving as ever. Han was there, visiting the show for the first time to gather some insights. And Carl was there for his first visit as well. It was the beginning of our efforts to cross-pollinate between the various international programs, and Han was taking it all in. While Brussels has always been known for its pickpockets, it was especially bad during this visit. We noticed people standing close to the cash machines, so we were very vigilant. And Molly's husband had his wallet stolen that first night. The situation was so bad, that the following morning – in broad daylight, I was followed by a group of young men -about six or seven. I could tell they were going to roll me and take my video camera, computer bag and all, so I started running, They started running too – but then I ran even faster, down the street, and into the Metropole Hotel to hide. I waited inside for 15 -20 minutes; long enough for them to give up the chase. Then, when it finally looked clear. I carefully walked back up the street to my hotel.

On the last day of the show I was riding in a taxi with Carl. I explained to him that our European reps were losing a lot of money due to the swing in exchange rates – about 30% in what they had received before, due to the weakening of the Dollar against the Euro. But my pleas fell on deaf ears, as he did nothing. So, I decided that I was going to have to take matters into my own hands to rectify the situation.

Next thing I knew, it was the middle of May. I came into the office to find a memo from EAS that revealed their concern about our failing market position in the Australia market. They were issuing a warning that unless we made major changes to the program, they were going to remove the funding for the program. I called EAS right away to talk at greater length about the issues with the program. It was pretty clear – we were still selling the same old canned product into the market that we had for decades. There had been no movements by the industry to innovate the product format - we were still promoting the same old product, the same old way. I told EAS that I would do what I could to sway the board to address this issue; I was warned that if we did not make immediate changes, the funding would be removed from the program, and it would cease to exist. I faxed a copy of the memo to the Juneau office, called Carl, made him aware of the situation, and requested a teleconference with him, the Chairman, and Kelvin Nash, the Chairman of our international marketing committee.

A day or two later we had the teleconference. I had made my case to Kelvin before the call, and I was trying to get him to support my position, that we needed to address this and make radical changes to the program if it was to survive. We started the call, and I made my case. But Harry and Carl did not grasp the sense of urgency in the message. The talked about tabling the discussion for the next board meeting in 5-6 months. Again, I tried to tell them that they needed to act immediately, but they acted totally dismissive of me, and totally shut me down. And then Carl asked Harry to follow up with him on the call when they were done - and then it was done. I was furious. I was so angry that I picked up my chair and almost threw it through my office window. It was bad enough that they would not listen, but their dismissive attitude is what pushed me over the edge. I went outside for a walk and cooled off, and then I made the phone call to EAS. When I shared the news about the lack of willingness by our administration to respond, they politely and curtly said, fine. They were going to issue a memo that they were eliminating the federal support for the Australia program. A few days later the memo arrived. They were pulling the plug, and there was nothing I could do about it.

I had to shift my attention to what I could fix. The SARS epidemic had started in southern China at the previous year. It was in full swing, and there were serious concerns about travel to Hong Kong for the HOFEX show. Bobby and Ocean were attending a show in Australia, and they were supposed to circle back through Hong Kong for the show, but I made the decision that it was not worth the risk. Considering all the health advisories and concerns, Ocean was compliant with my determination. But Bobby was persistent, he said he didn't care of he got sick, that he was willing to take the risk. So, I asked him to call me and we spoke. I made a very simple argument. I said, "You may not mind getting sick, but do you want to bring it home to kill your kids?" My approach worked – he conceded to forego the show and return home.

Things were settling down, and I finally was going to have some time to spend with the family. Sherry was pregnant again and considering the last two attempts had resulted in miscarriages, we were being quiet about it. But by now, she was about seven months into it, and she was starting to really show. So I decided it was time to stay close to home, and let the others do all the traveling.

Chapter 45

A New Life

It was a very hot summer, and Sherry was getting bigger and bigger by the day, and more and more miserable with the heat. We sent Ocean to Japan with a few industry members. I always did my best to attend the show, but it was time to let Ocean spread her wings even more to manage the Asia programs. Meanwhile, I was driving everyone crazy at home. Women start 'nesting' the house to get it ready for a baby. Guys – we go nuts and want to build something. It was not enough that I had been building a banya (an Alaska-style Russian steam bath) in the backyard for the two previous years (which I finished two years later) – no I had to go, and sand and re-finish my classic 1954 Wagemaker boat right before our first child was to be born. It was a beautiful old boat – made of mahogany. It even came complete with a 1959 Johnson Super Seahorse with an electric start. I was channeling my nervous energy, probably my own way of keeping occupied before the birth. But it also served a purpose – I was refinishing it so I could sell it. It was time to make room for the next phase of life – a life with children. Sherry thought I had lost my mind, working on a boat right before the birth. But I was undaunted. Every night after work I would work on it into the darkness. After just a week or so, it was done. I posted it on eBay, and it sold in a matter of days.

July was getting hotter and hotter by the day, and the child inside Sherry was growing so large that you could see the butt poking out one side of her, and it was moving all the time. Sherry was overdue by a few weeks, so it was time to take her to the hospital to induce labor. The house was ready, and so were we, and off to the hospital we went for the birth of our first child. We knew it was a girl, so I chose the name Karina, and Sherry had chosen Amie for her middle name – the same as hers. It was a long day as Sherry was induced and given an epidural for the pain. And then the delivery began. Things were okay at first, but then Karina became stuck – her shoulders were so large that she was having trouble clearing the birth canal. First a few assistant nurses were called in, and they were still having difficulty clearing the child, so they started calling for more help. The next thing I knew there were 8-9 nurses in the room trying to help. It was really starting to worry me. And then she finally delivered. Sherry was in a terrible state, she had suffered a lot during the delivery, but managed to have the strength to tell me, "Go see her, and make sure she is okay." And I did, and I looked upon our little Karina, and I held her hand and spoke to her softly. Everything calmed down, and we were moved to a recovery room with our new daughter. And all the family and friends began to visit and meet the new child.

That night I helped Sherry to get around as she was in terrible pain. She did not sleep well through the night, and the next day she was trying to rest between all the visitors. The day was going well, and we had a few quiet sessions in between visitors, so I went down to the street to get a newspaper and a Jamba Juice for each of us. I will never forget the moment when I returned. It was just before 6 pm. I came back into the room to find Karina laying in Sherry's arms, crying and turning purple. Sherry said, "She won't stop crying". I realized right away from the Karina's purple color that there was something drastically wrong. Sherry could not sense the danger, for she was under the influence of morphine and was not lucid. I ran out into the hallway and yelled for help from the first nurse I could find. The nurse saw Karina's distressed state, grabbed her, and quickly rushed her to a nearby treatment room. The child's state was critical; her oxygen saturation levels had dropped to the 30% level. She was provided oxygen, but her levels were not recovering, so they rushed her immediately to the Pediatric Intensive Care Unit on the top floor. By then, I had Sherry out in the hallway in a wheelchair, and all she could do was ask, "What is wrong with her?". But I had no answer. We followed them as they flew down the corridors to get her there as quickly as possible.

By the time we got upstairs, little Karina's situation appeared graver than ever. She was crashing, and they could not get her oxygen saturation levels to increase. But the staff in the ICU acted quickly and stabilized her situation; they intubated her, placed her on a respirator and provided an arterial oxygen feed through her umbilical. In hindsight, we were so fortunate, as it was just 6pm – time for shift change – and there were two entire sets of staff there to treat her. She was stabilized, but still no one knew what the cause was. They immediately summoned the cardiac specialist that was on call, and she began to conduct an echocardiogram. We had been watching the actions of the ICU with amazement, but since she was stabilized, they encouraged us to return to our room to get some rest. After an hour or so the cardiologist came to our room to explain Karina's situation. By then Sherry's parents were there, as were her sister and brother-in-law. The doctor began to draw a normal heart on the whiteboard, and then she drew a picture of Karina's heart – the right side of the heart did not work right, because the atrium (the upper chamber) had grown too big, and the ventricle (the lower chamber) was too small. The defect was called Ebstein's Anamoly, and it was very serious, and there was no guarantee that she would survive. Here was our first child, not even 24 hours old, and she might die? I could not help myself, I began to weep at hearing the news. She then explained what caused Karina's oxygen levels to crash. A child receives oxygen from the mother when in the womb, but when they are born, within a day or two there is a duct called the PDA (patent ductus arteriosus) that closes as the system switches over to the child's own cardiac system. When Karina's PDA had started closing, oxygenated blood was no longer backflushing from the pressure from the left side. Essentially the right side of her heart could not pump the blood to the lungs to get oxygenated. We were all mortified upon hearing the diagnosis, and after the cardiologist left, we began to pray for dear Karina's survival.

Karina clung to life through the night and was transferred to Children's Hospital the next morning for observation and treatment. Her legs were so long, and she was such a long baby, that when they brought her into Children's the nurses took a double-take at her chart. One of them said, "There is no way this is a two-day old newborn – the child looks like it is six months old. It was true – she was so long that her legs were hanging over the edge of the 'baby tray' that she laid on. The team at Children's' put her on prostaglandins, which kept the PDA open, but made her shudder and shake. It was hard to hold her and watch her little body tremble in such a manner, but there was no other way. The head of cardiology disagreed with the original diagnosis, and we sat for about a week in the Neonatal Intensive Care Unit, while they ran more tests, waiting for the determination. Ebstein's Anomaly is the rarest of all birth defects. It was so rare that the staff could not remember when they had last had a child there with the malady. But it turned out the original cardiologist had been correct with her initial diagnosis. Karina had Ebstein's – Type 3, which was severe, but not as bad as Type 4, which was almost always fatal. But Type 3 was very serious. Type 1 and 2 can be repaired to make the right side of the heart work to various degrees. But with Type 3, the right side cannot be repaired, and the only procedures are to bypass the right side and allow the unoxygenated blood to return to the lungs by gravity. So, the left side of the heart does all the work.

We were fortunate to have a great cardiac surgical team at the hospital. There were two head surgeons, and they always operated on a child together as a team, to make sure the highest success rate. We consulted with one of them, Dr. Quinn – he was a very warm and caring man. He would say, "if it were my child, I would do this...". His sense of empathy made us very confident. So, it was time to get Karina started on her first surgery. They were going to insert a Blalock-Taussig (BT) shunt to replace the PDA, so that she could come home until she had grown enough for the next surgery. For a newborn, the heart is the size of a strawberry, so it makes it very challenging to perform surgery. The surgery went well, but the recovery was a nightmare. The hospital was in a expansion phase, and there was very limited space, so we were sharing a room with three other children. I stayed night's with Karina, as Sherry spent days with her, and was totally worn out from the entire ordeal, and needed to get some rest. My God, they were long nights. I was the only parent that stayed the night with their (we would not let Karina to be left alone for a minute -throughout all of her surgeries and stays) So here were three other babies/toddlers, waking up and screaming, all through the night. The one next to us would keep spitting out its pacifier and then would cry for it to be put back in. The nurse would come by every now and then and put it back in. I wasn't supposed to do, but I started putting the child's pacifier back in to keep it from screaming. And one of the children on the other side would make very disturbing groaning noises all night long – sounding almost like a wild animal. It was terrible. But we endured for those five nights while Karina recovered. I would sing the Animals' song 'We Gotta Get Out of This Place' over and over to her, while I would rock her in my arms.

And then finally, we brought her home. Finally, after 2-3 weeks, our child was finally coming home. Sherry took her into her room, and quietly held her and rocked her in her rocking chair, and I filmed her and we both began to weep tears together – mixed both with joy, and with worry for our dear daughter's future. But I was bound and determined that she would survive. I had studied every article about Ebstein's Anomaly I could source, every spare minute I had. I also created a medicine planner, to make sure Karina was receiving her long list of medications, with the proper dose, at the proper time. If she was asleep (she was quite lethargic after first coming home), I would run her feet under cold water in order to wake her to take her medications. Sherry thought I was cruel to do such a thing, but I was letting nothing get in the way of Karina's survival – even the child herself.

In one fell moment, this child had changed my perspective on life. I had been driving myself so hard and was always ready to leave town and fly all over the world at a moment's notice. Now suddenly, I did not want to leave. I wanted to stay home and share every moment I could with her. Every minute all of a sudden was a precious commodity. Since we were unsure of her survival, we decided we would celebrate her birthday every month – which we did, for the entire first year of her life.

During my extended leave due to Karina's needs (I started calling her Kari Bear, because she would growl at night while I held her and rocked her), my staff and contractors had to conduct the annual strategic planning session without me. Carl did compliment me that I had created a great team, as they carried on without me with no problems. I was truly proud of all of them for managing the program in my absence. And they were all so happy to do it, as they had all felt so bad after hearing the news of Kari's challenges.

Chapter 46

Researching the Past

I could only hide from work for so long. During our Export Marketing Committee meeting in August, I was successful in convincing the committee to officially change the name of the Export program to the International program. My argument was strong. For years there had been confusion about the Export program. People would contact us and think we oversaw exporting product for the industry. I had even had a harvester call me and say, "I heard that you'll export my fish for me.". So, we changed the program to 'International. As well we changed the names of our program representatives from 'Foreign Promotion Agents' to 'International Promotion Representatives.' And we changed the committee's name from 'Export Promotion' to "International Marketing'. I may have seemed like I was being anal, but it was time to re-brand the program.

Next was a board meeting in Anchorage in September. There weren't too many changes, and things were plodding along under the new leadership. A few days later, I went to Europe to conduct trade meetings in northern France and Belgium with Elise. As we drove around to all the different sites, we began to talk about how Carl was hired so quickly. While Betty might have put him in front of the Board as a candidate, it turned out it was Sam that had made the call to hire him without really grilling him on his abilities to manage a marketing program. Elise had questioned Sam how he could make such a snap decision as Chairman, of which he had replied, "Who am I to question him, (Carl) he was an admiral." What great reasoning that had been.

Meanwhile, Molly attended Conxemar without me, as I was trying to reduce my travel schedule with the new child, and I had the China Fish Expo trade mission in October. For that mission we started in Shanghai as usual. After having an introduction dinner with our mission members, most went to bed to rest from all the jetlag. But I was revved up to go this time. Bobby and Billy asked, "Where would like to go?" I was sick of seeing all the high class, new establishments that were supposed to impress me. I wanted to go local. So I replied, "I want to go where you go – when I'm not here." The looked at me and said, "Really?" of which I replied, "Damn right!" So, they took me to Mao Ming Road. It was a fun little strip of bars on a road in the old city, with 'province girls' (street hookers from the provinces) lined up and down the street. I had a blast. We drank and danced and took in all the nightlife that the locals enjoyed. The next night we hosted a trade reception in the evening. And afterwards we talked Ocean into going back to Mao Ming Road with us.

Bobby's cousin, Gina, joined us this night. She had previously owned one of the bars on the block, and was good friends with another one of the bar owners. So, we took Ocean into this bar/club that was packed with 'working girls'. Rarely had I seen a bar where the women outnumbered the men so much. We drank for free the whole night and I danced with 'working girls' the entire night with Ocean. Shortly after arriving she had a few drinks and relaxed, and we were having a lot of fun. I had many women hit on me, but Gina was always getting in their face when they would offer a price – and laugh at them and insult them. The next day, Ocean was feeling bad, and said, "Oh my God, we were dancing with a bar full of prostitutes last night!" And I replied, "Yeah, it was a lot of fun, wasn't it?" That was definitely one of the more memorable experiences of that trip. They held the Expo in

Shanghai that year. It was a different venue, but it did not seem as enticing as Qingdao, and I remember Hans Heinz lost his wallet at his booth at the show to a pickpocket – which kind of left a bad taste in our mouths. It was not the best way to end the trip.

In early December, I conducted a research trip to Germany to interview some men that had served with my grandfather during World War II. I had spent months arranging all the meetings for this trip, so even though we had Kari at home, I was committed to finish this activity. My brother met me in Frankfurt, and we drove near Bonn to meet with the first veteran, a 90 -year- old man named Vogt. When we arrived, we expected to meet an old man sitting in a chair, waiting for us. Instead, we found him in a suit and tie, standing outside like an excited young boy, very enthusiastically waiting to see us. He had served as a fellow officer during the early stages of the war. The had attended War School together, and he was able to confirm a lot of our grandfather's activities during the early stages of the conflict. He had confirmed that he had served with the Legion Condor in Spain in 1936 for six months (there were no official flight records of this in most cases, as these were supposed to be secret operations). And he confirmed the time served in France, as well as during the Battle of Britain. He said our grandfather fell sick with appendicitis and had to be moved to Berlin for treatment. They never saw each other again through the remainder of the war, but remained friends afterwards.

For our next stop we met up with our aunt, who would help us to translate. We went to Braunfels, in southern Germany to meet with Dr. Karl. He had served under our grandfather during the later stages of the war in Bordeaux-Merignac. He had been a young man then, and he said he admired our grandfather, as by then he had been promoted to the group commander. He shared an example of his character. He said one night he found an enlisted man asleep at his post – this was a very serious offense - the penalty many times was to be shot. But our grandfather had woke him up and kindly said, "Please don't do it again." The doctor shared some great reflections, and let us view his flight log (which he had somehow kept), as well as showing us his library – which included one of the most comprehensive Luftwaffe book collections I have ever seen. He was also very generous in sharing some wonderful copies of images of our grandfather.

Our next stop was to Stuttgart, where we met with Schmidt. Schmidt had also been a young man while he served under our grandfather, and their air group had flown north to Norway in the autumn of 1944, and my grandfather had approved for him to return home to Stuttgart to get married. It was a dangerous journey, first by boat, and then by train across Germany, where he was constantly being attacked by Allied forces. He made it home for his wedding. And during the day of the event, right after the ceremony, a bombing raid started. The wedding party fled into the bomb shelter for safety. After the attack, they emerged to find the entire banquet for the reception had been destroyed, but they all laughed, because they were still alive. It reminded me that sometimes we forget to be thankful for the little things in life. Shortly after, I returned home for our first Christmas for Kari. It was a joyous occasion, and were thankful for our blessings to have this new child with us, regardless of her challenges.

Chapter 47

A New Board

It was time for another action-packed mission to Japan. We started with another Seafood Lunch Party and Seminar in Sendai. But this time we had a special guest - the very well-respected Sato of the Sato Culinary Institute. After that we visited Osaka and Kobe in order to negotiate some retail promotions. After that we headed back to Tokyo to perform for a TV cooking show in which we were educating children about seafood. I demonstrated how to fillet fish, and then we had the kids get together with their parents, to learn how to cook Alaska seafood meals together.

In February we sent Ocean to Hong Kong to conduct a trade mission, which was to make up for the activity that was canceled the previous year due to the SARS epidemic. I was happy for her, since she finally had her chance to experience Hong Kong, especially without having to be in my shadow. Besides, I really needed to stay home to work on the new CMS application, as well as to prepare for all the impending changes. By this time the Alaska Fish Council was getting into full swing – with a war chest of about $50 million. A first round of money had been allocated to salmon processors, based solely on how much salmon had been purchased the previous year. So, while some major buyers like Magic Mermaid and Harpoon received over $1 million, on the other end of the spectrum small buyers were allocated $11.

What the hell was somebody going to do with $11 to promote their brand? It was ludicrous – and laughable. They stacked the board with some old guard fisherman – Hal Cedar, Tommy Johansen, Geoffrey Shaftman and Calvin Meadows. And they grabbed two small processor representative – Mike Tucker and Hal Cale. And then there were the cronies – Hendrix McDonell (lawyer and lobbyist) and Senator Joe Clemons, who was all of a sudden the President of the Alaska Senate (go figure) – no favoritism here, even though his father, Red, was the one that had make sure the money was allocated for formation of the organization. And then they also added Carl to a seat as well, which many of us thought would be a conflict of interest, since he was running the marketing organization for the state. Indeed, it would seem that the planets were aligning in a different direction.

ASA was changing before my eyes too. At the February board meeting there were two plans being proposed for the re-formation of the ASA Board. There was Senator Justin McLaughlan's plan to scale the board back from 25 seats to 15, with seven seats to processors, seven seats to harvesters, and one layman swing vote. And then there was Senator Joe Clemons' plan to scale the board back to seven seats, with five processor seats and two harvester seats. The ASA board voted for the Justin McLaughlan plan. But somehow the Joe Clemons plan was the one that was to be adopted. I was sorely disappointed with what I saw coming, but I had to focus on completing the CMS, as I was about to have my hands fuller than ever.

Kari was scheduled for her second heart surgery in late March, the Glenn Shunt procedure. With this procedure they detach the superior vena cava (the vein that returns blood to the heart from the upper portion of the body) from the heart, and reattach it directly to the pulmonary artery. She looked miserable the first day after the surgery, as her head, and her whole upper body were massively swollen from the drastic changes in blood flow and pressure. But she endured and was recovering well. But after a week or two, the fluids in her chest area were not reducing like they should. So they ran some tests and procedures and realized that she had a fold in her blood vessel next to where the surgery was performed. Dr. Quinn – who had performed the surgery again, was beside himself. He apologized, but he said there was no choice to resolve the issue than to perform another surgery. So, she had to have her chest cracked open again, and start the whole recovery process all over again. The doctor apologized again and said that in all his years of practice this had never happened. In my attempt to comfort him, I told him, "Well, this way you will always remember her." She endured the surgery again, and another couple of weeks in recovery. I was working hard to finish the new application and juggle her surgeries and recovery, so I did not get much rest. By the time she came home, it was late April. Considering all of this, I did not go to Brussels, and stayed close to home to assist Kari with her recovery.

May arrived, and so did our new ASA Board. They appointed one of my old bosses, Dave Simpson, CEO of Magic Mermaid to be Chairman. Brendan Robins, Senior VP of Harpoon, would be another board member, and there was Daryl Lloyd, President of Crystal, Josef Watts, President of Captain Hook Seafoods, Calvin Meadows of Uyak Bay Cannery, Chad Fry, harvester, and Benny Bernal, harvester, who would serve as Vice-Chairman. Basically ASA was going 'back to the future', stacking the board with a majority of large processor interests. The harvesters had voted to remove their tax assessment to ASA, so they really weren't paying into the organization directly anymore. It was a disruptive trend, but it was happening.

Next we were asked by Carl to assemble presentations in order to educate the new board members. He called it the 'Captains of the Industry' session. So off we went, building presentations to educate the new body. Dave Simpson could not make the session, so we had to follow up the next week with a special session at Magic Mermaid headquarters. So, I found myself back in the Blue Room at Magic Mermaid, being berated by Dave. After I presented, he said, "You could shut down the Japan program down tomorrow, and nobody would notice a year from now." I kept my mouth shut, but I thought to myself, "If that's the case, why are we do we even have an international marketing program?" But I endured the criticism, and kept quietly moving along.

After the first educational session, Calvin made a visit to our office. While my conversation with him was friendly at first, he started questioning the activities of the international program. He started telling me that we needed to do more for canned salmon (and of course, he owned a stake in an old cannery). I could not help buy reply, "Calvin, you could give me $ 20 million a year to promote canned salmon, but you are asking me to promote black and white TVs in today's color plasma/LCD market. He responded with, "Maybe they (the consumers) don't realize that there is a benefit to buying that black and white TV. Maybe the color plasma puts off radiation." I couldn't help but think, "Ahh...another one in denial." He was missing the point. The intention of my message to him was that the product was okay, but the format was antiquated. Shelf- stable products are a viable market, but the packaging and format sorely needed to be updated. Again, we were going to have to start the education process all over again. Obviously nobody was paying attention with what had just happened with the termination of the Australia program just a year earlier.

But there was not much time to ruminate on these new developments, there was plenty of immediate attention required for our existing program. Once again, we were going to receive an increase in funding – we were continuing our upward trend, receiving $3.6 million in federal funding (a 150% increase compared to the budget four years ealier), making our total budget $4.5 million. And we were continuing to make progress in the markets – exports continued to increase at a healthy rate, with a total value of over $1.8 billion by the end of the previous year. I do remember sharing with Ocean that I was frustrated and was seeking better leadership for us. Her response to me was prophetic; she said, "BJ, I think that you are looking for someone to lead you, but it's not coming. I think that you need to look inside yourself for that." Those words would resonate with me for some time.

But there was little time to ponder the situation. I needed to run off to London to help conduct a number of trade meetings, as well as support another press luncheon. We had a very important work session with a small company called New York Seafoods. They had been working with frozen Alaska chum salmon for a few years, and now they were interested in launching fresh sockeye salmon promotions in the UK retail sector. A number of our industry members dismissed the idea, stating that the UK would never be anything but a market for canned salmon. But the staff at New York begged to differ. So Daniel and I started work with them to help in sourcing fresh product throughout the summer. Our theory was that by promoting fresh during the summer months, it would ultimately lead to frozen sales on a year-round basis. It was worth a try.

It was very hot that June, and the Euro Cup was taking place in Portugal. Being so close, I was very tempted to fly to Lisbon to attend some of the matches but realized it would be very expensive. My last night in London I was on my own. So, I headed over to a pub down the street from the hotel. I was having a cider and I couldn't help but notice that the guy sitting next to me looked very much like Dick Van Dyke, the famous actor from Mary Poppins. I had to share that he looked like the actor. He started to laugh. What an insult it had been to Englanders to have an American play the lead male role in that movie, with a fake British accent an all. But he was not too offended. He began to sing to me all kind of limericks. One was better than the next, but there was one that was so memorable that I will never forget it: "I'll be up your flue in a minute or two, and I do know where to find it. It's in the front, it's called the cunt, and the asshole's right behind it." It turned out the guy was a major bank vice president, and he was getting very drunk. He talked me and his buddy into going to a 'gentlemen's club' (strip joint) with them. But there was one slight problem. When we arrived at the door, I was stopped due to their dress code. I had jeans, t-shirt, and tennis shoes on. So, my new friend gave me his jacket to wear, in order to appease the bouncer at the door. But it was not working. So, I bid them goodnight and headed back to my room to prepare to head home the next day.

Chapter 48

A State of Flux

Ocean and I had also been busy getting prepared for another major reverse trade mission. We were bringing a new group of Chinese trade members to Alaska – a group larger than ever there were eight trade members accompanying Bobby and Jane. The group looked like another fun bunch of people, including Mr. Chu. Bobby had pointed him out to me and said, "See the guy with the black teeth? He had $200 million dollars in sales last year." That was the beginning of some fun times with Mr. Chu. He was such a personable character. He liked me so much, he said to me at first, "When you come to China, I will have four girls pouring you drinks." By the end of the trip, the number had increased to 24 girls. It seems he was really enjoying his time with us.

After the usual meetings with industry members in Seattle, we shuttled the group north to Cordova. I had never been to Cordova before, so it was going to be a new experience for me as well. The weather was beautiful, and the first day there was the longest day of the year. Salmon from the Copper River fishery kept flowing in, so the group was able to see some very high-quality fish being processed. That night we wound up at one of the local bars, and we drank well into the night. The Chinese kept on buying me beers, and would say, 'gam bei' which in Chinese means 'bottoms up'. I got a little drunk and started sharing jokes and funny saying. One of my favorites was a saying I had heard by a native woman years before. She said, "You buy me whiskey, I love you." I shared the saying with the Chinese members, and they broke out in laughter. But sometimes things do not translate well, as I was to discover a couple days later. We continued to drink until midnight, and then we made our way out to the center of the street to take pictures of the team under the midnight sun. Then a police car approached. They slowly crept up and asked what was going on. I had Ocean quickly guide the rest of the group off to the hotel, while Bobby and I explained to the cops that we worked for the State and were conducting a trade mission. They laughed and waved us along.

The next day we took the long drive up the Copper River Highway to visit the Child's Glacier and the Million Dollar Bridge. The glacier was magnificent to see. As we stood just across the river from it, every now and then there would be a loud pop or crack, and a big piece of ice would drop off into the river. We also toured the bridge, which was still being repaired from damage that occurred during the 1964 Good Friday earthquake. It had originally been built a century before for the railroad that ran north to the Kennicott copper mines.

We had planned to fly to Sitka the next day, but when we arrived at the airport, we discovered that Sitka was having serious weather issues, and so we had to cancel the visit. We quickly shifted gears and re-routed the group to Juneau. Our Juneau staff did a great job of getting us last minute hotel reservations, including a quick dinner with Carl and some of the staff. The first night there were not enough hotel rooms, so Ocean and I wound up sleeping at Bobby Olson's apartment – she took the couch, and I gladly took the floor. The next day we visited several processors, as well as the Alaska Beer Factory. The head of marketing for the brewery was providing us with a vertical tasting of their smoked porter beer. It was a very strong flavored beer, that do not appeal to most. I asked Bobby what he thought of the beer, and he got a sour face and said, "It tastes like soy sauce." I couldn't help but get a chuckle. At least he had said it when the brewery staff was not in the room.

Lanie had managed to quickly organize a dinner with a few industry members in attendance, as well as Carl and his wife. As I conversed with Carl and his wife, one of the Chinese girls from the mission came up to me and said in broken English, "BJ please tell us again how you ask for the sex with the native girls in Alaska." I was mortified. She had totally misinterpreted my joke from the previous night in Cordova. I had to take her aside and explain to her that she had misunderstood the meaning of what I had said. God, that was an embarrassing situation. That night we hit the town and had a wild time with the group. Having that large of a group was always a challenge, as it was always like herding cats, which required one of us in front, leading the group, and one in the back to keep the stragglers from getting lost, as there were always a couple that would wander off. This night was no exception. In fact, we managed to lose two of the group members. Bobby went out to look for them, but we could not find them. This could have been quite the problem since neither of them spoke English very well. Turns out to be they wound up in front of one of the liquor stores to take pictures with the police, who pointed them the way back to the hotel.

The next morning, we took the group to tour another processing facility to see black cod, and then we sent those that wanted out on a fishing charter – including Mr. Chu – who managed to catch a nice 20-pound king salmon. That night we headed back to Seattle, and watched them all depart back to China the next day. Even with the change in the schedule, we still managed to pull off another memorable activity.

A few weeks later, and it was time to go back to Japan for the Tokyo Seafood Show. Ocean and I both attended the show this year. It was a fairly standard affair. We ran through the motions, including holding an 'Alaskan Night' trade dinner where both Sato and I gave speeches. While I always enjoyed visiting Tokyo, I was happy to head back home, as it was about to be my daughter's first birthday. It was a wonderful party for her – all of the grandparents were there, as well as my sister. We all felt so blessed that she has survived her first year of life.

August that year was very eventful. At the start of the month Elise had a nervous breakdown. I had called to speak with her, and she kept saying, "Everything is ruined". She had been under tremendous stress for months, as her sister had basically lost her mind, and had to be committed to an institution. All the years of workaholism probably did not help much either. But my only concern was for Elise as a person. She clearly had snapped, and someone needed to help her – immediately. I called Carl right away and let him know about the situation; he was in full agreement with my suggested course of action. So my next call was to Molly. She was on vacation right then, and I did not want her to have to break away from time with her family. I gave her a choice, it could be either she or I, but somebody was getting on a plane the next day to deal with Elise. Molly decided to go, and I quickly made her reservations. When she arrived in Paris, she was able to meet with Elise, who was being hospitalized. Molly worked with her other sister, Simone, to get all the business in order at her office, as well as to visit Elise and lend moral support. Simone wound up staying around on a permanent basis at the Paris office after that. Elise took a few months off to recover and get her life back together, and the rest of us stepped up to make sure things kept running smoothly in her absence.

Meanwhile, Ocean was busy working with a photographer to conduct photo shoots in Southeast Alaska. They went out on several different fishing boats to get some shots of fisherman with real, fresh caught fish. I had spearheaded this program months before, as we really needed to update our image media library. Our theme was 'real fish from real fishermen' – kind of a punch back at the Norwegian Fish Export Board, who was displaying images of fishermen in their promotional materials, even though the vast majority of their products were now farmed. We had tried to secure existing imagery, but it was hard to find good images that had not been already been used elsewhere, and a lot of the photographers wanted way too much money per image to have the rights to use them. So, we had decided to just spend the money to hire some photographers to take new photos. In addition to the images from Southeast Alaska, I hired a photographer from Kodiak to capture images of fishermen and seafood from that region. The project was a success, which resulted in a new library of images for the organization and industry to use.

We were also in a state of flux, as the new board members were demanding that the office in Bellevue be relocated to Seattle – preferably in the Ballard area. This was going to create potential commute nightmares for us, as two-thirds of the staff lived on the Eastside. But board members were firm about their wish, so the search had begun, and we were starting to view potential properties for a new location.

Late in August, for the annual strategic planning session we took the international team to Kodiak. Everyone was there except Elise. My father had said that he was going to put on a party for us for the first night – and he did. After arriving to the island and checking everyone into their rooms, we headed up to my parents' house. We had a bunch of activities scheduled for the first day, but look so many other times, we experienced flight delays all through the day, and we had to cancel all the activities. When we arrived at my parent's house, we couldn't believe it - they had a big cooking pot out front, and they were cooking up fresh Tanner (snow) crab, as well as some fresh king salmon.

The next day we conducted processing plant tours, and then held a reception that night with local community members. We had a huge amount of seafood available for everyone to enjoy – but it still probably wasn't as tasty as the fresh, hot crab they had eaten the night before. It was Saturday night, and first we visited Bernie's Bar, where Molly and I sang some karaoke together. Then we all wound up down at the Mecca – the same bar that I had so much fun with the Chinese during the first mission. Everyone in the group was flying out early the next morning, except David, Bobby and Billy. Most turned in after a few drinks, but Ocean kept on going. I stayed with her a little while, but felt like turning in, as I had plenty to do the next day. She asked me to stay with her at the bar, as we had been drinking buddies several times during some of our trips, but I wouldn't have it. I reminded her that she needed to leave early the next morning, but she ignored me.

I found out later that the next morning Ocean overslept and created difficulties for those that were leaving – almost to the point of missing their flight. That next day I grabbed one of my best friends, Ted, and we piled Bobby, Billy, and Roger and his family (they all came with him for a vacation) onto my brother's boat. My brother was out of town, so Ted and I were going to drive it. I made Ted the skipper, and I ran the deck in order to teach our visitors how to fish. We brought a small gillnet with us and bunch of fishing poles. We caught a couple of salmon in the net, but the rest could not catch anything on their fishing poles. But we had another treat in store. My father was taking his crab boat out to pull pots to get some more Tanner crab. So we drove out there as well to let them see a crab pot being pulled. Everyone was having a great time and they loaded all the crab onto my brother's boat, to make it easy to offload. When we got back to the harbor, we pulled the truck down to the launch and loaded the crab into the back of it, and left Bobby, Billy, Roger and his family with the truck, while Ted and I went to tie up the boat in its slip. We were almost done when Rogers's son came running up to us to tell us that there was trouble with the police. We headed over back to the truck, and there was a Fish and Game enforcement officer, asking about the crab. Ted had his subsistence license, but it was not enough to cover the number of crab we had – we had exceeded the limit. So the officer seized all the extra crab and wrote Ted a big fat fine for about $500. My dad and I paid for most of the fine, but more importantly, we were relieved that it did not make the news. We could just see the headline, "ASA Staff Busted Stealing Crab". It was a good lesson to demonstrate to our ASA reps how strict the government was to protect the resources.

Shortly after I returned to Seattle to deal with our website project. We had been working to rebuild the international portion of the site since the Spring. During the summer we had been going back and forth with the Juneau office about where to locate all the international webpages. We were doing a total overhaul of the international site, and we were creating the first ever pages for each specific country program. The administration and the lead webmaster wanted all pages uploaded to one central server in Juneau. This made no sense to us, as each country specific site was dynamic, and need to be regularly updated by the respective contractor. If they were all housed in Juneau on one server, how were our overseas contractors to update the pages quickly and efficiently? So, I devised a compromise. We would create master pages for the international program that would include an international gateway that would be the portal the various country program pages – which would be based on the Juneau server. We put it all together and did the official launch during the Fall International Marketing Committee meeting. It was a big success, and visitor traffic increased tremendously in comparison to the old site.

September would be another busy month. Molly and I were off another mission to Europe. First stop was to Dusseldorf and Koln to attend the InterCool show in Koln. Many people asked us at the show where Elise was, and if we were replacing her. But we assured them that she was on extended leave with her family and would be back soon.

I took a day or two of personal leave to visit my family in Germany, and then I flew to Paris and met up with Elise. I spent a few days with her to see how she was doing. She was on a new medication and was starting to get back on track again. I was happy to meet her sister and see that she was getting back up to speed again. After two days I headed south to Vigo to join Molly and Roger for the Conxemar show, and then returned home.

Chapter 49

The Fellowship is Broken

We had another Asia trip coming up for the Fall. We were going to hit Japan and then China. As part of my cross-pollination initiative, we were having Molly attend the session in Japan. Ocean and Molly were supposed to fly ahead of me to conduct a promotion in Tokyo, and then I would join them a couple days later in Shiogama for another groundfish promotion. Unfortunately, Ocean was out having drinks with friends the night before she was supposed to leave, and she accidently left her passport at the bar. Since she could not get her passport until later the next day, she missed the flight and Molly had to fly on to Tokyo alone. Ocean and Molly had never gotten along well during the past three years together. No matter how I had tried to get them to work together, they just clashed. Ocean had not provided Molly with the itinerary and instructions for the hotel, or where the promotion was to be, etc. So when Molly arrived in Tokyo alone, she managed to find the hotel, but she had no idea where or when the first promotion was to take place. And with Ocean arriving a day later, there was no one to support the promotion. Han did not tell me about this situation until a few weeks later, and so I had no idea what a mess it had been.

I flew over to Japan a few days later and arrived on a Friday. I decided to go out and have some drinks, and I ended up staying out too late. The next morning I slept in late, and woke up to Tanaka's call to my room. Jim and I were supposed to catch the Shinkansen to Shiogama together.

I flew out of bed and made my way to the hotel lobby as quick as I could. Fortunately, there were other trains to catch, but due to me being late, we arrived late to the first round of seminar sessions. Ocean told me later that I looked like death warmed over when I walked in the door. But I managed to pull off some presentations anyway. The event ran all through the next day, and then we headed back to Tokyo. Molly had a tight schedule, so she split with us at that point, while Ocean and I continued onto China for the China Seafood Expo.

The first night of the show, we were having dinner with just the staff and a few of the trade members from the June mission. They wanted to return the hospitality by having us try some local Qingdao food. Bobby and Billy usually had at least two or three assistants at the show by now, so we had a full table. We went to a local restaurant that had very local Qingdao style food. Most of us didn't find the food very appetizing. And then we tried the local China whiskey. It was disgusting – it tasted to me like kerosene, and it made me nauseous. I tried to drink more, but it was just too foul to swallow. We were doing our best to be polite with the food, but it was hard to consume. I was starting to wonder how we could get away from this food without being impolite. Then all of a sudden, this tiny little woman came walking into the room. She bowed to us and said with one of the squeakiest voices I have ever heard, "Mr. Chu would like to invite you to the KTV bar."' We all started laughing, and she began to laugh with us. So, we all got up and followed her out to taxis to go and see Mr. Chu.

Now a KTV bar in China is basically a karaoke bar – but with the twist that it has hostesses. I had almost forgotten Mr. Chu's promises to me when he was in Alaska that he was going to surround me with women to pour me drinks. We entered into the bar – which was more like a private lounge with a big dance floor surrounded with a huge half-circle of booth seats. And there was Mr. Chu, smiling and laughing, and waving us inside. I was the guest of honor, and he sat me down, and started parading dozen of girls in front of us. I was blown away – I could not believe this was happening. But Mr. Chu insisted to pick out 24 girls to pour us all drinks. I wound up having three girls on one side, and two on the other, doing nothing but pouring me drinks and feeding me snacks, and dancing around and petting me. Then Mr. Chu called out a line of guys for the girls to choose from and told Ocean and the other ladies in the group to pick out a dozen guys to pour them drinks and dance for them. We had a blast, and of course there were plenty of 'blackmail' pictures that they took of me – but I never got to see any. I still wonder to this day what those pictures must look like.

The next morning, we were driving together to the expo, and Ocean was very upset about our visit to the KTV bar (even though she had been drinking and laughing all through the night). She kept on saying over and over, "I can't believe it, we were in a whorehouse last night." I tried to explain to her that it was not a whorehouse, it was just a karaoke bar with hostesses. And then Bobby came to my rescue by interjecting with his adorable Chinese accent, "Actually China is a very conservative country, not sex country like Thailand or Vietnam." Finally, Ocean was quiet. I had to turn and chuckle to myself, for what Bobby had said was so true.

The rest of the trip was fairly tame. Mr. Chu and most of the members from the June trade mission came and visited our booth. We had shipped two kegs of Alaska beer over to the show, but they had been stopped by customs agents in Shanghai. Every day we called and worked to get the kegs released, but customs would not let release the shipment. This was the first time that a shipment of beer had not made it. I joked that next time we needed to tape a 'tester' six-pack to the outside of the keg for the customs agents. We were going to have to find a better way next time. The highlight of the show was that for a third year in a row, pictures of our booth were in the front page of the newspaper. No matter how much the Norwegians spent, they couldn't buy that space – it was ours. After the show was over, we flew to Shanghai. This next morning Ocean

flew back home, while Bobby, Billy and I flew back to Thailand. For years Bobby and Billy had tried to convince me to go to Thailand with them. It was very affordable to visit from China – like flying from Seattle to Los Angeles. So, I had Sherry fly a day or so ahead of us to Bangkok, and then we met her there. She had become pregnant during the summer, and she was starting to show, being about 3-4 months along with the pregnancy. After arriving at the hotel, we found her hiding in the room. She had tried to venture out, but all the strong smells on the street were too much for her. It was Friday night, so we talked her into heading down to the Patpong market. We were walking around the night market, and we could not help but notice all the bars full of women – each bar had girls in matching bikinis. In one bar they would be all green suits, the next one pink, and so on. And then there were the vendors cruising the market. They would walk up, yelling out, "Ping pong show, ping pong show.", and they would have a little guide sheet that listed all the different 'performances' I could see. For those that have never heard of it, the ping pong show is watching a women shoot ping pong balls out of their vaginas across the room. There were so many shows to choose from on the list besides ping pong balls. You could watch them put a banana inside, and then cut slices of it with their lady parts. And you could pick so much more – candles, whistles, eggs – even goldfish. Here I was standing there with my pregnant wife, and they kept asking me if I wanted to watch a show. Again and again, I would politely decline. Sherry urged me to go watch the show if I wanted. But I couldn't bring myself to leave my pregnant wife alone to stand in the market down below while I went up to some bar to watch a woman shoot things out of her vagina.

We spent another day in Bangkok after that, and then Sherry and I headed south to Phuket, to enjoy a couple days on the beach. We stayed at a beautiful hotel with a giant swimming pool, and a swim up bar. The workers at the hotel were very friendly people. And the beach was nice too. With Sherry being pregnant, we were limited as to what we could do. She encouraged me to rent a jet ski, or go parasailing, but I felt like staying close to her. Every day, we couldn't help but notice all the old white men with young Thai girls it just looked so strange. The one highlight was that we went and watched the 'katoy' show. It was a performance by 'lady boys' – transvestite men dressed like women. These 'girls' were truly beautiful, and the show was very entertaining. After watching the show Sherry said, "I would be scared to be a man here. The lady boys are more beautiful than the regular women. How could you tell them apart until you get them home?"

After a few days, it was time to head home. We were flying through Tokyo on the way home, and I got the news from Han. She sent me an email and told me all about what had happened between Ocean and Molly at the start of the Japan mission, and how it had affected the promotion. I started to break a sweat as a read her words. Sherry could tell that I was disturbed and asked me what was going on. I thought to myself – enough is enough - for three years the two had been going back and forth, and I had done my best to manage the situation, but now this was really starting to impact the program. When I arrived home, the first thing I did when I arrived back into office was to get things straightened out with them. I called them both in and was very frank with them. I started with, "You both are different people, and I don't ever expect you two to be friends, but this is gotten beyond the point of tolerance – it has to stop." We talked about how we could work to find solutions. The situation could not continue like this any longer.

A few days later, and it was time to head back to Baltimore for the annual UFEA session. The big new initiative with EAS was to start the Global Based Initiative (GBI) program, which was an idea to make cooperators from different commodity groups to conduct synced promotion at the same venues at the same time. Great idea, but it was going to be a challenge to implement due to the seasonal differences between a lot of products. Still, it was the new mandate, so we worked to move forward with it.

We headed home for Thanksgiving, and then the following Monday Ocean told me she was resigning. While I knew that she was not happy with the

situation with Molly, and had created tension with Han lately, I was still a little surprised. But what was there to do? She had been there for three years and had done so much to help strengthen the programs. In reflection, those three years with Ocean were really the only time I did not have to do two jobs. I had been able to really grow as a manager, and it was the most productive years of my time with the organization. It was the only time we were truly running on 'full power'. She and I had cultivated a good relationship during those three years – she was my first protégé in the corporate environment, and I was kind of sad to see her go, but nothing lasts forever.

At least there was the relief that the problems between Molly and her were to be resolved. It was December and things were winding down, so I devoted my energies to working to finish the image library that Ocean and I had started. It took a bit of time, but I was able to organize the entire library and create hard copy binders for users to easily review the image when they visited the office, as well as organizing them all in digital format as well for online use. It was Ocean's final contribution to the program and I wanted to make sure the project was finished properly. I waited for the beginning of the year to post the job opening for the Asia position. Christmas was different that year. My brother had been in Phuket and flew back on Christmas Eve to celebrate the holiday (and his birthday) with us. He happened to leave Phuket on the 24th, just two days before the infamous earthquake and tidal wave that struck the region on the 26th. We were a day behind in Seattle, so we got the news on Christmas Day. My brother lost people he knew – he was so fortunate to leave just before the wave struck. And we had been there just six weeks before. I could not imagine what it would have been like, trying to survive a giant tsunami wave, with a pregnant wife in tow.

Chapter 50

The Second Born

January was a quiet month for a change. We had discontinued the Sendai Lunch Party event, so I was not traveling to Japan for the first time since I had started with the organization. The energy was glum, for we were starting to pack the office up to move to the new location in Seattle. They had selected a place near Ballard, along the canal, down the street from Magic Mermaid. Many of us were not looking forward to the commute, but we really had no choice. At least there was a pizza restaurant and an espresso shop across the street. In February we made the big move. I always said, "There is no good way in or out of Ballard.", and I was quickly being reminded of it. My office was a corner one with a lot of windows and a considerable amount of space. Molly's office had only one window and brick walls on two sides. But it was better than the third office, which was much smaller. I liked to refer to it as 'the closet'. I decided after the first week of traffic that I was going to change my work patterns. I had previously been the type to sleep in and come in late and stay late. But it was time to switch to - come in early/leave early (if possible, to leave early). The energy was not the same for me anymore. I had the new board to face, and I had to create new executive summaries for them, as Carl did not think they would want to read the full reports we created. That's all I needed was another set of reporting documents, but I built them with no complaints.

I had started the hiring process again, and there was a healthy group of applicants. I was candid during the interview process and let people know what the job paid. Many declined to move forward when they heard the salary – and I was not surprised. Most marketing jobs pay a lot more than this one did. So, we distilled the candidate pool down to a couple of people, and we started doing some group interviews. I selected a new candidate – she was a bubbly young Filipino girl that had recently graduated from one of the local universities. She seemed enthusiastic about the job, and Molly and Susan both thought she would be a good choice. We were excited to get her started before we got too deep into the new CMS application. Most of it was done already, but I needed her to start managing the Asia operations so I could finish the new plan. March flew by, as I had to help to teach the new hire how to edit the Asia program components, complete the final editing of the CMS, as well as attend the Boston Seafood Show. Meanwhile, we were dealing with another really challenging situation that was coming to head. Months before, a representative of the Alaska Air National Guard had called and requested for us to supply seafood for them to take with them on their flight to Japan to participate in joint exercises with the Japan Self Defense Forces. I explained to him that all my budget for product was dedicated to current international promotions, and that it was not within the regulations to support such an activity. I encourage him to work directly with our Juneau PR staff to provide product for such an effort. We had been 'ASA the Miracle Caterer' so many times before, but this was taking it too far, as it would be a domestic donation, and better that it be handled by the head office in Alaska. Unfortunately, no one at the head office had addressed the need, and here we were in March, with Carl being approached by the Air National Guard again to support the dinner reception in Japan. I tried to explain to Carl that this was not an approved international activity, and that considering the current political environment with the war in Iraq and Afghanistan – that it might not be very well received by the public if word got out. Han was also very concerned about the political ramifications of us supporting this effort, with similar concerns being shared by FEO and DOC agents in Sapporo. Han nicknamed the situation 'Mission Impossible'.

Since Han's salary was paid by federal funds, it would potentially involve conflicts with federal agencies. When Han brought up her concerns, Carl was not pleased. When I approached him to support her position, he told me, "If she doesn't want to do it, maybe we should hire a new contractor in Japan that will." He was basically threatening to fire her if she did not cooperate with this ethically questionable activity. I let Han know we had to perform this activity – whether we liked it or not.

As Han so well pointed out to me, since the activity ran well outside our planned set of activities or federal-mandated performance measures, had there been prior approval from the ASA Board or the Governor's Office? And then there was the absurdity of the idea that $5,000 was going to properly cater an event for 1,000 soldiers – when it typically cost us the same amount to have a similar event for 100 people. So, Han and I sourced another $4,000 or so to make the event happen. The Japan staff wound up literally having to buy food at a grocery store for the caterers. In the end, we spend about $9,000, and a considerable amount of time and energy, to feed military operatives in Japan.

By then it was the end of March. Sherry was on schedule to be complete with the new pregnancy in April, so I did not plan on doing any more travel for the next month or two. It was early in the morning on April 1st, and Sherry and I were heading out the door to the hospital to induce labor. And then I got a call from Bantu. He wanted to know if I planned to use all the program's money for the rest of the fiscal year (through June). I thought it was a strange question from our fiscal officer. Of course, we were going to spend all of the program's money – even though the budget was increasing every year, we still spent practically every bit of funding we received. But I was heading on my way for the birth of a new child, so I quickly forgot about his strange request.

We arrived early at the hospital that day, and we spent the entire day in a room, waiting for our turn. We must have been waiting almost ten hours, and we were told that, "Sorry, but you were an elective procedure, and we had some emergency births, so we need to send you home." It was April 1st – April Fool's Day – and the joke was on us. There were no calls on Saturday, but then early Sunday morning they called us back in again. We rushed over to the hospital, and spent a good portion of the day waiting, but then Sherry was induced into labor, and a few hours later, with much less stress, our second child – a boy – was born. We had spent months discussing possible names but had not come to agreement. I was picking some crazy names, like 'Tobias' and 'Kaiser' – Kaiser was definitely my favorite. But she would not have it. So here we were with a new child with no name, just the name 'Baby Kreiger' on the charts. Since we had so many problems with the first child, we were being very cautious this one. We stayed in the hospital for a couple days for them to allow for tests of the cardiac system, etc. Two days later and he still had no name. Finally, I suggested the first name 'Kelly' – she agreed. But she wanted to pick the middle name, so she chose 'Alan' – I agreed. I quickly filled out the paperwork for the birth certificate to submit the name to the hospital.

About a week later, Jeff gave me a call to share some news. It turned out that Bantu and Carl, without informing me, had approved to 'borrow' the International Program's spending authority – to the tune of $1 million. It turned out that AFC had provided funds to support expansion of domestic promotions. Instead of waiting to secure the spending authority from the State of Alaska, they chose to take it from our program. Essentially what this meant was that we could not pay our bills for the last two months of the year. Not only did I consider this to be gross mismanagement, but it was practically criminal. Our contracted representatives always had to pay for bills with their own funds (and credit cards), and then submit the bills back to Alaska for reimbursement. So essentially, our reps were stuck with close to a million dollars in debt on their own personal accounts. And as well, we could not purchase a lot of other items or pay for needs, since there was nothing to bill it to in the State system. It was about the middle of June before we were able to get the spending authority returned to our program.

I was not happy at all about this action – the security of the people in our program – and the program's needs - had been totally compromised.

This was about the time that I was starting to get tired of Carl 's disregard for the welfare of the staff and contractors. I had been so accustomed to Betty's management – who always went the distance to protect the staff. In contrast, it seemed like Carl had no problem with putting us in difficult positions – and without prior warning. I was starting to have some real issues with him, and my attitude was not improving. I had jokingly referred to Carl as 'Admiral Doolittle' for the past year. It seemed that the situation was continuing to become more stressful for all of us. But there was no time to grumble, it was the end of the month, and we were off to Brussels for the European Seafood Exposition. This was another big year for us – the Alaska pavilion had grown larger than ever, expanding across the aisle to allow Harpoon to have a double booth. And for the first time, we added a second story to the lounge, to better handle the increased activity and traffic. We had more food and Alaska beer than ever, and all the trade members seemed really pleased. Many of the staff were beginning to feel the frustration of the actions of the new Board. As we sat in one of our hotel rooms, I made a prophetic joke about our new Board members. I said, "We have a Daddy's boy (Brendon), a delivery driver (Dave), an iceman (Darryl), two lawyers (Josef and Calvin) and two idiots (Benny and Chad).

Everyone laughed, but on reflection now, it was probably not my best move saying such a thing. I should have kept my thoughts to myself.

Chapter 51

A Bad Hire

J ust a few weeks later and I was back in Seattle, preparing for a two-week trip to Asia. Our new Asia Specialist, Rowena, was joining Bobby Olson and I for the mission. As well, we were being joined by Benny Bernal, our new Board Vice-Chairman. We were kicking off the mission by having a booth at the Hofex show in Hong Kong, and then we were going to jump the border and conduct a chef seminar in Guangzhou, China. We arrived in Hong Kong, and I met up with Benny in the hotel lobby. He came up to me with a very worried look and asked if he could talk with me. He asked, "What are we doing here?" He had read the FEO reports for the region, and according to the reports it looked like Hong Kong was not a very good place for our products for the food service sector. I listened to his concerns, and then I asked him to put the reports away, keep an open mind, and watch what we did for the next few days, and then I would answer his question at the end of the mission. We had a nice booth again at the show. We shipped in some Alaska beer for patrons to enjoy, and sampled smoked salmon and snow crab. People really loved the crab and beer, and we had quite a few visitors that did not want to leave the booth. But problems were starting to surface with Rowena. She was late the first day of the show, she had overslept and did not get up on time, requiring the team to wait in the lobby for her, and arrive late at the show to prepare the booth. This became a regular occurrence almost every day with her during the mission. And she did not seem very enthusiastic anymore about the event, or any of the work we were doing. When I asked her if she had any questions, she always said, "No." She just was not very engaged about any of the work. But as soon as it was night, she wanted to stay up all through the evening to go shopping at the night markets. I wasn't impressed.

After the Hofex show I split up with the team. Everyone else took the train to Guangzhou, while I jumped the border into Shenzhen. I had been invited by Mr. Chu to come visit him, as he wanted again to return the hospitality to me for the support I had provide him during his previous trip to Alaska. It was great to see him again, and as we sat and had dinner, he showed me all the $100 bills in his wallet. He complained that he did get have enough entertainment and fun while he was in Alaska. I promised him next time that I would show him a better time – unfortunately I did not get to return that favor. The next day he showed me his factory and told me the story about how he came from the provinces, and how he had nothing and used to walk to work. Now he was worth millions, had a nice BMW and was building the largest private cold storage in southern China. He was a perfect example of the new economic miracle appearing in China. We talked about promotions, and he agreed to help me get beer into China for the next China Seafood Expo. The plan was to ship it to Hong Kong, and then transport it across the border into China.

That night I headed to Guangzhou to meet up with the others. We were conducting a chef seminar, and it went really smooth. Southern China was so much different than the northern region. It was warm and humid, and the atmosphere seemed so much more relaxed and festive. And while we sat at the hotel for breakfast in the morning, I saw what must have been two dozen baby girls – all Chinese – being adopted by Western couples. It made my heart melt. Here were all these little girls, who were essentially 'throw away' children, that were being rescued. It made me think of doing something similar.

After the event Bobby and Rowena headed to Dalian to participate in another chef seminar, and then to Beijing for visits with the FEO. Benny and I headed back together to Hong Kong on a train. As we drove through the countryside we sat together, and I told him I was ready to answer any questions he had. In the days he had spent with us, his eyes had opened. He had a much better understanding of what we were doing there; for Hofex, we were using Hong Kong as a hub for promoting to the food service sector for all Southern Asia. And the chef seminar activities were essential for reaching the food service sector in China. He really was starting to grasp the importance of the program, and the impacts that we were making in the market. It seemed like he became a huge fan of the program after that.

Shortly after I returned to Seattle I followed up with Bobby to see how Rowena had performed with him during the trip to Dalian and Beijing. He reported it had been more of the same. She was late for work almost every morning but had no problem going out all night to shop. Han had reported performance issues as well. After conferring with Molly and the rest of the staff, it almost felt like I had hired an entirely different person than who had interviewed. While she had seemed very enthusiastic and energetic during the interviews, her performance was not the same at work. She would barely come out of her office and had been very quiet and introverted. After she returned from the trip, I brought her into my office, explained that she was not performing as we had originally thought she would, and I let her know that I was letting her go. Since we always had the six-month probationary period for new hires, the paperwork was limited. I wrote her a letter, and I let her go. Again, I found myself with two jobs again, but I would rather have done that than, then have another sub-standard employee to detract from the Asia programs.

By late June, and it was time for a Japan press mission to Bristol Bay. This was a joint activity with the Real American Pollock Producers Association (RAAP), with ASA leading the beginning of the trip with a focus on salmon, and then having RAAP take over in Anchorage for the second leg of the mission, with a visit to Dutch Harbor to learn about the pollock industry. We welcomed the mission members – along with Han, in Seattle. After conducting several meetings there, we flew the team to Bristol Bay to see the salmon fishery. As had happened so many times before, Alaska Airlines delayed our flights, making sure that we were not able to conduct many of the plant tours we had scheduled. Both our flights in Seattle and Anchorage were severely delayed, and the press team spent a lot of time waiting at the airport. We arrived in King Salmon in the evening, and we were able to conduct at least one plant tour at Skipper Creek Fisheries with James Mitchell and his team. James was very helpful, and we were able to get some great images. Right after that we hosted a dinner at Chad Fry's house, and we entertained the mission members with fresh sockeye salmon and scallops. Early the next morning we were also able to visit the Harpoon plant to get more press footage. The rest of that day went as planned, with Chad providing a tour of the Naknek River on his fishing boat. As we came out of the mouth of the river, I realized that one of my father's boats was in the area. Tied to the dock was the Snow Petrel. As we pulled up we were greeted by my father and my sister. Several Japanese members were very excited to meet my family since they were actual fishermen. That night, we held a trade dinner in King Salmon at one of the hotels, and my family was able to attend near the end of the dinner. Considering it had been my 40th birthday that Spring, my father bought me a huge Bowie knife and handed it to me at the dinner. The Japanese were blown away by the size of the blade, as they passed it around the table. It was a truly impressive piece of polished steel.

The next morning, we took a very short flight to Katmai National Park. Katmai is notorious as a place to see a very high concentration of brown bears, and it is also the location of the McNeil River, which is a famous locale for taking very iconic shots of bears catching salmon in the river. As we walked to the river, we stopped to talk with one of the rangers. He was pointing to some of the active volcanoes that were venting. All of a sudden, just a few feet from us, a giant sow and her two cubs came stomping out of the brush and brushed right past all of us. Even with all my years of being around brown bears in Alaska, I had never been quite so close. I could only imagine how many press members must have peed themselves at that moment. After visiting the river to get some great pictures we returned to King Salmon to head back to Anchorage. Once again, Alaska Airlines was doing the best they could to destroy our mission with another severely delayed flight. We had a major dinner scheduled at the French Grill in Anchorage, with a very famous Alaskan chef, Archie French. I called all the guests to let them know we were going to be late, and we almost had to cancel the dinner, but at the last minute we finally caught the flight to Anchorage. Archie was kind enough to keep the grill open late that evening just for us, and we were able to get some great footage. We even set up a table in the parking lot to get some beautiful plate shots under the midnight sun. The next morning, we went to the airport, and I handed the team off to the RAAP reps for the trip to Dutch Harbor. A few days later we met up with the mission members in Seattle to conduct some more joint activities, and off they went back to Japan. Before they departed, I asked the press members what they thought of the trip. One of them commented, "Part of the Alaska experience is to spend a lot of time waiting in airports." All I could think was, "Thanks for the lasting impression, Alaska Airlines

Chapter 52

And Another Bad Hire

A few days later I was taking the day off to take my children to get their passport photos. We were having a problem getting Kelly's picture right, as his head was too small (being only two months old), and we keep having to do re-takes. In the middle of it all, I received a phone call from Carl. He told me to call him back when I had a quiet place to sit. All I could think was, "What did I do now?" After returning home I called him back and he let me know that he was hiring Kevin Steele to be our new Asia Specialist. I was dumbfounded; Kevin had been the Commissioner for the Department of Commerce – basically the boss of our division (they always had to sign off on our international travel).

Just earlier that week it was in the news that Kevin was resigning from the commissioner's position – the official story was that there was possible conflicts of interest being construed, due to his position on the Chugiak Corporation board. As Carl described it, Kevin needed a new position with the State, and so we were going to provide him the position for a place to lie low until the media storm blew over. Carl told me that he needed me to be a team player and make this work. I complied and told him I would do my best to facilitate the change.

For years, I had posted significant news reports on my office door, and most in the office would stop when they walked by to read it (remember, these were the days before social media). The commissioner of our department resigning was significant news, and so I had posted an article about it on my door. As it was a Friday, and Kevin was supposed to be in the office Monday morning to report for work, I quickly called the office, and asked them to please take the articles off my door.

On Monday, Kevin arrived about 9 am to report for work. I went to greet him as he arrived, and he looked at me and said, "I suppose you are supposed to be my boss now?" I could detect the look of humiliation on his face. He had obviously forgotten who I was, as I had warmly greeted him two years earlier when he had toured our offices. My how things had changed. I showed him where his office was and provided him with a copy of the current CMS plan, as well as the usual documentation to get a new hire up to speed. I asked him to get settled in, and then when he was ready, that to please come to my office for a talk.

A short while later he stepped into my office. I quickly shut the door and said, "Let's not waste each other's time, let's get right to the point. Why are you here?" He relaxed a little, and told me, "The only two positions currently available with the State were a position with the Governor's Office in Washington, D.C., and this position. My Mom doesn't want me to be too far away." He went on to talk about how he how missed the window to apply for a teaching position with one of the universities, so he needed a place to stay and hide for a few months until the application window opened again. He also was working under the impression that he could go to Alaska on a regular basis to help take care of his mother.

So basically, he wanted to be close to his mother, and wait until things were fine for getting one his old jobs back. I did not hold back. I said, "If you were looking for a place to hide, this was the wrong place. This is a marketing arm of the State, and we are constantly under scrutiny for our performance.

Basically, you just signed up to be in a fish bowl." I went on to tell him about the requirements for the job, and that we actually had a high workload, and had a lot of responsibilities. And then I let him know that one of his first tasks was to take the minutes for our next upcoming committee meeting. He was pretty quiet and went back to his office.

I let Carl know what had occurred, and then I continued to monitor the situation carefully. Kevin did not talk with me much after that. He spent most of the time on the phone, and the rest of the time out of the office. I watched closely, and calculated that he had spent at most, maybe 12 hours in the office that week. But on Friday, I had his time sheet on my desk, with 37.5 hours written in for the week. I faxed a copy to the head office, and then told Carl, as his supervisor, I was not going to falsify his activities and sign off on the document. I told him that if he wanted to do it, fine, but I was not going to start supporting such behavior. Carl told me he would confer with him and let me know what would happen next. On the next Monday, I was informed that Kevin was resigning from the position and returning to Alaska. Rumor on the street later was that the reason that Kevin had resigned from the commissioner position was due to the fact that he had been having an affair with one of his male assistants, and that the assistant had quit, and was suing him for sexual harassment. I never heard from him, or of him, again.

Shortly afterwards I was working to help support Stanley Wilkes' Korea trade mission. Stanley was the FEO agent that had worked with me previously in Japan (and had shared a room with me up in Mt. Fuji, drank all the Scotch in the mini-bar, and then left me the bill). Stanley was going to go through Seattle and Anchorage to lead buyers on a trade mission. I let him know that I was short-staffed, but that I would lend all the support I could. Moon Park had been made aware of the mission and had offered to help with setting up visits in Alaska. A day or two later, Stanley called me and told me that Moon had hijacked the mission in Alaska. Basically, she greeted him at the airport, and had told him that she had created a new schedule for meetings and demanded that he had to follow her schedule now, and if he did not, there would be major problems for him. Shortly thereafter, I got a call from Ben Stiller at WCFEA; he had heard from Stanley (WCFEA had helped orchestrate the mission), and he was not pleased with what was going on. I shared my previous experiences with Moon, and encouraged him to document what had occurred, and to share it with the proper authorities at both the State of Alaska and EAS. When the mission hit Seattle, Moon hijacked that portion as well. Clint Houston and I had worked to set up trade meetings at a venue in Seattle, but we could see that Kim was continuing to reset the schedule in Seattle for her own benefit. Clint and I tried to help but we knew it was a mess. While industry members had been scheduled all day long for meetings with the Korean trade members, we had been informed by Moon that after the morning introductory session, she was taking the team to meet with Magic Mermaid and Harpoon for the rest of the day. This was in total conflict with everything that had been planned. So that morning, Clint and I met at the venue, provided some quick presentations, and then went to get coffee as we waited for the bomb to go off. I returned to my office, to get calls all the rest of the day from angry industry members that had gone to the venue to have no trade members there to meet and conduct business. My hands were tied. I apologized to all of them and let them know that Moon had chosen to take the members instead to two of the major companies. I advised Ben and Stanley to write letters of what had occurred, which they did. Sadly, it was a sign of worse things to come.

About this time, Carl told me about the Herring Roe Committee that was being formed. There was a new herring roe initiative being pushed by AFC. Essentially, herring roe was a declining market in Japan. Herring roe was known as 'kazunoko' in Japan, and it had been traditionally marketed as a salted product in a box for gift giving at Christmas time. But a generational change had taken place, and gift giving kazunoko was now considered old school, something your grandfather used to do. So, the processors and harvesters wanted to do something to bolster the market. Instead of doing something to create added value, like creating new product formats, or marketing to a new consumer segment, instead they had a big bag of cash that they wanted to hand over to buyers and distributors in Japan to 'move the pack' (make immediate sales). And ASA and I were supposed to facilitate it. So here we were, dealing with a new temporary organization, the 'Alaska Herring Roe Processors Association' that was supposed to be administered by ASA, but wasn't really ASA. Another clusterfuck, approved by Carl.

Great, as if I did not have enough to do already, now I had to try and coordinate this new committee, and help steer this new channel of cash handouts to help subsidize sales. Still, I tried very hard to work with the industry and trade to work to create a new image for herring roe. I used the example of Jägermeister, an herbal-based liquor from Germany, that only old German men drank at the bar with their beer. But Jägermeister had somehow found a way to market its product to a new consumer sector worldwide as a sexy new 'shot bar' drink at clubs. It was the perfect example of using the power of marketing to get consumers to alter their perception and accept and crave a previously undesirable product. My idea was this – we would work to create a new image for the roe, by infusing it with vodka, or some other type of liquor and flavors, and introduce them at the club level as 'love roe'. Kazunoko did have the reputation in Japan of raising sexual virility in men, so with a little bit of marketing creativity, we would convince a new generation that if you consumed it, it would boost your sexual powers – hence the name 'love roe'. Unfortunately, my ideas were not heeded, and they went back to trying to use monetary support of current activities (basically cost subsidies) to move the pack. As I watched the committee members argue and maneuver to how much each of them got for funding for their customers, I had to just reside myself to the fact that nothing would change.

This was about the time that I realized I was getting burned out. I was getting very limited sleep, due to Kelly being very colicky during the first six months of his life. Every night I would return home from work, hold him in my arms, and rock him to sleep all night. If I stopped, he would awake, and start screaming. I would continue to rock him until I fell asleep, and then the process would continue again, almost every night. I had reached my limit, finally. Bobby's words that he had shared at the beginning of my career echoed in my head, "Watch out buddy, this is a marathon, not a sprint." For almost six years I had been sprinting all through a marathon, and it was finally taking a toll on me. I did what I thought I was supposed to do – I reached out to my boss for help. I called Carl and asked for help. I told him that I had been running too hard, for too long, that I had realized that for over three out of the six years at ASA, that I had held two jobs, and I was burning myself out. His response was muted. There was to be no help. After the disaster with Kevin, he was afraid for me to post for a new hire, as he was concerned of the political winds, and that Moon Park might try to apply for the job. I felt totally defeated, but somehow, I found the strength to carry on.

Chapter 53

Cooking Show Host

July arrived, and it was time again for the Japan Seafood Show in Tokyo. And this time Carl was joining me for the mission. We had a trade reception, so as I had done so many times before, I wrote a speech for the reception – but this time I wrote it for Carl. The speech was very candid again, and the words spoke to how the markets were changing, and while Japan was still a very important market for the industry, there were new markets that were emerging that were creating new levels of competition. When Carl read the speech, he thought I was setting him up. I reminded him that I wrote the speech as if I would deliver it myself; still, he was hesitant to deliver it. So, I encouraged him to share it with Han, since he did not believe me. Which he did – and she re-enforced what I had originally said, that the words and thoughts conveyed would be accepted by the Japanese trade – that they would respect us for our candor and honesty. He delivered the speech as I had written it.

The show was another good one –we were using the new images that Ocean and I had secured the year before, so our imagery and brand looked stronger than ever. We had two seafood displays, one on each side of the booth, and they were highly popular, jammed full of a broad variety of brightly colored species of seafood. The show was going well, and I had spent some time with the members of the Ocean Steward Board (OSB). They had a booth that year, as they were making a major push on the Asia market. The night before the last day of the show, I ended up partying with the OSB guys all night. I lost them somewhere along the way as we made our way through the clubs in Roppongi. By the time I got back to my room, I realized I only had one hour to sleep. So, I set my alarm, and I dragged myself out of bed and headed to the show site.

When I arrived, I instantly broke into a sweat, when I saw the mess in front of me. The power had been turned off at the booth, and all the fish and crab were swimming in giant puddles of water in both displays cases. There was only about 40 minutes before the show was to open, and I was going to need to move quickly. I laid garbage bags out in front of both displays and quickly laid all the display products out on top of them. Then I started to bail out all the display cases into a bucket with cup. Carl arrived during the middle of the process. While he could see that I was working at a feverish pace to fix the mess, he just sat down and watched me. Once again, he was demonstrating his character – he did not even offer to help me. But I did not miss a beat, I continued to clean out the cases, and then ran and got fresh ice by the bucket to fill the cases again. By the time Han and her staff arrived, I was almost finished. I was covered in sweat – but I had prevented a major disaster before the doors had opened for all the trade to see.

After returning from the show, Carl gave me approval to start hiring for the Asia position again. I could only hope that Han had helped convince him of my need to fill the position. We started the process of advertising again. It was hard to believe that we were barely halfway through the year but had already gone through two hires for the Asia program.

About this time the entire 'Salmon Thirty Salmon' incident was coming into the public eye. AFC had decided to give money to one of the airlines to paint one of their planes with a giant king salmon on the side. The paint job had cost about $300,000, and they prominently placed our Alaska Seafood logo on the front of the plane. I wasn't totally against the idea, but I had inquired as to what the airlines was doing to support the effort in return. I had suggested that they at least provide meals of Alaska seafood on the plane to educate consumers about the superior quality and taste of our products. But instead, it was just another big spend of money to create a giant, $300,000 flying billboard in the sky. The media had caught wind of it, and it was on national news, just about the time I was arriving in Washington D.C. for the summer UFEA Attaché Conference. We were the butt of all kinds of jokes at the meetings, as people asked me what I thought of the situation. I was happy to let them know that I had nothing to do with it.

In early August, I was finally having my left ankle operated on; after spraining my ankle horribly and playing soccer on it for almost seven years, the pain had become so intense, that if I learned too far forward, it felt as if someone were sticking an ice pick into the top of my ankle. I had a great doctor, and he had advised me a few months before that I had several torn ligaments, and that the cartilage was starting to tear loose from my bone. He also recommended that, since they were already performing surgery in the area, that they were going to cut the back of my ankle bone off, spin it and screw it back together so that it would have the proper angle. It was time to get it fixed. Sherry was angry with me that I was having surgery on my foot while having a newborn in the house, but I could not wait any longer. After the surgery I spent a week in recovery at home. I had been prescribed Oxycontin, and boy, was I high. I thought about writing some emails, but then I thought again it might not be such a good idea, considering how altered I was by the heavy opiates. I just laid around for the week and did my best to try and relax.

The applications for the Asia position started to roll in. I was not seeing anything special in the stack, and then Kylie came to me and suggested a possible candidate for the role. Her name was Jena Gardner, and she has grown up with Brendan Robins, and was very familiar with the industry, so I decided to consider her as a candidate. She came in for an initial interview, and I asked for some writing samples. I explained to her as usual, that there was a lot of writing required for the job, strong communication and organizational skills were going to be very important. The writing samples she supplied looked good, and she looked like she was a good fit, so I offered her the role, which she accepted.

I submitted the papers to the state for approval, and then I headed off for vacation with Sherry, the kids, and her parents to Kauai. It was kind of crazy trying to go to Hawaii on a pair of crutches and a boot on my foot, but we made the best of it. While I could not go swimming, I did my best to hobble around with the kids to enjoy the time.

When I returned, Jena had been approved to hire, so we put her right to work. I was hoping that I could finally have a good fit for the program, as well as someone that might mesh well with Molly as well. Molly had tried to help me with the workload this whole time as well, so it would be good to have a full-time staff member again to help shoulder the load, and provide us both a little relief. At least we had a good solid month to get Jena trained and up to speed before a long travel schedule for the Fall.

At the beginning of October, we were kicking off another long trip to Europe. First, we were heading to Conxemar in Vigo. I was really having a lot of fun traveling with my crutches, and I was reminded very quickly in Madrid how Spaniards did not care much about helping those disabled. People pushed past me to get on the plane – there was basically no help or assistance at all. I was beginning to understand and empathize for those that had physical disabilities. It was a real wake up call. I had tried to ship kegs of Alaska beer to Spain for the show, but we were afraid that Spanish authorities would not clear them, so instead I had a couple of cases of bottled beer shipped over as extra luggage. It was a total pain in the ass to pack around on crutches, but I somehow found a way to make it work. The Conxemar show was nothing too different – we had a nice booth, and some good presence, and we even added an octopus into the display case, in hopes of marketing that species to the trade. And the industry members appreciated having the beer at the show to enjoy. The hotel managed to get my reservations wrong, and I was kicked out of my room for the last night there. Roger was gracious enough to let me stay in his room for that last night, so he and I shared a bed. There were a few days in between the show in Spain, and the rest of schedule in Germany and France, so I flew to Hannover to visit my family once again. My uncle enjoyed my company again, and this time we decided to go visit the town of Goslar – which was only about 30 miles or so away.

Goslar is situated right at the foot of the Harz mountains. It is significant in that not only was it the Kaiser's winter palace, but it is also one of the only towns in Germany that was not bombed during WW II. During the war the town had served as a POW internment camp for British prisoners. And the British royal family had owned land in the area, so the town had been spared the horrors of aerial bombardment. If you ever get the chance, it is one of the few towns in Germany that reveal what most of Germany must have looked like before the war.

After a few days visiting with the family, I headed off to Dusseldorf again for the Gastrovision and ANUGA shows, where I met up with Molly, Bobby, Elise, and Daniel. We had a great time at the show, but Molly became very angry with me for negotiating a new promotion without her. She had nothing to be angry about – the negotiated promotion was truly accidental. Elise and I had been invited at the show to meet for a quick beer with one of the members of the trade. While we were enjoying the drink, we simply negotiated a promotion with the contact. I explained this to Molly the next day at breakfast; it took her a while to accept the fact that she had not been left out of the discussion intentionally, but I was finally able to appease her. After a few days in Germany, Bobby, Elise, Molly, and I traveled to the Netherlands for some trade meetings, and then on to Paris to conduct a major press luncheon. After what seemed like forever, I was finally heading back home again, after two long weeks in Europe.

After just two weeks at home, it was time to head to China. Finally, the China Fish Expo show dates had been moved to take place after Halloween – for years we had been going to the show and experiencing that holiday in China. And having young kids now, it was going to allow me to share the time with them at home to share the joy of watching them get dressed up to get candy. It was Jena's first trip out of town since she started, so it would be interesting to see how she would do. This year the venue of the show had been changed to Guangzhou. We arrived at the show site the day before to help with the setup. After we arrived at our booth, I set my computer bag into one of the kiosks. It had not been one minute, and Jena asked me where she should store her bag. I told her to put it next to mine. But she said there was nothing there. I could not believe it – it had not even been one minute, and my computer bag had been stolen! It turns out that there was a very high crime rate in the region. Shortly afterwards someone found my bag outside the show and turned it into police. Of course, the computer was gone, along with my new iPod Mini that I purchased that summer. Still, Billy and I had to go the police station at the show site to claim my property. What was interesting is that victims are fingerprinted when making statements in China. They made me stamp all my statements with my thumbprint in red ink, I believe to prevent me from committing perjury.

The show was pretty intense after that. Whenever we would walk outside the show site, there were so many 'province' people crowded outside, eager to try to sell us things and try to pickpocket us. To clear the way, Billy would start swinging his bag at the people to clear the way. This became a daily procession for us, and I would follow closely behind him, trying to keep the crowd at arm's length.

For some strange reason, every time I got together with Bobby and Billy, it seems that our dinner conversations would get very colorful. And this time during this show was no exception. About a night or two into the show, we sat down to dinner, only to have Sherry call me. It seems that during the day she and the kids had gone to the park with her sister and her kids, and their cousin had managed to get some dog poop on his shoe. She went on to describe how he had climbed up the ladder onto a slide playground slide, and tracked the poop all over it, and then the other kids started to climb the ladder and get it all over themselves – on their hands, on their coats - everywhere. I started to laugh out loud at the table as she described what had taken place. I got off the phone and the others were asking what had happened. I could barely describe the story, as I kept breaking down in laughter as I described what had transpired. Soon, I had the entire table smiling and laughing, as they envisioned all the little children running around with dog poop all over them.

The second day of the show Jena came to me and asked for help. We had a fisherman from Alaska at the booth that was complaining that we did not have any rock sole, flathead sole, or rex sole in our display case. I sat him down and tried to explain to him that those were products that were not being consumed in China. They were products that were only exported there for reprocessing and then were shipped to other countries for final consumption. Still, he was insistent we should have them in the display case. I asked him, "What would be the purpose of that? Did he want us to spend our limited funding on educating re-processors how to re-process fish?" It made no sense at all. Still, he continued to complain that we should be promoting those species. He went on to threaten that he was going to complain to Harpoon, who had a booth just around the corner. So, I called his bluff. I said, "Sure, let's go walk down there together and have a talk with them about it." He fell silent, but then started up again that we should have those species on display. I had had enough. For the first, and only time during my entire career at ASA, I had to finally utter the words, "I am sorry, but I can't help you." Finally, he walked away, as frustrated as ever. There went one of the 20% that I could never make happy, no matter the effort.

One of the planned activities for me during this mission was for me to fly to Beijing with Bobby and perform on a TV cooking show. I had been requested to assemble several Alaska recipes for the activity, but I was operating under

329

the impression that I was just watching and providing technical advice. But then the day before the show, they informed me that I was going to be the one doing the cooking. It took me by total surprise. I had not prepared for it at all, but then I start reflecting on all my days of cooking in the past, to reassure myself. When Bobby and I arrived in Beijing, we met with the producer, and they explained the situation to me. It turned out that the film site was on the grounds of the old university, and that foreigners were not allowed to be on the campus. So, they put me in a trench coat and sunglasses, and had me sit slumped down in the backseat of the car, as we drove past the security checkpoint. For a minute it felt like a scene from a James Bond movie – having to sneak in to perform the mission. When we arrived at the site, it was an old, dilapidated concrete building, that looked to be at least a half a century old. As we walked up the old stairwell, I could not believe we were to be shooting a cooking show there. But when we arrived at the studio, the room was well-lit and brightly colored – it looked nothing at all like its surroundings. We got to work, and we spent the next few hours rehearsing, and then cooking the dishes for two episodes. I had worn a black dress shirt and tie, and Bobby had a bright orange sweater with black stripes. The host of the show started joking that Bobby looked like Nemo, from the Disney movie of the same name. He started saying that we should call the show the 'Captain BJ and Nemo Show'. Then we went on to finishing shooting the episodes, where I cooked salmon, black cod, and crab. I must have done something right, because at the end, the crew all sat down and ate every bit of the food. I learned later that at least eight million people watched the episodes. I never dreamed of being a TV chef, especially one in China!

After that trip, the rest of the year was fairly quiet. We did the annual visit to the UFEA sessions in Baltimore, and then we wound the year down for the Christmas holidays with the new member of the family. And it was good to have some time to provide Jena with more training for her new role. The new year was going to be the 25th Anniversary of ASA, so I was working on a set of special edition hats and other trinkets, to celebrate the occasion.

Chapter 54

Gone for Easter

The year started off in an interesting fashion. I was called up to Anchorage to meet with the ladies of the Division of International Trade in person. I was not quite sure what was needed of me that required me to fly up for an in-person visit, but I was soon to find out. Since we had worked together for so many years, when we sat down, they went right to the point. They said, "It is (Governor) Terry's last year in office, and he wants to visit his cousin in Poland for Easter – we need to build a mission around it for him." As crazy as it sounded, and while I was a little shocked by their candor at first, I had been there long enough to realize that this is how things go in the world of politics. So instead of resisting at all, I shifted gears to find a solution. I suggested that we could conduct some activities in Germany and England. After all, I always considered the Governor to be the ultimate PR tool for our programs, so I returned to the office and let Molly, Daniel and Elise the news. We all went to task to build a set of activities for Terry.

As usual, the beginning of the year was very busy for us, as we were working on the CMS plan, and we were having to train Jena on how to edit the plans from the Asia reps, due to their English translation skills. As I reviewed her edited documents, I realized that her abilities were not as originally described. I reached the conclusion that the writing samples that she had provided at her original interview were probably not her work. I called her into my office and pointed out her deficiencies and revealed that she had basically misrepresented herself. She was very quiet – she had no arguments back. But trying to be a good manager, I asked her to start looking at writing courses that she could take to help strengthen her capabilities. There was always money in the budget for supporting such efforts, and I really encouraged her to take advantage of it, as I wanted her to succeed in the role. She thanked me, but unfortunately, she did not make any effort to find any classes.

Next came the really hard news. Doctors has originally told us that Kari to have her next, and final stage surgery – the Fontan procedure - to take place when she was about five years old. But since she had grown so much physiologically, she was ready for the next stage surgery before she was even three years old. And it was coming about at a very challenging time again. We were still in the final stages of crafting the CMS, we had Board meetings to prepare for, and I needed to crunch the newly released export figures. Still, she was the priority, so we were going to find a way to juggle all of this, as well take care of our newborn, Kelly. Kari went in for the surgery in mid-February, and we were on pins and needles again, wondering if she would survive. But she made it through the surgery okay and spent almost a month in recovery. Meanwhile I covered a double-shift, staying with her every night at the hospital, and then watching Kelly during the day while Sherry was at the hospital. Somehow I managed to work on all the new export numbers throughout those very trying four weeks. Of all the work I have done, those were some of the toughest days I have ever endured. I became so sleep-deprived near the end that session that I started to have auditory hallucinations.

My personal life had been challenging enough, but now I was facing another great challenge – the deterioration of my professional life and career. It had begun with the passage of the Crab Privatization Act. U.S. Senator Red

Clemons had crafted this new act that would privatize access/ownership of the Alaska crab fishery resources. The Act would create a 'two pie' system, with one pie being comprised of harvest quota shares, and the second pie being comprised of processor quota shares. Essentially, it was privatizing a public resource, and introducing restraint of commerce and trade. Several government agencies spoke against it for obvious reasons. But what was most interesting is how it was passed. Senator Clemons was the Chair of the Appropriations Committee at that time, so to avoid the Act being introduced as a separate bill – which would have been more than likely reviewed by the Commerce Committee and subsequently died or been defeated, he waited until the 11th hour and attached it as a rider to the Appropriations bill. This way the Senate had no choice but to either pass the bill or watch the U.S. government shut down due to lack of appropriations. Once this was discovered, several people became very vocal about this action – which included my father and brother.

Now about this same time, Red's son Joe (who was now President of the Alaska Senate, and Chairman of the Board for the AFC) was introducing Alaska State Bill 111, which would privatize access and ownership of the Alaska State water groundfish fisheries. My brother decided to be one of the leaders to oppose this new bill publicly. This included him flying to Juneau to level attacks at Joe Clemons while the State Senate was in session. Considering my very similar last name, I found myself getting calls from industry members, asking if I was related to these other Kreigers that were speaking very loudly during public sessions. During that Spring, my father walked into an Alaska Fish Board (AFB) meeting and threw multiple pairs of hand cuffs on the table in front of the board members and told them that they should arrest themselves as criminals for approving the Crab Rationalization Act. His follow up act about a month later was to walk into the next meeting dressed in a rat outfit to protest the rationalization of the crab fisheries. I would hear these reports and wince. I could feel that all my hard work and commitment to build my career as an international marketer and manager eroding away in front of me, due to my family's actions. I warned my father and my brother that they were probably jeopardizing my career, but they could not help themselves. They continued with their course of action, and I continued to count my days before I would start feeling the heat.

In between all the madness, I managed to fly to Kodiak again, to help support our booth during the annual fishery show. It just so happened that at the same time, there was a debate taking place between all the candidates that were running for Governor. Fred McCleod, who was the leading authority on salmon production data with the State, happened to be sitting next to me during the debate. Fred and I had worked together through the years, and I respected his opinion. This is the first time we had seen the new female candidate, Kerri Baldwin. She had a red dress on, and some men had been commenting how 'hot she looked'. But I was more concerned what was between her ears, then what was under the dress. Fred and I sat and watched as the candidates answered questions. And Kerri's response also seemed to be the same, canned response: " I come from a fishing family, and fishing issues are important to me." I was not impressed. She was not really answering the questions, and it made start to question her competency. I learned over to Fred and whispered in his ear, "What do you think of her?" And Fred replied, "I think she doesn't know enough, to know she doesn't know enough." I chuckled quietly with my hand over my mouth. Truer words were never spoken, as she was to reveal later in her career.

Moon Park had decided to conduct a seafood mission to China in late March, and they had requested that someone from ASA support the effort. Being the 'miracle caterer' that we were so well reputed, we needed to ship over display fish and some fish for consumption to support the effort. Since Jena was still new to the program, I made the choice to travel and act as the organization representative for the mission. I had worked closely with her to select the right fish for the mission, and had gone over the packing list, and she said she would take care of it. Unfortunately, by the time I left for the mission I received a call from our freight forwarder to tell me that

CHAPTER 54

Jena had screwed up the shipment and had not packed the right fish. There was no time to fix it, we needed to let the shipment continue as planned. I arrived in Shanghai for the session and had to deal with the fact that we did not have the complete set of display fish needed for the event. The hotel staff did their best to make it look good, but I knew that I was going to receive criticism from Moon Park — we had just given her more ammo to make arguments against our effectiveness in the market. I was forced to 'eat crow' and presented at the event like there was nothing wrong at all. I tried to let it go afterwards, but I knew we had provided an opportunity to lose face to our adversaries.

After the event, Bobby and I took a whole bunch of their staff members out to a club, one with girls in 'go go' boots. They had a pole on the bar, and one of the staff girls invited me up to dance, which I quickly replied, "No, they will kick me out for sure." The female bartender heard my response and quickly said, "No, please go ahead, I would like to see." So sure enough, I jumped on the bar, and started to swing around and around on the pole, to the delight of many of the people in the club. After that, we danced all through the night with the staff members, as I tried to forget about what had just taken place at the promotion.

I barely had time to be home for more than a week, and then it was time to head back out. At least I was able to be home to celebrate Kelly's first birthday — which I was really looking forward to. But first it was time to get down the ugly business of dealing with Jena for screwing up the shipment for Moon Park's promotion in Shanghai. She knew she was in trouble when I arrived back to the office — you could see the anxiousness on her face when I walked in. I called her into my office and shut the door, and sat down very calmly and said, "I want to apologize to you." She looked up at me with disbelief in her eyes. And then I continued, "I have worked very hard for the past 8 months or so to train you and guide you, and I am sorry, because I must be failing you as a manager, because there are some very basic things you are not getting right." I think that she had thought that I would start to berate her, and 'chew her out' for making a mess of the shipment to Asia. But I had grown as a manager enough by that point to recognize that I had to take responsibilities for my subordinate's actions, whether I was in control or not – that is just something a good manager needs to accept. She began to cry, and say she was sorry. And then she went on to tell me that I was one of the best bosses that she had ever had. I thanked her for the compliment, and then I shifted gears, and asked her what we needed to do to take make sure things like this did not happen anymore. I reminded her that I wanted to see her succeed in the role and challenged her to work closely with me to see that happen. I was hoping she would take the words positively.

A few days later it was time to head to Europe for the Governor's mission. Molly had her hands full getting ready for the Brussels show – so I was going it alone again. I flew into Hamburg first, where we met the Governor's staff to brief on the activities, and then had an informal delegation dinner that night. It was my first time to meet Governor Baxter in person, and he was very cordial, and wanted to know what my thoughts were about the market. The next morning, I met with Elise and she and I toured one of our promotions at a local Caremorre store. After that we met with the Governor's staff to present at a media reception, and then conduct a seafood buyers' luncheon. Then we took the delegation out to visit our old friend Simon Dunkel at his state-of-the art smokehouse out in the countryside. I must admit, the Governor was quite impressed with the operation. After the session, we bid the group farewell, as they left to travel for activities in Poland over the weekend.

The next morning, I headed by train to Hannover, to spend the Easter weekend with my family. I was really looking forward to some rest, but when I arrived I found my aunt had come from southern Germany, and had brought my cousins' girlfriends with her. The boys were gone in Asia on vacation, and she decided to bring the girls with her, as they had never been to Hamburg, and were hoping I would take them there for a tour. I had just come from there, so I was a little perplexed about the situation, as I was looking forward to a little rest and relaxation. But they kept on asking me if 'Uncle BJ' would take them to Hamburg to show them around. So, we went out and had a couple drinks that night, and then the next morning we got up and went to Hamburg. It was Saturday, so we toured some of the shops and sights before everything, and then as the night arrived, I took the girls down to the Rapperbahn to see the infamous nightlife. We started at my favorite bar, Herzblut, and after a few drinks, I took the girls out to the empty dance floor to 'break the ice'. It worked, as other people saw us dancing, and started streaming onto the floor to enjoy the music. We wound up partying late into the night, and then I packed us onto an early morning train to head back to Hannover. By the time we arrived back in the early morning, I was totally exhausted, and slept through most of Easter Sunday. Later in the early evening I awoke, walked out to great everyone, and declared, "I have rose from the dead!" Then we all sat down to enjoy a beautiful dinner together and laugh about what we had seen in Hamburg.

The next day I flew out of Hannover to head to London for the rest of the Governor's mission. The following morning, we met up with Daniel and some of the delegation to perform some retail store audits, as well as check out the venue for the next day's press luncheon. The locale was the world famous Nobu Restaurant, so we wanted to make sure everything would go off precisely as planned. The following day we held the press luncheon, and as the British would say, "It was a smashing success." I sat to Terry's left during the luncheon, and we chatted quite a bit about the seafood industry and our programs. It was great to get the Governor's ear for once, and he was so impressed with our efforts that he wound up pushing for more state funding to back our program – to the tune of about $ 1 million. Later in the day, we held a business reception in his honor at the U.S. ambassador's house. It was quite a busy affair, and Daniel and I spent most of the time shuffling food and drinks out for the crowd, as well as continually thanking the ambassador and his family for allowing us to conduct the reception at their home.

The following day we took the Governor and his entourage to the brand new, New York Seafoods plant. This was the same 'little' company that just two years earlier had been bold enough to take the gamble to promote fresh Alaska salmon in the market. And it had worked out well for them – they were now moving millions of dollars of frozen sockeye salmon into the market, and Terry was there just in time to cut the ribbon on their new state-of-the-art processing and distribution plant. Overall, it had turned out to be a very successful mission. The Governor and his staff very pleased, and I was very relieved that we had been able to take what appeared to be a 'vacation junket' and turn it into a PR powerhouse mission to promote the brand of Alaska.

I flew home the next day and arrived in the office on Monday to get the news from Jena that she was quitting. The decision had not come easily for her, as she had a young son that was autistic, and she just could not take being away from him for extended periods of time. I had known that this could have possibly been an issue when I first interviewed her, but I had to be fair and give her a chance. So, while it was frustrating to see her go after spending over eight months training her, I had no choice but to accept her letter of resignation. Here I was, stuck with two jobs again, as well as facing the fact that in just over a year, I had three different people in the role. How was this going to reflect on my management capabilities?

I tried to not think about it too much, as I was getting ready to leave a day later for a much-needed vacation to Hawaii with Sherry. Much had happened the last year with the arrival of our second child, Kari's third major heart surgery, and my ankle surgery. We had not had much time between ourselves with all my travel. We headed off to a nice quiet condo in Kihei and tried to spend a little alone time together. We were there for about a day, and I could sense there was something wrong with her. She was acting cold to me, and when I asked her what was up, she said, "I want a divorce." She told me that she had her dad writing up the papers, and that she wanted out. I was never around, and the relationship had become very strained. I was totally caught off guard and fell silent. The rest of the day and night were pretty quiet, and I waited for her to go to bed, and then I called my parents to share what had happened. They were very sad to hear what was happening and encouraged me to try and work things out. The next few days we were there, I tried to talk with her and repair the obvious damage that had occurred in our relationship. In hindsight, I think that it was her way of asking for help. This was her way of saying, "I miss you, and I need you in my life again." And I could understand her point. With all the work I had been living a very unbalanced life – it was mostly work, and very little personal time. All the travel and long hours were taking their toll. As she had joked before, "I am married to the invisible man." Now I was watching not only my professional life heading for the rocks, but my personal as well.

Chapter 55

A Canceled Vacation

With Jena's departure, I had decided that I would forego the show in Brussels. Molly and Carl were going, and Jeff Prince as well for the first time. Instead, I needed to turn my energies back to the Asia programs again. There was the Restaurant & Bar show in Hong Kong about the same time as the Brussels show, and I needed to support the effort.

My biggest problem was trying to get approval for my old friend from Magic Mermaid, Ed Mackey, to attend the show with me. He had left Magic Mermaid recently, and was busy devoting all his energies to the Alaska Live Company that he had been operating for years. He was a perfect industry member to take, considering the high demand for live crab products in the Hong Kong market. But I was getting a bit of resistance from the head office. They were giving me a bad time for trying to get Ed's approval on such short notice. It was because the travel clerk in Juneau had been dragging her feet on submitting the approval, which made it appear last minute. I went back and forth with them and was finally able to get approval at the last minute.

So off Ed and I went to Hong Kong for the show. It was in the same venue as the HOFEX show, and it reminded me a lot of it. We had a nice booth at the show, and Ed was making some great contacts. We had one girl from a wine booth that kept coming by and asking us if she could join us later – she was obviously attracted to me. After about the third time of her coming around, Ed made the observation, "She is a real cling on." Bobby caught the statement and asked, "What is a cling on?" Trying to explain American slang could be tough. So I said, "It is like a dingleberry." And Bobby asked, "What is a dingleberry?" I was digging myself a deeper hole. This was going to be a tough one to explain, so I told him to let me think about it for a while. A few hours later we went to dinner, and he asked again, "So what is a dingleberry?" I kept on trying to explain, but I kept cracking up and laughing every time I tried to utter the words. After about the third or fourth time, I finally was able to blurt out, "A dingleberry is a ball of poop that is stuck to your butt hair after taking a shit." I just did not know how to explain it any other way. Bobby's eyes grew wide, and then he started howling with laughter. Then he explained to the others at the table in Chinese. They all began to howl in laughter together. Here we were again with Bobby and Billy, sitting together at a table in Asia having dinner, and talking about poop. Then I took it a step further. Bobby and Billy had represented the U.S. Cranberry Promotion Council, so they knew what Ocean Spray Cranberry Cocktail was. I started making jokes about launching a new flavor- 'Ocean Spray Dingleberry Cocktail'. The whole table broke out in laughter as we came up with ideas about how we could promote the new 'Dingleberry Cocktail' in the China market. I don't know why, but every time the China staff and I would get together, we would come up with some of the most outrageous things to talk and laugh about.

I had a few weeks back at home, and then it was time to head to Germany for the soccer World Cup. I had been anticipating this trip for a year or two, and Elise and I had been working for the past year or so to develop some strong promotions for this major global event. I had planned well in advance for this, including taking a few weeks off for leave after the promotional activities had been completed. Unfortunately, Elise was having problems finalizing the activity schedule, which had made it hard to finalize my final travel plans. Having to spend so much time and effort on coordinating the Moon Park and Governor mission activities had not helped either. But I had submitted the travel approvals to the Juneau office prior to departing to Hong Kong in early May. Again, it appeared that the travel clerk had sat on the request, and waited to the last minute to submit the documents for approval. I could feel the tension growing from the head office towards me. It was continuing to make me very wary. At the last minute I was given approval, and off to Germany I went. We had researched the cost for flights in and out of Munich. Since the opening ceremonies and first match would take place there, the prices were astronomical. Instead, we booked a flight in and out of Hannover to save on costs.

After arriving I visited with the family for a day, and then drove with a friend to Munich. After we arrived in Munich, I conducted some retail store audits, and the following day I met with a major distributor called Taufer. Elise had negotiated the World Cup promotion with them, and they were serving Alaska seafood products at the VIP lounges at all 14 venues across the country. It was quite a significant promotion, which wound up serving over 188,000 meals of our seafood – quite the marketing punch for only about $20,000. Originally, I was scheduled to attend the opening ceremony, and then conduct PR visits at select venues around the country. But due to security concerns, we found that I would not be allowed into any of the venues. It was unfortunate, but not the first time I had experienced a change in plans during an activity, so I made the best of it. I spent the rest of the day touring several of Taufer's various outlets, including one of their retail outlets, as well as one of their restaurants and quick service bars. During meetings with the staff, I managed to negotiate a Fall promotion, and as well as garner their interest in purchasing even more Alaska products.

My cousins had traveled by train to meet us to enjoy the festivities taking place in Munich. Since I could not visit the VIP event at the stadium, I made my way back to my hotel to meet them. The town was full of soccer fans from all over the globe – there were colors from so many different countries, just like I had seen in Seoul a few years before. We went out to watch the opening match at one of the major outdoor venues. At first, we were going to try to go to the Olympiastadion to watch the match, but as we were to step on the light rail train, we were told that the venue was full, so we made our way back up the street to another major venue in one of the squares. But at the last minute, they shut the venue down, due to security concerns about a possible bomb threat. People were scrambling up and down the streets, looking for a place to watch the match at the last minute. We found ourselves in the same predicament too, until we finally found a bar that we could slip into to get a seat in front of a screen. Germany beat Costa Rica. After the match, we made our way through the streets to watch a town that was going nuts. There were many major streets shut down, there were beer steins and bottles and cans strewn about everywhere, while bands of drunken fans roamed across the town. We made our way into another bar and found ourselves dancing with Brazilians and Costa Ricans through the night. We returned to my room at about 2 am and found ourselves out on the veranda, enjoying the view. We noticed several fire trucks had pulled up outside the hotel, and we were wondering where the fire was. We did not have long to wonder, for next came a knock on our door by the firemen. It seems that all the cigarette smoke in our room had set off the fire alarm, so they had come for us! After they inspected the room, we began to have a laugh about the whole affair, had another cigarette, and then we were finally ready to sleep. The next morning, I received a call from Carl – while he knew that I had planned on staying an extra week or so on leave when I was done with the activity schedule, he really needed me to come back to attend a special Board session in Anchorage to help defend the China program from Moon Park and Ronald Reynolds, as they were making movements against us. As much as I wanted to stay, I complied and let him know I would be returning in a few days, and work on a presentation that help bolster the effectiveness of our efforts.

I said goodbye to my cousins, and I headed back north to Hannover to take a few days off before heading back. The next day I received a call from Sherry

– and she was laughing. To her dismay I had nicknamed Kelly 'Hellboy', due to him crying all night, and his tendency to pull his diaper off at night and spread poop everywhere. As she laughed, she said, "You were right, he is Hellboy." It turns out that he had pulled his diaper off again and spread poop all over the pack and play crib, as well as painted his face and body. I could only imagine the mess. I asked her to take a picture, but it was already too late – they had cleaned it all up. I spend the rest of that day catching up on all work emails, as well as starting to prepare the presentation for the board session.

The next day I flew back home to attend the board meeting. I did not have any time to stop at home, I just bounced through Seattle and on up to Alaska. The next morning, I was up and ready to defend the program. Carl had been correct – the international program was under attack, or more specifically the China program. Ronald Reynolds and Moon Park were to give a special presentation about how ASA's efforts in China were ineffective. They made accusations that products in the stores were mislabeled, and that the current operatives for the program were not providing adequate results. And then they talked about how the China program needed to have a real Alaskan involved with the program, and that they should be living in-country on a full-time basis to carry out a more effective mission. It was pretty obvious that they were trying to make a case to create new jobs for themselves in China. The AFC program (and Sun's special funding from the Governor) was only temporary, and when it ran out, they were going to need to find new jobs. As they insulted and slandered the China program, and my management of it, I calmly sat there and took notes. My domestic colleagues would look over at me during all of this, wild-eyed, and probably expecting me to break into a rage. But I had mentally prepared for this attack, and I remained tranquil, and continued to take notes for a rebuttal. I was scheduled to follow directly behind Bill and Sun, and as I took the podium, I provided updates on the program, and provided updated figures about the rise in exports to China, as well as the achievements of our efforts in the country. They could make accusations all they wanted – we had the numbers to back up the effectiveness of our efforts, which were stronger and more focused than ever. While I was not happy about having to forego my leave in Germany with my family, I could at least take comfort in the fact that I was able to effectively defend the China program and put to rest these unfounded accusations.

After the session, I pulled Carl aside, and let him know that the World Cup promotion had not gone as planned, and that I was not able to attend the intended venues but had done my best to negotiate some new promotions. He acknowledged what I said and agreed that sometimes these missions did not go as planned. There was no further discussion about it, and we moved onto other matters in front of us.

Chapter 56

Another Chinese Invasion

I returned to Seattle a few days later, and had to quickly prepare for another reverse China trade mission. This was the largest group we had ever had – including Molly and I, it made for 20 people, and it was a mix of both trade and media members, as well three federal government officials. It was such a large group that I had enlisted Molly to join me for the mission, as I needed someone else to help me 'herd' all the Chinese visitors around. It was one of the most intensive reverse missions I had carried out – we had several locales to visit throughout Seattle and Alaska. I had learned from previous missions how hard it was to keep so many group members on track, and on time. So, I brought a rubber fish with a string necklace, and I explained to the entire group that whoever was the last team member to meet at the lobby, or to board a bus for an activity, was the one that had to wear the fish around their neck until the next meetup. Of course, it worked, as no one wanted to have to wear the fish around their neck all day.

After spending a day or two in Seattle, with tours of retail stores, restaurants, and processing plants, we headed for Alaska. We started out in Anchorage, and after a wonderful dinner, we met at the Crow's Nest Bar at the top of the Captain Jack Hotel. Mr. Chu's voice was echoing in my head from the last Chinese mission, when he had said that I did not show him a good enough time. I quietly whispered in Bobby's ears that we could go visit the Great Alaskan Girl Company. Now 'The Girl' is the most famous strip joints in all of Alaska, a place that everyone should see – if they are into watching beautiful strippers perform. I had expected Bobby to come back with a handful of people that were interested, so I was a little shocked when he came back to me and told me that all the mission members wanted to see 'The Girl' – even the ladies. We patiently waited for the rest of the industry members to depart, and then I quietly shuffled all the members into taxis for the strip joint. Unfortunately, two of the girls had forgotten to bring their IDs, and were turned around at the door, and had to return to the hotel. But the rest were eager to get inside. Most of them had never seen buxom blonde woman like those inside, so we took turns buying them table dances. After a while they got even with me and bought me a table dance from a beautiful Asian girl. While I was a little concerned about the bad press we might get if we got caught, it was worth the risk to see the Chinese laughing and enjoying this once-in-a-lifetime experience to see all the beautiful woman at 'The Girl.'

The next day we were all up early for a day trip to Seward. We had a full schedule of activities, including a whale watching boat tour. While they were all excited to see whales, I found that the most entertaining for me was to watch several of them get seasick and start puking. After watching them feed their breakfast to the seagulls, we stopped in for a visit at the Aleut Shellfish Hatchery. It is a research center that is dedicated to expanding shellfish fisheries in Alaska, and there was a wide assortment of marine creatures to see, including geoducks – which almost all the Chinese couldn't wait to hold and take pictures with. After the hatchery we visited the local processing plant, where they had a chance to see halibut and salmon being processed. After the busy day in Seward, we headed back north to Girdwood to have dinner at the Alyeska Resort. After taking the tram to the top of the mountain (where the restaurant was), it turned out there was a special treat in store for the Chinese. Even though it was the middle of the summer, there was still snowpack at the top of the tram. None of the Chinese had seen snow before, and to them it was almost magical. They were like little kids, having snowball fights, and rolling around in it and taking pictures. For many of them, I think it was the highlight of their trip.

The following day we took them on a tour through downtown Anchorage, including some shopping and a trip to the museum. After that we took them to some of the State offices to meet with state officials, and well as to conduct trade meetings with local industry members. That night we had another special dinner planned at the French Grill, with Archie serving his usual delightful assortment of Alaska seafood dishes. We had several state officials there that night, including Carl and Senator Joe Clemons. I was busy for most of the dinner, coordinating photo shoots in the kitchen, and making sure everything was going as planned. Joe sat on the other side of the room with other state officials, keeping a safe distance from me. When it was time for him to go, he was shaking hands with all of those in attendance, and when he came to me, I stood up to shake his hand, and he said, "Thanks for inviting me, Sam (my brother's name)." He started to turn a beautiful shade of red, as he realized his slip – as I am sure my brother was heavy on his mind, after all the public attacks he was making on him. He quickly apologized for the name mistake, and as I shook his hand, I smiled and looked him in the eye and said, "It's okay Senator, I am the friendly Kreiger." It was the last time I ever saw him.

The next morning, we flew to Kodiak. We had another action-packed schedule, with plant tours, interviews at the radio station, as well as visits to the Fish Tech Center and the local museums. The following day we flew to the south end of the island to visit the processing facility at Alitak. I had spent my youth in Alitak – it had been my introduction to the seafood industry, and it was the first time I had returned there in 15 years – it was a bittersweet experience for me, to see so many faces and places from my past. This is the place that I decided to start my journey into marketing, and here I was, so many years later, returning as a marketing executive, fulfilling the dream that I had envisioned in my younger days. After enjoying a quick lunch at the bunkhouse, we boarded our planes to head to Red River for some bear viewing – and we weren't disappointed. We were able to get some great shot of a couple of bears in action, which was totally thrilling to all the mission members. While I had already spent so many years with the bears, for them, this was a truly another once-in-a-lifetime experience.

We returned that afternoon, and went to tour the road system, including a trip to the top of Pillar Mountain to secure a panoramic view of the town. Unfortunately, the weather was horrible, and after reaching the top of the mountain we could not see anything. As we got everybody back on the bus, I was the last one on board – and they were waiting there with me with the rubber fish. One of them said to me, "BJ, today you get to wear the fish." And they all began to laugh very loudly. I proudly put it around my neck and wore it the rest of that day and night. We held another big industry dinner that night, which was well attended by the community. It was great to see the interaction between the visitors and the locals, each sharing their differences and their stories. There was always so much work we put into these missions, and these were the moments that seemed to really make it all worthwhile. As I always used to say, "The reverse missions were a lot of work, but in the end, they were a labor of love." The next day we flew back to Seattle, and the spent another day conducting technical seminars and buyer's meeting (we had learned that it was better to educate the buyer's first, and then set them up for sales meetings after they were more knowledgeable about the products).

After we finally got the mission members back on their way home, I went home and collapsed – I must have slept a day and a half, recovering from the sheer exhaustion of all the work. I returned to the office to find myself accused of throwing the domestic programs under the bus. Carl called me and let me know that there was dissent in the office, as the international program was to receive additional funding from the State – to the tune of $ 1 million, and that there was the general feeling from my domestic counterparts that I had 'badmouthed' their programs; he was asking me to meet with them and address the issue. I agreed to meet with them to try and smooth the situation out. For years I had worked with a very small staff to accomplish seemingly insurmountable tasks – at the cost of my own personal life. I had to speak up and question, "Why is our program being recognized as more productive than the others? Was it possibly not because of negative things I was saying about domestic programs (which I had not)? Did you think that maybe people had drawn their own conclusions?" I did not have time, nor the inclination, to 'bash' the other programs – I was too busy trying to make the international program be successful. It really appeared to me that I had worked too hard for too long (as well as Molly and the other international team members) and had raised the bar too high for others to wish to follow. As Elise used to say to me when she visited and watch me work so hard, "BJ, why do you work so hard? None of the rest do." Of which I replied, "I can't help it, I am just built that way." I called in the domestic staff, and I apologized for any bad feelings that they may have had, but I assured them that it was not due to anything I was saying about them. Whatever they were hearing out in the network was being misconstrued. Again, I could feel the tide of ill will and bad sentiments rising up against me. I felt it was only a matter of time before it would get worse. I could not help but think how many more days I had before the situation would become intolerable. And to make matters worse, Carl would not let me post to hire a replacement for the Asia position. I could not help but feel that things were just going to get worse.

Chapter 57

MoonMart

And the situation was continuing to deteriorate. We had been preparing for our annual strategic planning, which was to take place in Tokyo in conjunction with the Japan Seafood Show. For the first time, the entire international team was to meet together at a locale overseas, instead of Seattle. Just a few days before we were to depart, Carl contacted me and let me know that Moon Park and Harpoon needed help with shipping instructions for shipping promotional products to China for a promotional mission she was to be conducting. She had informed me about a few weeks earlier that she was planning on conducting a generic promotion, with several Alaska suppliers, but at the last minute all of them had bailed, except for Harpoon. Since there was only one brand now, that made it a branded promotion. ASA's charter forbids any type of branded promotion, so I warned Carl that, while we wanted to try to assist this effort (even though it appeared duplicative of our efforts in China), we should only lend advisory support. Carl was convinced it was a generic promotion, and for some strange reason wanted to provide funds to pay for the import fees into China. I told him I did not think it was a good idea, but he was insistent that he would provide the funds from his administrative budget. He was also under the impression that we could receive the product, but I explained to him that our contractor in China did not have an import license, so we referred them to an importer that could help clear the product. I sat down and wrote detailed instructions for how to ship promotional products to China, which included providing a copy of one of our latest pro-forma invoices, as well as contact names for our freight forwarder, in case they had any further questions. I emailed the instructions to Moon and the contacts at Harpoon and encouraged them to follow up with me if they had any questions. Still, I thought it strange that the largest producer in Alaska, that already had a strong presence in China, needed our help to ship over something as simple as a promotional shipment.

What I didn't realize at that time was that Moon was planning on doing in-store promotions at Hal-Mart locations in China. Hal-Mart was celebrating ten years in the China market, and we had been approached earlier by the federal agricultural officials in China to support a giant U.S. food promotion as part of the celebration – which we gladly were participating in as a fellow cooperator group. I wish I would have known what Moon was planning, because I would have alerted the FEO offices in China and tried to halt her actions.

But I needed to turn my attention back to the strategic planning session that we were coordinating. We were really excited to have the entire international team together in Japan. I was invited to be one of special dignitaries for the ribbon cutting event to open the show. It was a proud moment for me to have my whole team there, watching me and cheering me on. But the good feelings were short-lived. Han and I had a miscommunication, and she thought I was bringing over a new slide deck to share with the Japan press. I had totally misunderstood the request (probably because I was overwhelmed with all the other tasks I had in front of me), so Jim Tanaka had to come in and save us with a bunch of USDC generated facts and figures. Still, Han was not pleased with me. She was under enough pressure already, as just that Spring there had a review performed of the Japan program, and it was not flattering. I had gone to bat for her, and had stood up for the program, and dismissed the flawed review, which had seemed very biased.

Still, she was feeling the heat, and it was starting to show.

To make matters worse, Bobby and Billy were totally under duress from all the requests and demands by Moon Park. She had been targeting their program for months now, and they were starting to crack under the pressure. They had always been so calm before, but I sat in their hotel room and for the first time I ever, I watched them screaming at each other. Bobby yelled out, "Moon should be fucked by a dog." Then Billy responded, "No, she should be fucked by two dogs." Then Bobby yelled back, "She should be fucked by a pack of dogs!" I could feel their frustration. Moon was tearing the China team apart, and I assured them that I would do everything I could to keep her at bay. But they were so stressed that they had Billy fly back home to prepare for dealing with Moon Park's activities. I did my best to keep the team on track in Tokyo, and we tried to do a lot of team building exercises, including touring the Tsukiji market together. While I was feeling a lot of pressure, Daniel continued to assure me that everything would work out. He had always been my moral compass during my journey at ASA, and I trusted his judgment.

I returned home in time to celebrate Kari's third birthday. It was a wonderful party, and we had most of the family from both sides in attendance. I was trying to forget about work and having so much of my family there made it easier for me to relax and enjoy the moment. A few days later I was off on leave for a week to spend some time with Sherry's family on a nice beach house on Whidbey Island. We were not allowed to have dogs, so I took them up and left them with my friend. Sherry's siblings were all there, and we were relaxing and having a great time at the beach.

And then my mobile phone rang. It was Bobby, and he sounded frantic. Harpoon had shipped over an entire ton of products for Moon Park's promotion, and they had horrible undervalued it – just $210 to be exact. Chinese customs suspected that it was an attempt to smuggle product into the country, and they had seized the shipment. And now Moo n and one of the Chinese representatives from Harpoon were threatening Bobby that he needed to go to customs and sign a statement accepting responsibility for the shipment, or he would never work for Alaska again. Basically, they were telling him to write his own ticket to prison. For a Chinese national to accept such responsibility, he could be arrested on the spot, and imprisoned until proven otherwise. He was working himself in to a total panic as he told me all of this. I told him to stand down. Under no circumstances was he to take responsibility for that shipment; if any one asked, he had direct orders from me. For the next day or two, I bantered back and forth with Bobby and Carl about what had happened. I explained to Carl the situation that Bobby was being put into, and that he could not be asked to do such a thing. I tried to explain that I had provided directions on how to ship products to China, and that they must have totally disregarded them, and this was the result. Either way – it was not our fault, and we shouldn't be involved with it. Meanwhile, I asked Bobby to quietly take pictures of the Moon/Harpoon promotion that was taking place. My family vacation was getting ruined, while Moon Park and Harpoon were busy walking all over the U.S. promotion at Hal-Mart.

As if things couldn't get any worse, at the end of the vacation I went back up to pick up the dogs from my friend. Sherry's dog, Tonto, was missing. When their son had opened the gate, he bolted past and ran down the street, never to be seen again. I picked up my dog, Bingo, and brought her home. When I got to the house, she ran inside to look for Tonto. But when she could not find him, she started to get frantic. The two dogs had been very protective of the children, and now Bingo was left there to guard them alone. The next day I returned to work and noticed a thick brown envelope sitting in my inbox. I opened it and found to my dismay that I was being accused of going to the World Cup promotion in Germany under false pretenses, and that I had only gone there for vacation, and was being asked to re-imburse the State of Alaska for the entire trip. I slumped back in my chair and thought, "It's finally happening, they are trying to frame me and destroy my reputation." I read through all the documents – basically the administrative staff had turned on me and had tried to cook up a case against me. I immediately scanned a copy of the letter and emailed it to Daniel, and then called him. I said to him, "They are trying to frame me." He agreed that it was low what they were trying to do to me, but he felt that their case was very weak. He and I went to work on writing a response letter to address the accusations. He assured me that he would support me through this. My next call was to Elise. When I told her what had happened, her response was, "Oh my God, have they lost their minds?" She told me she would go right to work to get a letter from Taufer that would verify and support the work I did, including the new promotions I had negotiated while I was in Germany in June. How ironic it was – I had flown to Shanghai for just one day of work in May to support Moon Park's promotion, and I had spent almost two weeks in Europe in April to support the Governor's junket, but now I was being accused of flying to Germany for a vacation when I was had been implementing our program's promotion? I found it almost laughable, considering I had canceled my vacation in Germany at Carl's request, to come back and defend the program. The situation was deteriorating rapidly. Then I got the call that afternoon – the boat my brother was on had just sunk. He was okay, but he could have been killed. I thought to myself, "How much worse could things get?"

But they did. I went home after work that night to learn that my beloved dog, Bingo had a stroke that day. She was losing her balance when she tried to walk and would fall over. I held her in my arms, and I hoped and prayed that she would recover. But the next day she had another stroke and could barely hold her head up. I made the hard decision to let her go. I called my friend that worked at a vet, and had my sister drive me while I held Bingo in my arms. We took her to the vet nearby, and I had her euthanized. I held her in my arms while they did it, as I felt her life slip away. I held her in my arms while they did it, and I felt her life slip away. It was a very somber moment for me.

Meanwhile the whole situation with Moon Park and Harpoon in China had melted down. By now, I had nicknamed the whole affair the 'Moon Mart' promotion. The entire shipment of seafood had to be abandoned, because if Harpoon changed the value of the shipment, they would be basically admitting that they had falsified the value of the product. Harpoon was trying to point fingers at us, accusing us that we had not been cooperative enough, when in reality, we had done everything we could to provide information to avoid issues. I had Bobby send pictures of the branded promotion to Carl, which clearly showed Harpoon banners hanging up prominently at the stores, with Harpoon staff working underneath them. Considering this, Carl all of a sudden had to change his tune about the organization's ability to support the effort (something I had warned him about from the start). Not only had they conducted a branded promotion, Moon Park, Ronald Reynolds, and Harpoon had managed to walk all over the US promotion that was taking place, which had angered the federal authorities. Still, it didn't stop Carl from trying to chastise me for my reluctance to support the effort – when I had tried to warn him from the start that it was going to create nothing but problems.

Chapter 58

Losing My Cool

It seemed like the whole world was melting down that week. The FBI had been investigating corruption charges into what was now being heralded as the 'Corrupt Bastards Club', which was a group of Alaska legislators that had been receiving funds from corporate interests – including Senator Joe Clemons. This group was so arrogant that they had actually created 'Corrupt Bastard Club' baseball hats for themselves. And the latest news was that the FBI had just raided Joe's office in Juneau.

Meanwhile, I was busy writing a four-page response letter back to Carl about the allegations being leveled at me. Daniel and I fine-tuned the letter, diminishing all the weak and false accusations against me. After all I had done for the State to support so many efforts – including all the time I had dedicated to activities that were outside the scope and responsibilities of our program. How many times had we played 'ASA the Miracle Caterer' for other state organizations? I had been so careful all during my career at ASA to remain ethical, and to follow procedures. It didn't seem to matter now. We finished the response letter and I sent it to Carl.

A few days later, Carl came to Seattle, and he scheduled a meeting for me in the afternoon. He walked into my office and sat down and started telling me about how he had just spent the morning getting his ass chewed by Harpoon employees for the whole Moon Mart affair in China. And then next he took the four-page response letter I had sent him and tossed it back on my desk in front of me and told me that it did not respond to any of the allegations being asserted again me. I could feel the rage build inside of me. I lost it. I had had enough. My composure was gone, and out the door. I told him, "For five years I have put up with you. I have supported you publicly, regardless of all the questionable situations you have put me and my staff into, but enough is enough." I went on about how I had warned him about the not getting involved in the Moon Mart affair. How he had allowed Bobby to be put in harm's way. How insulted I was about these accusations that I traveled under false pretenses. I had answered the weak allegations against me. As the anger began to rise in my voice, I watched all the rest of the staff leaving the office and scrambling to their cars in the parking to get the hell out of there. I told Carl to 'fuck off', and I flipped him the middle finger at the same time. I didn't care anymore. I told him what a 'fucking bitch' Moon Park had been this whole time, and how I was sick of getting put in an awkward position by the 'fucking processors' like Harpoon. I just couldn't take anymore – it had been too much.

Then I caught myself, and I shifted gears. I looked at him again, I took in a deep breath, and I explained how I had always had my team look up to me as their leader. That they had counted on me to keep them out of harm's way and defend their position. And then I told him that I had looked to him for years for support but had never fully felt like it had been provided. I looked at him again and asked, "Would you please lead us? Would you please defend us?" He said nothing. He was without words. I am not sure if that he was a coward, or maybe he had never had a subordinate speak out against him in such a manner. Whatever it was, he looked visibly shaken as he left the office, got in his car, and drove away.

The next day he came back in the office, and he called me into the conference room. I started by apologizing for the way that I had spoken to him yesterday,

358

but I had been pushed to the limit. He put a letter in front of me that he had written, and he asked me to read it, which I did. The letter cited my behavior and language, and it stated that I was to be on a probational basis for the next six months. Then he said to me, "You can't refer to another member of the State staff as a 'fucking bitch'." I could not help but immediately retort back, "But she is." That person had caused so much stress for all of us at the organization. I was going to remind Carl how many times I had heard him cuss during discussions with him. But it was no use making such arguments now. It was obvious to me that I was being put into an awkward position. I had gone from 'golden child' for the organization to a political target rather quickly.

A day or two later, EAS had 'invited' me to attend an FEO cooperator meeting in China – and I knew that I was about to the 'face the music' about the MoonMart promotion. Earlier in the year, we had started preliminary work for our first efforts in Russia – some members of the board had wanted to start a small pilot program in Russia/Ukraine – mainly to promote salmon roe/caviar sales. Originally I had planned on traveling to Russia for the World Food Moscow show, but with the FEO meeting on the horizon, we made the decision to send Molly and Daniel to attend. Since only two of us were on the staff since April, we were spread pretty thin. Our IMC chairman, Kelvin Nash had recognized how being short-staffed was wearing thin on us, and so he had written a memo to Carl and Dave Simpson about how the staff shortage, and implored the administration to provide us with additional staffing resources – but it fell on deaf ears. I began to suspect that they were purposely wearing us down. But we were undaunted. Molly would attend the show in Russia and Conxemar in Spain, and I would take care of business in China.

So off to China I went. I flew into Shanghai first, and Billy and I visited the FEO for a briefing. The new director was Dave Daskin; Dave had served at several other posts during my days with ASA, and we had built a rapport through the years. We spoke about several different issues – the need to increase messaging in the market, as well as to garner more industry support. And then came what I had expected – he shared his opinion that the Alaska state agencies's efforts had been duplicative of ASA's efforts referring directly to what had taken place during the MoonMart promotion. As he so well pointed out, EAS had invested over $200 million in China the past few years, and that the duplicative actions of other Alaska agencies were endangering EAS's position in the market. We assured him that we would do our best to avoid such duplication in the future. My original assumptions were correct – that MoonMart was going to create a lot of problems in many ways.

The next day we traveled to Qingdao for the FEO cooperator session. During the second day of the sessions, we had individual cooperator sessions with FAS staff. The director of FAS, Wayne Dee, was in attendance, as well as Morgan Chase, a special attaché from Beijing, as well as the new directors for the FEO programs in Beijing, Chengdu, Guangzhou, and Shanghai. We started out covering strategic and tactical efforts and changes to ASA's China program. And then it got fun. The MoonMart promotion and the actions of Moon Park and AFC were raised, and several the directors voiced their displeasure of having another Alaska state agency operating promotional seafood efforts in China – especially during a promotion that had already been sponsored by the FEO and ASA. They requested that such duplication cease in the future. And Morgan even went as far as to ask why the State did not give the money to ASA to increase promotional efforts, that if there was additional funding available that it could have bolstered the existing program. I had no answer – all I could do was apologize on behalf of the State.

I implored them to write a letter to the ASA Board to make and official request to resolve such duplicative efforts in China to stop – but it never came. As I walked out of the meeting, Ray Kurt, who was now the director the FEO in Chengdu, followed me out. He told me that he knew it wasn't my fault, and that it would be okay. I turned right around and looked him in the eye and replied, "I am going to probably lose my job over this." He didn't believe that it would happen. But I had a feeling that this was the beginning of my end at ASA. I returned back home, and Billy and I began to write the trip report for this session, and what FAS thought about the 'MoonMart' affair.

About that same time, reporters were starting to investigate the 'MoonMart' affair in China. I had spoken with a few of them about it, but I was very careful about what I revealed about the affair – just confirming that the seafood shipped had been undervalued. Billy and I finished the trip report and made sure that Moon Park and AFC had been named in the discussions. I made sure that I sent a copy of the report for Carl to review – but it appears that he never read it, or paid no attention to what it said.

Chapter 59

Into the Fire

It was early October, and things were settling down a little bit. I was trying to stay positive in face of all of this, but it wasn't easy. It was Tuesday October 10th, and suddenly my right knee started to ache. I had just played soccer the night before and did not remember any type of injury taking place, so I couldn't understand what was going on. An hour or two passed, and the pain became worse, and I could see that the knee was starting to swell, so I left work and went straight to a clinic to get it checked out. The doctor looked at and said that I must have injured it, and that it looked like inflammation. He prescribed me some pain pills and anti-inflammatories and sent me home. By the next night the pain had increased so much that I couldn't' stand it. It was the most intense pain I had ever experienced. Sherry was getting ready to call me an ambulance, but instead had her father come pick me up and take me to the hospital. I could not even bend my knee at this point, and I had to lay down in the back of his Suburban for the ride to the emergency room. As they checked me in, I was doubled over in pain – they asked me how bad it was on a scale of 1 to 10 – and I replied, "It is a 10." They put me in a treatment room, and I asked if they could please give me something for the pain – it was so intense. I got upset with the nurse, and he said that he would step outside the room and let me calm down. I couldn't believe it. A couple minutes later he came in and finally gave me a shot of morphine to dull the pain. They then shoved a needle in my knee to draw a sample of fluid from the knee joint -but found no infection. They gave me more pain medication, recommended that I visit an infectious disease specialist, and sent me back home.

The next day I went saw a specialist at the hospital, and he said it just looked like inflammation, but gave me some antibiotics, just in case. The next day I looked at my knee, and noticed that the inspection was spreading. It was Friday the 13th, and on top of it, it was Sherry's birthday. We were supposed to being going out to dinner that night to celebrate, but I had a feeling that wasn't going to happen. She took one look at my knee and said, "I'm taking you back to the hospital right now. There I was, back in the emergency room again for a second time in three days. But this time was different. On call was this brilliant young orthopedic surgeon, that happened to be a knee specialist. I told him how I had been in and out to medical facilities every day since Tuesday, but to no avail. He asked, "Did they poke the top of your knee to take a sample?" I told him, "No." He couldn't' believe it. The top of my knee was bigger than a grapefruit. He took a syringe and poked the top – and sure enough – he drew out a massive amount of pus. They rushed it to the lab for testing, and sure enough, it was a massive infection of MRSA bacteria – a very serious staph infection. The immediately gave my intravenous antibiotics, and then the doctor said, "You have two choices: We can cut the knee open, put a drain in, and monitor for the next week or two, or we can do emergency surgery. Considering that I had to travel to China in a little over a week, I told him, "Surgery, please." Suddenly I was being rushed off to surgery upstairs. I woke up a few hours later, with a giant row of stitches on my knee, and an IV in my arm hooked to a morphine pain pump. The massive swelling was gone, but the cut and stitches in my knee looked horrendous. Still, it was hard to suppress my sense of humor. I told the nurses that I was having a luxury weekend at the 'chateau'. They were amused by my sense of humor, and I did my best to relax through the weekend.

They released me from the hospital on Monday, just in time for me to attend the week -long special board meeting, joint committee meetings, and a reception to celebrate ASA's 25th anniversary. The anniversary was on that Thursday, and I had made 100s of custom baseball caps to hand out at the reception. I had also created some certificates for the three industry members that had served at ASA for the entire 25 years. I was on crutches but was being my usual jovial self throughout the sessions.

The next day things were not so much fun. We were conducting an IMC meeting and included in the packets were the trip report from the FEO meetings that had taken place in September. Moon Park was at the meeting and she grabbed a packet and started going through it. I noticed her get up and leave the room while we were in session. A few minutes later Carl came rushing into the room and asked that the trip report be removed from the packets and provided to him so he could destroy them. It seems that Moon had seen her name in the report, and immediately complained to Carl that she would make 'big trouble with Governor Baxter' if the report was not rescinded. I quickly remembered that I had provided a copy for Carl to review a few weeks before (and I had sent electronic copies of the report to all the committee members). It was a little late to make the report totally disappear. Still, I was dumbfounded. After the session, some of the committee members were quietly asking what the issue was about. I tried to play it down, but I explained the circumstances. I was just doing my job – as I always had – and was just reporting what had taken place during my sessions in China.

Shortly thereafter I walked downstairs to the main session room, and Carl walked up to me and said, "I thought you would know better than to name State employees (and AFC) in a report." I replied, "I don't see what the problem was". This was especially true considering I answered to both the State of Alaska and the U.S. Department of Agriculture and needed to report what had been said. Then he said to me words that I never thought I would hear, "Your problem is you are too honest." I was floored – here was my boss telling me that I was being too honest. Meanwhile Moon avoided me but glared across the room at me when she saw me. And then there were industry members coming to me asking me what the issue was – I tried to change the subject. Again, I was in trouble for doing my job like I was supposed to. I was not going to be complicit in a promotional activity that I had warned should not have taken place. The possible outcomes I had warned about had pretty much all taken place – and now I was in trouble for it.

I went home, wondering if things could get any worse. But I did not have much time to worry about it, as I needed to fly to China two days later. Carl and I were flying together to attend the China Fish Expo. Carol Hopper, who was the legislative aide for Senator Joe Clemons, was joining us. When I had been coordinating the travel for this mission a few weeks before, I inquired as to which agency was paying for Carol's travel to China. I was told that Magic Mermaid was paying for her travel, and to not worry about it. I could not believe it. Since when was it okay for a private company – one that had received a healthy amount of AFC funding under the chairmanship of Senator Clemons – okay to pay for a state employee's travel for official business? This did not seem right at all, but with the way things had been going, it was best not to argue the subject.

We arrived in China, and Carl requested that I have breakfast with him the next morning. During breakfast he of course started chastising me for writing the report that named Moon Park and AFC. I politely tried to explain the circumstances – that I had a duty not only the state, but also to the federal government to officially report this. I was caught in-between, and in a rather tough spot. His point was that I should have not named the actual people and agency involved. I had to disagree. I was not trying to be argumentative, but I was sticking to my guns on this one. He warned that I had created more problems, and that further disciplinary action might be required.

But it was time to manage the booth at the show. We had managed to supply Alaska beer to the show this time – by shipping it to Hong Kong, and letting our connections take care of getting it 'cleared' across the border into China. I tried to keep calm, but I was feeling a little uneasy with Carl and Carol. She knew who my brother was, and it was kind of an awkward situation, considering that my sibling had been politically attacking her boss. Thankfully, Carol and Carl went to Beijing for a different food show. It was not part of the approved mission, so I found it kind of ironic that they could just suddenly add a trip to Beijing in the middle of the mission – when I had been in so much trouble for my trip to Germany in June that had gone afoul. Still, I kept my mouth shut, and I made the best of the mission. When we arrived back in Seattle, Carl and I were both picking up our luggage. Before I headed out the door, I turned, shook his hand, and said, "Please let me know if you have to fire me for writing the report; have a safe trip home."

The timing had been just perfect on all this. It turns out that the day the report was rescinded Dan Krass had released a news article that exposed the MoonMart affair. He had submitted a Freedom of Information Act (FOIA) request to the Alaska Department of Commerce - that was requesting all electronic and hard copy communications related to the promotion in China. When I read the story, I called Dan to follow up on details of what was revealed from the FOIA request. He informed me that all of my and Billy's communications with Carl and Moon about the activity had been withheld from the FOIA requests. State reports generated by Moon Park and Ronald Reynolds claimed that during the promotion $140,000 of seafood had been purchased by Hal-Mart. As well, representatives from the state and Harpoon all claimed that the promotion had been a huge success. But no Harpoon product had been purchased, and Hal-Mart had reported that the increase in sales was a little over $15,000. Essentially they had conducted a branded promotion that had trampled all over the FEO/ASA promotion, and resulted in sales of Alaska seafood that did not sell one bit of Harpoon product. And on top of that, two state agencies were working in conjunction to cover up the whole mess.

I was continually getting more disgusted about the whole affair. A week or so later we traveled to Baltimore for the annual UFEA meetings. While there I quietly set up a meeting with Wayne Dee. Wayne made sure there was three other FAS staff members there to witness the session. I reported to him that I was working in a hostile work environment due to the report I had written, and provided him a copy of the report. I revealed the cover up taking place, including the rescinding of my trip report, and that I wanted to go on the record about it. Wayne assured me that my information would be kept confidential, and that he would do the best he could to protect me in case the situation deteriorated. I thought about the predicament and started to form a backup plan – to form a new U.S. seafood promotion board that would represent all American seafood – not just Alaska's. Kelsey and I had spoken of this a few years back, and I started to re-approach her on the idea while we were together for the meetings.

Meanwhile, back at the office I was receiving complaints about Molly. It was being claimed that she was not being cooperative with other staff members. I talked with her again about the situation, but I wasn't sure what we could do to fix it. I had done my best to reach out to the domestic staff members to try and improve relations, but the relationship remained strained. It seemed like it did not matter what Molly and I were doing, people from both offices were continually hostile to us. Molly and I decided to look for an employment lawyer to represent us. We talked with one she knew, but he wasn't much help. I continued to search for one, but it was hard to source, as so many were already hired to represent legislators and other government contacts due to the FBI corruption investigation in Alaska.

Chapter 60

Asking for Help

About that time, I was provided with a connection to Rod Baldwin, husband to Kerri Baldwin, who had just been elected Governor. My brother had insisted to me that Kerri was a 'white knight' that was going to come in and clean up all the corruption. One of her campaign promises had been that she was going to take on the 'good ole boy' system that was so pervasive in the state government. While many people believed her, I was still skeptical. For some reason my gut instinct told me that this would not be the case. In hindsight, I should have trusted my gut. Still, I coordinated to speak with Rod. So he gave me a call and asked me what he could do for me. I explained to him that I was in a hostile work environment, that potentially there were laws being violated, and that I would like to request to be shielded under the Alaska Whistleblower's Act. He told me he would talk to Kerri and get back to me. The proper channel for filing a complaint would have been the Chairman of the Board for ASA, but I did not trust him – or any of the rest of the Board, to act in my interest. I was in a tough spot. A few days later I received a call from the newly appointed Attorney General. He inquired as to what the situation was, and said he would look into my request, and get back to me.

Meanwhile I had located a lawyer in Anchorage that would possibly represent me. I asked Molly if she wanted to seek representation. But by then she had consulted with her husband, and she said that they were worried about their future in the industry. So I flew alone to Anchorage and started the process of revealing my situation. The lawyer felt that I potentially had a strong case and agreed to represent me. Immediately he sent an acknowledgment letter to the Attorney General's office. The only response that was received was a call back from the Attorney General, informing my attorney that, "...it was too political to get involved."

It appeared that the new administration was going to do nothing to shield me. Quietly, I let Dan Krass know of my predicament, specifically my attempts to contact the Balins to seek relief. Shortly thereafter, he interviewed the Governor, and inquired about me. She denied having any knowledge of me. Now considering that Rod did not work for the state, and that after speaking with him I was contacted by the Attorney General, the natural conclusion was that Rod spoke with Kerri about my situation, and she delegated that task to the Attorney General. Of course, I have no proof of this, but I always wondered what the level of communications about me must have been. Kerri was later involved in an email scandal known. It turned out that she had conducted a high level of state business on her personal email account and was accused of abusing her power for personal reasons. The case wound up in the release of 13,000 emails – though there were thousands more that were suppressed due to 'executive privilege'. I still wonder if communications about my situation remained in the stack of withheld messages.

I had to come to the realization that I was being left out in the cold to hang in the wind. The situation continued to worsen. It was January of 2007, and I received a written quarterly performance review. Carl was still pressuring me to rewrite the FEO China trip report. According to him, it was inappropriate that I wrote a report that criticized a state official by name, and that the Board was extremely upset that I would do such a thing. Moon Park had been running around for the past few years, walking all over so many people, trying to leverage her relationship with the Governor's wife to force others to comply with her wishes. While it may have appeared that I had singled her out, in fact I was only reporting what the FEO staff was complaining about – how else was I supposed to resolve the issue, unless the perpetrator was identified? Carl was also accusing me of consuming too much alcohol at the China Seafood Expo in October – it was noted that both he and 'a staff member of the Alaska State Legislature' (I wonder who that could have been), claimed that I had consumed too much beer during the first day of the show. I found that almost amusing, considering that if I had actually appeared drunk during the event, common sense predicated that I would have been reprimanded almost immediately – instead of waiting almost two and half months later to accuse me in writing.

And then there were ongoing issues with Molly. She was being accused of being rude and arrogant, and that staff at both offices were complaining about her attitude. And as well, there was the general concern being voiced by staff that, while I had improved my interactions with staff, that they were still skeptical that I would return to a pattern of negative behavior. And then there was the presumption about my ability to work with other state officials. After all the years of working in conjunction with so many departments with the state, after one bad incident – a situation that I had advised would have negative outcomes – now I was the bad guy, being singled out as a 'problem area'. The picture for Molly and I was continually being painted darker and darker by the day. By the end of month things had not improved. We couldn't even book a trip or make a change to her travel schedule without it being turned into a major issue. No matter what we did – it seemed like it was a problem.

The final insult came at about that time. Bantu and I were splitting hairs over the upcoming fiscal budget. During the board meeting almost a year before, the Board has assigned a cash match of $2.2 million for the coming year's budget. But the cash match was never actually allocated to the international program. There was $1 million that the program never received – even though the State had slated it for us, and the Board had assigned it. And when I pointed out the shortfall, all Bantu could say was, "I answer to the Board, not you."

The only good news that came to me was that Sherry was once again pregnant – she had wanted a third child. While I had been resistant to the idea, I had given in to it. And sure enough, she was pregnant with twins. When she brought the ultrasound image home, it showed two fetuses – one large one, and one small one. She informed me that the doctor had said that the small one would not survive, but I disagreed. "Oh yes it will survive.", I replied. "You wanted one more, and now you are going to get two." I said wryly.

I was really beginning to lose faith in the ability to rectify the situation, so I made an appointment with the Vice-chairman of the IMC, Devon Whitfield. I copied an entire pile of documentation that revealed all the questionable activities that had taken place the last year or two, and then drove to his office for a visit. While I was there, I explained the decaying situation for Molly and me, gave him a number of specific examples, and provided him with the copies of the documentation, letting him know that if anything happened to the staff, that he would at least have written proof of what had taken place.

A week or so later I had my brother call me and ask me why I had not responded to industry members that had questions about the program and activities. I told him that I never received any such requests. He forwarded copies to my private email address to prove the requests had been sent. That is when I realized that the staff in Juneau had been intercepting emails addressed to me. A few years before we were on a State server – as we should be – as all electronic and written communication by State staff was supposed to be public record (and we had been warned about this regulation a number of times through the years). But for the last year or two, somehow the Juneau office had gotten permission to take us off the State-run servers, and so the messages were running directly through the Juneau office. Obviously, they had been monitoring my emails for some time, and blocking emails from the outside that they did not want me to see. Day by day, I was continuing to lose faith in my administration, as well as my ability to carry out my duties.

I was not committing to any international travel, as there was only two of us to work on the CMS application, and as always, there was much work to do. February was upon us, and it was time for the winter Board meeting. We had just scheduled a committee meeting right before that. Carl was in attendance, and one could see that there was a lot of tension between us. In fact, I had one committee member tell me that he had appeared 'imperialistic' in his approaches and statements. The next week I traveled to Juneau to face the board. When it was my turn to speak, I had prepared for the worst. I brought a glass of water up with me to the pulpit – because I knew I would need it. I started by giving a slide deck presentation that included updates, achievements, and issues. And then it was time to light the grill. As I had expected, there was a barrage of questions about the program – all intended to make me falter, stumble, and look ineffective as director of the program. But I was unshakeable. Every question was provided a solid answer. Every accusation was proved to be unsubstantiated. When they questioned the validity of decisions, I consistently re-directed questions to committee members to answer, demonstrating that decisions were made with the guidance and support of industry. The questions went on and on, but the entire time I never broke a sweat. I never stammered or hesitated. Somehow, I stayed calm and collected throughout the entire process. I could see that some of the Board members were getting frustrated, as no matter how they attacked me, I was able to deflect. Of all my board meetings, I think this was the most time that was ever dedicated to a discussion about the international program. After I finished, Bobby Olson walked up to me and said, "I'm proud of you – you didn't let them get to you." By the energy in the room, I felt that this would be my last meeting with the Board. While I was in Juneau, I made my peace with Lanie Freeman. We had some bumps in the road through the years, but for the most part our relationship had been harmonious. When I said that things didn't look good, and that there were complaints from both offices about me, she replied, "BJ – you and I have always had a special relationship, and none of this will ever affect that." Those words meant a lot to me, considering the space I was in at the time. At least one person had not turned their back on me.

I made one last ditch effort to rectify the situation. Mark Montrose and I had helped each other several times throughout the years, and he understood the predicament I was in. He agreed that he would try to help fix the situation by having the Chairman of the Board intercede in our behalf. He reached out to Dave in my behalf to try and protect me, but the answer that came back quickly and curtly was 'no'. Shortly thereafter, I had lunch with Ivan Metcalfe. Ivan had always been a good friend and confidant. He had helped me during the early days as director to steer through the politics of the Board and the organization in general. I trusted Ivan, so I shared my dilemma with him. After hearing what was taking place, Ivan said without hesitation, "Sue everybody. Even if you don't follow through, do it for a point of positioning." In hindsight, I should have followed his advice.

Chapter 61

Waiting to Be Freed

Molly announced that she was resigning. She had had enough. She shared that all the negativity and stress was starting to affect her health, and that she needed to move on. I could totally empathize with her position. It was not a healthy environment anymore – for either of us. As sad as I was to see her go, I went through the archive of images from the years and found some great pictures. I had them all framed, along with certificate of appreciation, that thanked for her years of contribution to the program. Reflecting, I could not help but remember all that we had been through together. She had been my 'right hand' during all those years. We had endured a year or so together with Ryan when were his subordinates, and she had been unwavering with me all those years after I became her supervisor. We had our spats, but we had literally spent more time together than we had with our spouses during those seven years together. I could not have accomplished with I did without her – and I let her know that.

So now I was truly alone. Soon after I traveled back to Kodiak for the annual fishery show. By then it was mid-March. I did the usual appearances – provide interviews for reporters, help support the booth at the show, and join meeting and forums. The whole time I felt like I was just going through the motions – that I was a dead man walking, just putting in my hours, waiting for the boom to come down on me. I had lost all of my enthusiasm and energy- it had literally been drained out of me. While I was there I saw my father. He could see how dejected I was, and he was helping me pay the lawyer fees for what we felt like was an impending lawsuit. We were just waiting for the players to act. There had to be some formal action against me being crafted – and we felt it was surely coming soon.

A few days later I flew to attend the seafood show in Boston. When I arrived at the show, I did the usual – I helped to man the booth and answer questions, but I could feel the tension in the air. Still, I did my best to support the program and organization. As I walked to other booths and visited people I had worked with for years, I kind of felt like I was saying farewell to all of them. During that time, Kelsey and I got together. All those years we had been there for each other. I had helped her during her challenges, and she was there to support me still. We talked again about creating a U.S. wide promotion board but realized that there would be a lot of challenges to creating a structure and implementing it. She could tell that I was not doing well, but there was not much left to say, except reflect on all our past accomplishments. Years of joint activities and shows together had created a bond between us. She encouraged me to keep my chin up. That was the last time I ever saw her.

At the last night of the show there was an Alaska reception. I attended, but was being shunned and avoided by most industry members. It was obvious that I was a 'marked' man. Then I noticed who was there – of all people, it was Dick Thompson – it was true serendipity that the guy that had berated me on my second day on the job at Magic Mermaid was now here with me. I had not seen Dick for years, and there he was, standing in front of me, a changed person. He shared how he now cared how people thought of him and had really tried to change his ways. It was ominous, because Dick had been the last one to speak with me when I left Magic Mermaid all those years before, and of all people, here he was, talking with me again. It was virtually a reminder to reflect on the lessons I had learned during my days with the agency. I left the reception early, as I had an early flight back home. I headed out the door, and who did I run into on the way out it was Bud Robins, of all people. The founder of the 800 - pound gorilla of the industry, the grand poohbah, the big enchilada. I greeted him and he shook my hand, and he asked me how I was doing. He was obviously totally oblivious as to the current state of affairs about me, even though his son was a board member. I replied that things were going great, and that it was really good to see him. It was truly ironic that the 'captain of the industry' would be the last industry member I would ever see.

The following Monday I headed to the office. A few days before Carl had informed me that he was coming to Seattle, and that he needed to schedule a meeting for me in the afternoon. I knew the blade was about to fall. I could just feel it. I called EAS that morning on the way into work and told them that I thought I was about to be terminated. They assured me that EAS would allow no such thing to happen. I called Daniel and shared what I was feeling – considering that the CMS application was not completed yet, his response was, "It would be stupid of them to do such a thing." I went about my business all morning and calmly waited for my afternoon session. When Carl came into the office, he asked me to come into the conference room – and he asked the retail program director to join us. The poor guy had to be the witness. We sat down, and Carl put a memo in front of me and said that I was being placed on administrative leave with pay. The accusations were that I was not acting in the interests of the program anymore, and that I was attempting to divert funds away from the program. I was instructed that I was to go home, and that I had to stay at home to be ready to report for duty at any time. I was not to have contact with any industry member, government official, or member of the media. Essentially I was to be under 'house arrest.' The retail director's eyes grew wide during the accusations. He was probably expecting me to lose it and go into a berserker rage with the accusations leveled against me. But I kept my cool the whole time. Carl asked me if I had anything to say, but I told him I did not. My lawyer had instructed me to keep my mouth shut and not be resistant, and I followed his instructions precisely.

He walked me back to my office to have me turn over my computer – I was allowed to keep my phone in case I needed to be reached during the leave. I had some private files on my computer, and I let him know that I needed to download that information to my own media. He asked that I not destroy any business documentation. I assured him I would not, and he sat there in my presence as I downloaded the files. In the meantime, I started to make a list of all of the active projects and needs for the program - I wanted to make sure that nothing fell through the cracks because of this action. Carl was actually shocked that I was so helpful. He said that in all the years he had dismissed or suspended people, he had never seen someone that was so helpful. I could not help it; regardless of my personal predicament, I remained a professional to the end. It was taking some time to get all my files to download, and Carl was getting impatient, as he had a dinner date. I apologized, but I was undaunted. I wanted my private data, and sure as hell was not going to leave it on the computer for State officials to review. Finally, I was finished with the download, and I gathered the rest of my personal effects, and headed out of the office. He walked me out, and as I waited for the elevator, I shook his hand and said goodbye.

The first person I called on the way home was James Krylos. I told him – now I am you. I could not help but reflect how he had left under similar circumstances, and almost within the same time frame too. We could not help but laugh at the predicament. As soon as I arrived home, I shared the news with Sherry. She was not happy to hear it, but in a way, she was probably relieved – the stress had been building for some time. The next day I contacted my lawyer and advised him of the situation. His opinion was that my civil rights had been violated, and that there was potential for a major lawsuit. So, I let my lawyer do the talking. Several industry and media members attempted to contact me to ask what was going on, but I had to tell them I was not allowed to speak with them, and could not make any comments.

A day or two later, Molly called me and told me she was being contracted temporarily by ASA to help complete the CMS application. She wanted me to hear it from her directly – as she did not want me to feel betrayed by her actions. I could not blame her for doing it – it would not be fair to the program reps to have the application not be completed properly. Still, deep inside, I could not help but feel a twinge of betrayal. At the end, all had turned their backs on me. Kylie's words from years ago echoed in my head: "Why do you work so hard, a few years after you leave, no one will even remember you were here."

For a month I sat at home, working with my lawyer to negotiate a deal. During that time my father said to me, "You are going to get blackballed; we need to sue them." I could respect his perspective, and I wanted to continue with a lawsuit to protect my reputation – or at least receive a reasonable settlement to compensate for the damage. But Sherry felt differently. She had endured many months of stress with me, and she begged for me to just walk away. She reminded me that a lawsuit would be long and drawn out. She implored me to just resign, walk away, and find another job. Considering that she was pregnant, I was very worried that the continued stress might cause her to miscarry the twins, so I agreed with her to resign. I requested a letter of recommendation from the Board, but they refused to provide one. I wound up settling for six months of severance pay and agreed to resign. My last official day was the last day of April. I had made it seven years and seven months. The dream was over. The beacon was finally sinking into the pool to be extinguished. But I was free again.

Epilogue

After I left, the next day I flew back to Kodiak to go halibut fishing with my father. The crazy thing was this – the plane for my flight north was the infamous 'salmon-thirty-salmon'. I felt it was a beautiful and ironic touch to the situation. After ten years away from the fishery, here I was, boots on deck again – almost like I had never left.

A few months later I officially opened a consultancy. It was a good test to see if my reputation had been tarnished – while many thought that the industry would be lining up to utilize my services, I found that I was indeed blacklisted. I was never really able to get any sufficient work in the industry, nor in the giant and vast international network, I had built. Most of the international reps were kind to me and made sure they visited me when they came into town. Billy told me that things were just not the same at the organization – that when I was there, I had made the team feel like a family, but that it did not feel the same anymore. It was one of the greatest compliments I could hope to receive. The visits lasted a few years, and then the connection slowly started weakening. Slowly but sure, the connections just faded away.

The most important thing that occurred by leaving that career behind was that it saved me, and my relationship with my children. I had been absent during so many of the early years of life of my two oldest children. But now I was fully present in their lives, making an impact like I had never done before. Sherry had a tough pregnancy that summer, but the twins arrived in September. We truly had a full house now. Unfortunately, I was never able to secure a job that had the same premise and prestige. I drifted for years, bouncing between commercial fishing, consulting, and creating a couple of different startups. For over a decade, I did not travel outside the country again.

It took years to get over the anger– this is probably one of the reasons I had a hard time finding a 'real' job again. People could feel that energy when I entered the room. And there were always the questions of why I had left the organization – which was difficult to answer. At the urging of my father, I sent a formal letter to Governor Baldwin, requesting that she start an investigation into the matter, and provide me with a letter of recommendation. A month later I received a written reply back from the AG's office which stated that an "...independent investigation was conducted...". I found this astounding, as neither I, nor my legal counsel, were ever contacted or notified of such an investigation prior to this notification. I questioned how an impartial and independent investigation could be performed, when the claimant and their legal counsel were never informed or interviewed. But it fell on deaf ears.

A year or so later I sent a letter to the new Alaska Attorney General, requesting he start an investigation of the matters. But there was no response. By then, I was fed up with the whole situation, and just gave up, and moved on with my life.

When people ask me now why I left, I have just two words: 'Mission accomplished'. In retrospect, it was time for me to move on. I had done what I had come to accomplish – I had taken a brand that had fallen from grace, and worked with an industry to re-position it to prestige at a global level. In a five-year period, we had raised export values by more than $1 billion. There wasn't much more to be done – I just could not see it at the time.

Life teaches us many lessons, and my years at these organizations were no exception. Here are some of the lessons learned that I hope can be of value to others:

- Keep an open mind. Don't limit yourself by what you think you already know.

- Stick to your guns. Don't compromise your principles. Be brave, have moral integrity. But be prepared to pay the price for doing this – which may include your, job, your career, and your reputation. I know all too well that integrity can come at a very heavy cost.

- Try not to get angry. Find a way to diffuse it in a healthy manner. Don't let it build up – it will poison you, and lead to an explosive episode like the one I experienced.

- Stay positive. This can be hard to do. It is easy to become negative when life's circumstances don't work out as you would like. Find gratitude in each day, remembering what you have, instead of what you don't have.

- We all have something to learn from each other—whether your role is the student, or the teacher. Never stop learning – no matter the source.

- Keep it professional. I let my emotions get the best of me and acted less than professional a number of times. Speaking expletives on a regular basis debases your value. Try finding better, kinder words to express yourself.

- Don't be afraid to ask for help. And if the answer is no, keep asking. Find a way to get the help, even if your boss won't give it. That means put it in writing. Leverage your connections and your network. By nature, human beings are highly sociable, so don't be afraid to be vulnerable and reach out to others.

- Get out before it is too late. When you see things going dark or moving down the wrong path, heed the warning signs and prepare to quickly move on. My reputation was trashed and utterly destroyed by being forced to resign. And it took years to build my confidence and reputation back up.

- When you leave, don't go into exile. If lies and dishonest words are spread about you, your presence can help to alleviate such defamation. But if you just 'go away', then rumors and stories will run wild. While the inclination is to run, be ready to stand up for yourself in an effort to protect your reputation.

- Watch out for 'extortionist 'bosses– they will play games and continue to pile dirt on you. Don't let them make you feel cornered. Stay nimble and elusive if you are going to play the game – or just see the warning signs and get out as quickly as possible.

- Be ready to forgive. That includes yourself. My mother taught me that, "Hatred is the poison you drink every day, thinking it is hurting your enemy." Forgive quickly and move on – it is the path to healing and being whole again.

- Don't lose hope. The human spirit is amazingly resilient and strong. Most importantly, don't give up on yourself, and your abilities. You are stronger than you realize. We never truly lose, if we never truly give up.

Life is a journey, a series of lessons. These lessons build character and spirit. Don't be afraid to learn, challenge norms, step forward bravely when no one else will, or have the nerve – it is a part of the journey, and you will be a better person for it. Be an inspiration for others. Be a beacon when you find yourself immersed in a pool of darkness. The light inside of you will always guide you back home.